The California Saga

The California Saga

Chunichi

www.urbanbooks.net

Urban Books, LLC
78 East Industry Court
Deer Park, NY 11729

ISBN 13: 978-1-60162-544-1
ISBN 10: 1-60162-5544-8

First Printing April 2013
Printed in the United States of America

10 9 8 7 6 5 4 3 2 1

*This is a work of fiction. Any references or similarities
to actual events, real people, living or dead, or to real
locales are intended to give the novel a sense of reality.
Any similarity in other names, characters, places, and
incidents is entirely coincidental.*

Distributed by Kensington Publishing Corp.
Submit Wholesale Orders to:
Kensington Publishing Corp.
C/O Penguin Group (USA) Inc.
Attention: Order Processing
405 Murray Hill Parkway
East Rutherford, NJ 07073-2316
Phone: 1-800-526-0275
Fax: 1-800-227-9604

Acknowledgments

Thank you to my almighty God for continuing to bless me with the opportunity to write. Some careers are short lived and to others reaching such places is nothing more than a dream. But God has taken me places that I had never imaged and is still opening doors. To Him I give all the glory.

Thanks to my continuously growing fan base. I appreciate all the e-mails on Myspace and Facebook and all the wonderful comments. You all give that extra push to get these books out.

Much love to my literary fam. Thanks to Carl Weber of Urban Books and Mark Anthony of Q-Boro for tolerating my divalicous attitude and only being a phone call away. To my personal Urban Books chaperone, Denard aka G Buggy, you're irreplaceable. Thanks to my super agent, Marc Gerald, for seeing the vision and setting the path. To my literary big sister, Nikki Turner, love you boo!

Thanks to all my girls for keeping me full of ideas. Toya, Tracey, Kicia, and Chele—your loyalty will never be forgotten. Anthoinette and Sophie, you both hold a special place in my heart. NeNe of Major Creations Hair Studio, you know I can do nothing with this head without you.

I send never ending hugs and kisses to my family. Mom, thanks for always shining so bright. No matter how dull my day is I can always count on you to

Acknowledgments

brighten it. Dad and little bro, thanks for your support. Thanks to my wonderful husband, Aron, for being tough enough to keep me on track when I veer, yet loving enough to pamper me when I'm weak. To my Jamaican fam back home, don't worry yuhself, mi soon come a yard!

I could go on forever with this section. I've learned so much in this past year about bad-minded, envious people, and haters. But rather than talk about it here, I'll just write a book on it. So to all my haters, thanks for the continuous inspiration and making me rich! Smooches!

Prologue

California Jewel—Who in hell would name their child some shit like that? That's the first question that comes to mind when someone hears my name. Jewel, the name I actually went by, was given to me by my grandmother. She said I was more precious to her than a priceless stone. Now, California, that shit came from my whore-ass momma. She named me California because I was the product of a one-night stand she had in California.

Although I hated the name, as reckless as it seemed, I was damned if any other name was more appropriate. California described me perfectly. Just like the state of California, I was full of sunshine. My pussy was wetter than a ripe California orange. I was definitely Hollywood when it came to my divalicious attitude, wanting what I want when I want it. But if you ever tried to cross me, I'd become more dangerous than the LAPD. To say the least, I was off the Richter, like a California earthquake which would know exactly what I meant.

As if my flawless five-foot four-inch frame wasn't enough, I just had partnered up with a beast by the name of Michael Burroughs. He was Mike to his family and baby mothers, but to cats getting money on the streets, he was known as Calico, short for "California Connection." And every nigga in the drug game dreamed of having a person like him on his side.

I, on the other hand, had made a different kind of connection with him, but little did I know just how far that connection would take me.

Chapter 1

"A Drunk Person Speaks a Sober Mind"

Jewel

"Fuck you, bitch!" I held up my middle finger as I grabbed my oversized Chanel bag then stormed out of my now ex-manager's office. "And take this and shove it up your big, white, cottage cheese ass," I said to the overweight, unattractive wench that had just fired me. I knocked over the carnation flower arrangement that sat in the waiting area of the medical office then slung a few magazines across the floor on my way out the door.

Thinking of how that wicked witch had just tried to humiliate me, I just wasn't quite satisfied with my tantrum, so I stopped in front of the huge window that covered the entire front of the office and pulled down my pants. "Oh, and you all can kiss my big, plump, juicy ass!" I yelled as I smacked my butt cheeks then ran off laughing. Now my heart was content, and I was able to get in my truck at ease. *That bitch had some nerve calling me out in front of the entire staff and patients, making it seem like I was some sort of incompetent young black chick,* I thought. I started up my white Range Rover, the words *datbitch* on my license plate, a message to let everyone know who was driving this here whip, and zoomed out of the parking lot, leaving nothing but dust.

Evidently that chick didn't read between the lines of my resume. Of course, I had plenty of medical billing experience, but I also was first a born hustler that could game any nigga, and second a ghost writer, which translated to, "I'm not dependent solely on your fucking pissy-ass check, bitch!" That working shit was never for a chick like me anyway.

If it wasn't for my homeboy Touch, I would have never been working in the first place. His words were still fresh in my head as I pulled out the parking lot and onto the busy street. "Keep you a li'l gig on the side, Jewel," he'd say. This nigga insisted that I should always keep a plan B, no matter how much loot I had coming in. I enjoyed having the extra cash on hand, but I didn't know if that advice was for my benefit or his. I think that was simply a way to keep me out of his pockets.

Touch was my boy, so if I were to ever fall on hard times, he would've definitely come through for me, but he knew that I liked keeping my pockets swollen. Regardless, I was on my grind and had money coming in from every direction. My new career as a ghostwriter was really taking off, and I always had a nigga or two that I was constantly gaming. Hell, that's how I was able to afford my whip and my crib. Me getting fired from that job was actually a blessing in disguise. Now there would be less stress, and more time to focus on my writing, the real money-maker.

I connected my iPod to the radio and blasted the tune "Glamorous" by Fergie as I headed to the bank to deposit my check. I thought about my manager on the way. *That bitch didn't know I was already living the fucking glamorous life. She ain't doing no damage here.* I laughed as I pulled up to the bank's drive-thru.

From the bank, I headed to the nail shop. I began to laugh again as I thought about what was happening. *How many people get fired from their job then go get their nails done? Only a real fucking diva like myself.*

I had to call my girl Sasha and let her in on my drama for the day. I smiled as I scrolled to her name in contacts and the picture of her from the back, wearing only a thong, with a whip thrown over her shoulder, popped up on the screen of my iPhone. Sasha was my girl. Although we'd only been friends a couple of years and we'd met on some strange terms at the strip club, she was still on a different level than any of my other friends. She and I had a little closer connection, a connection that I shared with her only.

I waited patiently for Sasha to pick up as I sang along to the reggae tune "Can't Breathe" by Tanya Stephens, which she had set as her call tone. You can always tell what a bitch was going through by her call tone or voice mail.

"Hello?" Sasha answered right away.

"What's up, Boobie?" I called her by her pet name. "I gotta tell you about my day at work."

"Oh Lord! What the hell that fat bitch done this time?" Sasha was aware of the daily drama I had with my stupid-ass manager.

"Bitch, why that fat cow fire me?"

"For real, girl?" Sasha asked in disbelief.

"Yes, bitch. She gon' come at me with some bullshit about the collections versus production is showing a huge gap"—My sentence was disrupted by the sight of a fine-ass nigga passing by in a black drop-top 2008 Mercedes Benz SL550 that screamed, "I'm that nigga!" My eyes were glued to him as he passed by slowly. I saw nothing but his cornrows, dark chocolate skin, ice grill, at least a three karat diamond stud in his right ear, as he chatted away on his cell phone. It was as though everything was moving in slow motion. I gave him my most seductive look, and he glanced at me from the corner of his eye.

"Jewel! Jewel!"

"Oh, shit. Sorry about that baby. I just saw this fine-ass dude, umph!"

I felt a shiver in my pussy as I thought about what I could do with a guy like him on my team. He could possibly take the place of my MVP and turn him to a bench-rider. His looks were one thing, but his money was what really made my pussy wet. And after getting fired, I was definitely in search for a new player on the team to compensate for my lost wages.

I'd learned the rules to gaming a dude at a very young age. I'd watched my mom use and abuse men my entire life. Her father had left her at a young age, and it seemed liked she was never able to get past it. As a child, my mother taught me to trust no man, never wear my heart on my sleeve, and to always stand my ground, because kindness was a sign of weakness. A while later she taught me the power of beauty and the booty.

As an adult, I'd fallen right into my mother's foot-steps. I guess it's true what they say, the apple doesn't fall too far from the tree, because I'd mastered the art of gold-digging, just as she did. It was like a gift. I could look at a guy and assess him in a matter of seconds and know approximately how much dough he was holding, and where it came from. In my book, looks alone didn't get a man anywhere, but money would get him every-where. Don't get it twisted though, this book I'm refer-ring to isn't titled, *The Whore Handbook*. It's more like *The Gold-digger's Guide to Financial Security*.

***

"Girl, you crazy. You ain't never gon' change," Sasha said in a disapproving tone.

"Why you sound like that? Did I say something wrong?"

I could tell by the tone of Sasha's voice that something was bothering her. It was a tone I was way too familiar with. I just didn't know whether it was something I said, or if it was a personal struggle.

When we'd first met, her life was going downhill, but we pulled together to turn things around. Sasha started off stripping at Blue Light in Hampton, a city about thirty minutes from Virginia Beach, and life was good for her. She had a house she lived in, a townhouse that she rented out to Section 8 recipients, and a nice car. She needed for nothing. But when she stabbed a chick during an altercation, she was fired from the club, and her world began to crumble. Sasha decided that the strip scene was no longer for her, and wanted to work.

Although she had little work experience and education, I was still able to put something together for her. Luckily, she'd actually gone to school for medical assistance and worked in a couple of medical offices. But during her time as a successful dancer, she figured she would never see this kind of money working a regular job, so she let her certification expire. Even though odds were against us, I created an exaggerated, yet professional resume and cover letter for her, and used some of my connections in the medical field to land her a job with Sentara Healthcare.

At first, everything was smooth sailing, more or less, but it didn't last long. Nearly a year later it had almost become routine for Sasha to call me with some depressing news. It was as though someone had put a curse on her ass or something. In six months alone she'd gotten in trouble with the authorities for welfare fraud. Then she lost her investment property, and as if things couldn't possibly get any worse, her baby father got robbed.

"I can't take this stress anymore," Sasha said, bursting into tears.

"What stress, baby?" I asked, wanting to know what was bothering my friend.

"It's like everything is going so wrong so fast. I'm working my ass off, but with my monthly bills, plus the money for daycare and gas, it's just not worth it. I can't keep living like this, Jewel."

"So what you want to do?"

"I don't know. I guess I'm gonna have to start back dancing. I've got to get these bills caught up. Since Rick got robbed, he ain't been able to help out, and I'm at risk of losing everything I own. I'm gonna lose my house."

Now my first instinct was to tell her about that deadbeat-ass baby father of hers. There ain't no way a broke-down dude would be living up in my shit and can't even pay a light bill. Who gives a fuck if he got robbed? That's part of the fucking game, and a real hustler always knows how to get back on.

Besides, where the fuck was his stash? I didn't even bother going into that with Sasha because I'd heard all the excuses once before—"He decided to get out of the game since he got robbed. He's trying to start his own business." Trying to stay focused on Sasha's needs instead of her downfalls, I directed my attention back to her statement.

"So how you gonna do that, Sasha?" I knew that once you got a bad rep in the stripping world in this area, your career was basically over. "I thought you were blackballed on the whole dance scene in this area?"

"Well, I heard girls be going to Atlanta and New York and be racking up. Maybe I could just go to Atlanta for a couple of weeks and then come back and hit New York on the weekends. All I need is money to get my business licenses and plane ticket. Plus, my mom lives in Columbus, Georgia. That's only an hour away from Atlanta. I could take the boys there to stay with her until I get on my feet, and I could crash at her crib the weeks I'm there dancing. What you think?"

I knew Sasha wasn't so much asking me what I thought of her idea, but more so what I thought about giving her the money to carry it out.

"Hey, I've always supported your decision. If you think this is what's best. So I take it you're gonna quit your job?" I asked, since she so conveniently forgot to mention her job when explaining her master plan.

"I have to. I mean, I have no other choice. I need fast money, Jewel. They 'bout to foreclose on my house."

"A'ight, Sasha," I said, disappointed in my her actions. We'd gone through a lot to get her that job, and now she was leaving it to go right back where she started. "How much you need for the business license and plane ticket?"

Almost before I could finish my sentence, she quickly responded, "Like six hundred."

"Okay. I'll call you later, and you can come get it."

"Thank you so much. I promise I'll pay you back," Sasha said, full of excitement.

"Yeah, Sasha. I'm 'bout to get my nails done. I'll hit you later."

I wrapped up the call knowing damn well I would never see that six hundred dollars again. I'd lost count of the number of times I'd lent her money and never saw it again, so I never held my breath on a promise to pay. That was always a promise waiting to be broken.

"Love you," she sang into the phone.

"Love you too, Boobie." I disconnected the call and jumped out the truck and headed for the nail shop.

"Hey, Kim," I said to my nail tech as I walked in.

She said, "Me not Kim. Me tell you every time."

And she was right. She did tell me every time, but I always managed to forget, until she reminded me.

"I want a manicure, pedicure, eyebrow wax, upper lip wax, and eyelashes," I said, running off my list.

"Sit here," she said, directing me to the spa pedicure chair. Then she asked about my homeboy, Touch, who regularly came to the nail shop with me. "Where ya friend?"

"Good question." I turned on the chair's massager then pulled out my cell phone to give him a call.

I relaxed as I waited for him to answer. Boy, was I drained. I didn't know if it was just the events from the day or Sasha's constant issues that drained me, but whichever it was, it was nothing a little pampering couldn't solve.

"You have reached the voice mail box of . . ." the recording began to say, letting me know that Touch wasn't available.

Maybe to the average chick or someone else he wasn't available, but he was always available for me, so I dialed his other cell phone number.

Touch was like my brother. We'd been friends since high school. When I'd first moved to Virginia Beach from Compton, California, all the chicks were hating on me, and all the dudes were loving me. But it didn't take long for me to sort out the real gangsters from the fake ones, and when it was all said and done, there was only a couple left standing. One, Diablo James, I made my high school sweetheart, and Touch, the other, I made my best friend. We clicked immediately.

As a native Southerner, I was used to seeing many black people and few white people. Sure, segregation was over, but deep in the South, black people stuck together, and the white people did the same. You might call it voluntary segregation—They didn't bother us, and we didn't bother them. So when I came to Virginia Beach, it was way too many white people, and way too many black people that acted white for me. For me, it was like moving from Compton to the Valley.

Touch, coming straight from the streets of Norfolk to the center of Virginia Beach, experienced the same culture shock as me. He felt my pain. It was like we were in the fucking twilight zone. So being the natural rebels we were, we acted out and did our own gotdamn thang.

A born hustler, Trayvon Davis knew how to get money by any means. People said that everything he touched turned to gold, so he was given the name Touch by the streets. Unlike most dope boys, Touch had never experienced a loss, never had a nigga buck on him, and never had weak product. He'd been dealt the best of hands in this here poker game of the streets.

Touch's parents moved their family to Virginia Beach during his high school years to keep him out of trouble, but with my help, he was able to get back and forth to Norfolk on a daily basis. But he couldn't stay out of trouble at all, which was why he ultimately got sent to the penitentiary.

My homeboy spent three long years of his life locked up. But since he got out, shit had been nothing but uphill for him. Keeping the truth to his name, he was still turning shitballs to gold nuggets.

"What up, bay?" Touch answered right away.

"Nothing. I'm at the nail shop. Meet me here. I need some company. Then afterward we can go have some drinks." Drinking wasn't my thing, but Touch's borderline alcoholic ass loved it.

"A'ight. I'll be up there." He already knew I was at our regular spot, which was just around the corner from his crib.

"Hey, sexy," I said to Touch as he walked in.

Never the flashy type but always dressed tight, Touch demanded attention as he entered a room. He always wore the latest styles but never any jewelry. You could catch him with a different color Prada or latest Gucci sneaker on each day of the week, but you won't catch him with an iced-out chain. The most he would have on was a watch. He didn't even have his ears pierced. No jewels, not even a tattoo, he was the most humble nigga around, with enough charisma to charm anyone. Touch managed to get any bitch he wanted. Now, how many niggas would love to be in his shoes?

Before Touch had a chance to respond to my sexy comment, another nail technician directed him to sit beside me. "You can sit here."

Touch sat down and slid off his Gucci slippers and rolled up his Antik Denim jeans to prepare for his pedicure then focused his attention to me. He looked at me with his thick cornrows and with those big brown eyes as another nail tech grabbed his hand to begin his manicure.

"What's up, homie?"

"I got fired today." I laughed.

"Stop playing," Touch said in disbelief.

"Yep."

"You a'ight?" he asked.

"Hell yeah. You know I didn't want to work anyway."

"So you gonna look for another job?"

"I have a job, damn it!" I yelled.

"A'ight, a'ight," Touch said quickly.

"And answer your damn phone." I said, acknowledging his phone that had been ringing constantly since we began our conversation. "I'm sick of hearing that shit ring."

"It's my baby mother. She on some bullshit right now, and I ain't into that arguing shit."

"Your baby mother is a trip." I grinned as I thought back to the many stories I'd heard about her. "What you do now, Touch?" I asked, automatically assuming it was his fault.

"I ain't did shit. She just pissed about my new girl. They stay into it. My baby mother be calling her phone and all kinds of shit."

I couldn't do nothing but laugh as Touch continued to tell me about his baby momma drama. Normally, I would be the first bitch to snap when he would tell me about a chick doing him wrong, but when it came to his baby mother, it was nothing but love. I had to respect her because she was just so gangster with her shit. Real talk, she reminded me of myself. Everything she did was some shit I would do.

I felt sorry for the nigga that ever decided to make me his baby mother. A nigga better marry me because, trust me, the shit I would do if my baby father left me would make them give baby momma drama a whole new name.

"It's okay, pookie face. We'll go drink our problems away in a few minutes." I reached over and rubbed the side of his face, careful not to smear my freshly painted nails.

Sticking her little-ass nose all up in my business, the one I called Kim said, "You like him. He not friend. He boyfriend."

"What?" I balled my face up.

"You like him." She pointed to Touch.

"Go 'head wit' dat shit," Touch told her. "Dis my fucking sista."

Although I was pissed that bitch was all in my business, I knew where she was coming from. It wasn't the first time somebody had said that same shit. Hell, all of our friends swore we were fucking. Anybody on the outside looking in felt it was a little more than a tight friendship between us. As crazy as it may seem, they were all wrong. Touch and I hadn't even held hands before, let alone kiss. That nigga was truly my best friend, nothing more, nothing less.

"Yo," Touch answered his other cell phone as I headed to the back of the nail shop to get my waxing done.

"Don't make my eyebrows too thin," I instructed as I lay on the bench to wait for my wax.

"It not too thin," the nail technician tried explaining in her best English. "I do nice for you."

"Okay. I hope so, 'cause last week you made them way too thin."

As a mixed breed, Panamanian and black, my eyebrows were naturally thick, so thin eyebrows did me no justice. A full face, a head full of thick, curly hair, and little skinny eyebrows wasn't the business.

"Shit!" I yelled as the nail tech ripped the tape from beneath my eyebrow.

I knew getting wax was no piece a cake, but I didn't ever remember it being that painful. For a moment I thought that little Vietnamese bitch was applying a little extra force on some get-back shit.

Ten minutes later my waxing was complete. I looked in the mirror closely to examine the wax job I'd just received. Surprisingly, it was perfect.

"It looks good. Can you do it like this next week too?" I asked as I handed back the little woman the hand mirror.

"I told you, I do nice job for you," she responded as she headed out the door, and I followed her to the cash register.

Touch sat in a chair near the register. "You done, yo?"

"Yep."

"Let's roll." Touch pulled off four twenties from a stack of money he carried in his pocket and paid for our services.

"Keep the change," I said, as though I'd just paid the eighty dollars for our day at the nail shop.

"See, me told you he your boyfriend," Kim said, as Touch and I walked out the door.

"Whatever," I said, choosing to no longer entertain her foolishness. "See you next week." I asked Touch as we walked to our vehicles. "Where we headed?"

"I thought we was gon' get a drink?"

"Said like a true alcoholic," I said, noticing the panic in Touch's voice. He was like a fiend needing his daily fix. "We are going to get a drink, hon. I was just asking where."

"Oh, shit. Let's hit the beach," Touch said, now much more relaxed.

"You want me to jump in with you, or should I drive?" I asked, knowing Touch's tendency to want to stay at the bar longer than me.

I couldn't count the number of times I'd left him at the bar alone. And the funny shit was that no one would ever know he was there alone. Being the social type and loving white people, he had no problems mingling and fitting right in at the bars on the oceanfront. You would think they would single out a young black dude with cornrows from Norfolk. But, I guess, when you got something they all wanted, they wouldn't care if you dressed like André 3000, had hair like Bob Marley, and spoke like Ozzy Osbourne.

Touch was a real businessman, and knew how to pick his clients, suppliers, and workers.

On top of all that, this nigga was just so fucking reserved, never the greedy type. Although it rarely showed, Touch also had a dark side that would come out and show its dirty little head when a nigga got out of line. Even with all that, he still didn't think like the average dope boy. He had bigger goals like businesses, houses, investments, and setting up college funds for his twin daughters, his pride and joy.

"Go 'head and drive, 'cause I gotta meet my man there and I don't know how long this nigga gon' take."

"Okay, lead the way." I pressed the unlock button on my keychain and headed to my truck.

I knew exactly what it meant when Touch said he had to meet his man. Touch tried his hardest to exclude me from his dealings with the drug game, but I knew him way too well. Although I can honestly say I'd never saw a drug transaction go down or even seen the product, I still knew what was up. Of course, Touch had legit businesses, but I still knew he had his ties with the game, quiet as it was kept. I'd have been a fool to think otherwise.

I hopped in the truck and grabbed my iPod and set it to some riding music. I could kiss the muthafucka that invented that shit. The radio was nearly nonexistent in my world. No time for a bunch of commercials and constantly changing the station, trying to find a song I enjoy. Then when it came to CD's, I hated shuffling through a big-ass CD case and loading and unloading CD's into the deck. My heart goes out to those still living in those prehistoric ways.

Not even ten whole minutes had passed before we reached Atlantic Avenue at the oceanfront, better known as "The Strip." I pulled into the beach parking lot behind Touch as he paid for the both of us. By the time I was parked and getting out of my truck, he was already headed to the bar.

I yelled at Touch across the parking lot, "Gotdamn, you fucking wino! Slow down. They ain't gonna run out of liquor before you get there."

Touch waited for me at the door of the bar and held the door open for me to walk in. "Do you have to be so damn loud? You used to be a little prissy-ass beach girl, now you ghetto as fuck!"

I paused in the doorway and looked him in the eyes. "I'm prissy when the time calls for it, and I'm ghetto when the time calls for that," I said and proceeded to walk past.

Touch smacked my ass as he followed me in the bar. "Whatever, nigga."

"Ugh! Don't ever touch my booty," I said, surprised at Touch's actions.

"You just started getting an ass. Back in high school, you were straight up and down, *Miss Nasatall*." Touch joked as we grabbed a seat at the bar.

"Oh, I know you didn't. You trying to say I had *no ass at all*." I laughed at Touch's taunting.

Our conversation was interrupted by Touch's incoming call.

"Yo."

I could hear the person ask from the other end of the phone, "Where you at?"

"The front," Touch said, trying to give his location without actually saying the words.

Niggas kill me with that shit. They act like every phone is tapped and every phone call is being recorded by the damn feds. I grinned to myself as he continued his conversation.

The overly tanned white woman with obvious breast implants laid napkins in front of Touch and me. "What cha having to drink?"

I ordered Touch's usual. "X-rated and Sprite for me, and Grey Goose on the rocks for him."

After ending his call, Touch asked, "You ordered for me?"

"Yeah," I lied. "I got you a Hennessy and Coke."

"What? Why the fuck you do that, Jewel?"

I continued to lie just to see how aggravated Touch would get. "I thought that's what you drink?"

"Man." Touch sucked his teeth and called for the bartender. "Yo!"

The bartender put up one finger as she made our drinks, signaling that she would be right over in a moment.

"You goin' to drink that fucking Hennessy too." Touch pulled out a cigarette.

I didn't even respond as I watched the bartender bring our drinks over and sit them directly in front of us.

"What can I get for you, hon?" she asked Touch.

"Man, let me get a Grey Goose on the rocks," he ordered, not even noticing the drink sitting right in front of him.

"Another one?" the bartender asked.

Touch looked down and grinned. "Nah, this good," he said to the bartender then mushed me in the side of my head.

I busted out with laughter. I teased him, saying, "I told you, you're an alcoholic. See how mad you got over that drink?"

"Nah, man. Me and my girl just got into it last night over that same shit. Before I go to the bathroom, I tell her to order me another drink. I come back and this crazy bitch ordered me gin on the rocks. I almost threw up when I sipped that shit. I was like, how the fuck this bitch don't know what I drink as many times as we been out together? Damn, I don't drink but one kind of liquor."

"That is pretty bad. Sorry, I didn't know. She should know you a little better. Next time you're with her, ask her what color your eyes are." I figured that would be the true test. There was no way anyone could miss those big brown eyes. Hell, that was one of his greatest assets.

"My eyes? What? I don't even know what color my eyes are."

Damn, that's crazy, I thought to myself. "They are brown, Touch. Haven't you noticed your eyes are a tad bit brighter than the average black person? I mean, they aren't hazel, but they are definitely not the average dark brown eyes. Here look." I searched my bag for my M•A•C compact then pulled it out to hand it to him.

He pushed my hand away. "Hell nah. Put that shit up."

"Come on, look." I opened the compact and shoved it in front of his face.

"Go 'head, man. Stop playing." Touch struggled to take the compact away from me.

"What's the matter? You too cool to look into a woman's compact at a bar?" I laughed. I finally gave up and put the compact back in my bag.

"You full of games, I see. Well, I got a game for ya, jokesta," Touch said in an I-dare-you-to-play-along tone.

"Okay, what's up?" I quickly accepted the challenge.

"We gon' play a drinking game—"

"Oh, hell nah!" I yelled, cutting him off. That was definitely a challenge I would lose. I was always up for a fight, but I knew suicide when I was faced with it.

"Gotdamn! Hear me out, homie. The game is not about who can drink the most. I already know I got your little buck-and-a-quarter ass beat when it comes to that. The game is, you order my drinks, and I order yours, and no matter what the next person orders you have to drink it. Cool?"

"Okay, but no off-the-wall shit."

"A'ight, drink up. After we're done with these drinks, the game begins."

I swallowed my drink down, and Touch threw out the straw from his Grey Goose and took the drink to the head.

"Yo!" He flagged down the waitress then signaled for me to order when she arrived.

I looked at all the different liquors that sat behind the bar. "Let me get, uuummmm . . . a shot of piss," I said. Then Touch and I burst out laughing at the same time.

The waitress said nothing. She just stood there with a puzzled look on her face. She probably thought we were already drunk.

"I'm joking. I'm joking," I said, noticing the waitress was starting to get a little impatient with our foolishness. "Let me get a shot of tequila, the one with the worm. Matter of fact, if possible, can we get the worm in the glass?"

The waitress shook her head, as if to say okay, then looked at Touch for his order.

"Let me get a Long Island Ice Tea."

"Thanks," I said, feeling as though Touch had given me a pass on the first round. I was surprised that he'd ordered it. I was expecting something crazy like I'd ordered for him. I knew he only drank clear liquors, so I was expecting him to pitch a fit right away over the tequila, but he didn't even seem moved by my order.

The waitress came back and placed our drinks in front of us. We switched drinks, and Touch downed his first. Then I began to sip on mine. "Whew!" I said after the first sip.

"Yeah, nigga." Touch sang. "Thought you was getting off easy, didn't you? It's about five different liquors in that shit. Drink up." He laughed.

We laughed and joked as Touch waited for me to finish my drink. I was down to my final sips, and I really felt like I could go no farther. I was really feeling the effects of the liquor.

As a stall tactic, I decided I'd take a little bathroom break. "I'll be back," I said. "I gotta tinkle." I pushed my stool away from the bar.

I looked myself over in the full-sized bathroom mirror. My eyes were glassy, a sure sign of intoxication. I made my way to the handicapped bathroom. Of course, I was nowhere near handicapped, but those bathrooms were always so spacious. So whenever I had the option, the handicapped bathroom was my first choice. I hung my purse on the hook that was posted to the back of the door. After struggling to get my pants down, I squatted over the toilet seat. That was the biggest challenge of all. I was so tipsy, I couldn't even squat steadily.

With the forceful flow of urine, I got pee all over the seat, and even some on the floor. I couldn't do anything but laugh as I pressed my hands firmly against the walls beside me to try to hold my balance. Once done, I flushed the toilet and cleaned up the area around me nicely.

As I stepped out of the restroom, an older white lady shot me an evil look as she leaned against the wall, her arms crossed. Ignoring her, I walked right past to the sink and began to wash my hands.

I could hear her mumble from the restroom stall, "You don't look handicapped to me."

Neither do you, I thought in my head, but chose to respond, "I'm not."

I began to fix my make up and straighten my hair when I heard the toilet flush. I rushed to finish touching myself up so that I wouldn't have to stand next to the rude lady as she washed her hands. Just as I finished applying my lipgloss, the lady came limping from the bathroom, one leg shorter than the other.

She groaned then positioned herself against the sink so that she could wash her hands. "Well, if you're not handicapped then stay out the bathroom."

"Okay, so I used the handicapped bathroom. Sorry. Write me a fucking ticket!" I then pranced out the bathroom, taking extra-long steps like a runway model.

Normally, I would have felt bad and been very apologetic, but I'd had my share of rude white bitches for one day, and I think, more than anything, the alcohol was talking. Besides, how many times had anyone really been in the restroom using the handicapped stall and someone handicapped was actually waiting? I don't know about you, but it was a first for me.

Touch greeted me as soon as I walked out the bathroom. "Jewel, come over here. I want you to meet someone. This is my boy, Calico."

I almost swallowed my tongue as I looked at the person before me, realizing it was the guy I'd seen near the nail shop earlier in the day. "Hello. Nice to meet you. I'm Jewel."

I extended my hand, and this flawless man before me grabbed my hand and kissed it. "Hello, beautiful. Same to you."

I only prayed that I didn't look as drunk as I felt. I cut my eyes in Touch's direction to say, "Help."

In his best drunken mannerism, Touch tried to find out what was wrong. "Jewel, are you feeling okay? Do you need to sit down or something? You look crazy."

"Shut up," I said softly between clenched teeth as I got comfortable on the bar stool to his right.

Touch directed his attention to his friend that sat on his left. I couldn't believe my luck. I didn't know what to do. I wanted this man, but I was so drunk, I hadn't a leg to stand on.

I snatched out my cell and sent a mass text message to all my girls. I had a special distribution list for emergencies just like this one. I needed some advice, and fast. I sent them a quick message that read:

OMG grls I need hlp! I'm drunk & there's a dude here I'm tryn 2 impress. Wht do I do? Dnt wnt 2 make fool of myself.

It took less than a minute before the responses started rolling in. The first text received was from Sasha. It read:

Do nothing. Leave. Guys come dime a dozen. U got enuff on the team. Besides, I need 2 c u neway.

I thought to myself, *Typical response. That's why you home with the broke-ass boyfriend right now.*

I went to delete Sasha's text just as fast as I had opened it, but before I could even hit the erase button, she sent another message.

Ur @ a bar every 1 is drunk. Just go talk 2 him. He's prob drunk 2.

That was two strikes. The final text was from my girl Shakira. I prayed this was the answer.

Is he there w/friends? If so u have 2 stall. Drink a
RedBull and order food 2 try 2 sober up then talk to
him. Or on ur way out have waitress send him a drink
and your #.

Finally, some advice I could use. I began to text Shakira back when Touch grabbed my phone. "What you
so busy doing over here?"

"Nothing that concerns you. Now can you kindly give
me my phone back, Touch?"

I reached for my phone.

"Nah." He put my phone in his pocket then stood up.

"Damn, you that drunk just off two drinks?" I said,
observing how childish he was acting.

"Hell nah," he said loud enough for his friend to hear
as he headed to the men's restroom. "I had two more
shots while you were in the bathroom."

I noticed his friend was laughing. "That's so not
true." While Touch was in the restroom, his friend
came over to chat with me.

"Oh shit," I said to myself as he came over. I didn't
get the chance to order a Red Bull. I saw an unopened
can sitting in front Touch's stool, so I grabbed it,
opened it, and took a big gulp.

"I didn't catch your name," he said as he sat next to
me.

"I didn't throw it," I snapped back. *What a corny
response,* I thought. *I need another gulp of Red Bull.* I
felt like an idiot as I took another gulp, nearly finishing
the whole can.

"Well, you may want to throw it, because I don't
wear the catcher's mitt for too long," his friend said,
completely throwing me off.

Hold up? I know this nigga ain't coming out his mouth sideways. Does he think he's flier than me or something? "Excuse me," I said, trying to make sure the liquor didn't have me tripping.

"I'm saying. I'm not the type to chase a broad—"

"Broad? You obviously don't know who the fuck I am. Please, baby, check my resume. I don't wear the 'broad' title, boo. But since you think you're fly, let me kick something to you. Yeah, no doubt, I was interested. I was even gonna put you on the team. But you wasn't even gonna be the star player, baby. Sad to say, you were gonna ride the bench. But don't worry, I would have pulled you off when another nigga was injured— well, his pockets, that is." I looked at him like he was a li'l bitch then pulled out my American Express Black card.

I then called for the waitress. "You can wrap the tab up, baby," I told her. I handed her the card then gave Touch's friend a condescending smirk.

Just then Touch walked up. I don't know if it was the fumes rising from my head that sent that nigga a smoke signal or if he saw tears in his boy's eyes, but as soon as he walked up, he could tell something was definitely wrong.

Touch stood beside me. "What the fuck going on, bay?"

"Ask your disrespectful-ass friend." I looked his boy straight in the face.

"Gotdamn, Calico, what the fuck you say to her?"

"Man, it's this area. I can't kick it with these East Coast bitches. They just don't see it the California way."

"What the fuck he say 'bout me?" I asked, when I heard him say *California*.

"Is your name *California*?"

"Yes, the fuck it is."

Touch noticed the stupid-ass look on his boy's face. "Yeah, it is, for real, man. California is her first name. She just go by Jewel. Look, I'm 'bout to order another round. Everybody cool out and have a drink," Touch suggested, assuming liquor was the answer to everything.

"Let me get this one. What you having, Miss California Jewel?" Calico said, offering me a truce drink.

"I don't accept drinks from people I don't know," I said with a slight smile.

He began to say, "I'm sorry—"

"Oh, I know you sorry . . . sorry-ass nigga." I just had to take that. I owed him one. "I'm joking, sweetie," I said, seeing the wrinkles of disapproval in his forehead. "Okay, let's start from the beginning."

"I'm Calico," he said as he extended his hand.

Now just being a spoiled-ass little bitch for the hell of it, I folded my arms and refused to shake his hand. I wanted to be sure I had the upper hand.

"Come on, don't do this to me," he begged.

I still refused, pushing it a little further.

"Yo, you just make a nigga wanna . . ." He paused and took a deep breath, as though he was trying to refrain from doing something terrible. He added, "You just make a nigga wanna hug your little ass," then grabbed me tight.

Totally surprised by his actions, we all laughed together.

Damn, I'm glad this nigga hugged me and didn't haul off and hit me, I thought, realizing I would have been caught totally off guard and probably knocked the fuck out.

Now that things were back on track, I figured I'd better wrap things up. I needed to get his number and get the hell out of dodge. I started a little small talk as I waited for the perfect time to execute.

Meanwhile, Calico ordered a round of Cuervo 1800. The last thing I needed was another drink, but I didn't want to take the risk of insulting him by turning it down. So, on the count of three, we all tapped glasses and threw the drinks down.

"Okay, that's it for me, fellas," I said as I attempted to stand up.

"Oh no, you don't." Calico grabbed my purse. "Friends don't let friends drive drunk," he said between laughs.

"Whatever! I'm not your friend, so it's okay to let me drive," I said sarcastically.

"Damn, are you always this vicious or just when you're drunk?" Calico asked.

"I'm a Scorpio, baby. We never stop."

"Well, Scorpio, I'm not letting you drive. I'll take you home."

I looked at Calico from head to toe. I thought back to the first time I'd seen him. *Boy, you just don't know. If you came home with me tonight, you'll be handing over the keys to your Benz tomorrow. As horny and drunk as I am, who knows the tricks I would turn to-night?* My thoughts were interrupted by Touch's call.

"Jewel, come on, I'm taking you home." He pulled my hand with his right hand, and my purse sat comfortable on his left wrist, just like it belonged there.

Calico followed behind us as we walked to my truck. Touch unlocked the door and threw my purse and cell phone on the driver's seat.

I climbed in the passenger side and began to fumble with my iPod as I waited for him to gather some things from his car.

"Oh shit," I yelled as Calico tapped on my window, nearly scaring me to death.

He opened the door. "Let me see your phone."

I reached over and grabbed my phone from the driver's seat and handed it to him without hesitation. I'd been a bitch enough for the night. Now it was time to settle down and handle business.

Calico entered and stored his number, called his phone, then handed me my phone back. "Can I get a call tomorrow?" he asked.

The words, "You sure can," slurred from my tongue, as my head began to spin.

"Cool. Have a good night, sweetie." Calico buckled me in and closed the door.

Touch hopped in and gave Calico a wave as we pulled out of the parking lot.

As quickly as we pulled out, I was knocked out. When I opened my eyes we were in front of my home.

"Come on, drunken monkey." Touch dragged me from the truck and into the house.

As soon as I opened the door, I was met by a ringing house phone. My head still spinning, I couldn't make it past where Touch had laid me on the couch.

Touch grabbed a pillow and blanket for me and placed the pillows beneath my head, and the blanket over my body. "You need anything?" He grabbed a Heineken from the refrigerator and popped it open.

I noticed my cell phone was now ringing off the hook. "My purse."

Touch passed me my purse then headed to my bathroom to relieve himself yet again.

By the time I'd pulled my phone from my purse, I'd missed the call. I looked at my list of missed calls. I had ten missed calls, seven from Sasha, and three from a private number that I was sure was Sasha as well. *Damn! I forgot to give her that money I promised.* I immediately called her back.

"What the hell are you doing?" Sasha said as soon as she picked up.

"Cut this bullshit right now. I'm drunk," I snapped back.

"Obviously," Sasha stated. "When are you going home?"

"I am home."

"I'm on my way," she said, as though I'd invited her to come over or something. Then she hung up.

Touch sat an empty garbage can next to me and finished up his Heineken. "You straight?"

"Yeah, I'm good. Sasha is on her way."

"Good. 'Cause ol' girl is blowing my phone up. I'm out, bay." Touch gave me a hug then set the alarm to the house and locked the door behind him.

"You stink!"

I thought I was dreaming, until I opened my eyes to a tiny blurred butter pecan five-foot frame with curly hair that stood before me. As my vision cleared, I saw Sasha standing in front of me, her hands on her hips. Not wanting to be bothered with her nonsense, I immediately grabbed my purse and pulled out my wallet. I didn't say a word to her as I counted the cash in my purse. Seeing that I only had three hundred in cash, I pulled out my checkbook.

"Uh-uh." Sasha shook her head. "Don't write me no check."

"All I got is three hundred on me, Sasha. I figured if you came all the way out here in the middle of the night, you would expect to leave with the entire amount." Personally, I figured it wasn't that serious and she could have waited until the next day.

I guess she thought the same thing when she replied, "I'll just get it tomorrow," and then walked into the bathroom.

I could hear the water running from the bathtub faucet shortly after. Sasha yelled from the bathroom, "Who the hell been here?"

"How the hell you get in here?" I answered with a question, realizing I didn't let her in.

"I used the spare hidden beneath the rock. Now back to my question, please."

"And the alarm?"

"One, two, three, four. You use the same pass code for everything, bank account pin number, voice mail, alarm.

I mumbled loud enough for Sasha to hear, "Umph. Note to self, change all pass codes tomorrow, especially voice mail."

"Jewel, I know a nigga been here. So who was it?" she asked again.

"Why?"

"I know you ain't bring that nigga home from the bar." Sasha walked back into the living room.

"You think you know so fucking much, don't you?" I sat up on the couch and headed into the bathroom.

Sasha was right on my heels. "So who was it, Jewel?"

"Gotdamit! It was Touch." I realized Sasha wasn't gonna let it rest. "Is this for me?" I touched the water that filled the bathtub to test the warmth then turned the faucet off.

"Yes."

I got undressed and slowly stepped in the steaming hot water. Once I got comfortable in the tub, I rested my head against the bath pillow and closed my eyes.

A few minutes later Sasha returned. She reached over me and grabbed the shea butter body wash and loofah sponge. She lathered the sponge and began to wash my body.

Five minutes later I was rinsing the soap off and wrapping my bath up. I dried off, threw on a robe, and gave my teeth a much-needed brushing, and rinsing with Listerine. Now it was definitely time for bed.

I walked into the bedroom and took off my robe, sliding in bed beside a naked Sasha, who wrapped her arm around me and began licking the lobe of my left ear.

I grabbed her arm and gently placed it beside her and rolled over. I did it for a few of reasons. One, I was drunk as hell and not in the mood. We had gotten down like this once before, and it was good, but I really didn't prefer the girl-on-girl thing. And, two, I was no trick. I didn't need a fuck to give her that money she asked for.

"What's wrong with you?"

"Nothing. Go to sleep, Sasha."

"Go to sleep? Do I look like a child to you?"

"No, but sometimes you act like one."

Sasha had turned me off from the time she'd walked in the door, not to mention how she irritated me with this whole quit-my-career job-to-take-up-dancing decision she'd made earlier in the day.

I'd first met Sasha about a year and a half ago. I had gone with one of the niggas from my team to the club she happened to work at. It was time for her act as we walked in. She was sexy and turned me on. Our eyes were locked on each other her entire performance.

When she was done with her set, she came over, and we talked for a while. She even gave my dude a lap-dance. When I was getting ready to leave, she wrote her cell phone number on a napkin and gave it to me, telling me that I could call her anytime.

I always tried to take a picture of a new person I was putting in my phone, so I know who's calling. When I asked her to pose for the picture, she turned around and bent down, showing me her thong and fat ass. I laughed at the gesture, took the picture and then gave her my number. The next day, she called me and invited me to come to the mall with her. The rest is history.

Everything was cool for a while, but it seemed like the more I learned about her and the closer we got, the more she turned me off. And this particular night, her mouth was really pushing me over the edge.

Sasha sat up in the bed and began to yell, "What? Who the fuck do you think you're talking to?"

"You notice you're the only one yelling? You might want to bring it down a couple of notches and stop cussing at me." I constantly had to remind Sasha to watch the way she talked to me. Besides being with a tired-ass man, her anger was her biggest downfall.

Sasha let out a big sigh and flopped back down on the bed. I could hear her sniffles, a true sign she was crying.

Fuck! Now I got to kiss this bitch ass! "Why you crying, Boobie?" I rolled over and pulled her close to me.

"I'm just so stressed-out. I know you don't deserve to be talked to like that. You never cuss or yell at me. You're always so calm no matter how much I go off. I'm sorry, Jewel."

"It's all good," I said, although deep down inside I really wanted to tell her about herself.

"That's why I love you."

Sasha rolled on top of me and kissed me passionately, her kisses traveling from my lips to my breast and ending with an explosion between my thighs. "Sweet dreams," she whispered in my ears and wiped my wetness from her lips.

Chapter 2

"Truth Be Told"

Sasha

"Jewel, your phone," I mumbled, bothered by the constant ring of her house phone. She didn't even budge as I sat up in the bed and looked around the room for the cordless phone.

My first thought was the nightstand. "Nope, not there," I said to myself as I continued to search. The phone wasn't on the cradle, but I could hear it was near. I noticed the time as I glanced at the clock on the nightstand. It was nine o'clock in the morning. *Who the hell would be calling Jewel so persistently and so early on a damn Saturday?*

Shit never seemed right from the night before, so I made it my business to find out who was calling. I got out of the bed and followed the sound of the ringing phone. It led me to the walk-in closet. I opened the closet door and saw the phone sitting on top of some shoeboxes.

I shook my head as I picked the phone up. For a chick that always complained she didn't have shit to wear, she surely had an overflowing closet. I shuffled through a few pair of jeans that still had the tags on them; two hundred thirty dollars was the cheapest pair. Hell, that was about how much I owed on my past due phone bill.

As I walked out the closet, I scanned through the
caller ID to see who had been calling all morning. I
flipped to the last person that called and stopped there.
The caller ID read: Griffith, Shakira.

"Shakira Griffith," I said, knowing exactly who it
was. "Jewel." I walked over to the bed and shook her as
though I was trying to give her shaken baby syndrome.

Jewel sat up and looked at me as though she wanted
to smack me. "What, Sasha, what?"

"The feeling's mutual, mama," I said, letting her
know I was just as pissed as she was. "Why the fuck is
skank-ass Paradise calling you?" I addressed Shakira
by her dance name purposely, trying to demean her.

"Why not? And why the fuck you all in my caller ID?"
Jewel stood up and snatched the phone from my hand.

Her sexy, naked frame caught my eye for a second,
but it wasn't enough to distract my focus from the conversation at hand. She knew damn well how I felt about
Paradise, and I wasn't gonna let this shit ride.

Paradise to the strip scene, Shakira Griffith was a
young chick that Jewel and I both knew from the strip
club. She and Jewel claimed they had this "little sister-
big sister" friendship, but I'd always believed it was
more to it.

I for one knew exactly how those so-called "sister"
friendships worked. I was once like Paradise, young,
fresh, and naïve to the strip world. Then my girl Ceazia
came and took me under her wing. She was a big sister
to me too. Until we became lovers. She was my first
and would have been my only, if she hadn't had passed
away.

So when I saw the way Jewel and Paradise made eye
contact with each other when Paradise was on stage
dancing, I knew exactly what was about to come of
their so-called sisterly friendship. It was as though they

were the only two people in the club and no one else mattered. They acted like they wanted to jump on top of each other right then and there. That look was way too familiar to me because it was the same attraction that me and Jewel shared when we'd first met. And to think they had the nerve to say Paradise didn't even swing that way. Well, one thing for sure, if she wasn't already there, she was on her way.

"Why the fuck is she calling, Jewel?" I asked again following Jewel into the bathroom.

"That's what friends do, Sasha. Don't you call?"

"Are you insinuating that we are on the same level? If so, I can take that one or two ways, either I'm just a friend, or she's your lover. So which one is it, Jewel?"

I grabbed a robe for myself and handed another one to her, and we both threw them on.

"No. You are crazy." She laughed and shook her head as she began to brush her teeth.

I didn't know if Jewel was intentionally trying to rub me the wrong way or what, but she was really starting to piss me off. "You're right, I am crazy. I'm crazy for thinking I could trust your ass. I should have known what was up from the jump. I mean, I did meet you at the strip club."

After Jewel rinsed her mouth and washed her face, she said, "So what?"

"So, I had to be crazy for hollering at someone from the strip club. Just like you had me, now you're scoping out the next bitch, Paradise."

"I had you? More like you had me. Did you forget you were my first? You sought me, Sasha."

"Yeah, and now it's like you've lost your fucking mind.

"You got a taste, and now you're so confident, you're seeking pussy, huh? Yeah, I had to be crazy to think you and I could really have something."

"What? Are you serious? Nah, boo. You crazy for being with that nothing-ass nigga of yours." Jewel headed
into the living room.

I couldn't believe Jewel went there. I knew she always wanted to say something about Rick. I was just
waiting for the day. "You happy? You finally said it. You
finally got it off those thirty-six D's. Do you feel better
now? I knew you felt that way about him anyway."

"Oh, that's just the beginning. To be honest, I think
he is less than a man. You haven't been the same since
he moved in with you. You don't keep yourself up, you
always broke, you never go out. On the real, I hardly
even talk to you. It's like you gotta sneak and call or
something, and when you do call, it's because you need
something." Jewel paused then shook her head. "And
how the fuck you got a nigga living with you, yet you
got to dance in Atlanta just to keep from losing your
house? What good is a nigga if he can't do shit for you?
What you want—dick? Dick don't pay the bills, boo."

I finally had to tell Jewel how I felt about her using
men for money. "I'm sorry, I don't fuck for money—I
fuck for love. That 'gaming-a-nigga' shit is your style."

"Ha-ha-ha!" Jewel laughed as though I'd told a hi-
larious joke. "Baby, let me explain something to you.
Listen carefully because this is some real knowledge
I'm about spit to you. But, before I begin let me just
say, don't forget where you came from. If I'm not
mistaken, gaming a nigga is how you got your money
back in the day. Now, before I get down to business, let
me just point out a few things to you. I drive a Range
Rover, I own my own condo in a gated community here
in Kempsville Greens, and I am a ghostwriter but have
a background in certified medical billing and coding. I
have a closet full of designer labels, and I have investments and a nice chunk of savings. I have no children

and have no problem paying my bills. And all this comfort at a sweet age of twenty-three. So I think we all can agree that I am accomplished.

"Now, my secret to success is, I started with me. I made sure I had something solid that I could always fall back on. I have an education and a career. Then I used the power of my beauty and my booty to take things to the next level. If you want to call it fucking for money, fine, but I beg to differ. One of the standards I have for my men is that they have money, and plenty of it. So the way I see it, mami, if you wanna fuck for love, love his money. Or, better yet, fuck for the love of money. Phrase it however you like, but you better get with it."

Jewel ran down the law to me like she had invented the game herself.

"Well, Rick was there for me for five years when he had money, and now just because he's down, you want me to kick him out? And, did we forget, this is my baby father we're talking about?"

"Nope, not at all. But you need to do you. Fuck that nigga. He can't even take care of his son." Jewel walked over to answer her ringing cell phone.

I walked up to her and began staring her in the face. "We're in the middle of a conversation, Jewel. That shit can wait."

She attempted to answer. "Hello?"

"Give me the muthafuckin' phone." I tried grabbing the phone from her ear.

"Hello?" she called out again. She directed her attention back to me after realizing she'd missed the call. "Yo, you are really bugging."

"I know you fucking that bitch Paradise too," I said. Since I'd been speaking my mind all morning, there was no sense in holding that in.

"Your mind is real fucked-up, Sasha!"

"Fuck you!" I yelled. That's all I could form my mouth to say.

"Besides, if I'm fucking Shakira, why are you here?" Jewel gave me a plain look.

"You right," I said without thinking, and began to get dress.

It took all I had to keep my tears in. There was no way I was going to let Jewel see me cry. I had my clothes on in two minutes flat and was headed out the door.

She yelled, "Key, please," as soon as I opened the door.

I reached in my pocket and pulled out the single key and tossed it on the counter. I ran to my car and rushed out the neighborhood.

I pulled in the gas station on the corner and burst into tears. I didn't know what was wrong. So much was running through my mind at once. I loved Jewel, but I just didn't feel like she loved me the same. Little did she know, if she just loved me wholeheartedly, I would leave Rick and be with her. But she would rather fuck a nigga for money than kick it with me.

I couldn't help but compare our relationship with my relationship with Ceazia, a lover and my best friend that I loved her with all my heart. I would've done anything for her. My relationship with Jewel was almost similar to my last one, but for the life of me, I just couldn't understand why she didn't feel the same. Then to think she may be the first to sleep with Paradise was even more nerve-wracking.

I knew Jewel had my back in time of need, but I just didn't feel that connection I wanted. Here I was crying over her, but I was sure she had never shed a tear over me. Hell, at times I even felt like she resented me, or like I just wasn't good enough. It was like I lived in her shadow or something.

From the time I'd met her, everything was so perfect for her. And it seemed like every chance she got, she was throwing it in my face. *"Fuck that nigga. Dick don't pay the bills. I drive a Range Rover." Blah, blah, blah.* My pity began to turn to anger, the more I thought.

"Fuck that shit. Jewel is no better than me," I said, giving myself a pep talk. "Little does she know, easy come, easy go. Just as fast as she got on top, in a blink of an eye, she could be on the bottom. And when she hit, I'll be sure to be on top, so then it will be me she'll be crying to."

That was all the motivation I needed. My mind was made up. I was going to get on the grind, dancing in Atlanta and New York, and get shit back to the way it used to be.

I wiped my face and got myself together then looked above, asking Ceazia, who was now my angel above, for help. "I need you, *C.* I know you got my back."

Chapter 3

"Bag That Bitch"

Calico

I answered the phone on the final ring, in an attempt not to seem too anxious. "Hello?"

"What's up?" Jewel sang from the other end.

"Nothing much. What's up witchu?" I remembered how drunk she was the previous night. "You feeling all right?"

"Yeah, I'm good. I may have had a slight hangover when I woke up, but I had so much drama this morning, I wouldn't have even noticed," she said, sounding a bit agitated.

I sensed her stress. "Damn! Sounds like you need to do something nice for the rest of the day to make you forget about your morning."

Jewel jumped at the opportunity. "Any suggestions?"

"Well, I was going to the outlet to grab a few things. You want to roll?"

"Potomac Mills?" she asked. Her response let me know off the top what type of spending she was interested in. "Nah, Williamsburg."

"Calico, there aren't any really good stores there. Have you even tried Potomac Mills?"

"Nah," I said, playing stupid. "Where is it?"

"Up I-95 North, like you going toward DC."

"That's too far, baby. I'm just trying to shoot there and shoot back."

Jewel realized she was fighting a losing battle and finally gave in. She gave me her address, and I agreed to pick her up at two o'clock, which gave me time to take care of a few things before we left.

"Hello?" Jewel answered in a sultry tone.

"I'm out front," I replied, Shawty Lo's "Dey Know" blasting in the background.

"I'm coming out now."

I watched as Jewel walked toward the car. Her lips seemed extra lip-gloss shiny. She was sexy as hell, dressed in a white stretched tank top that accented her perky breasts, and matching white jeans that were so tight, if she bent over, I could see the print of her pussy lips.

"Hey, Miss Lady." I greeted her with a hug. *Damn, your ass is phat!* I thought as she sat her perfectly round ass down on the black leather passenger seat of my black drop-top. My dick was getting hard by the minute.

I looked at Jewel's full lips again and started to imagine myself getting my dick sucked, riding down the interstate with the music blasting. I looked her up from head to toe one last time, while pretending to look for a CD.

My peep show was interrupted by her yell and look of disgust. "CD's? Are you serious?"

Confused, I asked, "What? You want to listen to the radio or something?"

"No, boo. iPod," she replied with that same sassiness she was giving me last night.

"Oh, I forgot who I was dealing with. Sorry, Miss Prima Donna. I don't have an iPod," I said as I inserted Jay-Z.

"Well, the next time we meet, please have one. So are we still going to the Williamsburg Outlets?" She asked as though I'd changed my mind or something.

"Yeah, I wish we could go further, but I have some business to take care of later on tonight," I said, a mischievous grin on my face as I checked out her smile.

"All right, what's so funny?"

"Nothing. I'm feeling the wife-beater on you. That's real gangster for a diva like you. All you need is a fresh pair of Air Force One's to match." I took another look at her.

"For the record, fresh white Prada's, not Nike's. And thank you for the compliment, but honestly, I think I look a little fat." Jewel grinned back at me.

"What? You're crazy." I took this as an opportunity to look her over quickly. "You have a killer frame."

"No, honey. I have one of those borderline frames. I'm one Slim-Fast away from Beyoncé, and one burger away from *America's Next Top Model* contestant, Toccara."

We both laughed.

"Look, let me tell you something about skinny chicks. Don't no man want a skinny chick. For one, no one knows how she got that way. The bitch could be sick. The way I see it, give me a fat bitch. At least I know she healthy," I said.

We both laughed uncontrollably.

"You enjoy yourself at the bar last night?" I asked, changing the subject as we headed toward 64 West.

"Yes, I did, but I don't do the whole bar scene too often."

"I know." I nodded at her.

"How so?"

"Well, it was one of the first things I noticed.

I meet Touch at that spot all the time, and last night was the first time I'd seen you. If you hung out at the bars often, I'm sure I would have seen you there before."

"Yeah, clubs, bars, and lounges aren't really my thing. All it consists of is guys wishing they could get a second to talk to you, and the girls, you know how that goes, they wish they could get a second to talk to a nice guy. But when he doesn't want to holler at her, she will hate all night on the chick that can accomplish what she can't."

"Well, I will let you know right now that I've never been turned down," I said with plenty of confidence.

"Neither have I."

We both gave each other a smirk.

Just then, Sean Kingston's "Beautiful Girls" started playing on the radio, and Jewel started singing to the lyrics.

> "You're way too beautiful
> That's why it'll never work
> You had me suicidal, suicidal
> When you say it's over"

She sang like the song was talking about her specifically.

I gave Jewel a playful shove in the head. "You ain't gon' have nobody suicidal."

"Whatever. We'll see about that." She rolled her eyes and neck in unison then said to me, "Tell me about yourself."

"It's not much to tell. My name is Calico, and I'm from Los Angeles, California. My pops was a drug dealer-turned entrepreneur. He had a hot li'l jewelry spot in LA back in the day, but when we had those riots back in ninety-two, he lost everything. For the first time, my father couldn't provide for his family. He tried everything to get back on his feet. Everything, except going to back to the dope game. He'd promised my mother that once he was out, he would never go back to it. Eventually my father could no longer take the pressure of not being able to provide for his family, so he drank himself to death, and my mother slowly but surely picked up the pieces.

"Seeing my mom struggle as a kid really fucked me up, so I decided I was going to be the man of the house. I automatically had respect on the streets because of my father's street cred. After some good deals came through that put real money in my pocket, I stepped up to the plate and took care of the house. Still, my mother has never been the same. I can't tell you the last time I've seen her truly happy."

"Any brothers or sisters?"

"Yeah, I have an older brother and sister. I'm the baby. I will let you know now, I'm a serious momma's boy. Whatever momma wants, that woman gets."

"Of course, I understand. So you and Touch are good friends?"

I felt like I was under interrogation as Jewel came at me with question after question. "We're more like business partners, splitting the profits right down the middle." I then turned the tables on her. "What do you do?"

"Right now, I'm a ghostwriter full-time. Yesterday, I was a medical biller and coder. Tomorrow, I'll be the girl of your dreams, and soon after that, I'll be running that part of the business you have with Touch," Jewel said without a doubt.

I grinned. "Damn! You got big dreams, shorty." I knew there was no way in hell she could ever reach any of those dreams she had set for tomorrow and thereafter.

Jewel looked me directly in my eyes and gave me a seductive look. "It's not a dream, baby." She paused and gently caressed my chin. "It's very, very real." She ended the statement with a kiss into the air.

I took a swallow in an attempt to break the trance she had just put me in. She watched and gave a slight smile, as though she knew what I was thinking.

"So"—my voice cracked, making me clear my throat—"do you make a lot of money ghostwriting?"

"Yes, you can. It depends on who you write for, and how many jobs you get. The job can be tiring at times, but I enjoy it."

"Is it hard?" I asked, really intrigued by her profession.

"Not really, but I feel as if my job is never complete. I'm only as good as the last song that I wrote."

"So why not just be a rapper? I thought everybody wanted to be a rapper."

"Yeah, when they're like thirteen. Rapping is not for me. I could never get on stage and perform like that. I'm more of a behind-the-scenes type of chick. I'm good without the fame. I already got my share of it. All I want is my check, you feel me?" Jewel chuckled.

"I heard that. You already got your fame, huh? A'ight, Miss Local Celebrity." I laughed.

Jewel snapped back, "No, baby. I'm a star wherever I go."

"Damn, girl. One thing about you that I'm gonna have to get used to is that mouth." I shook my head, wondering if it was really possible for me to get used to it.

"That's me. You have to accept everything about me, smart mouth and all. Take it or leave it. I put it all out there straight, no chaser. Now it's up to you to decide what you want."

"I'll take it." I laughed, knowing I could break her little ass down to Reese's Pieces in a matter of days.

Jewel joined in on my laughter. "I know."

Time passed by quickly as we talked and laughed together, and before I knew it, we were at the Williamsburg Outlet. I parked and opened the door for Jewel.

"What store do you want to start at first?" she asked.

"Lead the way. I'm with you," I replied with a smile that consisted of a upper blue and white diamond grill.

I followed Jewel as she headed to our first stop, the BCBG store. Next, we hit Michael Kors. Then we hit a few stores for me, like the Timberland store, Cole Haan, Izod, Nike Factory, and Vans. After that, we were back to Jewel's picks, Guess, Coach, Perfume World, and Sunglass World. Knowing that Jewel was watching my every move, I didn't complain the entire time. I never even lifted an eyebrow, no matter how much her total ran up to.

"Before we leave, I want to hit Gymboree and Nautica," Jewel requested.

"Gymboree? Isn't that a kids' store?"

"Yes, it is."

"I didn't know you had kids," I stated.

"I don't."

With a puzzled look on my face, I began to wonder if Jewel was straight trying to play me for a sucker. I watched as she picked up little girls' clothing, two of each. My first reaction was to cuss her ass out, but I chose to roll with it. I figured at least I could get a fuck out of it, if nothing else. I prepared to pay as we reached the counter.

"Thank you for your generosity, but I got this one."

Jewel's response surprised me. "So who's it for?" I asked out of curiosity.

"Touch's twin girls."

"Oh yeah? Y'all tight like that?"

"Yep! Tighter than these jeans I have on." Jewel laughed.

As I watched her ass bounce with each step, I thought, *Damn! And my nigga ain't never tried to fuck that?*

"I want cookies and cream on a waffle cone," she said like a kid at the ice cream truck as we passed Ben & Jerry's.

"Come on, baby, I know you don't want that junk. I'm in the mood for steak." I looked at my watch.

"Okay," she quickly agreed. "Steak is better than ice cream on any day."

"Unless that day happens to be the day you get your tonsils taken out." We both laughed.

"So, are we eating here or back near the beach?" Jewel asked as we loaded the bags into the trunk of the car.

"It's up to you."

"Ummm, the beach. I don't know much about this area, except the outlet stores."

"Okay." I took her right hand and kissed it. "Well, let's go get lady Jewel her filet mignon."

Chapter 4

"Baby Momma Drama"

Touch

I spotted my homeboy Calico as soon as I walked through the door of Mo Dean's Jamaican Restaurant and Lounge. "What up, ace."

"What up, fool." He gave me a hardy pound and pat on the back. "Yo, I'ma tell you right now, your fucking baby momma in here, nigga, so put the brakes on."

"I ain't worryin' about her, man," I said, quickly glancing around the bar. It didn't take long for me to spot her. She sat at a booth on the other side of the place with her partner in crime, Monica, and a couple of their ghetto-fabulous girlfriends. I contemplated on whether or not I should just blow the joint. Knowing her ghetto ass, at first sight of me, she would want to make a scene, and I wasn't the one for drama. Still, I wasn't going to be intimidated by her, nor was I going to let her keep me from getting my drink on.

I grabbed a stool and sat in the corner, out of their sight. The cute waitress with a phat ass wasted no time coming my way. "What can I get for you, Touch?"

I imagined bending her over and pounding that ass from the back. "A back shot," I said.

"Whatever, nigga! I'll be right back with your Grey Goose on the rocks," she said then walked off, her booty bouncing each step of the way.

For some reason I felt like she put an extra bounce in there just for me. She knew I would be looking as soon as she walked off. I pulled out a cigarette and lit it. I took a few pulls. *Damn,* I thought to myself, *I even have to take a smoke to mentally fuck this bitch. That shit is crazy.*

When the waitress came back with my drink, I told her, "Thank you, baby. I got you," letting her know I'd take care of my tab at the end of the night.

"Don't be trying to run out on me," she said playfully. "You know I'm supposed to hold your credit card."

"Come on, sweetheart."

It was a damn shame that I'd been going to that lounge nearly six months and this same waitress had always been there, but I didn't know her name. Me and the niggas always referred to her as the cute waitress with the phat ass.

"How you gon' play me like that? What's your name, ma?"

"Diana," she said, looking straight in my eyes.

"Okay, Diana, you win. I'll pay for my drinks as we go." I pulled out a twenty to pay for my drink.

"That's okay," she said, finally seeing shit my way. She pushed my hand away. "I'll see you at the end of the night."

Like with every first drink, I threw that shit down my throat in just a couple of swallows, and as soon as my empty glass hit the table, Diana was there.

"Ready for another one?"

"Yeah. Make this one a double shot," I requested.

"A'ight. I'll be right back."

Calico came over and grabbed a seat next to me. "You good, nigga?"

"Yeah, I'm straight."

"Gotdamn, nigga, you gon' make your baby momma force you to stay in the gotdamn corner all night?"

"Hell nah. She ain't forcing me to stay nowhere. I'm chilling, nigga. After a few drinks I'm out anyway."

"So how shit looking?" Calico wanted to know how quickly the coke he'd given me the day before was moving.

I told him, "Shit right, nigga. Cats loving this white girl. She different from the last one you gave me."

"A'ight. So when we talking?" Calico asked, referring to the one hundred fifty grand I owed him.

"In a few days I should be straight."

"Here you go," Diana said, interrupting our conversation. She winked an eye at Calico.

I noticed the double shot of Grey Goose on the rocks plus two shot glasses filled with liquor. "What's this?" I asked.

"Patrón. Let's take a shot together. It's on me."

I tried declining the drink the best way I knew how. "I don't do Patrón, ma."

Calico shook his head from side to side. "Man, go ahead and take the shot, nigga."

I thought back to the last time I had Patrón. I woke up on the steps of my mom's front porch, and my car was parked in the middle of her front yard. Patrón was definitely not my thing, and Calico knew it. I had to wonder if he was trying to set me up.

Diana folded her arms and gave me a slight pout. "Oh, so you gonna disappoint me like that?"

Calico said to Diana, "Give that man some motivation. A nigga ain't trying to take risks for nothing." Then he cut his eyes at me to take it from there. He'd set up the bait; now I just needed to catch the fish and reel her in.

I really never needed help bagging a girl, but Calico thought he would lend a hand. I figured

since he had gone through all this trouble, I would at least play along and take the drink, so I played into the setup.

"I'm saying, if I get sick from this shit, who gon' take care of a nigga?"

Diana smiled. "I'll take full responsibility."

"Let's do it," I said, feeling Diana was down for whatever.

We tapped glasses and downed the drinks.

"Damn!" The liquor felt like it was burning a path down my throat to my chest. I grabbed my Grey Goose and drank it as a chaser.

As I sipped my vodka, I looked over at Diana, who was whispering in Calico's ear. He didn't seem to be fazed by the tequila shot at all.

Diana diverted her attention back to me, while twirling the end of the braid of my cornrow between her fingers. "You okay, sweetie?"

"I could be better," I responded to her subtle flirtation.

"Well, can I help?" Diana licked her lips.

I grinned then glanced at Calico to see if he was picking up on the same vibes I was getting from her. He cut a small grin back as an indication that he was. Now that I knew this shit was real and it wasn't just the liquor talking, I fed right into the game she was playing.

"Yeah, but I'ma need you to come with me to do that." I came on strong, to see if this bitch was really with it and not just talking shit, but she said exactly what I wanted to hear.

"A'ight. I get off in a couple of hours. Hang out and we can leave together."

As Diana walked away, Calico said, "Damn, Touch! It's like that, nigga?"

"It is what it is, baby."

We both laughed as I pulled out another cigarette.

I stood up to head to the bathroom and stumbled a bit on my first step. *That Patrón must really be getting to me*, I thought as I passed the booth that my baby mother and her girls sat at. I didn't even look in her direction as I went through the double doors leading to the bathrooms.

Before I could hang a left and go into the men's bathroom, I was stopped by a familiar five-foot-five frame. I didn't say a word as I looked at her voluptuous breasts. My mind was too busy thinking about how nicely my dick would fit between them. Then I looked down to see a small hand massaging it softly. I opened my mouth to tell Diana to chill, but before I could get one word out, my mouth was filled with her tongue. I didn't even resist.

I ain't even the kissing type, especially not with a jump-off, but for some reason I was really feeling that shit this night. I moved my hands all over Diana's plump ass and between her ass cheeks. I couldn't wait to get inside her.

My first thought was to pull her into the men's bathroom and bend her over the sink and bang her out in there, but the real nigga in me just wouldn't let that shit happen. "Save this for later, ma," I said, and I pulled away from her and headed into the bathroom.

After relieving myself of the liquor I'd consumed, and the blood rush that Diana provoked, I washed my hands and headed out the door. Just like I was stopped going in, I was stopped coming out, but it wasn't as pleasant as the first time.

Ciara, my baby mother, said, "I know you saw me when you came back here."

Not even you can ruin this night, I thought, playing it cool with her to prevent argument. "Yeah, but I had to piss."

"Give me some money, Trayvon," Ciara said, addressing me by my government name. She felt my pockets to see if I had the usual wad of money in there.

Without protesting I pulled off five twenties, handed them to her, and walked away.

When I arrived back at my table, Calico was sitting there with a couple of chicks. I already had my meal planned for the night, so I chose to sit at the bar rather than disrupt him. Who knows, maybe he was trying to set up a little late-night snack for himself.

I sat at the bar playing the computer game as Diana constantly fed me drinks. Every time she passed by, she would either blow me a kiss, stick her tongue out seductively, or give me some other type of sexual notion. This bitch really had me going.

I pulled out one of my phones to check the time. *One o'clock. One hour to go*, I thought. I sat my phone on the bar beside me and turned my concentration back on my game.

My bothersome baby mother came over again just to annoy me. "Why you sitting over here instead of with your friends? What you looking for—some pussy?"

"Nah. I'm letting Calico get some time in with the hoes."

"Whatever," she said then walked off.

There was no way in hell I could tell Ciara what I was doing. That bitch would fuck up anything I had with another female. I never understood why Ciara acted such a damn fool. I hadn't slept with her, finger-fucked her, or even kissed her since I came home from jail nearly three years ago. Again I turned my attention back to my game.

Not even five minutes passed before my cell phone began to ring. I answered my girlfriend's call, "What's up?"

"What the fuck you mean, 'what's up'? Have you lost your mind, Touch? If you going to be with your baby mother every night, why don't you go live with her?" My girl went on and on.

"What the fuck you talking 'bout?" I asked as calmly as possibly. I looked around the bar to see if maybe my girl was at the lounge and assumed me and my baby mother were there together.

"I just got off the phone with Ciara, Touch. She called me from your other phone."

I looked around the bar for Ciara as I listened to my girl talk.

"She told me she was calling from your phone tonight to prove that are y'all are together."

I got a glimpse of Ciara sitting in the booth, looking in my direction, with a stupid-ass I'm guilty smirk on her face. I hung up on my girl as I headed toward the booth.

Once I arrived at the table, Ciara was sitting there with my phone in her hand. She stared me dead in my eyes with a look that said, "Yeah, I did it. So what you gonna do about it?"

I wasn't that nigga that hit chicks, but if pushed, I would set a bitch straight quick. And this night I was just about seconds away from beating the shit out of Ciara. I ain't even bother to entertain her bullshit. I just snatched my phone out of her hand then walked out the club.

Diana and Calico both called out to me as I stormed out the front door. I didn't even pause to see what they wanted. I was fuming inside. I knew if I spent another five seconds in Ciara's presence I would end up at 811, better known as Norfolk City Jail.

I rushed to my crib to try and explain shit to my girl. As soon as I pulled up, I noticed little pieces of burning paper falling out the window. I figured she must be doing that shit chicks do when they get mad, like ripping and burning pictures of us. Normally I didn't make it a practice of explaining shit to a chick, but this time I had no choice.

I rushed to the house and opened the door. The smell of bleach smacked me in the face as soon as I walked through the foyer. Now, I'd heard of people doing a lot of things when they get upset, like exercise, write, go for walk, but this was the first time I'd seen someone go on a cleaning binge then burn pictures. I followed the scent of bleach and burning paper up the stairs to the master bathroom. There I saw my girl sitting at the bathroom window with stacks of my money, pulling off twenty after twenty, setting them on fire, and throwing it out the window.

Without thinking I rushed toward her and grabbed her throat. My first instinct was to set that bitch on fire and throw her ass out the window, but her gasps for air snapped me back to reality.

"Bitch!" I pushed her to the floor and began to gather my money. I grabbed a Gucci duffle and threw my money in there then began to grab some clothes.

Even though this was my house, I wasn't going to stay a second longer; otherwise I was definitely catching a charge tonight.

As I rambled through the closet to pick out a few key pieces of clothing, my girl screamed, "I hate your trifling ass!"

I ain't say shit to her ass as I gathered my things. I just needed to get the fuck out of dodge, and fast.

In five minutes flat, I had my bag packed with enough clothes to last me a week. I glanced around the room one last time before exiting.

My girl lit a blunt and took a pull from it. She said calmly, "Don't forget your shit in the bathroom."

From the look on that bitch face, I could tell she'd done some real fucked-up shit. I tried to think of the worst possible scenarios as I prepared myself to enter the bathroom.

I walked in and glanced around, but didn't notice anything strange. "What the fuck you talking about?" I asked, anxious to get out of the house.

She shot me a devious smirk. "The bathtub."

I took a deep breath as I pulled back the shower curtain. I almost fainted when I looked down. Both of my chinchillas that I'd spent twenty thousand dollars on each were in the tub, soaking in bleach. I could feel my blood pressure rise, the more I looked at them. I ripped the shower curtain down, pulling the rod with it, and stormed out the bathroom.

My girl stood in the middle of the floor, a Kool-Aid smile on her face.

Although everything in me said, "Beat that bitch, stomp that whore, whup that trick," like I was Terrence Howard on *Hustle & Flow*, I used every ounce of strength I had and walked right past her.

"Yeah, that's what you better do—Walk away, you little pussy!"

I stopped in my tracks as my girl's words pierced my ears. "Bitch!" I smacked her, and she fell to the floor. I yelled, "You ain't shit without me!" and proceeded to rip every piece of clothing and jewelry off her. Then I pulled her down the steps, ass naked. "And get the fuck out my house!" I pulled her out the front door and locked it behind me.

Once outside, I hopped in my car, leaving my girl standing in the nude as I pulled off. I sped out of the neighborhood and never looked back. My head was racing as I drove. I didn't know what to think. And the constant ringing of my cell phones was driving me crazy.

I looked at my phone to see who was blowing me up. It was my man Calico. Then it hit me. *Oh shit! I forgot to pay my tab! I know that bitch is tripping too. I did exactly what I told her I wasn't gon' do. Damn!*

I busted a U-turn and headed back in the direction of the bar, where I arrived ten minutes later. I jumped out the car and rushed in.

As soon as I walked through the door, I saw Calico holding Ciara, whispering in her ear. *What the fuck y'all doing?* I thought as I walked up to them.

As soon as Calico noticed me, he said, "Touch, get your baby momma, man."

As I examined the situation before me, I thought to myself, *What the fuck for? It looks like you got her right where you want her, nigga.*

"Trayvon, don't need to do shit," Ciara snapped. "That's why that bitch 'bout to get her ass whupped now . . . because of Trayvon."

I was wondering how so much shit could happen in one night. For a nigga like me, this was unheard of, and I was close to becoming undone. No one wants to see when that happens. "What the fuck is going on?"

"Man, she tripping on ol' girl," Calico said.

I looked over at Diana standing at the bar getting some drinks, oblivious to what was going on. I shook my head and pulled out a hundred dollars. "Pay my tab for me, man." I handed the money to Calico. "And you"—I grabbed Ciara— "let's go."

Ciara looked over her shoulder first at Calico then gave Diana an evil glare and grabbed my hand and came without hesitation. I wasn't sure what that eye contact with Calico was about, but I was sure gon' find out later. I didn't trust Ciara one bit, but I was more irritated because I didn't want Diana caught up in no bullshit because of me. I knew how Ciara and her girls could get, and I didn't even want Diana caught up in that.

I was drained as hell as I drove all the way to Chesapeake to take Ciara home. I was glad when I got to her crib. I didn't even park, I just pulled up in front and hit the unlock button, a sign for her to get the fuck out.

"Damn, you ain't even gon' come and see your kids," Ciara spat.

"Don't even come at me like I'm some deadbeat dad. They should be 'sleep anyway."

"So what?" She yelled as though I was around the block somewhere and not right in her face.

I wouldn't mind seeing my li'l fat rats, I thought. I swung the car around in a parking spot and hopped out. Then I followed Ciara to her apartment.

As soon as she put the key in the door, I could hear the twins.

"Mommy's home!" they yelled. They ran and hugged Ciara as she stepped through the door. "Hey, Mommy."

Kennedy was the first to see me. She yelled, "Daddddyyyy!" and rushed over and hugged me tight.

I picked her and Reagan both up in my arms and kissed them. "What y'all still doing up?" I said as I sat on the couch.

"Watching this damn Beyoncé DVD," their aunt said, sounding exhausted. She'd been watching them all day while Ciara ran the streets.

"A'ight, girls, time for bed." I held my hands out for each of them to grab one. As we walked to their room, Reagan said, "Can you read us a bedtime story?"

"Yep. What y'all want me to read?"

"*Dora*," they both said in unison.

"*Dora*? Nah, she a punk," I said to tease the girls. "What about Diego?"

Kennedy said right away, "Daddy, Diego is for boys. We are girls."

"A'ight, a'ight. *Dora the Explorer*, it is."

Once I got the girls tucked in and started to read Dora, they fell fast asleep. I looked at the time. It was already 3:00 A.M. Since I was comfortable, I decided to get in a quick nap.

Three minutes after I closed my eyes, Ciara yelled, "Trayvon! Trayvon, wake up!"

"Yeah?" I wondered what the fuck she wanted.

"Come get in the bed," she said, grabbing my hand.

I looked at the girls, who were both out for the count. I got up and kissed them on the cheeks then headed to Ciara's room. I pulled off everything, except my boxers, and lay down, and she slid in beside me.

Just as I was dozing off to sleep, I felt a hand glide against my dick. I turned on my back and looked over my right shoulder at Ciara. She was ass naked.

Although my dick was saying yes, my mind was saying fuck no! There was no way I could fuck Ciara. She was already a crazy baby momma. If I fucked her, the bitch would really lose her mind. In her mind, that would mean we were getting back together, and no way in hell was that ever happening.

"Come on, chill with that bullshit, Ciara."

"So you trying to tell me you gon' lay up in here next to me and not fuck me, Trayvon?"

"Basically." I rolled back over on my side, putting my back to her.

"Well, then get out." Ciara shoved me with her foot, forcing me off the bed.

I wasn't up for another argument or fight, so I put my shit on and broke out. There was no way I was going back to my house. I figured my girl had probably called the police and everything, so when I got in the car, I hit Jewel up.

"Hello?" Jewel said in one of those deep-ass sleep voices.

"Damn, you sound like a man. I'm homeless," I said, knowing she would offer her place.

"Come through, Touch. You know where the key is." Jewel then hung up the phone.

I looked up at the sky as I drove to her house. *It's gotta be a full moon*, I thought, recalling the crazy night I'd had.

Fifteen minutes later, I was at Jewel's crib, knocked out in her guest bedroom. Finally, I had the opportunity to let my guard down and get some much-needed rest.

"Damn." I woke to the smell of bacon and a growling stomach.

I dragged myself out of the bed and into the bathroom. As I stood in front of the toilet to take a piss, I looked down at my hard dick and wished I had some hot, wet, morning pussy to push it in. For a moment, I actually fantasized about ramming my dick up in Jewel. I quickly shook that from my head, flushed the toilet, and washed up before following the smell of bacon into the kitchen.

I walked up on Jewel as she chatted away on the phone. "You made enough for me, yo?"

"You the only reason I'm cooking, nigga," Jewel responded as she poured the blueberry waffle mix into the waffle maker. "I don't do breakfast."

"Damn, man! You always got that phone glued to your ear. Ain't you afraid of getting ear cancer or some shit?"

We both laughed at the thought, and I grabbed a seat at the breakfast bar. I listened to Jewel talk on the phone as I waited for her to finish cooking.

I heard her say into the phone, "What? Please don't trip. That is Touch. I told you we were tight. He's like my brother."

I wondered who the fuck she was talking to. It seemed like we had to go through this same shit with every nigga she fucked with. Every single one of those cats assumed me and Jewel had something other than a friendship.

"Okay, I'll call you later." Jewel hung up the phone.

"Who was that?" I asked, my face balled-up.

She smirked. "Your crazy-ass friend."

"Who?" I wondered who the fuck she could be talking about.

"Calico."

"Calico? Are you serious?" I asked, hoping she was joking.

"Yes, Calico."

"I just saw this nigga last night. He ain't even say shit about y'all kicking it."

"Yeah. We were together all day yesterday. We went shopping and everything. Which reminds me, I got the girls something."

"And that nigga already tripping?"

"Nah, he was saying to call him when I was free," Jewel said, already making excuses for him, "and he didn't know we were close like that to be spending the night together."

"Yo, give me the phone and let me call that nigga." I reached for the house phone.

"Ahh . . . no. Me and him ain't even like that for him to be trying to trip, so don't waste your time." Jewel grabbed the cordless phone and pushed it out of my reach. "So what the hell happen last night?" she asked as she made my plate.

"To make a long story short, my baby momma fucked with ol' girl again, and the bitch went crazy. When I went home, the bitch had bleached my furs and was burning my money. So I released her from all the shit I bought, which left her naked, and I pitched her dumb ass out my house. I went back to the bar where Ciara was beefing with a chick I was hollering at earlier in the night. So I grabbed her and took her home. My fat rats were awake, so I chilled with them and ended up falling asleep in their bed and shit. Ciara wakes me up and tells me to go get in her bed. Then the bitch wants to fuck. Now you know the worse thing I could possibly do is fuck her, so I refused. Now she starts to trip, so I dip out on her. I thought the other bitch might have called the cops, so thinking the block was hot, I called you for a place to crash, and here I am."

"Damn, Touch, you had a busy night. You're always gettin' into shit because of your baby mother. Why don't you check her on that crazy shit she be doing?" Jewel asked as she placed my plate in front of me.

"Ain't no talking to that girl, Jewel."

"Whatever." Jewel passed me a glass of orange juice. "Deep inside, I think you don't want her to leave you alone. You like the fact that she be going crazy over your ass."

"Nah, man. I can't stand the drama."

"So why y'all ain't together anyway? You never really told me the whole story, you know."

"She fucked up," I said, trying not to really go into details. "I could never trust that bitch again."

Jewel really started digging deep into my business and inquired more, just like I knew she would. "What did she do?"

The truth was, that shit Ciara did really fucked me up. And that shit her and Calico was doing the night before was kind of suspect. It took me back to that shit she'd done before. A nigga was hurt and I hated reliving that moment. But I'd never kept anything from Jewel for this long, so I thought I'd come out with it.

"When I was locked up, she started fucking one of my little worker cats, a nigga I put on the corner."

"What? Are you serious?"

"Yeah. A li'l nothing-ass nickel-and-dime cat." I shook my head.

"I can tell that shit really hurt you, Touch." Jewel stared me in my face, seemingly waiting for a reaction.

"Look, I ain't never lied to you before, and I'm not gon' start now. My baby mother is the only chick I've ever loved," I said, confessing my feelings for Ciara for the first time, "so you damn straight—that shit fucked me up when I found out she fucked my man. But, you know, it is what it is."

"I know you still love her, and I know you love your twins, so why don't you just be with her and have one big happy family?" Jewel said it like it was an easy fix.

"Can't do it. I don't go back."

"Nah. You just got too much pride. You know niggas would clown you." Jewel's words were painfully true.

"You might be right."

"I know I am. Just try it. You don't have to dive into it headfirst. Shit, what do you have to lose? I know you ain't trying to get back with ol' girl. She probably ain't even trying to fuck with you like that anymore, anyway. So why not holler at your baby mother?"

I let what Jewel said go in one ear and leave out the other. "We'll see."

"Well, can we see my truck?" Jewel said, reminding me that I still hadn't brought her truck back to the crib.

"Oh, shit. It's at my mom's house in the garage. We can go get it after breakfast."

"That's cool. I need to holler at Ma Dukes anyway."

"Yo, I told you about that shit."

My mother loved Jewel like she was the daughter she never had. For some reason, they clicked from the first day they'd met. Every time my mother would see or speak to Jewel, the first thing I'd hear was, "I really like her, Trayvon, I really do."

"Don't hate because Ma loves me!" Jewel cleared the bar then walked into her bedroom. "Momma knows best, baby boy. Momma knows best."

You might be right. I reached for a cigarette then massaged my rising dick as I watched the silhouette of Jewel's ass bounce beneath her satin robe.

Chapter 5

"One Love Out and Another One In"

Jewel

A week or so had gone and, for the most part, my life as I knew was pretty quiet. That silence was interrupted by a familiar ringtone. "It's your baby. Pick up. It's your baby. Pick up," the voice from my cell constantly repeated.

I sat up in the bed and rubbed my eyes as I tried to figure out where my phone was. I finally found it on the dressing table and quickly flipped it open. "Hello?" I said through a cracked voice.

"Hi, Jewel," Sasha said faintly.

"What's up, Sasha? How are you doing?"

"Not too good. I miss you, Jewel. I'm leaving today, and there was no way I could leave without seeing you."

"Damn."

Reality had finally set in. It wasn't until that point that I realized how much Sasha really meant to me. True, she irritated me at times with her constant nagging and the poor decisions she made, but she was still my boobie and I loved her.

"So that's all you have to say?" Sasha asked.

"No. Actually, I don't know what to say. This is all of a sudden."

"Well, I already did a quick sale on my house, sold my car to a used-car dealer, turned off all my utilities, and broke up with Rick."

"Well, at least one good thing came out of all this," I said, referring to her breakup. "So what's next? You just gonna live in Georgia now?"

"I'm gonna stay with my mom, and dance in Atlanta. Hopefully, I'll get my money right and be able to get back on my feet."

I tried to give some encouraging words. "Sounds like a plan. Sometimes you just gotta start over, in a fresh environment, you know what I mean?"

"Yeah, I feel ya. So what do I have to do to get me a baller when I hit the A?"

"Oh, now you want advice from the gold-digging whore," I said in a joking tone.

"Jewel! You know you're not a whore. I'm sorry for anything I may have said the last time when we spoke. I was angry and jealous about the whole situation."

"Apology accepted," I said, with no hesitation.

"I swear, that's why I love you so much. You have the biggest heart in the world! *Muah!*" Sasha kissed the phone.

"Kisses back at you, Boobie."

"Okay, now to business. Tell me how to get my rich man!" For once Sasha seemed really interested in my advice.

"All right, listen carefully. Matter of fact, you might need to jot this down." I laughed then continued. "First, you have to look, act, and talk like a top-notch chick. Your persona can't say stripper, groupie, or gold digger. Show that you are pretty and intelligent, not some dumb chick. You should familiarize yourself with upscale places in the area.

"Next, you have to know your target. You have to be able to identify real money, know the difference between dope boy money versus athlete, entertainment, and distinguished money. Don't be fooled by exotic car rentals, fake jewelry, and fake clothes. Men with genuine money are reserved and on the low. They have nothing to prove, and therefore they're not flamboyant, and never seeking attention.

"Once you've identified your man, you have to get his attention. Do this by sending him and his boys a drink. On your first date, pull out your wallet and prepare to pay. Although he will stop you, he will find it very impressive. If things go farther, when you're out shopping, bring him back something significant, like his favorite cologne. When you're spending the night at his house, tidy up a little, and more importantly, get up and go to work in the morning.

"Now this is the part where most women fuck up, so pay close attention. Play your position. I repeat—play your position. Know that you are more than likely not the only female in his life. Nine times out of ten, he has a wife at home, which makes you a mistress. Never compete with the home front. Don't smother him. You will receive monetary support and gifts for the lack of attention. And, last but not least, satisfy your man sexually. Have a huge sexual appetite, learn what turns him on and off, and be prepared to fill his every fantasy. You want to do everything that his wife or the next girl won't do. So if that means threesomes, sucking dick, licking ass or fucking in the ass, be prepared and willing to do it." I ran down the dos and don'ts like I wrote the manual.

"Damn, it's that serious, huh? I think I got it, though. I'm gonna put it to the test in Atlanta. I'll let you know if it works."

"It's foolproof, baby," I assured her. "I promise you, if executed correctly, it will work."

"Oh, I know. If anybody knows how to get a man or woman, it's you. Hell, you even got the power to get straight bitches." Sasha somehow managed to turn this conversation around to talk about Shakira.

"Blah, blah, blah, blah," I sang to cut her off. "I'm not trying to hear that shit. This is your last day here. You supposed to be over here fucking me like you will never get another piece of pussy in life." I knew that would grab her attention.

"That's why I was calling. I want to spend my last hours with you. Are you going to come get me?"

"Is everything in order?" I asked, to be sure she had mended all her loose ends.

"Yep. They closed on the house today. The family I sold the furniture to came and got the last of it yesterday. I dropped off my truck this morning, and the boys have already made it to Georgia." Sasha ran down everything to me.

"Okay, I'm on my way." I hung up the phone, freshened up, and headed out the door. Thirty minutes later, I was in front of her house. Sasha hopped in, and I put the truck in drive to pull off.

"Wait." Sasha placed her hand on top of mine at the gearshift.

I put the truck back in park. "What's wrong?"

Sasha didn't respond. She just stared at her house.

"Did you forget something?" I asked, confused by her actions.

Again she didn't say anything, but she did shake her head no. I had a feeling that something was really wrong. I gently grabbed her by her chin and turned her toward me. And, just as I'd thought, tears were rolling down her eyes. I didn't say a word. I just grabbed her

and hugged her tight. I listened as she cried hysterically.

"This is my house, Jewel," she said, forcing out the
words. "This is all I had left. Now I have nothing, absolutely nothing. No car, no furniture, no home, nothing.
All I have is a shitload of dance costumes and heels,
and a single suitcase of daily clothes."

Damn, I thought to myself, *she doesn't deserve this.*
I truly felt bad for her.

"Baby, I wish I could make it all right," I told her.
"Look, before you know it, things will be better. Just go
to Atlanta and stack your dough. When you get a little
saved up, I'll put it in the right places and make things
happen."

"Okay, baby." Sasha wiped her tears away, and I
pulled off.

It wasn't until I got home that I realized I was really
gonna miss Sasha.

The next couple of hours were spent in pure ecstasy.
Sasha had made me feel things I'd never felt before and
in places I've never felt before. I'd never felt such pleasure in my life. She definitely left her mark.

As she was washing up to prepare to leave, I went
through my dresser drawers and my closet and collected things I knew she would like. When she came
out the bathroom, I had a number of jeans, dresses,
shirts and bags waiting for her.

"Too bad you don't wear my shoe size," I said as she
looked as the things I had laid out for her.

"This is for me?" Sasha said in disbelief.

"Yes. I want you to have them."

"Your True Religion, Joe's Jeans, and Rock and Re-
public? They still have tags on them!" Sasha said, still
in doubt.

"Baby, it's all yours," I reassured her.

"Even your Prada bag?"

"Everything on the bed, Boobie."

"Damn!" Sasha rushed over and kissed me passionately. "I love you so much!"

"I want it back when you come back to VA, though." I shot her a quick look. "I'm just joking."

We laughed together.

The trip to the airport and the good-byes were heart-wrenching. I drove home depressed like a little girl who'd just lost her puppy. I turned on the TV and flipped through the channels as my mind wandered. I thought about all the good times and all the bad times we'd shared. I never thought I would miss her as much as I did.

My house phone began to ring, interrupting my reminiscing.

"Hello," I said without even looking at the caller ID.

A male voice said, "May I speak with Mrs. Burroughs, please?"

"You have the wrong number," I said and prepared to hang up.

"I believe I have the correct number," the person said on the other end of the phone.

The voice began to sound familiar to me.

"Who is this?" I asked

"Mr. Burroughs," he responded.

"Calico?" I said, figuring it could only be him.

"What up? How you gon' be my wifey and not know your last name?"

I snapped, "You never offered to give me your government name. I figured you would tell me when you wanted me to know."

"Michael Burroughs. You happy?"

"Nah. I need a social security number, permanent address, and the name and phone number of your nearest relative," I spat back.

"Damn. What am I doing, applying for a line of credit?" Calico laughed.

"I'm just fucking with you. So when am I going to see you? I'm real lonely right now."

"I'll be there probably in a week or so."

"What if I can't wait that long?" I said, just to see how he would respond.

"Then I'll come sooner."

"Yeah, right," I said, knowing he was just talking shit.

"I'm serious. I'll do whatever makes you happy."

"Well, in that case, can you make everything right so my girl can come back to Virginia?" I said, really missing Sasha.

"Huh?" Calico was thrown by my request.

"My girl Sasha just left to go to Georgia. She had to move because shit was really fucked-up for her here. So she's going down there for a while to try and get things back in order. She just left, and I already miss her."

"I'm sorry, baby. I wish I was there to pamper you. You want me to catch a flight tomorrow?" Calico asked.

"Are you serious?"

"Yeah, but you can't let nobody know I'm coming. Niggas gon' expect this to be a business trip, and my phone gonna be blowing up the entire time. I'll have to hide out at your crib or something, and we won't be able to hang out."

"First of all, no one sleeps in my bed except rent-paying tenants. And, lastly, what fun would that be if we have to be cramped up in the crib anyway? I'd rather wait."

"That's cool. We can wait. I was just trying to be there for you. And, for the record, I don't mind paying rent. How much is it?" Calico asked like it was nothing.

"My mortgage"—I put emphasis on the word *mortgage*—"is twelve hundred a month."

"A'ight, I got you. Do I need to put down a deposit too?" Calico said, cool as a fan.

"I don't know. Maybe I should ask for a deposit, since you refused to supply information to put in a credit application." I giggled.

"I ain't got no problem putting down a deposit. So when is my move in date?"

"We'll discuss that when the funds have been secured. I accept cash only, Mr. Burroughs." I spoke to him in a professional tone as though I was a property manager.

"Okay, well, I guess we've got a contracted lease. You can pick your funds up at a Western Union in about an hour."

"Okay. Bye"

"Gone." Calico ended the call.

I watched the clock constantly as I counted down the minutes. After about forty-five minutes, I couldn't wait any longer. I hopped in my truck and headed to the grocery store to check on the wire. I filled out the Western Union form and gave the cashier my ID. "Do you know how much?" she asked.

Now my first thought was to say, "Did I put in an amount on the form?" Instead I chose to be nice and replied, "No, I don't."

The cashier huffed and puffed as she entered the information in the computer. "Do you have the money transfer control number?"

Now this time I just had to respond, "Do you see one on the paper?"

The cashier must have gone with her better judg-
ment and decided to keep any comments after that to
herself. She handed me the money order and directed
me to sign at the X.

I glanced at the amount. "Three thousand, umph," I
said to no one in particular.

The cashier counted out my money, and I pranced
out the store with a big smile on my face.

I called Calico as soon as I reached my truck.

"Okay, it looks like I have a new tenant. When would
you like to move in?" I asked as soon as he answered,
pretending to be a landlord.

Calico played along. "When will the place be ready?"

"Immediately," I responded, wanting him to come
right away.

Calico laughed at my eagerness.

I figured, since we'd touched the money subject, this
would be a good time to talk about exactly what type
of business Calico had. Deep inside I already knew the
deal, but I wanted to see just how he would carry it. I
wanted to know if he was gonna be up front with me or
keep playing the "I'ma-businessman" game.

"Do you remember the first time you saw me?"

"Of course, I do," he answered confidently.

I knew he thought I was referring to the bar, so I
figured I would use this as an opportunity to get a little
deeper in his pockets. "I bet you don't."

"I'm a gambling man, so I'm game. Set your wager."
Calico was enthusiastic about our little competition.

"Okay. If you win, I'll give one sexual pleasure of my
choice. If I win, you have to take me to Potomac Mills
Outlet for a day of shopping." I said, laying down the
rules.

"That's cool with me. I just hope you can keep up
your end of the bargain," Calico said as though he knew
he was going to win the bet.

"Okay, so what's the answer?"

"It was a Friday," Calico began to say very carefully. "The day I saw you at the bar with Touch."

"Wrong!" I said right away, interrupting him. "So when are we going shopping?"

"Damn, you ain't even let me finish."

"No need, hon. You are wrong. Now the answer to my question, please."

"As soon as I get there," Calico responded, no longer putting up a fight. "Okay, and I'm holding you to this too."

"No problem."

"Why you so quick to give money up?" I asked, directing the conversation to where I really wanted it to go.

"What make you say that?"

"Well, you took me shopping on our first date. You sent me three grand like it was nothing, and now you just agreed to take me shopping again with no problem. The average dude ain't coming off no money like that, especially with a chick he's only known for a couple of days."

Calico gave the safest answer he could, but that wasn't gonna stop me from finding out what I wanted to know. "I feel like I've known you for years."

"I'm sure, but that doesn't answer my question. I've noticed you're pretty good at avoiding subjects that you rather not talk about, but in order for this thing we have to go any further, I have to know exactly who I am dealing with."

I heard him chuckle on the other end of the phone. "I like you, Jewel, but there are things that I can't tell you. Not yet anyway. I am good at dodging bullets and questions. It comes with the territory. I do this for a reason, and I shouldn't have to defend that at all."

I listened as Calico talked. I heard what he was selling, but I wasn't sure if I was buying. Calico had so
much game, it was almost impossible to tell when he
was lying from when he was being sincere.

"When you're in my position, it puts even the ones
you care about at risk. That's why I do my business on
the East Coast. When I was working in the area where
I lay my head at, shit got too hot. I'm constantly worrying about the safety of my kids and their mothers as
well as the rest of my family. Withholding shit from
friends and relatives in my line of business keeps niggas breathing for at least another day."

I wondered what type of girl he figured I was. "So
what are you saying, Calico?"

"You ain't ready for all the shit that goes down in my
line of work. You ain't no 'ride-or-die' chick. You ain't
that chick that can sit through interrogation and not
rat. You're not that chick that can go deliver a package
or hold shit down if I get locked up. I mean, would you
even know how to bail a nigga out?"

Calico's words cut me deep. If any other nigga would
have said this to me, they would have certainly found
themselves alone, but his words, however harsh, were
true.

Although I had a gold-digger's eye and could easily
categorize a man based on his wealth, I had never been
"a gangster's girl." Frankly, because dope-boy money
had never been long enough for a bitch like me, but I
wasn't gon' let this nigga know that. Something about
Calico was different from those cats, particularly because he was the nigga giving out the orders and not
taking them. But, besides that, I think I was really
starting to like him.

I didn't want him to know that his words affected me
in the least, so I did what any bitch would. I put on a
front.

"You've just proven I am good at what I do. Don't let the image fool you. That's why I'm never suspect, because even though I know the game inside and out, I look like Miss Corporate America," I lied.

"That's hard to believe, but I'm not the one to call anybody a liar. Trust me, time will tell."

"It sure will."

"It's more to it than just standing by your man side though. You gotta always be on point. You can't be distracted by any nigga that pass you in a shopping center in a drop-top Benz. I bet you know how many karats were in my ear," Calico said, proving he did know the first time he saw me. "You tricked me!" I yelled, shocked that he really remembered that first glance.

"No, I didn't. You cut me off. You were too eager. You moved too fast. That could fuck you up in the game. But a real ride-or-die chick would know that, right?" Calico tried to make a point.

"Whatever! Finish what you were saying."

"All I got a chance to say is, it was a Friday, the day I saw you at the bar. If you would have let me finished, I would have continued by saying, you passed me as you chatted away on your cell phone going downtown, probably on your way to the nail shop."

"And how do you know I was on my way to the nail shop?"

"Observation, another skill that comes with the territory."

"Okay, okay! Maybe I'm not 'married to the game,' but I can be that chick by your side, and I'm not afraid to prove it."

"Action speaks louder than words. Don't talk about it, be about it."

On that note I was ready to end the call. "Enough said."

Chapter 6

"Juggling Chicks"

Touch

Damn, I ain't even trying to see this bitch, I thought as I rounded the corner, heading toward my crib. I had been chilling at Ciara's crib for the last week and a half, so I wouldn't have to kill a bitch, but since I had run out of clothes, I had to come back. Although I thought it was gonna be hell staying with Ciara, shit turned out all right. We had a few arguments, but all in all, it was cool being around my girls. For a split second, I actually thought about really getting back with her, but that shit flew out the window as soon as it entered my mind.

"Yes, sir!" I said to myself as I put the car in park and jumped out.

The house was empty. Everything was in the same order that it was left that night I fought with ol' girl. Tired of her constant bullshit, I packed her shit and told her to come through for it. She was trying to act different on the phone, being all calm and cute, telling me that she'll be by in twenty minutes. While I waited, I tried to straighten up.

When she got to the house, she pleaded with me to forgive her, but like I said once before, I don't go back. She finally realized my mindset when she found her stuff in two plastic garbage bags. I told her that I had something to do, so we needed to make this quick.

She flipped out. "Where you in a rush to? You still running after your baby momma, huh? Well, she can have your sorry ass then!"

"Bitch, whatever," I said. Truth be told, this was a good move for me. I never even clicked with her like that anyway.

"I was a good fucking girl to you," she yelled as she was reaching for her car door.

"Nah, what you lost was a good man. What's sad, you don't know shit about me." Me and ol' girl were together for a good minute now. You would think she would know how I flex and that I wouldn't even roll with my baby mother like that. This bitch ain't even know my drink! I thought about what Jewel said and decided to put her to the test.

"What color are my eyes?"

"What? What kind of fucking question is that?"

I gave her another chance to answer. "What color are my eyes?"

I faintly heard, "I don't fucking know," and she got in the car and then quickly sped off.

Exactly! Eat dust, bitch. I looked at her from my door, confident that I'd made the right decision. I took her two garbage bags full of stuff to the curb and then went back into the house.

After about an hour of flipping TV channels, I realized I hadn't talked to my road dawg in a while, so I pulled out my cell phone to hit Jewel up.

"I was just about to call you," Jewel said as soon as she picked up.

"Oh, yeah? So what was stopping you?"

"Whatever! Where the fuck you been? Boo'd up somewhere?" Jewel snapped.

"Chill out, man. I been at my baby mother crib."

"Ah shit, now! You been doing the family thing. I'm cool with that. I told you, you need to get back with that girl anyway."

"I don't know about that shit. I can't lie, shit was cool when I was there. She made sure a nigga ate. I had my fat rats around me all the time. I had to admit, that shit was a'ight."

"Well, I'm glad to hear that. I just want you to find you someone and settle down. You're a good guy, and you deserve a good girl."

"You know I ain't even that nigga that got a bunch of bitches. I do my thang, but I don't mind having a steady bitch. You know me, I do the relationship thing," I told her.

"Yeah, I know, but you just be picking the wrong damn chicks."

"Yeah, yeah, yeah." I wasn't trying to hear that shit Jewel was talking. "I'm gonna need you to take me to the airport next week. I'm going to the A."

"Okay, I got you. But, anyway, on to me, I talked to your boy today."

"Yeah? What that nigga talking 'bout?"

"Well, I think I really like him. He sent me three grand today," Jewel said full of excitement.

Oh, shit. This nigga 'bout to pull one on Jewel, I said to myself. I knew exactly how Calico moved. He was known for running game on bitches and giving them money and gifts and shit to win them over then convincing them to let him chill at their crib, and the next thing you know, he doing work out their crib and have them doing runs for him. But I was hoping that Jewel was smarter than that.

"So what's three grand, Jewel? That ain't no money, and you for one should know that," I said, wondering if my homegirl was slipping.

"I know that, Touch. Of course, I've gotten much more than that from dudes, but the difference is, I ain't even known him that long, and I ain't put in no work. This nigga took me shopping and sent me three grand in this little bit of time. Plus, this is dope boy money, not entertainer or athlete money that I'm normally dealing with."

As I listened to Jewel speak, I thought, *Damn, he told the truth about what he does.*

"Touch, you hear me?" Jewel asked in reaction to my lack of response.

"Whatever you say, li'l homie," I said, uneasy about the whole situation.

"I need to know some things, though."

"What's up?"

"Does Calico have a chick here?"

"Come on, Jewel. You know I'm not into shit like this. You not 'bout to turn me into Mr. Palmer," I said, referring to this Jamaican cat around here. He would call the cops in a moment's notice if he saw you hanging out on the corner two seconds longer than you should be. For business, he was a real pain in the ass.

"So it's like that, Touch. This nigga is going to be staying with me when he come here, so I need know what the deal is."

My fucking stomach sank when she said that. *I can't believe this fucking chick. Has she lost her fucking mind? This ain't even her. She on some bullshit right now.*

"Jewel, what are you doing? I thought you were smarter than this. You don't even know this nigga."

"I actually know a whole lot about him. We've had extensive phone conversations."

"A'ight den. If you know so much, you don't need to be asking me shit. You on your own with this one.

You're a smart girl, you know the game. Hell, you run game. And game always recognize game, right?" I left it at that.

"Fa sho!" Jewel yelled back, and we ended the call soon after.

My dick was aching as I drove back to my baby mother's house. I needed some pussy bad, but I wasn't trying to fuck her. That shit was like committing suicide. Ciara was already on some bullshit when I wasn't fucking her, so I could only imagine what would happen if I started. In her mind, that would mean we're back together.

Just then, Diana popped in my head. I wondered if Ciara had fucked things up between the two of us as I took a quick exit off the interstate and headed toward Mo Dean's instead of my original destination.

The parking lot was packed as I pulled up to the restaurant. I circled the block and parked on the street. I figured that probably was best as I walked up. At least, that way if my baby mother or one of her snitch-ass friends passed by, they wouldn't see my car in the parking lot and be tempted to come in and ruin my night.

I scanned the club from the entrance and proceeded with caution, to make sure the crowd was to my liking. I walked in and grabbed a seat at the bar. I ordered my usual as I looked around for Diana. I didn't see her in my immediate area, and hoped that she was just at a booth or something, where I couldn't see her. To waste a little time, I began to play one of the many computerized games that sat in front of me.

Just as I was getting into the game, someone hugged me from behind and whispered in my ear, "Hey, sexy."

My dick rose as though it had ears and recognized the voice. I turned around to greet Diana. "Dirty Diana," I sang. "What's up, baby?"

"You." She looked at the imprint of my swollen penis in my Five Four jeans.

I got right to the point. "You gotdamn right. So what you gon' do about that?"

"I'm down. I've been down. You the one with that baby momma drama."

"Baby momma drama?" I played stupid because I knew Diana had no idea what was going on the other night at the club.

"Yeah, baby momma drama. Our boy, Calico, told me all about it."

What? What kind of bitch shit is that? I wondered what type of trouble Calico was trying to start.

"Fuck all dat. Let's do this. Can you leave now?" I wasn't trying to waste no more time talking about bullshit and take the risk of my baby mother blowing my spot up again.

"Right now? I'm working."

I pulled Diana between my legs and grabbed a handful of her ass cheeks with each one of my hands. "He want you right now," I whispered in her ear as I pressed my manhood against her thigh.

"Well"—she paused as she glanced around the restaurant—"it's slow, so I guess so." She untied her waitress apron and headed to the back of the bar to notify them she was leaving.

As we hopped in the car, my mind was spinning about where I could take her and not run into anyone else. I thought about the dope house, but it was just too many niggas at that crib. I needed to find a spot fast. My dick was rock-hard, and I needed to bust a nut before I caught a bad case of blue balls.

"My electric bill is due. I'm gonna need something," Diana whispered in my ear, while rubbing on my dick.

Spoken like a typical chickenhead. *No wonder this bitch was throwing the pussy at a nigga. She out for money. It is what it is. At this point I don't even give a fuck. I don't mind a jump-off. It ain't like a nigga trying to wife her*, I thought to myself but decided against voicing it.

Temples sweating, I answered, "A'ight, I got you." I pulled out a hundred-dollar bill.

Normally, I would only throw a jump-off sixty or seventy dollars, but at the time, I was thinking with my dick instead of my mind.

Shortly after, we passed a Roadway Inn, hiding off to the side near Shore Drive. *Perfect*. I busted a U-turn and headed into the parking lot and parked. Diana stayed in the car while I checked in.

Minutes later, she was following me to room number 208.

"What you want? What you want to do?" she asked with a slight attitude, pulling off her clothes as if she was going to bed. She didn't even try to undress in a sexy way to keep me turned on. It seemed like Diana had the same intentions as me, fucking and bucking.

"It don't matter, but first, a nigga need to piss." I headed for the bathroom, unbuckling my pants.

A minute later, Diana was standing at the bathroom door ass-naked with one hand on her hip. She looked at her watch on the other. "Hurry up. I got some things to take care of. For a hundred dollars, you can't get much," she said like the trick she was.

"Soon as I bust, we can go," I answered. I shook the last few drops off my dick then grabbed some tissue to wipe my tip.

I walked into the room and sat on the edge of the bed and signaled Diana to come over. Then, I pulled her head down to my dick. Bobbing her head up and down,

Diana was beginning to choke, but I didn't give a fuck. Plus, I didn't like her nasty attitude. This bitch acted like she was into a nigga, but all she really was into was a nigga's pockets.

But what I did like was the way this bitch sucked the skin off my dick and was playing with my balls at the same time. A service like that deserved payment.

"Ah fuck! Suck that dick, bitch!"

Diana stopped her dick-sucking duty for a brief moment. "I don't swallow, and you get one more position, nigga."

Damn, this bitch is a trick for real! The realization set in as I registered her last statement. *Well, better make the best of this, since I'm officially a john.* "Yeah, a'ight."

I picked Diana up and both of us landed on the dresser against the mirror. Her legs were wide open while she played with her pussy. I quickly put on a condom. One thing for sure was, I didn't need any more fat rats running around, and definitely didn't need a trick-ass baby mother, or even worse, that monster that a nigga can't shake.

After placing my dick into Diana's wet pussy, I began choking her. I decided to use this as an opportunity to do that rough-sex shit. To my surprise, this crazy bitch loved it.

"Choke me harder, nigga," she screamed.

"You want it harder, bitch?"

"Yes, choke me. Fuck me. Give it to me real hard! Fuck this pussy up!"

The look of excitement and fear, plus her extremely wet pussy, made me come within minutes.

Damn, I needed that, I thought as she got up to shower.

I reached for a washcloth to wash off my dick. *That was the best hundred dollars I ever spent.* I pulled out a cigarette.

By the time I finished smoking, Diana was out the shower, and we were headed back to Mo Dean's.

I didn't even bother pulling into the parking lot as I pulled up. I just stopped at the corner and hit the unlock switch and signaled for her to get out. As soon as she closed the door behind her, I pulled off and headed to my crib.

I jumped out the car and headed in the house. I rushed upstairs and started a hot shower. After bathing, I opened the drawer to get toothpaste and toothbrush to finish my hygiene session for the night.

Today was a good day, more or less. I finally got some ass, for a hundred dollars, and there was no baby momma drama. "Finally, a nigga can get a good night sleep," I said aloud to myself.

Chapter 7

"Saved by C"

Sasha

"Come back home!" Jewel yelled as soon as she picked up the phone.

"Girl, you're crazy! I ain't even been gone but three days!" I laughed.

"I know, but I miss you already. So how's everything?"

"Well, I'm pretty much settled. I dropped my oldest boy off at his dad's house, and me and the youngest are comfortable here at my parents' house in Columbus. Girl, why this nigga have a big-ass five-bedroom house on a finished basement! He making major bread, and I'm up here struggling! That's some bullshit!"

"Don't worry about what he has. That's motivation for you to get your own shit together. Then you don't have to ask a nigga for nothing! You have your own and anything a dude wants to contribute is extra! Understand?" Jewel quickly shared some real knowledge with me.

"I feel you," I replied. "I checked out a few strip clubs in Atlanta, and I think I found one I want to work at. It's called Bottoms Up. They have one chick there by the name of Juicy that is supposed to be like the star chick. She got a nice body or whatever, but she doesn't really do any shit that's so amazing to me. I don't feel like it's any real competition there, and the club stays pack. I figure I'll be able to stack dough and get back on my feet in no time."

"Good! It sounds like a plan to me!" Jewel said.

"You know I've even thought 'bout moving out here. I noticed they are doing a lot of building up in Atlanta and the houses are dirt cheap. Plus, it would be good for me to be close to my baby father and parents."

"You know I don't want you away from me. But what you saying is true. Just do what's best for you and your family, baby. Hell, it's a flight from Norfolk to Atlanta daily." Jewel tried to make the best of the situation.

"Well, let me get off this phone. I need to go get my business license and go talk to the manager about a job at the club."

"A'ight. While you at it, why don't you register with a staffing service." Jewel always made me feel like I wasn't doing enough. "It wouldn't be a bad idea to have a job as well, especially if you plan on buying another house or getting a car."

"Okay. I'll talk to you later." I rolled my eyes then ended the call.

I rushed in the bathroom and hopped in the shower and threw on some clothes. I had an hour drive to Atlanta and wanted to miss the traffic.

By noon I'd already gotten my business license and was on my way to the staffing service.

The redhead lady called from the back, "Sasha Lewis."

"Yes?" I stood to my feet and headed in her direction.

We shook hands as she introduced herself and directed me to follow her to the back. She reviewed my resume.

"Oh, you have so much experience in the healthcare field. It shouldn't be hard for you to find a job. I noticed you listed you were interested in medical front office jobs, but it says here you went to school for medical assisting. Why not pursue that route? You could make more much more money."

"Well, I am not certified. I let my certification expire," I said shamefully.

"Oh my! How could you do that?"

Well, if you must know, I was shaking my ass making ten dollars every three minutes, so at the time ten dollars an hour was nothing to me. I told her, "I was in school working toward another career."

"Oh, I see. Well, it's neither here or there. You have a great amount of experience, so I'm sure we can get you a position. You will be hearing from us soon."

"Thank you very much." I shook her hand once more then left the office.

I rushed to my mom's car that I'd borrowed and headed to the strip club. That was my final stop for the day.

I pulled up at Bottoms Up. It was only three in the afternoon, and there was already a small crowd at the club.

I walked up to the security and explained to them I was there to seek employment. They escorted me to the front door and told me to ask for Chastity. I walked to the bar and asked for her.

Moments later, a medium-height, well-dressed, light-skinned female walked out. "How are you?" She held out her hand as she looked me over quickly.

"I'm just fine."

"You can follow me," she said, and we walked toward her office.

I felt comfortable as I walked in. This was unlike any other interview I'd had for a strip club. Chastity was so welcoming, and her office was a professional setting.

Unlike the usual let-me-see-you-naked interviews I've had with perverted club owners in the past. Maybe the mere fact that Chastity was a woman alone made me feel better.

"Please have a seat." Chastity handed me a clipboard with a pen and application attached.

Wow! An application? Never did this for a strip club before. I began to fill out the application wondering if I should give my real information. Giving false information was what kept me out of jail when I had my last strip club situation. A chick couldn't press charges if she didn't know a name. This bitch, Chastity, looked like she was about her shit though, so I figured, I'd better go with the real. After I was done I handed it to her.

"Identification and social security card please." Chastity waited as I shuffled though my new Prada bag I'd received from Jewel.

I handed her my cards, and she went over to the copy machine and made copies. She handed them back to me then sat in her oversized leather chair behind her huge wooden desk.

"So you're from Virginia, Sasha?"

"Yes, I am. I just moved here last week."

"I'm from Virginia myself. I have quite a few friends back home. It says here you danced at Purple Rain. I believe one of my friends use to dance there too. Do you know anyone by the name of Ceazia?"

My heart skipped a beat at the sound of her name. Before Jewel, Ceazia was my world. From the first day we met in the strip club she took me under her wing. We once shared that "little sister-big sister" relationship that Jewel swore she and Paradise had, but it turned to something more. Just like Paradise, I'd never been with a woman, but Ceazia changed all of that for me. She was my first and would always hold a spot in my heart.

"Yes, I do. She was a very dear friend of mine."

"Was?"

"Yes. You didn't hear?" My heart raced as I realized Chastity had no idea.

"Hear what?"

"Ceazia passed." I looked down as my eyes began to fill with tears.

"Damn, I had no idea." Chastity paused as she stared into space. "Well, our work here is done." She stood up. "You're hired. Welcome to the team. I have to tell you, I don't normally hire on the spot. Most girls who apply have to come in during the week on amateur nights until they prove they're ready for a scheduled set. But on the strength of C, you've got the job. When would you like to start?"

"Tonight!" I said, full of excitement.

"See you then."

"Thank you!" I walked out of the office. "And thank you," I said as I looked up to the sky. "I knew you were looking down on me. I love you, girl." I sent love up to Ceazia.

Chapter 8

"Sex with You Is Like . . ."

Calico

I don't know if it was the six-hour plane ride from Los Angeles to Norfolk, or if it was the weed that I had been smoking on my way to Jewel's house, because I was so high, I drove past her house three times before I realized it. But whatever was the cause, all I knew was, I was horny as a muthafucka, and I wanted some pussy.

"So you like my place?" Jewel asked me as we walked into her immaculate home.

I had to give it up to her because, from a quick look at things, her spot impressed me. And I wasn't the easiest person to impress. "Yeah, I'm actually feeling it." I smiled.

Jewel pointed out all the details and showed off at the same time. "I bought it brand-new about a year ago. So when they were building it, I had the builder put in all custom shit—Canadian maple floors, granite countertops, stainless steel kitchen appliances, all of that."

I nodded my head, but I didn't verbally respond to Jewel. I walked behind her and followed her from the living room to the kitchen and then back toward the living room.

Jewel had on an Ed Hardy wife-beater, and I could tell that she didn't have a bra on, because her firm, full titties were packed so tight into her shirt that I could see the full imprint of her nipples. She also had on some black Twisted Heart sweatpants and a pair of Gucci slippers. I couldn't keep my eyes off of Jewel's sexy feet, and as horny as I was at that moment, it didn't take much for me to get turned on.

As I walked behind her and watched her fat ass jiggling around in her sweatpants, my dick instantly got hard. "You ain't wearing no panties, are you?" I knew that my question had caught Jewel off guard, but I could tell that she didn't take offense.

She turned around and said with a smile, "Excuse you."

"You and your sexy-ass feet." I grabbed my crotch.

"Calico, stop playing. Let me finish showing you the rest of the house. Come on, let's go upstairs," Jewel instructed me as she reached the base of the semi-spiral staircase that led to the second floor.

"But am I right, though?" I asked.

"Calico, please."

"You owe me one."

"What you mean?" Jewel asked.

"One sexual pleasure," I said, reminding her of the bet she'd lost.

"Fuck!" Jewel yelled then turned toward me and smiled as she slowly pulled down on the front of her sweatpants, exposing her Brazilian waxed pussy to me. And just as quickly as she had flashed me, she pulled her pants back up. "Satisfied?" she asked, and she started to head up the steps.

"Oh, shit! That's what I'm talking about!" I said as I caught up to her and wrapped my arms around her from behind.

I started to caress both of Jewel's breasts and kissed on her neck. Jewel made a slight erotic gasp. I could tell that she was enjoying how I kissed and touched her body.

"Baby, you giving me chills," she said. "We can't do this now. Come on, stop. Let's chill." She removed my hands from her breast.

"I want chu right now," I whispered into her ear, kissing on it at the same time. And without her permission, I slid my right hand into her pants and started massaging her clit with my middle finger. "Oh my God!" Jewel said.

I could tell that she was turned on because of how wet her pussy was. I slipped my middle finger into her pussy and I started to finger-fuck her right there on the steps.

Jewel began moving her hips as if she was dancing to a reggae song and she was getting more and more turned on by the minute. "We gotta stop, baby," she said to me, while trying to remove my hand from her pants.

But I could tell that she wasn't really putting up any true resistance. She turned and faced me, and when she did, she dropped her cell phone on the steps.

I turned her back around so that her back was again to my chest, and I pulled her sweatpants down to her ankles.

"Calico, okay, wait, just let me get my phone," she said to me.

My dick harder than Chinese arithmetic, I could care less about her phone. "Fuck the phone." I stepped on it with my foot and slid it down to the next step below the one I was standing on.

While I palmed Jewel's ass cheeks with my left hand, I used my right hand to quickly unbuckle my LRG jeans. I was feeling like a dog in heat, so I didn't bother to take off my shoes, my jewelry, my shirt, or anything. I simply pulled my pants and my boxers down around my thighs so that my dick was fully exposed.

At this point, Jewel had slipped out of her slippers and had managed to fully work herself out of her sweatpants. I bent her over and slid my dick into her pussy from the back and started pumping like a porno star.

Jewel reached her hands forward and balanced herself by placing her right hand on the steps in front of her and her left hand onto the handrail next to her.

"Aaaahhhh fuck!" Jewel screamed out. "Calico, your dick feels so damn good!"

"Your pussy is tight as hell! I wanted to fuck you from the first day I saw you!" I steadily continued to fuck her.

I pulled her wife-beater forward so that her titties were fully exposed. I watched them sway back and forth as I hit her ass doggy-style. The sight alone of her big ass slamming against my stomach was enough to make me cum, but I knew that I couldn't cum before her. And from the way she was throwing her ass back at me, I could tell that she was really close to reaching her peak.

Jewel turned her head and said to me, "Baby, we ain't even using a condom."

"I know, I know. Don't worry, though. I'll make sure I pull out before I cum," I said, hoping that would be enough to persuade Jewel to let me finish fucking her.

Jewel didn't respond, so I took that as my cue to keep going. I grabbed a fistful of her hair and pulled on it, and fucked her even harder.

"Oh, yes! I love that! Fuck me harder!" she screamed.

I complied with her instructions, and about thirty seconds later she let me know that she was cumming. And not long after that, I could feel myself about to cum as well. Her pussy felt so damn good, I didn't want to pull out, but I had given her my word that I would.

"Turn around," I instructed Jewel as I pulled my dick out of her pussy. "I wanna cum on your titties!"

She turned around and sat on one of the steps and cupped her titties so that she was pressing them together. I stroked my dick a few times and then shot cum all over her breasts.

"Oh, shit! That was good! I needed that!" I said to her.

Jewel looked at me and smiled. And then she stood up and mushed me in my face. "Nigga, you better have a got-damn condom next time!"

"Definitely," I said. I pulled up my pants and I began to fix my belt buckle. I watched Jewel use her wife-beater to wipe the cum off her breasts. I was satisfied that I had accomplished my mission.

My mission was to get her to totally trust me so that she would be willing to do anything for me that I needed her to do. I had already pacified her with a little a bit of bread, and seeing that she had let me so easily fuck her "raw dawg" with no condom, I knew she had to trust a nigga. But, then again, at the same time I had to be smart, because Jewel could've just as easily been a hoe-ass trick who was just trying to set me up to snake me somehow.

Chapter 9

"All Chicks Are the Same"

Touch

"Jewel! What up, ace?" I answered my cell phone, happy to hear from my homie. "Hello?" I said, after not hearing any response on the other end. I held my phone forward to double-check the name that was on the screen, and it was definitely Jewel's name that appeared on my phone.

My first thought was that we had a bad cell phone connection, and I was about to hang up and call her right back. But then I heard some noise in the background. I listened more closely to try and decipher what it was that I was hearing. After listening closely, I realized that Jewel must have called my cell phone by mistake.

"Aaahhh fuck! Calico, your dick feels so damn good."

"What the fuck?" I said out loud. I balled my face up.

"Your pussy is tight as hell. I wanted to fuck you from the first day I saw you."

I couldn't believe what I was hearing. I was hoping it was just some kind of sick trick that Jewel and Calico were playing on me.

"Baby, we ain't even using a condom."

"I know, I know. Don't worry, though. I'll make sure I pull out before I cum."

"Oh, yes! I love that! Fuck me harder!"

As I continued to listen, I could literally hear the sound of skin slapping against skin, so I knew that Jewel and Calico were actually fucking. I twisted my lips and shook my head in disgust. *How the fuck Jewel gone sell out like that?* I couldn't believe this shit I was hearing.

"Turn around. I wanna cum on your titties."

"Oh, shit! That was good! I needed that."

"Nigga, you better have a gotdamn condom next time!"

"Definitely."

I listened for a little while longer and I could hear Jewel and Calico rummaging around and making small talk with each other. It sounded like they were done fucking. Fuming, I hung up on my end. I didn't know what pissed me off more, the fact that Jewel was acting like a naïve schoolgirl and was actually falling into Calico's trap, or that Calico would disrespect the game and fuck with Jewel on that level.

I tried to go back to watching sports highlights on ESPN, but I had to admit, hearing that phone call had fucked my head up. Jewel was my female road dawg, and although we had never really caught feelings for one another, there was a small part of me that kind of made me feel like she was my girl. So listening to that phone call and hearing Calico fuck her was kind of like me hearing some nigga fuck my bitch. I could just picture that shit. I ain't gon' lie, a nigga was real fucked-up.

I got up and went to my kitchen to get a Heineken. After I cracked it open and took a few swigs, I decided to call Jewel. I dialed her number, and her cell phone just rang out to voice mail. I waited a few minutes and called her house phone, and again she didn't pick up, and it rang out to voice mail.

Yo, I can't believe she fucking falling for that clown-ass nigga, I said to myself as I walked back to my flat-screen television.

What was wild was, as I sat and watched ESPN, the announcers started talking about that old beef that Kobe Bryant and Shaquille O'Neal had a few years ago when they were on the same team. Stuart Scott from ESPN, the cool black dude that all of the other announcers try to be like, kept it real, saying how it was wrong for Kobe to snitch on Shaquille O'Neal like he'd done when he got caught cheating on his wife. He continued on and was saying how in his mind that was probably the last straw for Shaquille O'Neal and that was probably what made him demand a trade to the Miami Heat.

Then he summed it up by saying that at the end of the day it also was probably just a situation where Kobe's ego and Shaquille's ego were just too fucking big for the two of them to be on the same team together.

It was crazy for me to be hearing the commentators talking about that because, in a lot of ways, that was how I was feeling about me and Calico. Here that nigga was from Cali-muthafuckin'-fornia, and he was all the way on the East Coast, in my town, coming across like he owned the muthafucking key to the city, and like he was the man and shit. Granted, Calico was a big reason why a lot of niggas was eating, and he and I had done a lot of business together, but that nigga had crossed the line this time.

At one point this nigga used to be humble and about his bread. Fast-forward a year or two, and the nigga is all Hollywood all of a sudden. Now the nigga wants to fuck every bitch, floss in all the clubs, and do all kinds of high-profile shit. I'd learned a long time ago, whenever a nigga stops being humble and it starts becoming all about them, that's when it's time to cut niggas off and stop fucking with them. I mean, I seen it time and time again, niggas go and get Hollywood, and then they get fucking sloppy and fuck shit up for everybody. Hell, that's how I ended up in the penitentiary.

Calico was my man, so I knew exactly what he was trying to do. He was planning on using Jewel's ass so that he could use her crib as a stash house, like he was doing with a bunch of other chicks. He was gonna chill in her spot for a spell and run his product from there, cook up, stash some money and a few guns. Then when he felt like her spot was getting hot, he would be on to the next chick.

Fuck that nigga Calico! I thought to myself. *This is my motherfucking town!* I was gonna play shit cool, but it was definitely time for me to start making moves so that I could phase Calico out. I had a plan, but to be honest, the easiest plan would have been to pay one of those young-ass cats trying to make a name for themselves to make his ass disappear. It wasn't like he was untouchable. And, after all, my name was *Touch*.

Chapter 10

"Love & Hate"

Jewel

Sexy muthafucka. I looked at a sleeping Calico. My body ached from a night of continuous fucking as I rose from the bed and headed toward the bathroom. I looked at my reflection in the mirror with shame. I spoke to my reflection. "You are officially a bona fide whore!" I couldn't believe the shit I'd done. Not only did I let this nigga fuck me as soon as he got there, but I let him fuck me raw! I guess when a bitch is on a one-month drought, the pussy has a mind of its own. I ain't gon' front—I wanted some dick, but a bitch should have at least had a little class about herself. All I can say was, at least that shit was good. I knew it had to be some-thing golden about this nigga for him to have so many bitches, yet no drama. Shit, the money and dick alone was enough to keep my mouth shut! Plus, this nigga's body was as flawless as a coin in mint condition.

I jumped in the shower and threw on some clothes so that I'd look my best when Calico woke. The time was nine o'clock. Remembering Touch needed me to take him to the airport, I called him up.

He answered the phone with little emotion, "What's up?"

"Ugh! What's wrong with you?" I said, noticing he wasn't himself.

"Nothing. What's the deal?" Touch responded with the same tone as before.

"Well, I just remember you said something about the airport the other day. When you going?"

"Today."

"Today? Why didn't you call me?"

"I was gonna just use short-term parking."

"No, I'm taking you. What time is your flight?"

"Three o'clock."

"Okay. Meet me at my house, and we'll leave from here."

"A'ight."

"Cool," I responded then hung up the phone.

Realizing I only had a few hours before it was time to take Touch to the airport, I rushed to cook Calico breakfast. Thinking of something quick, I decided to cook omelets.

Before I was finished, Calico was on his way into the kitchen. "Yeah, I better have some breakfast waiting. Especially when you be cooking that nigga Touch breakfast." He hugged me from behind.

"Whatever, nigga. Don't think you gon' be getting this kind of treatment every morning, though." I let him know the deal right off the bat.

"I ain't trying to hear that shit. You gon' do whatever it takes to keep a nigga happy," Calico said confidently.

Yep. As long as you keeping this bitch happy by keeping the money coming, I thought.

"What you smirking at?" Calico asked.

I guess my thoughts were written all over my face. "Nothing. Just thinking about what you said."

"So you ain't trying to keep a nigga happy?"

I responded with a question just as important, "You trying to keep a bitch happy?"

"No doubt. I got you. I thought you already knew that."

"Nah. That could just be preliminary game you throwing. You can see from how I do things that I'm not your average chick. I like nice things and love having my way. So are you really trying to hold me down?" I asked, to see where his head was really at.

"Jewel, I got you, baby. Relax. Let shit take its course." Calico took a seat at the breakfast bar.

"Okay then. Well, I got you," I said, as I handed him his food.

I cleaned up the kitchen and straightened the small mess we'd made in my bedroom as Calico ate.

When he finished he met me in the bedroom. "I'm about to run out," he said. "You didn't tell anybody I was here, did you?"

"Nope," I said, just now remembering he'd told me not to tell anyone of his visit. Luckily, I hadn't told anyone.

"You sure about that? Not even your homeboy?"

"I guess you're referring to Touch but, to answer your question, no, I didn't tell him."

"Cool. Well, I'm going on a few runs. I'll hit you up when I'm done."

"Okay."

Deep inside, I wanted to put up an argument, because this trip was supposed to be all about me, but I knew that I had to take Touch to the airport and I'd told him to meet him at my house. So I kinda needed Calico to leave so that I didn't blow his cover. I kissed him on the lips before he headed out the door.

"Damn, I've got another winner!" I said to myself as I watched Calico jump in his rental car from my bedroom window.

Just then my phone rang, interrupting my thoughts. "Hey, Boobie," I answered, realizing it was Sasha.

"Hey, baby. I've been dancing at the club, and it's turning out great! I'm really making some money!"

"That's good. I'm so happy for you. I'm making me a little change myself." I quickly began to share the news of Calico with Sasha.

"Huh? What you doing? I know your ass ain't on no pole!"

"Hell nah, girl. I finally got this nigga Calico where I want him."

"Who?"

"Calico. Touch friend. The one from the bar that night, remember?" I tried refreshing Sasha's memory.

"Oh, okay. Damn, how you do that?"

"Well, you know he took me shopping on our first date. That was an indication of how he breaks bread. But, anyway, I talked him into coming to VA, and this nigga sent me three grand, Western Union, before he even got here," I bragged.

"And what did you have to do to get that three grand?" Sasha asked, sounding all sarcastic and shit.

"What chu mean?"

"I know you gave up some ass."

"To be honest, yeah, I did, but that was *after* I'd received three stacks and a shopping spree, enough to ensure there was more to come. And if not, it still covered the expense," I spat back, letting her know I knew what I was doing.

"Umph . . . well, good for you, I guess. I got three stacks too, but it took me a few days in the strip club to gain that."

"Well, why you not there looking for a nigga? I gave you the rules. Shit, utilize those muthafuckas!"

"I hear you."

Just then I heard a horn blow in front of my house.
Touch was out front.

"Well, let me go. I have to take Touch to the airport.
He's coming down your way, as a matter of fact. You
gon' be at the club tonight?"

"Do I have a choice?"

"What's that suppose to mean?" I asked, hoping she
would elaborate. I'd had just about enough of Sasha's
sour-ass attitude. I really hoped it wasn't envy I smelt
in the air. Sasha and I had the same opportunities in
life. She just chose an alternate route. Was I to blame?

"I ain't got it like you. I got to struggle to get mine."

"Well, I'm trying to help a sister out. I'm gon' send
Touch up there to show some support."

"Thanks . . . I guess."

"Yep," I said, totally ignoring her stupid-ass attitude.
Bitch! I thought to myself before ending our phone call.

I headed out the door to meet Touch. "What's up, big
homie?" I pressed the unlock button to my truck.

"Ain't shit." Touch climbed into the truck.

I tried to figure out what was up with my buddy.
"Damn, you still down, nigga? What the fuck? Guess
you got baby momma blues and too ashamed to tell me
or something."

"Nah, it ain't my baby momma this time. Someone
else is fucking up. Looks like that shit is contagious,"
Touch said, confusing the hell out of me.

I could tell from the way Touch was talking, he was
very disappointed in someone, and it didn't look like he
was trying to talk about it, so I chose to leave it alone.

"Well, you know Sasha is in Atlanta now," I said,
changing the subject.

"Oh, yeah?"

"Yep. She's working at this club called Bottoms Up.
You and some of your boys should go check her, show
her some support."

"I'ma make sure I do that," Touch said, showing interest in something for the first time since we'd been together.

Fifteen minutes later, we were at Norfolk International Airport. I pulled up to the Delta departure terminal. "Here's your stop."

"Thanks." Touch pulled out his wallet, pulled out a fifty, and handed it to me.

"Have a safe trip." I grabbed the money with one hand and leaned forward to hug him with the other.

"Nah. You be safe. You're gonna need it more than me." Touch jumped out the truck without hugging me.

I sat in awe for about thirty seconds, trying to register what the fuck had just happened. When I finally came to my senses, I looked up to see him walking through the automatic doors and into the airport. The nigga never even looked back.

He's on that Gemini split-personality bullshit for real, I thought to myself before peeling off.

Chapter 11

"Down-ass Chick"

Calico

By the time I got back to Jewel's house, it was close to seven o'clock, and I knew that I hadn't kept my word.

"You know you done lost a whole lotta points with me, right?" Jewel said to me as soon as I walked into her crib. She didn't even give me a chance to respond and kept going in on me. "I thought this little trip you took out here was supposed to be all about me! I sure as hell can't tell, from the way you running the streets. Can *I* get some attention, gotdamit?"

I couldn't help but look at Jewel and smile. I loved her sassy-ass attitude and her whole style. "What the fuck are you smiling about? I don't see shit funny!"

I didn't answer Jewel. I just walked up to her and smacked her on her ass and continued on my way to her kitchen to get myself something to drink.

"Mr. Burroughs, don't fuck with me! You said this trip was supposed to be about me, and that no one was going to even know you were here. But, from the looks of it, this trip seems like it's all about you. You already got some pussy, I cooked and fed your ass, and then you have the audacity to spend the entire day on the street. What the fuck?"

"Jewel, I told you that I got you."

"Yeah, whatever, nigga. I can't tell. You just seem a little too damn comfortable."

After Jewel said that, I sipped on some fruit punch that I had just poured for myself and put the glass on her granite countertop. I walked out the front door toward my rental car.

"Where are you going now?" she asked with a major attitude.

I didn't say anything as I pressed the button on the key-chain to release the trunk. I reached inside and took out a shopping bag, and headed back into the house. "This is for you. I hope you like it," I said as I handed Jewel the shopping bag and walked into the living room and turned on the flat-screen.

"Ahhhhhhhhhh!"

When I heard Jewel screaming, I knew she loved the gift.

"Calico! I can't believe you!" Jewel came running and jumped into my arms.

"Oh, now I'm Calico again? A minute ago, I was Mr. Burroughs."

"Yeah, but a minute ago you hadn't given me a green crocodile Hermes bag."

I couldn't help but chuckle at Jewel as she loosened herself from me and proceeded to parade around the living room, showing off her bag as if she was a runway super-model.

"The girls are gonna be so sick when they see me rocking this bag."

"Yep! And they'll have nine thousand reasons to be sick," I said, alluding to how much I'd paid for the bag. "Now, do you believe me when I say I got you?"

"Yes, sirrr," Jewel playfully responded.

Jewel's mood had instantly switched up from pissed-off and agitated to warm and cheery. That was a sure indication of how to deal with her in the future.

"Come here and let me give you kisses," Jewel said to me as she walked toward me, her lips puckered up for a kiss.

I kissed her soft lips and felt on her ass, and two seconds later she was back admiring her bag in the mirror.

"So, listen, here's the deal. That bag is my down payment on a shopping spree. Tomorrow, we'll go shopping, but tonight let's just go out to eat and then hit the strip club or something," I said.

"Okay. But I thought you didn't want nobody to know you were in town? You sure you wanna go to the strip club?"

"Yeah. Actually, there's a whole lot of shit on my mind right now, and the strip club has always been the best way for me to unwind and get my head right."

"Ocean Cabaret? Hell, nah. That's not a real strip club. It's too fucking bourgeoisie for my taste. Let's hit up Purple Rain," I explained to Jewel as we headed out of McCormick & Schmick's Seafood Restaurant.

"Oh, so you like that ghetto shit then. Okay, Purple Rain is cool with me. I can check my girl Shakira. But, for the record, there you go with shit being about you again. Remember, your trip to Virginia was supposed to be about me."

I looked at Jewel and nodded my head as we pulled off in her white Range Rover. Jewel had forgotten her iPod, so she was forced to listen to the radio. When she turned on the radio, one of my favorite Jay-Z songs were on, "Can I Get a Fuck You."

"Oh, turn that shit up!" I yelled. I began reciting the lyrics along with Jay-Z. I reached over and turned the volume down, and then I asked Jewel, "So if I wasn't a nigga with figgas, would you come around me or would you clown me?"

Jewel just looked at me and smiled, and then she turned the volume back up. Right on cue, she began to recite the female lyrics of the song. She reached and turned the volume back down, and the two of us started laughing at each other.

"Wait, hold up. Don't you ever touch a black man's radio! What's wrong witchu?" I asked, trying to imitate Chris Tucker in *Rush Hour*. I turned the radio back up and started to recite the chorus to the song, doing the wop dance at the same time.

"Now can you bounce for me, bounce for me Can ya, can ya bounce wit' me, bounce wit' me . . ."

"Oh my God, Calico, you are so crazy!" Jewel laughed at me.

Not much longer after that, we arrived at the strip club. The shit was extra packed. There was some porn star chick named Pinky, who was making a guest appearance that night, so that was the reason for the large crowd.

As soon as I walked in the spot, it was like a freaking love fest. Dancer after dancer kept coming up to me saying hello, as did some of the fellas that I knew from the streets.

Jewel said to me, "I see you a little ghetto celebrity in here."

One of the dancers asked me, "Yo, Calico, you gon' make it rain tonight?"

"Nah, baby, not tonight. I'm just chillin."

When Jewel and I sat down, I ordered a bottle of Hennessy for myself, and a bottle of Nutcracker for her. As soon as our drinks arrived, Jewel started in with the questions. "Okay, so tell me, what got your head so fucked-up that you needed to come in here and get it right?"

I drank a glass of Hennessy and then I exhaled some air from my lungs. "It's just that I'm real hot right now," I screamed into Jewel's ear over the loud music. "It's a lot of jealous-ass snitch muthafuckas out here that wanna see me fall, you know?"

Jewel drank some of her Nutcracker. "You'll be okay, pookie face," she said.

I shook my head. I didn't totally let Jewel in on everything that I knew, but the fact was, I had just recently found out that I had been secretly indicted by the Virginia Commonwealth Attorney. And, from what I was hearing from my man who was fucking one of the female assistant Commonwealth attorneys, Touch had snaked my ass, and it was his testimony to the grand jury that really led to my indictment. I hated to believe that my man for so long would do some shit like that, but you could never really trust a nigga, when it comes to the drug game.

I knew that I was taking a big chance being in Virginia, with all this going on, and an even bigger chance being out at the strip club. But the thing was, deep inside, I knew that Touch had snaked me. I never wanted to show him the cards I was holding, so I purposely played things cool with him, hung out with him, and did everything as normal.

Truth be told, one of the main reasons that I had come to visit Jewel was so that I could collect on the hundred and fifty thousand that Touch had owed me, and to set him up to have him killed. I mean, I wasn't no dummy. I knew that a dead Touch couldn't pay me the bread that he owed me, so I had to get my dough first, and then hit his ass.

My plan was to butter up Jewel with gifts and all, just like I was doing, so that she'd be distracted. I needed her distracted because I didn't want her suspecting anything that was about to go down with me and Touch. This way, when Touch did get blasted, she would never suspect that I had anything to do with it. I knew I had to move cautiously.

Although Touch was a pretty chill dude, he did have a dark side that would surprise any unsuspecting nigga. Shit, that's one of the reasons I had originally partnered up with him. And that's why I'd conveniently sent Diana his way. So that I could keep tabs on him, and she could distract him when necessary. I knew if I threw her a few dollars I could rely on her to hold things down. Plus, I even had his no-good baby mother on the team. Although she had no idea, she was probably gonna end up causing his death.

With Touch on my mind, I pulled out my cell phone and placed a call to him. "What's good, baby boy?" I said when Touch answered the phone. I then excused myself from the lounge table that I was sitting at and made my way to the bathroom, where it was quieter and I could hear better.

"Everything's good. What's the deal?"

"You got that for me?" I said, referring to the hundred and fifty thousand.

"Yeah, yeah, no doubt."

"So where you at?" I asked.

Touch explained to me that he was down in Atlanta and that he would be back next week.

"Next fucking week? Touch, what the fuck is up? Your dough is straight or what? Keep it real with me. Last week you told me this week, and now you telling me next week? I ain't never had no issues over getting my bread from you—"

Touch cut me off. "Exactly, we ain't never had no problem, so no need to stress me. I got your dough. I'm just outta town. When I touch down, I'll get the shit to you, a'ight?"

"Whatever, man. Just hit me as soon as you touch down, and I'll head out there the next day," I said, not wanting him to know my whereabouts.

I made it back to where Jewel was sitting. I saw her chatting with one of the dancers that went by the name Paradise. Before I could blink, Jewel winked her eye at me and told me that she was going off to get a private dance.

"Oh, okay, do you, ma."

I sat and drank glass after glass of Hennessy, and within an hour I was fucked-up. Jewel was also twisted. And after being around so much tits and ass, we were both horny as shit.

"You ready?" I asked her.

Jewel said that she was, and without making my usual rounds to tell people that I was bouncing, she and I just got up and departed from the club. I quickly peeped out the parking lot as we made our way to Jewel's Range Rover. As we pulled off and headed back toward Jewel's crib, I noticed Diana's trick-ass hollering at a couple of dudes with New York plates.

We were no more than five blocks away from the club when Jewel said, "Something's up."

"What are you talking about?"

"The fucking police are following us."

"Get the fuck outta here."

"Yeah, it's a marked car. He been following us since we left the club."

"Muthafucka! And I'm dirty too! Shit, what the fuck was I thinking?" I started to stress out.

"You dirty how?"

"I got these fucking X pills on me," I explained to Jewel as I pulled out the bag of ecstasy pills to show her just what the hell I was talking about. Just at that point the cops signaled for us to pull over. My heart was pounding.

"Give me that shit," Jewel said to me as she kept driving, disobeying the cops flashing lights.

"What?"

"Calico, give me the damn pills!" I didn't know what Jewel was planning on doing, but I didn't want her to get bagged on no drug charge. "Nah, Jewel, I got this."

She reached over and grabbed the clear bag of X pills. She began unbuckling her tight-ass jeans with one hand, and steered the car with her other hand. "I'm putting this shit in my pussy. We'll be good."

Jewel was like a magician, the way she squirmed out of her tight jeans just enough to expose her pussy and stuff the bag of drugs inside.

I said to her as she pulled over, "My name is Martin Green, if they ask you."

She looked at me. "Okay."

Before we could blink, there was one cop on the driver's side window, and another on the passenger side. They were both shining their lights inside the car after Jewel and I had rolled down our windows.

The cop asked Jewel, "Miss, can you tell me why it took you three extra blocks of driving before you pulled over?"

"I pulled over as soon as I saw your lights in my rear-view mirror, officer."

The cop shook his head and asked for Jewel's license and registration and insurance. "Is this your car?" he asked.

"Yes."

"Okay, the reason I'm pulling you over is because of your tint," he explained. "You can't have your tint so dark. It's illegal."

Jewel responded, "I didn't know that, officer." "Okay, sit tight. I'll be back."

As soon as the cop walked off, Jewel exhaled. "I am drunk as a skunk. I hope he can't smell that shit."

"Nah, you good. Just relax."

"Damn, that was quick," Jewel said in reference to how quick the cop had returned to our car.

"Ms. Diaz, can you step out of the car, please?"

I yelled over to the cop on the driver's side, "For what?"

"Sir, just put your hands on the dashboard and relax," the cop on my side said to me.

The cop said to Jewel, "Turn around and face the car," and he whipped out his handcuffs and placed her under arrest.

"This is crazy! What are you arresting me for? Tinted windows?"

"No, ma'am. Your license is suspended. That's what I'm arresting you for." The officer frisked Jewel.

The cop on my side asked me, "You have a driver's license?"

I shook my head no, and at that point, my mouth became dry as shit.

Jewel spoke up and told the cop who'd handcuffed her that it would be all right for me to drive her car home.

"Not without a driver's license," the cop explained.

"Do you have any identification on you?" the cop asked me.

"No."

"Do you have a name? Date of birth?"

"Martin Green. Seven, twenty-two, seventy-two."

The cop walked Jewel to the back of the police car, while the other cop radioed in the information that I'd just given him.

For five minutes I sat in limbo in Jewel's Range Rover. Then the other cop that had walked Jewel to the squad car came back over to the Range Rover and whispered something into the other cop's ear.

"Can you step out of the car please?"

I obeyed, not fully knowing what was up.

"Michael Burroughs, you have the right to remain silent. Anything you say can and will be used against you . . ."

Muthafucka! I shook my head and clenched my teeth in anger, wondering just how the fuck was I gonna get myself out of this sling that I'd suddenly found myself in.

Chapter 12

"Payback's a Bitch"

Touch

After I hung up the phone, I shouted, "Bitchass nigga!" Calico was really becoming a pain in my ass.

I immediately called Jewel, and her phone rang out to voice mail. "Jewel, what's up? This is Touch. Call me back as soon as you get this message. Gone."

I made my way into Bottoms Up. I needed a drink in the worst way. I headed to the bar and ordered a double shot of Grey Goose and took it straight to the head.

"Oh, shit! Hey, Touch. What's good, homie? Is this like a fucking high-school reunion or some shit?"

I squinted my eyes, trying to figure out who the fuck it was that was talking to me. "It's me, man. Diablo."

"Oh, what's the deal, Diablo?" I extended my hand to Diablo and gave him a pound.

The deejay shouted into the microphone, "Coming to the stage, we got Juicy on stage one, and Malibu on stage two. Show them some love, fellas."

Diablo said to me, "That thick shit right over there on the stage, Malibu, that's what's up."

I looked over to the stage and saw Sasha wiping down the pole on the stage, preparing to do her thing. I have to admit, looking at Sasha instantly made my dick rise.

I hadn't seen Diablo in years. I'd heard that he'd moved to Atlanta from Virginia and was doing his thing and getting money down there. But I never really liked the dude. I always tolerated his ass, but I never really fucked with him like that. He wasn't an enemy per se, but he wasn't a real nigga. He was one of those niggas that always managed to get over and shit. Besides, that nigga ain't like me back in high school because he thought I was knocking Jewel off when they were kicking it.

Diablo ordered a bottle of Rosé, and we popped the bottle and drank champagne, and kicked it.

Just before Sasha was finished with her routine, I walked up to the stage and threw three hundred-dollar bills at her.

"Oh, shit! Thank you," Sasha said, looking at the money only and not even realizing it was me.

I screamed out to her, "Sasha, what up, girl?"

"Oh my God! Touch! What's up, baby? I didn't even realize that was you. Wait right there. I'll be there in a minute," Sasha said as she walked around the stage, butt-ass naked in her stilettos, picking up the money that she'd just made and tossing it in a tall, clear garbage bag.

I turned around to see Diablo hawking my ass like a fucking stalker.

"So, Diablo, where you gonna be? Let me get your number so I can kick it wit'chu before I bounce back to VA."

Diablo gave me his number. "So you down here buying them thangs?"

I knew he was referring to weight, but that wasn't the reason I had come to Atlanta. "Nah, I'm actually down here looking at some real estate that I'm trying to buy."

"Oh, okay. That's what's up. So, if you need them thangs, holler at your boy." Diablo gave me a pound and walked off.

Just as Diablo walked off, Sasha came up to me and gave me a kiss on my cheek.

"Sasha, I forgot you had all that damn booty up under them clothes," I said, still admiring her body. "You make a nigga wanna wife your ass."

"Nigga, please. Everybody wanna wife a bitch when she butt-ass naked," Sasha said jokingly.

"So what's up?"

"Nothing. I'm just up in here working, trying to get my swagger back. I been going through it lately."

I couldn't help but to continue to stare at her body.

"Touch, if you don't stop . . ."

"Yo, come on, I want a private dance. You working, right?" I grabbed her by the hand, and we walked downstairs toward the VIP rooms. "It's twenty dollars a song, right?"

"Yep." Sasha smiled at me and took the lead, walking in front of me toward a leather couch in the VIP room.

I handed her one hundred dollars. She sat me down and asked me if it was all right if she took off her shoes. I nodded yes, and she took off her shoes and waited for the next song to come on. When it did, she started dancing for me.

I asked her, "You know I always had a crush on you?"

"Yeah, whatever. You know you coulda had me whenever you wanted me, but your nose was always up Jewel's ass."

Sasha sat her soft, plump ass on my lap and started grinding on my rock-hard dick.

"So I *coulda* had you?" I asked. "So you saying I can't have you *now*?"

Sasha turned around and faced me in a straddled position. Then she leaned in and started kissing me on my neck and ear. As she kissed me on my ear, she whispered, "You know good and well that Jewel would have a fit if I was fucking wit'chu."

At that point Sasha had turned me on to the point where I was ready to stick my dick in her pussy right there and fuck her on the spot. Jewel and her feelings was the last thing on my mind right then. Besides, she was banging Calico. Maybe she needed a taste of her own medicine.

"We both grown," I said. "What we do is between me and you. Jewel ain't got to know what we do."

Sasha didn't respond. She just kept grinding on me and doing her thing. Then she reached her hand in my pants and started stroking my dick. "Ummmhhh," she moaned in my ear, "I didn't know you were working with all this."

"So now you know." I wanted to just stand up and bend her ass over and fuck her.

The last song of my five songs had just started playing, and I said to Sasha, "I know everything I say to you, you gon' go back and tell Jewel what I said. But ya girl's been on some bullshit lately, on the real."

"Oh my God! Who you telling?" Sasha shot back at me. "I thought it was just me, but I did notice she was acting funny and shit. It's like sometimes she can be there and care for me and look out for me, but it's like I don't know if it's always genuine 'cause, in the next breath, she's always flaunting shit and trying to down my ass and show off and shit."

I nodded my head, and then we both stood up because my time was up.

"So, listen," I whispered into her ear, "I'm staying at the Ritz Carlton in Buckhead across from Lenox. Why don't you come chill wit' me when you get up outta here?"

Sasha nodded her head. "Okay, but I probably wouldn't be leaving until around three in the morning."

"It's all good. I still be here."

She kissed me on the cheek then walked off. I watched her every move as her sexy ass walked in her stilettos and the white slingshot bikini that she was wearing. I couldn't wait to get her to my room so I could smash that ass.

Chapter 13

"In the Heat of the Night"

Sasha

Although I was dancing for a nigga and he was making it rain, my mind was on other things. I watched the clock constantly, waiting for three o'clock to hit. Hell, even two thirty. Anything just so that I could get the fuck out of dodge. All I could think of was Touch. That muthafucka literally had my pussy dripping. A bitch had to go to the dressing room and clean up with a baby wipe after lap-dancing with him. A few more songs and I could have busted right on his lap.

"Yo, shawty," the dude I danced for said with his deep down south country accent.

"Yes?" I responded full of attitude because he'd disrupted my day-dreaming about Touch.

"Make it clap or something for a nigga," he said, noticing my lack of energy.

"Okay, baby, I got you."

I figured I may as well straighten up and drain this nigga then call it a night. I danced for him and his boys for another ten songs then I was out.

I stopped by Touch's table on the way to the dressing room to let him know I was packing up. As soon as I packed my things and was ready to head out the dressing room door, the realization of what I was about to do settled in, and my heart began to race. I knew that Jewel would kill me if she found out. There was no way I could do it. I took a deep breath, grabbed my dance bag, and walked toward Touch to break the news to him.

He handed me a shot as soon as I walked up. "Drink this."

"What is it?"

"Patrón."

I took it down in one gulp. Hell, I needed that shit.

"You ready?" he asked as soon as I finished.

"Well—"

"Well, what?" Touch whispered in my ear then gently kissed me on my neck.

My knees got weak, and my head collapsed in his hand. I almost came from that alone. My neck was my weak spot, and it was as though this nigga knew it or something. I forced out the words, "Touch . . . I can't do this."

There was a slight awkward pause before he spoke up. Surprisingly, he gave in without a fight. "A'ight, cool. I don't want to force you. Just have a few drinks with me before I bounce."

"That's the least I can do," I said, knowing I'd disappointed him.

We took shot after shot; Patrón for me, Grey Goose for him.

After the third one, I was feeling nice, a little too nice as a matter of fact.

I found myself getting lap-dances. I looked at Touch as Juicy, one of the dancers, gave me a passionate lap-dance. She moved across my lap slowly and caressed my body all at the same time.

I fantasized it was Touch's hands on me as she embraced my body. The feeling was too overwhelming.

My mind was made up. I wanted Touch, and I wanted him at that moment. I pushed Juicy off me and approached him. "I'm ready. Let's go now."

Touch didn't say a word. He just pulled his keys out and grabbed my hand, and we headed out the door. Once outside, we agreed that I would follow him. He headed to his car, and I headed to mine.

Minutes later, we were in front of the Ritz Carlton. I gathered my composure as we headed to his room. I gave myself a pep talk as I waited for him to open the door. *Get it together, Sasha. You can do this. It's just sex. You're grown. Do you. Shit, Jewel is doing her.*

"I need to take a shower first," I said as soon as we walked through the door. "Do your thing." Touch turned the light on in the bathroom then flopped down on the bed.

I jumped in the shower and lathered up. I was sure Touch would be asleep when I got out. I was kind of hoping he would be. At least, then I would have an excuse not to have sex. But to my surprise, Touch was wide-awake when I walked out the bathroom.

"Damn, you are sexy!" he said, admiring my naked body.

"Wait!" I said, stopping him as he proceeded toward me. "Just let me do one thing first."

I ran into the bathroom and opened my bag. I needed a little encouragement, so I pulled out an ecstasy pill and popped it in my mouth. I waited a couple of minutes and headed back to the bed.

"What? You had to shit? Don't be getting in bed with me with shit crumbs in your ass," Touch joked.

"Boy, shut up. Ain't nobody shit."

I slid beneath the sheets with Touch. His dick was already rock-hard as I began to stroke it. I didn't know if it was the X pill or just the freak in me, but I wanted to do all kinds of things with this nigga. I pulled the covers back and straddled him. Then I began kissing him on his neck and moved down toward his nipples. I licked his nipples and bit them gently, sending erotic chills down his spine.

Next, I moved my way toward his penis. Now that was my joy! Like a jumbo Blow Pop, I slowly licked all around his head. Then, out of nowhere, I began to rapidly deep-throat his dick. Touch's moans of satisfaction turned me on.

"You better not cum. I haven't even started with this dick yet." I stroked it with my right hand then began to suck it.

I took a pause and juggled his balls and licked that little piece of sensitive skin beneath them, causing him to quiver every now and then. Confident that I'd given him a blowjob better than the infamous Superhead herself, I strapped on a condom, using my lips only, then straddled his dick. Touch moaned as I sat my warm, fat, wet pussy on top of him.

"Look at this fat pussy," I demanded as I bounced up and down on top of him.

"Damn," Touch said as he watched my pussy grip his manhood with each movement.

I could tell the image alone made him want to bust, but not before I got mine. I fucked him like a dog in heat, until I felt myself reaching my peak.

"You want to cum, baby?" I asked him.

"Yeah," he said between moans.

"Okay. I want you to cum with me. I'm about to cum, baby. Cum with me," I yelled as I dug my nails into Touch's chest, and we busted together.

Moments later, while I was lying on the bed, trying to catch my breath, Touch's phone began to ring. I used that as my cue to get up and headed to the bathroom.

I heard him say, "Oh shit."

"What?" I rushed back into the room, thinking the condom had broke or some crazy shit.

"Jewel is calling."

"Don't answer it," I said frantically.

"You don't have to worry about that."

As soon as Touch's phone finished ringing my phone began to ring. I didn't know if it was a guilty conscience or what, but something was telling me that Jewel knew something was up.

Oh well, I thought to myself as I freshened up in the bathroom. *Sasha, what Jewel don't know won't hurt her. Now what you need to do is pop another one of those X pills and go back in that room for round two with Touch. As I'm sure Jewel would say herself, "Use sex to secure that nigga and his money!"*

With that in mind, I proudly headed back into the bedroom. Hell, I was just following the advice of a friend. Jewel gave me the tools, so I was utilizing them. Based on the rules I was given on how to trap a baller, Touch fit the description, and I was just being a good student by putting in the work.

Chapter 14

"A Real Gangstress or Not?"

Jewel

"Why the fuck isn't anybody answering their got-damn phone!" I said to no one in particular as I waited for the cab driver to pull up to Norfolk City Jail. I'd been calling Touch and Sasha both since I'd been released and couldn't reach either of them.

Since this was my first offense and my charge wasn't major, the magistrate had agreed to let me go on a personal release bond. Calico, on the other hand, wasn't so lucky. I was able to find out that he didn't get a bond at all. Just like Calico had said when we first met, I didn't know what the fuck to do to get a nigga out of jail. That's one reason I needed to get with Touch, so I could find out my next move.

I was ecstatic when the cab pulled up. I walked to the cab like a woman with a broom stuck up her ass. I still had the plastic bag full of ecstasy pills in my pussy, and it was really beginning to feel uncomfortable. I gave the cab driver my home address and made myself comfortable in the back seat. I wasn't even trying to go to the car impound right then to pick my truck up. I felt disgusting. I reeked of jailhouse funk. Three hours in jail had really taken a toll on me, and all I wanted to do was go home and shower.

I was relieved when I finally pulled up to my home. I paid the cabbie and rushed in the house.

I turned my shower water on so that it was hot as hell and got undressed. I shook my head as I pulled the bag of *X* pills from below. *What the fuck am I doing?* I opened the bag and poured out its contents into the toilet then urinated afterwards. "Fuck this!" I said aloud. I flushed the toilet then hopped in the shower.

I exhaled as the hot water from the shower ran across my body, rinsing away all the drama from the hours before. I reflected back to the moment I realized the cops were behind me. It was like second nature when I took those pills and pushed them inside me. Shit, I didn't know I had it in me. In that case Calico could eat his words about me not being a ride-or-die chick. Hell, if that wasn't a gangtress move, I didn't know what was. But the fucked-up part about it is, now that I'd proven my status, I had no idea what was going to happen with Calico. I'd put in the work, but with his arrest, shit was looking dim, like there might not be a reward for me.

It was episodes just like this that made me remember why dope boys were never on the top of my list. Not only was their money not long enough, but shit, the lifestyle wasn't secure enough. Too much risk.

Needless to say I was tired as hell from everything that I had been through. I desperately wanted to speak to Touch, but since I couldn't get in contact with him, I figured that the smartest thing to do was to just lay my ass down in the bed and get some rest. I needed some sleep, so I could best figure out what the fuck had just happened, and what the fuck I was going to do next.

I crawled in my California king-sized bed. My green satin sheets never felt so good as I got comfortable beneath them. Within a matter of minutes, I was out cold and getting some much-needed sleep.

About two hours later, I was awakened by what sounded like someone knocking on my front door. I woke up disoriented and confused. Although I felt like I had been hibernating for two days or some shit, the clock said 2:30 P.M., so I knew that I had only been sleep for a few hours.

"What the fuck?" I barked as I stepped into my slippers and made my way downstairs to see who was banging on my door like they had lost their fucking mind.

My head was throbbing from having woken up so quickly, but that didn't stop me from venting the major attitude that I had. I didn't even bother to ask who it was at my door. Instead, I unlocked both locks and flung the door open.

"Do you have a gotdamn problem or something? Banging in my fucking door like you done lost your damn mind?"

There were two dudes standing at my door. One of them was big, black, and ugly, and reminded me a lot of the Notorious B.I.G. The other dude was short and stocky like a running back.

The short stocky dude asked, "Yo, where Calico at?"

Without responding to his question, I squinted my eyes and tried my hardest to figure out, had I ever seen either of those two dudes before.

"Ma, did I fucking stutter? I asked you where the fuck is Calico at?"

"What are you talking about?" My headache had suddenly disappeared, and my heart rate picked up.

The fat, ugly dude remarked, "She playing games."

At that point something told me to just slam the door and lock it shut and try to get to my gun that was locked upstairs. But when I attempted to close the door, the short, stocky dude prevented it from closing by sticking his foot in the way. Instantly I ran as fast as I could, trying to make it to my bedroom.

"Ugggh!" I screamed after having a fistful of my hair grabbed from the back, stopping me dead in my tracks, and being violently yanked to the ground. "Get the fuck off of me!" I screamed as I tried to get back up.

"Shorty, calm the fuck down!" The short dude put one of his white Nike Air Force One sneakers to my throat and applied pressure. *Click-click*. Now with a gun cocked to my head, he continued talking. "I'm gonna ask you one more time—Where the fuck is Calico?"

Seeing my life flash before my eyes, I knew I had to speak up or else lose my life. This dude definitely seemed like he had the heart to pull that trigger. "Okay, okay, just don't kill me."

The dude gave in and released all of the pressure that he had been applying to my neck.

I started to blab, my heart still racing, "Calico was here, but he got locked up last night."

I knew I had broken the first and most important rule of the streets by running my mouth, but fuck that! This was the first time that I had actually had a gun put to my head. A bitch wasn't trying to die.

The big dude said, "She lying!"

"I swear to God, last night I was with Calico at the strip club, and the cops pulled us over when we were leaving and he got knocked." My chest was visibly inhaling and exhaling the air from my lungs, as if I had just run a marathon or something.

The guy holding the gun on me instructed the other dude, "Go check the spot."

As I sat on the floor scared as hell and at the mercy of the intruders, I could hear my house being ransacked.

The dude yelled from upstairs, "Ain't shit up in here!"

He was instructed to keep looking.

I tried my hardest to calm down, but I just couldn't. It felt like I was playing the role of Tommy's girlfriend, Keisha, in the movie *Belly*, when niggas ran up in her shit.

Five minutes more had passed by and then the Biggie look-alike came back into my living room. Once his fat ass caught his breath, he confirmed what he had said earlier.

"That's some bullshit! Get the fuck up!" the stocky dude ordered me.

I stood to my feet as I was instructed.

"We gon' get this shit up outta her! Fuck that!"

I stood up, and the room was silent.

"Yo, son, go turn on that stereo," he ordered his man.

After fiddling with my sound system, the fat dude finally figured it out, and I heard the sound of music coming from the surround-sound speakers.

"Take all your clothes off, shorty," the dude instructed me over the loud music.

"What?" I asked, looking like I was ready to shit in my pants.

"Take your muthafuckin' clothes off, bitch!"

I couldn't help but start sobbing because I knew what was coming next.

"You wanna take that pussy?" the short dude with the short-man complex asked his man.

"Hell fucking yeah," he replied, rubbing his palms together in excited anticipation like a man ready to dig into Thanksgiving dinner.

"What do y'all want? I already told y'all that Calico was locked up. I ain't lying. You can check the Norfolk City Jail," I pleaded, desperately hoping that I wouldn't get raped.

"Where the fuck is his stash at?" the dude asked me.

"I don't know. I don't fuck with Calico on that level," I replied, sounding aggravated.

The cocky dude nodded his head to the big dude, and without hesitation he began unbuckling his belt and loosening his pants. Before I could blink, his pants and his boxers were down to his knees. His fat-ass belly was so huge, it was actually covering up his little-ass dick that he reached for and began stroking.

The sight of that fat, disgusting belly and his ugly-ass dick and balls was enough to make me throw up. I knew that if this nigga's dick actually penetrated my pussy, I would have died right there on the spot.

I urged myself. *Think, Jewel! Think, think, think,*

"Okay, listen, I'm not sure, but I think Calico might have stashed something over here," I said as I walked toward a closet that was located near my front door. My heart was pounding and ready to come out of my chest, but I had to make it to my ADT alarm system keypad.

I reached for the doorknob of the closet door, and at the same time I placed my hand on the alarm system keypad that was located right next to the molding of the door and pressed the police button.

"Back up from the closet!"

I was so nervous that when he yelled, I practically jumped, but I knew that I had to hold the button down for at least five seconds. "I can't promise that there's something in here, I mean—"

"Move back from the closet," the dude said and pushed me away.

I was sure he hadn't realized that I had pressed the police button because he didn't say anything about that. He just opened the closet and began rummaging through it.

"I had just picked him up from the airport. If his bag ain't in there, it's gotta be around here somewhere," I said, trying my hardest to stall for time.

"Man, that bitch lying! Let me break her ass off real quick and let's get the fuck up outta here," Biggie Smalls Junior said. This dude still had his pants and boxers pulled down around his ankles. By now, his disgusting dick was rock-hard and three inches long, instead of the original two.

"Nah, just chill for a minute. That bitch said there was three kilos up in here, and we leaving with that shit."

Right after he was done saying that, my home phone began ringing. I was almost sure that it was the alarm company calling to check shit out before they sent the police. I wanted to answer the phone, but I froze in my tracks and waited for them to say something.

The phone stopped ringing, and everyone looked at each other.

"Go bring me the phone," the short guy said to his partner, who quickly retrieved the cordless handset. Then he instructed him to search through the caller ID. "That was probably that muthafucka Calico calling the crib."

I prayed it wasn't Calico. I was hoping like hell that it was Touch because he would have definitely known what was up, and who to reach out to in order to come check on me.

"Ain't this a bitch! Yo, son, that was the fucking alarm company," Biggie shouted.

Without warning, the short guy knocked me upside my head with the butt of his gun, spinning me around and sending me crashing to the floor, blood pouring out of the side of my head. I was literally seeing stars. I couldn't believe that I felt my own warm blood running down my chin.

The dude knelt down so that his mouth was right next to my earlobe. "You make sure you tell Calico that Sincere said that he's gonna stay all up in that ass!" After saying that, he kissed me on my earlobe and stuck his nasty-ass tongue in my mouth.

"Let's get the fuck up outta here, yo."

With that, they left, not even bothering to shut my front door and leaving me lying on the floor in my own blood, woozy and feeling like I was about to pass out. I couldn't believe what I'd just gone through.

Chapter 15

"Ready for War"

Touch

When I got the call from Jewel that some niggas had ran up in her crib and that she was hurt, I jumped on the next plane out of Atlanta and got my ass back to Virginia. I didn't know what was up, but I could bet that it had something to do with Calico. And if Jewel knew what was good for her, she would leave him the fuck alone.

I took a cab from the airport to her crib and jumped in my car. Then I headed straight to her girlfriend's crib and scooped her up and shot back to my crib with her.

I said to her while we drove toward my house, "Jewel, from all the years that I've known your ass, you ain't never lie to me. So why the fuck are you gonna start lying now? You telling me some niggas just ran up in your crib and pistol-whipped you, but they didn't take shit?"

"Yes, Touch. And why are you stressing me out? My head is killing me, and look at how I look. Look at my fucking face. Oh my God, I can't believe this shit!"

I paused because I wanted to make sure that I was acting rationally. But after thinking to myself for a moment, I knew in my heart that this shit had something to do with Calico. "So when the last time you seen Calico?"

"Touch, I don't know."

"Did you fuck that nigga?"

"Touch, what are you talking about? Look, what you should be concerned with is dude with a New York accent named Sincere. *Sin*-fucking*cere*, not Calico!"

I said sternly, "Jewel, did you fuck that nigga, yes or no?" then stared her in her face as to say, "I dare you to lie."

"No! Okay. All right? No, I didn't fuck Calico, got-damn!" Jewel yelled and turned her head and looked out the window, a definite sign of deceit.

I didn't have a short fuse, in terms of a temper, but whenever I felt like someone was trying to insult my intelligence or trying to play me for a fool, that shit would always cause me to lose it.

"Jewel, you fucked that nigga, and I heard the whole shit. You fucked up and called my phone by mistake, so don't sit here and lie to me. I'm ready to kill niggas behind your ass, go to jail for your ass. And you know I would die for your ass if some muthafuckas violated you the way them niggas did. But one thing I ain't gonna do is be blind to some Calico bullshit and start fighting that nigga's battles."

I looked over at Jewel as she sat slumped in the passenger seat. I could see the stress on her face. She had this look like she was ready to lash out with anger, but she kept her cool and didn't say a word.

"Now I'm gonna ask you again—Did this shit have anything to do with Calico?"

Jewel looked at me. She rolled her eyes and twisted her lips, and then she went on to tell me how Calico came to stay with her and that he didn't want anyone to know that he was in town, and that she had sworn to him that she wouldn't say anything to anybody. So, out of respect for him, she kept her mouth closed.

I slowly nodded my head, but I didn't say anything. Then there was this uneasy silence for a while.

"Touch, in case you ain't notice, I'm fucking grown. So, okay, yes, I fucked the nigga, but it was just one of those things that just kinda happened," Jewel said, giving me that same old bullshit line I'd heard a thousand other dumb-ass bitches say, including my baby mother. "It wasn't planned or nothing like that."

I smirked and then I reached for the radio and turned on the music, to break the tension that was clearly visible.

"Oh, so you're a whore now? Just randomly fucking niggas? The only chicks that I randomly fuck are tricks and whores."

"You know what—"

"What?" I asked, cutting her off.

"Yes, well then, if that makes me a whore, then I'm a fucking whore. Shit!"

"I told you from the jump how that nigga rolled. He fucks bitches, set up shop in their crib, and when shit gets hot, he bounce. You're just another fucking statistic."

The two of us finally reached my house, and I smoked a cigarette as we sat quiet in my car for a few moments not saying anything to each other. When I was done smoking, we exited the car and made it inside my crib.

For good reasons Jewel was scared to go back home and stay by herself, so I let her stay at my place, which I had no problem at all in doing.

"You know where everything is. Just make yourself at home. I gotta make some calls."

I went into my kitchen and started calling all my soldiers and told them that we was getting ready to go to war with some cat with a New York accent who went by the name of Sincere.

When I was finished with one of my calls, Jewel came into the kitchen and told me that her and Calico had gone to Purple Rain, and she told me about the arrest and all that went down with that.

"So you just had a real fucked-up run?"

"Touch, I'm all fucked-up right now."

All I could do was shake my head in pity. "Well, I'm just telling you this because, after I thought about everything, I realized that them dudes had to have seen us up in the strip club, and they must have asked around about who I was. That's the only thing I can think of as to how they knew there was a connection between me and Calico."

"Jewel, I'm gonna make everything better. I'm on the shit. You just gotta listen to me and trust me. I know how Calico gets down and what he does with chicks and how he uses them. So who knows who he ran his mouth to and about what?"

"How does my face look?"

"Jewel, you're fine. That knot is just a 'speed knot.' It's gonna go down. Besides, it's in your hairline. Once the swelling goes down, you'll be straight."

Regardless of what I said, Jewel couldn't pull herself away from standing in front of the mirror and staring into it.

"By you just staring in the mirror, it ain't gonna change nothing. Why don't you just go upstairs, get one of my T-shirts, go take a shower, and then fix yourself a drink, and we'll just chill for the night. And if you need me to, I'll chill with you at your crib for a few days until we find this nigga Sincere."

Jewel nodded her head, and then she took her shoes off and headed to my bedroom. Before long, she came back into the living room with my New York Giants Plaxico Burress jersey in her hands and asked if it was okay to wear that.

I gave her a look as if to say, "Why are you even asking me such a stupid question?"

Jewel immediately got my drift. Before she walked off, she said, "And just for the record, I wanna be clear that I ain't nobody's trick or nobody's ho."

I knew damn well that she wasn't a whore. And, truth be told, I loved the fuck outta Jewel, like a dude loves his wife. In my mind she was like a wife to me, and it was time that I started making that shit known.

"I apologize for saying that. Jewel, you just . . ." I paused as I gathered my thoughts. "It's like you just different than most women, so when I react a certain way to shit or say certain shit, I'm speaking out of love, you feel me?"

"All I know is, you called me a skank whore, so save all that nice talk, mister," Jewel said with a smile.

"So you accept my apology then?"

Jewel nodded her head and walked off.

I watched her sexy frame making its way back to my bedroom, and I couldn't resist. "I'm coming up there to take a shower with you. Don't make the water too hot."

Jewel turned and looked at me. She sucked her teeth and smiled. "Anyway."

Little did she know, I was dead-ass serious.

Chapter 16

"Lovers and Friends"

Jewel

My heart dropped when the shower curtain pulled back and a naked Touch stood before me. I didn't know if I should cover my body or turn my head from looking at his body. This was totally unlike him, and I was wondering where this was coming from. There'd been times when I got so drunk from the club that he would bathe me and then put me to bed, but that was back in the day, and he had never been naked with me.

As he stepped into the shower with me like it was nothing, I screamed, "Touch, no!"

"Chill out, girl. It ain't nothing but a shower." He reached for his Irish Spring body wash.

Oh well, I guess he's right, I thought to myself, feeling a little silly for reacting like a little schoolgirl. I studied Touch's physique as he washed his face beneath the running water from the showerhead. *Damn, was he fine!* Plus, his package was just right.

Touch caught me checking him out. "I see you looking."

"Boy, ain't nobody looking at you," I lied, embarrassed that he'd actually caught me.

I rushed to wash the blood out of my hair from my head wound. Then I went on to wash my body.

I noticed that Touch's whole demeanor was kind of nonchalant the entire time we showered. Don't get me wrong, I didn't expect him to be jumping on top of me and trying to rape me or anything, but damn, a nigga should at least be trying to get a peep in. There was no way I was goin' to have this nigga around me, fronting like he didn't want to touch me, so I thought I might break the ice a little bit.

"Can you wash my back?" I said, hoping to get a little attention from Touch.

"Nope. How you wash yourself all the other times when you're showering alone?" he said playfully.

"Boy, don't play with me. You do me, and I'll do you." I handed him my washcloth.

I don't know if I was tripping or what, but as soon as he placed the towel on my back, it sent chills down my spine, and with every stroke, a sensation was sent throughout my body. Just as I was getting into it, it was over.

"My turn." Touch handed me my washcloth then grabbed for his.

"Turn around." I grabbed his towel and instructed him to turn his back to me.

"Nah, you said you were gonna do me." Touch looked at me with a straight face.

"No, silly. You know gotdamn well ain't nobody talking about *doing* you! I was talking about you wash my back, and I'll wash yours. Now turn around!" I demanded.

"Nah. Do it this way. I don't want you looking at my ass." Touch laughed.

I didn't even have the energy to fight with his crazy ass, so I just wrapped my arms around him, as though I was giving him a hug, and tried my best to wash his back thoroughly.

Touch wrapped his arms around me and squeezed me tight, like he was going to war and this was the last time he would see me.

It kinda caught me off guard, so I paused and looked up at him. We locked eyes as he looked down at me with those big brown eyes that I thought made him irresistible.

Then, in one motion, he slid his hands behind my neck, forcing it back, and slipped his tongue inside my mouth.

I didn't resist the least bit. It felt so right. We kissed with so much passion that the fire inside me was burning hot, and I was prepared to take it all the way. I moved my hand toward Touch's penis, but he stopped me.

"I love you, girl," he said as he grabbed his bath towel and stepped out of the shower.

I stood in the shower alone and speechless. This was all taking me by complete surprise. Touch and I had been friends for forever, and not once, through all the assumptions and innuendo, did we or, at least, did I ever think that we could be more than friends. But in the last twenty minutes all of that had changed. Years of friendship had changed. Where did that leave us now?

Baffled, I finished up my shower, hopped out, dried off, and baby-oiled my body. I threw on Touch's jersey and then met him in the living room.

"I'm hungry," I said, trying to forget the awkward moment we'd just shared.

"Wanna order Chinese?"

"Sure." I grabbed the phone then shuffled through his junk drawer in search of a Chinese menu.

Once I found one, I ordered our food then flopped down on the couch beside him. I took the remote from him and started to flip through his cable's On Demand, to find a movie for us to watch. By the time we'd flipped through six or seven movies and watched the previews and bullshitted with each other for a while, our food had arrived. We made ourselves comfortable on the sofa and ate Chinese as we watched the movie *Halloween*.

Not a fan of horror movies, I balled up underneath Touch's arm and lay my head on his chest, my feet across his lap. With what I had been through, being pistol-whipped and all, this was the safest that I had felt since the ordeal.

Although most of the movie was spent with me closing my eyes, screaming and jumping, I was still able to catch Touch constantly staring at me. Tired of wondering what the hell was on his mind, I just spat it out.

"Why the hell you keep looking at me?"

Instantly becoming irritated by my question, Touch sighed heavily and said, "This is some bullshit." He then quickly got up from the couch and headed toward the kitchen.

I followed hot on his heels, yelling, "What? What the fuck is your problem?" *I know this nigga ain't sitting up here thinking about that shit between me and Calico.* I stared all up in Touch's face, waiting for an answer, but he didn't respond. He just shook his head and stared at me.

"So what? You think I'm pitiful now? That's why you shaking your head?"

"You have no idea, Jewel. I need to be with you, not that nigga Calico. That muthafucka almost got you raped. Maybe killed. All these years, and not once did you think to look my way, but this new nigga come into town and give you some money, now you ready to go down for his bullshit. I have protected you and cared about you all this time, and now you asking me some dumb shit? You know what? You right. You are pitiful because you here tellin' me I need a good woman and you can't see that you're it."

This was the second time tonight that Touch left me speechless. I just never knew that he felt this way. I mean, sure, he was fine as hell, but he had Ciara and the fat rats. Besides, Touch couldn't be some random nigga I put on my team. I would dismiss the whole squad just to be with him.

My thoughts were interrupted when I heard moving around.

"I need to step out for minute." Touch grabbed his keys and headed toward the front door.

I raced in front of him and stood in front of the door like a club security guard. "You ain't going outta this house, Touch," I yelled, tears of frustration welling up in my eyes.

"You want me to stay?" he asked calmly.

"Yes."

"You sure?"

"Yes."

"You don't know what you're asking for, Jewel."

"Yes, I definitely know what I'm asking for.
Just don't leave me. Please, don't leave."

Touch grabbed me by my throat, startling me. The pressure from his hand pinned my head against the front door. He pressed his body against mine, and began to kiss me passionately again, causing my pussy to get wet within seconds. He released my neck and used his leg to force my thighs slightly open. I could feel the solidness of his dick through his boxers as the force from his body pressed against mine. With each hand he gripped my outer thighs and lifted me off the floor.

Eager to have him inside me, I wrapped my legs around his waist. In only a matter of seconds, I had lifted Touch's jersey over my head, and he'd dropped his boxers. And in one big thrust, he was inside of me, fulfilling my every desire. I didn't say a word as he forced his manhood deep inside of me. Not only did my body yearn for more, but so did my heart. I wanted Touch.

For the first time, I'd felt that chemistry between man and woman that I'd heard so much about. It was surreal. I was reaching my peak so fast.

"Cum with me, Touch," I whispered in his ear, and like magic, we both came together.

Once again tears ran from my eyes, but this time they weren't tears of fear. They were tears of ultimate satisfaction.

After a session like that, there was nothing else left to do but wash up, and go to bed. And in Touch's case, take a smoke, wash up, and go to bed.

The next morning, I was awakened by a call from Sasha. "Hello?" I answered full of attitude.

"What's wrong with you?"

"Nothing now, but when there was a problem, you sure didn't answer your damn cell phone." I was still pissed that Sasha didn't answer her phone when I'd called her the other night.

"I'm sorry, Jewel. I worked late that night, and I was fucked-up when I left the club. Are you okay?"

"Well, I am now," I said, full of disgust.

"So what happened?"

"To make a long story short, me and Calico got arrested when we were leaving the strip club."

"Oh, you went to see your little bitch, Paradise, huh?" Sasha interrupted my story with her regular bullshit, totally overlooking the fact that I said I'd gotten locked up.

"Like I was saying, I spent a few hours in jail but was released on bond. Calico is still in there. Then after that some niggas ran up in my shit and pistol-whipped me."

"Oh my God! Jewel, are you sure you're okay? Where are you now?" "I'm at Touch's house." I smiled to myself.

"Oh, for real. What he doing?"

"Sleeping. I put that ass to sleep."

"What?"

"Bitch, you heard me—I put that ass to sleep!"

Sasha said in a tone of disapproval, "Jewel, don't tell me you fucked Touch."

"I sure did."

"But that's your best friend. I thought you would never go there with him. I hope this is not another one of your money schemes, 'cause if it is, it sounds pretty pathetic to me. Oh, let me guess, you gonna use Touch now because Calico is locked up. Jewel, that is foul."

Usually I can take Sasha's jealous rants, but today was different. She went on and on, like Touch was her fucking blood brother or some shit.

"Relax. It's not even like that. And why do you care anyway? I had no ulterior motive when we had sex. And the thing about it is that it felt so right. For the first time I have true feelings for a nigga. It's like he's my soul mate, and to think he was right in my face the whole damn time."

"Whatever. Well, I gotta go. I have another call coming in." Sasha hung up the phone before I could even say goodbye.

That was definitely new for her. She had never hung up on me like that before. *What's her problem with me seeing Touch anyway?*

No sooner than she hung up, my phone rang again. This time it was a number I didn't recognize. My first instinct was to not even answer, but I went against it. "Hello?" I answered with caution.

I heard a woman's voice say, "Hold on," then Calico chimed in.

"Calico!" I screamed, waking Touch.

"Hey, baby. Look, I don't have much time. I'm on a three-way, so listen carefully."

Although I wanted to blast him about that shit that happened the day before, I gave him an opportunity to speak first. I listened attentively as Calico explained he was granted a million dollars bail, and was going to pay the ten percent of that, one hundred thousand dollars, in cash and bond out. He also told me that he needed me to collect one hundred fifty thousand dollars that Touch owed him. Once received, some of the money was to be given to his attorney as a retainer, and I was to hold on to the rest, which he would need to make moves when he hit the streets.

"Okay, I got it, and I'm on it as soon as we get off the phone. Now let me share a few things with you," I said calmly.

I spent the next five minutes giving Calico a rushed version of how that nigga Sincere came up in my house. But with the automated voice counting down the minutes and with Touch constantly yelling at me in the background to hang up the phone, I just couldn't deliver like I wanted to.

Thankfully Calico had a bond, so he would be out, and as soon as he was, I would be the first to snap off on his ass.

Before I could even properly hang up the phone, Touch said, "Yo, you insist on dealing with that nigga, huh?"

"Touch, I just want to let him know what's going on and wrap things up. Once things are in order, I'm gonna back away. I just don't want to up and turn my back on him, not right now anyway. Right now, I'm all he has."

"So you think," Touch mumbled. "Trust me, that nigga got plenty of other chicks playing the same position as you." He got out of the bed and stood up and looked at the missed calls on his cell phone.

"Oh, and he wants you to give me the one hundred and fifty grand you owe him. I have to pay his lawyer with a portion of that."

"Yeah, okay. Whatever." Touch headed into the bathroom and closed the door behind him.

All I could do was shake my head. I damn sure didn't need no more stress in my life.

Chapter 17

"Opportunity Knocks"

Sasha

I so didn't feel like answering my phone when I saw Jewel's name pop up on my caller ID, but since she had called me four times in a row, I decided to pick up. I answered the phone with a sarcastic attitude, "Either you're a psycho bitch, or you're a stalker. Which one is it?"

"Sasha, what is your problem?" Jewel asked.

I wanted to tell her that I was tired of her bullshit, tired of her always flaunting shit and showing off, tired of her always making a come-up, while I was in a unending state of struggling to get mine. Instead, I kept my mouth shut. It had been about three days since I had abruptly hung up the phone on her, and to be honest, I had absolutely no intentions of ever calling her ass back.

"Helloooo."

"Yeah, I'm here. You called me. So what do you want?"

Jewel blew some air into the phone, as if she had a reason to have an attitude. "Look, I know you been going through some shit lately, and to be honest, I'm sensing something, like you have a problem with me or some shit—"

"Well, actually—" I cut Jewel off, ready to cuss her ass out and tell her to leave me the fuck alone, but then she interrupted me just as quickly.

"Wait! Would you just hear me out and let me finish?"

I kept quiet.

"What I was trying to say was that I got my hands on some money and I'm gonna be heading to New York to go shopping. I wanted to do something nice for you and have you come with me. My treat, all expenses paid."

"Damn, that must be some killer-ass pussy!" I couldn't resist making a smart comment. "So how much did you get Touch for?"

"Sasha, what the fuck is your problem? I call you with regular everyday shit, and you got an attitude. I call you trying to be nice, and you still got an attitude. I don't get it. Is it that time of the month or something?"

"You don't get it because you're not me and you ain't going through the shit that I'm going through."

"Yeah, but, Sasha, I'm your homegirl. You can tell me what's going on without taking things out on me. You already know that I'll be there for you and look out for you in any way that I can."

"Blah, blah, blah, blah," was what I felt like saying to Jewel, but I was no dummy. I was at least gonna get a free trip to New York and get some clothes in the process, so I held my tongue.

"So how much money did you get your hands on?"

"Well, Touch gave me one hundred and fifty grand."

"A hundred and fifty gees?"

"Bitch, dry your panties off, 'cause the shit ain't my money. Some of the money is supposed to go to pay Calico's lawyer, and the rest is going to Calico. It's just money that Touch owed him. But, the way I see it, ten percent of that has to go to me as a fee for my services. You know how I do."

Regardless of my attitude with Jewel, I couldn't help but laugh at her. I had to admit, I loved the way she got down, especially when my ass could benefit from it.

"Jewel, you are a true hot-ass mess."

Jewel laughed. "Nah, that shit is only right. It's a ten percent facilitation fee."

"Hooker, your ass can't even spell *facilitation*."

Jewel and I both laughed. Then she told me that she was gonna book my ticket and call me back with the details.

"So we good now?" she asked me.

"No, I'm still gonna fight you when I see you," I said jokingly.

Yeah, I switched up and went into a joking mood, but the truth of the matter was, I was just fronting my ass off. Jewel had her hands on one hundred fifty grand that I was gonna help her spend. As far as I was concerned, that was one hundred fifty thousand reasons for me to put on an acting performance.

Right after I hung up the phone, I sat straight up in my bed. My mind was registering what she really said. Then, suddenly I had an idea.

That bitch said she has her hands on one hundred fifty grand. Sasha, if you put on an Oscar award winning performance, you can leave New York and come back to ATL with at least one hundred thousand, I thought to myself. This was definitely it. It was time for my come-up. My panties really were getting wet just thinking about what I would do with a hundred thousand dollars.

I got up from out of my bed and paced back and forth in my room, trying my hardest to think of just what I was gonna say to her, and how I was gonna say it, for her to hit me off with that money. I just didn't know if I should call Jewel back and kick my game to her, or if

I should wait until we got to New York to give her my sob story.

Jewel ran plenty of game, and I'd learned from the best.

It was time to give her a taste of her own medicine. I knew I had to be careful because one thing for sure was, game recognized game. Jewel was an all-star at this, so she couldn't be easily manipulated. My hands were tied. This wasn't gonna be an easy task.

Think, Sasha, think! I pleaded with myself.

After a few minutes, it came to me that when Jewel called me back I had to go in for the kill. I couldn't wait because, if I waited until we got to New York, she might divvy the money up by then and pay the lawyer and hit Calico off.

Yeah, bitch, I'ma play your game. You think you the only one with that pot of gold between your legs that can fuck money outta any nigga, right?

I knew that I had some killer sex myself. A tongue and pussy that I knew Jewel would die over. That girl loved me and she knew it. And with one hundred thousand in cash, I was gonna make her prove it.

Chapter 18

"Back against the Wall"

Calico

As soon as I made bond, I made a few calls and had one of my chicks make arrangements to get me out. Then I headed straight to my attorney's office. I had been indicted on a racketeer influenced and corrupt organizations charge, better known as a RICO charge. Those fucking prosecutors were acting like I was John Gotti, talking all that organized crime bullshit. From what my lawyer was saying, the shit didn't look good. Her theory was that the state had a 97 percent conviction rate on this type of charge, and that I had to seriously consider taking a plea deal. If not, I could be looking at twenty years.

"Fuck that!" I told my lawyer bluntly. "I ain't copping out to shit. And I ain't no snitch, so there's no way I'm cooperating. They can forget that."

My lawyer was a sexy, green-eyed, blonde-haired Italian supermodel-looking chick. Besides the fact that she was smart as shit, what I liked about her most was that she understood the struggle. Her pops used to be in organized crime and got locked up when she was eleven years old and had been in prison ever since. The fact that she had grown up without him led her to want to be a lawyer.

"Michael, you know I'll fight for you till the bitter end, but make no mistake about it, it's gonna be a dogfight to beat these charges."

"I only fuck with the best. That's why I got you," I said before leaving.

I had explained to her that Jewel would come by to give her one hundred and twenty-five thousand. And she made sure to remind me that I would be looking at, at least, one million in fees by the time it was all said and done. But I knew that it would be money well spent because she would have to hire investigators, expert witnesses, and shit like that, on my behalf. Once I wrapped that shit up, I was on the next flight home to California.

I'd been in California for the entire five days after seeing my lawyer. That shit with niggas running up in Jewel's crib really had me fucked up. I had put a hit out on Sincere, and things were immediately dealt with. But something still didn't sit right with me. I couldn't understand how these dudes knew where to find me and how much coke I had. I wasn't a sloppy dude, and nobody really knew I was kicking it with Jewel like that. I knew I needed to talk to her more about the situation.

Since my arrest I had refused to talk on my cell phone. Instead, I was only using prepaid cell phones that I would get rid of on a weekly basis. Just to be extra careful, I made sure that Jewel and other people that I spoke to on a regular basis didn't call me from one of their regular phone numbers.

"You know this prepaid cell phone shit is for the birds," Jewel complained to me.

"It's a slight inconvenience for freedom baby," I explained to her. "Anyway, a couple of things real quick. I handled that shit with Sincere, just like I told you I would. Them fucking New York niggas think muthafuckas is just gonna get down or lay down 'cause they from New York. I guess niggas know different now."

"Oh, shit! Yeah, I heard about that. I had no idea."

"One thing, though . . . shit don't seem right. It had to be someone else involved, or something more to it. I ain't tell no niggas I was chilling with you or how much shit I had. Tell me any and everything you can remember about these dudes. You sure you've never seen them before?" I asked, fishing for more information.

I listened attentively as Jewel spoke. I thought about everyone I'd come in contact with on that visit. Then it was one thing Jewel said that stuck out.

I made sure I'd heard correctly. "You said a chick told them I had coke in the house?"

"Yep."

"Say no more." I deaded that conversation.

I knew exactly who had set me up, and that bitch was to get dealt with next. Shit had finally come together. That shiesty bitch, Diana, was the only chick I'd dealt with that day, and I remembered seeing her hollering at two unfamiliar dudes in a car with New York tags as we were leaving the strip club. I didn't even bother telling Jewel.

"Now about this money, you hit my lawyer off yet?" I said, changing the subject.

"No, but—"

"Jewel, listen, this shit ain't a game. I don't want you walking around with that kind of bread. Now, you said you wanted to be my ride-or-die bitch. I need you to prove it to me. Take the shit to over to her today."

"Okay, okay, I'm on it."

"So what is Touch saying?"

"Saying about what?"

"That bitch-ass nigga, I'm surprised he ain't give you a hard time giving you my loot."

"Calico, what are you talking about? Why you calling him a bitch? And for the record, Touch gave me that money with no problem."

I didn't go any further with that issue. I really didn't have the time to concern myself with Touch. My money was getting low, and I had to get my weight up. Those New York niggas had been coming down to Virginia and trying to supply the same market that I was supplying, and now I knew how. I was sure that trick-ass Diana was making it real easy for those niggas, putting them on to my customers and everything.

I admit that they had caught me slippin', and in the process, my money took a hit. It was nothing that I couldn't recover from, but I was experiencing a slight drought. And with that case that I had caught, it just seemed like the government and my competition smelled blood, and were moving in for the kill.

My back was starting to feel like it was up against the wall, but one thing about me was, I knew I was smarter than all the street niggas out there. And I was never the one to back down from shit. I was gonna lay low for a month or two in California and let things run their course, but I was definitely gonna be plotting shit out in the meantime. I ran Virginia. That's how it was, and that's how shit was gonna continue to be.

When I hung up the phone with Jewel, I poured myself a glass of Hennessy on the rocks and sparked a blunt that I had rolled earlier. I took the remote to my CD player, and I turned on the *American Gangster* soundtrack and went right to track 10 and blasted the song "Ignorant Shit." In seconds the lyrics had me amped as I took pulls from the weed. I turned the volume up even louder as I drank from my glass and recited along with the song.

My head was feeling nice. It was like, instantly, I could care less about my legal problems or anything else as I continued to rap out loud as if I was Jay-Z.

Chapter 19

"Money Scam"

Jewel

"Hey, Boobie!" I yelled as I raced toward Sasha, who was standing at the luggage carousel at the airport.

"Hey, baby!" She rushed into my arms, and I hugged her tight as she wrapped her arms around me and grabbed a handful of each of my butt cheeks and squeezed them tight.

I quickly removed her hands. "Sasha, we're in the airport. People are watching."

Laughing, Sasha grabbed her bag from her incoming flight from Atlanta, and we chatted as we walked to the counter to check in for our flight to New York. Sasha asked about the discussion we'd had about flipping Calico's money the previous day.

"So you reach a decision yet?"

"Yeah, I have. I ain't gon' lie, that shit sounds like a good idea. I'm just thinking about the risk," I said to Sasha, even though my gut was telling me to just look at Sasha's loser track record and to not go through with her grand money plans.

Sasha tried to assure me that her plan was foolproof. "What risk? Diablo is your homeboy. He loves you to death. You know he'll give you the product at a good-ass price. And you don't have to worry about a driver.

I'll drive to Atlanta with the money and bring the shit back up here to you. Baby, there is no risk. You have nothing to lose."

I flipped through my Gucci handbag, trying to locate my driver's license so that I could hand it to the clerk at the airline counter. "Yeah, I hear you, but Calico is on my ass about paying his lawyer."

"Just stall him, or better yet, just lie and say you paid the lawyer. What the fuck? Girl, don't act like you don't know how to game a nigga."

I looked at Sasha, just as the clerk handed me my boarding pass. "See, that's the thing, Sasha. This ain't a game. Calico is really going through it right now, and I can't fuck his money up."

"You won't fuck it up, Jewel. We got this, trust me."

Purposely ignoring Sasha and not responding to her on that issue, I walked toward Starbucks so I could get a grande caramel frappuccino. I asked her, "You want something from Star-bucks?"

Sasha shook her head no, and then she gave me this look, as if to check me for not answering her. "Jewel?"

Sasha looked so irresistibly cute, and she did have one helluva plan. Besides, a bitch could always use some extra dough, but I didn't want to just give in to her right there on the spot. This was no ordinary nigga I was going to game. This was the "California Connection." Shit could get really messy if this plan of hers wasn't executed properly.

"Let me think a little more. I'll let you know by the end of our little trip. Right now, all we need to be thinking about is spending this fifteen gees!"

The plane ride was quick. Sasha and I both slept through the whole flight into New York's LaGuardia Airport.

"Come this way." I instructed Sasha to follow me as we exited the plane, and I headed toward the limousine driver that was holding a sign that read C. Diaz.

"Damn, you doing it big, huh?"

"Yeah, I'm doing it big, but not on my dollar. I also have a little business to take care of while I'm out here."

"Business?" Sasha responded full of attitude.

I knew how salt jealous Sasha could be, and that was why I had purposely held back from telling her about the other reason for my trip to New York.

"Relax. It's only a quick meeting. This independent hip-hop record label that I've done some ghostwriting work for in the past referred me to this major publishing company here in New York. They want me to do some work on this book that TMF is putting out."

"TMF? Bitch, shut up!" Sasha yelled.

I knew Sasha would be impressed with those niggas. Who wouldn't be? TMF stood for True Mafia Family. It was a group of niggas that had just as much drugs, money, and power as the Italian mafia. They had the same organization and success as the Italians, but all these dudes were black. There were the Frank Lucas of their time.

"Yep. I'm just gon' run in there and meet with everyone, see what they talking about, and sign my name on the dotted line."

Chapter 20

"Temperatures Rising"

Touch

"So y'all doing it big up there in New York," I said to Jewel, practically shouting into the phone in an attempt to compete with all the noise in the background.

"Yeah, we met with the publisher, and I got the contract. I signed off on that shit, which I probably shouldn't have done without having a lawyer look at it. But, hey, fuck it, the dollars look right."

There was so much noise and commotion behind Jewel, I could barely make out two words of this conversation.

"We hanging out and I'm trying to get to know these niggas so I can write from their point of view. But I'll call you as soon as we get back to Virginia."

"A'ight, but one thing. I really called to ask you why the fuck is Calico calling and questioning me about his bread? You paid his lawyer right?"

"Touch, come on now, that bitch got her money, so if Calico is saying different, you tell him to call me."

"Enough said."

Jewel hung up the phone, and my next call was to Calico. He didn't pick up, but I let him know that I had verified with Jewel that she'd paid the lawyer and that I didn't appreciate his bitch ass calling me and insinuating that I was trying to play with his money.

The truth of the matter, though, was that I knew Jewel was bullshitting. I knew that she hadn't paid that lawyer. Now, exactly why she hadn't paid the lawyer and what she was planning on doing with Calico's money, I didn't know, and to be honest, I really didn't give a fuck. That was on Calico for trying to run game on a chick like Jewel. But one thing I did know was if that nigga ever tried to come at Jewel sideways, I would be the first to deal with his ass. And it wouldn't be a hit. That one I would have to handle face to face, because then it would be personal.

My baby moms was back to stressing me the fuck out. I was going to see her, so I could check that ass for some smart comments she'd made. This bitch had to nerve to say some shit about me not fucking her and that Calico was the only dude that knew how to fuck her like she wanted to be fucked. A broad can say anything on the phone, but shit is different when you up in their face. I was going to her crib, to prove that shit.

She knew how I felt about her fucking these cats out here in the streets. That's why I wasn't with her bitch ass anymore. If she really fucked Calico, I would lose my mine. I would really kill that bitch. She was the mother of my kids, yeah, that's true, but that wouldn't make a damn difference if she was even halfway telling me the truth. The way I was feeling about her and Calico lately, shit wasn't looking good for either of them, as far as I was concerned.

Chapter 21

"Seal the Deal"

Sasha

"Oh my God," I said as I opened my eyes and slowly sat up in the bed. A night of club-hopping with TMF had taken a toll on me. I was definitely feeling the effects of the Ace of Spades champagne I'd drank the night before. Or should I say Armand de Brignac, since Jewel's bourgeoisie ass kept reminding me of the proper name the entire damn night.

My head was spinning as I tried to focus my eyes to see the time on the clock. It was twelve o'clock, three hours before our flight. That left me roughly an hour and a half to give Jewel a little sexual persuasion so that this plan to flip Calico's money could happen.

Without waking Jewel, I ordered breakfast for us and had room service deliver it. Then I woke her to breakfast in bed.

"Thank you, baby," she said in a groggy morning tone.

"No. Thank you for such a wonderful trip," I said sweetly. Then I kissed her.

After we ate our food, I put the tray outside the door. Jewel was full and content as she sat in bed and flipped through channels on the television. Now it was time to bring up the money.

"So, baby, did you decide anything yet?" I asked as I lay beside her, my leg over hers.

"Well, I'm still not sure. Don't get me wrong, it sounds like a hell of a plan, and everything you're saying makes sense, but I'm still unsure."

"It's okay," I said, knowing I was about to do exactly what it took to make her confident.

I lay my head on the pillow next to Jewel and watched TV as she fell back asleep. Once she was sound asleep, I gently straddled her naked body without saying a word. With a feather-like touch, I lightly circled the outline of her nipple with my tongue then gave them small sporadic suckles combined with light nibbles.

Jewel moaned with pleasure as I slowly crept down her stomach, leaving a row of kisses on the way. Reaching her womanhood, I slid my tongue over her lips and even in her hole, purposely avoiding her clit. I sucked each lip separately, giving them special attention and heightening her desire even more.

Jewel moaned again and began to thrust her hips forward as she pushed her fingers between the tight curls of my hair and grasped the back of my head. This was a sure indication she wanted more.

Satisfied that she'd reach optimum levels of desire, I finally moved toward her clit. Using only my lips and tongue, I began to suck her pleasure zone.

Jewel moaned even louder, and her thrust became constant and more intense as she reached her peak.

Ready to send her over the edge, I shoved my middle finger and my ring finger inside her, certain to hit her G-spot, but sure not to disrupt the ultimate clit massage she was receiving. Moments later, like milk from a baby's bottle, her wetness flowed, and I drank.

I lifted my head from between Jewel's legs, my face still wet from her explosion. I asked her, "Are you certain about that money scheme yet?"

She laughed. "How could anyone say no to a face like that?"

"My thoughts exactly!"

"We'll do exactly as you said. When we get back to Virginia, I'll give you the money, and you can go meet Diablo."

"Perfect choice. Now we about to see some real money and do some real big things. Fuck niggas! Get money!"

We gave each other a high-five.

Or, in my case, fuck bitches! Get money! I then began to chant that verse of the song as I walked to the bathroom to get cleaned up. Cheesing from ear to ear, I was about to do me.

Chapter 22

"Don't Test Me"

Calico

I asked my right-hand man, "So you sure that bitch never came home?"

"The muthafuckin' mail in her mailbox is piled up and shit, no lights ever on at the crib, and ain't no noise coming from the house. That bitch ain't there. I sat on her block 'round the clock."

"What about her ride?"

"I don't see that shit. I been to all the spots. I seen Touch on occasion here and there, but she was never with that dude. I don't know what to tell you."

I ended my conversation with my homeboy who I had sent from California to Virginia so that he could locate Jewel, see what was the deal with my dough. Just like a scheming trick, Jewel wasn't nowhere to be found.

"Fuck!" I screamed. I stood up and punched a hole into the wall of my bedroom. I repeatedly called Jewel's cell phone, but she wasn't picking up. I called from block numbers and unblocked numbers, but it didn't make a difference. She was definitely ducking me. I knew that was the reason why she was screening her calls. I called one last time, determined that this was gonna be the last time that I called that bitch.

"Jewel, I don't know what kinda shit you on, or who the fuck you think you dealing with, but understand this, at this point, shit ain't even about the money, this shit is about being disrespected. Don't think that just because I fucked you that I won't personally murder your ass."

I ended the call, getting more and more vexed by the second.

It didn't make no sense on harping on the shit because I still had a lot of moves to make, and other shit to stay on top of. One thing was for sure, in the end, if that bitch didn't come through, her little pretty ass was definitely gonna pay.

I was planning on meeting one of my new lieutenants named Poppo at Roscoe's Chicken and Waffles. Since so much heat was on me and the people close to me, I felt that it would be smart to start adding new layers of people between myself and those I was doing business with. So my plan was to start grooming Poppo, who I trusted the most, to handle shit for me in Virginia, and that was what we were gonna be meeting at Roscoe's to discuss.

While I was driving toward Roscoe's, my cell phone rang. I noticed the caller ID had a 757 number on it. I answered the phone, "Yo."

"Calico?"

"Yo, who dis?"

"It's Jewel."

I immediately pulled my car over to the curb so I could speak to that bitch with no distractions.

"You got some big-ass balls, Jewel. You do know that, right?"

"Oh my God! Calico, what are you talking about? I heard the message that you just left me, and I'm like, 'What the fuck is going on?'"

"Jewel, let's not play this fucking game, a'ight? 'Cause I swear that if I was next to you right now I would choke the shit out your little gold-digging ass!"

Jewel was silent and didn't say shit. All I heard her do was sigh into the phone.

"Jewel, where the fuck is my money?"

"I paid that shit to your lawyer. Ask her where the fuck your money is. I really don't need this bullshit, Calico."

"Your ass is still talking shady? Yeah, a'ight. You and Touch can stay on that snake shit if y'all want to, but on the real, y'all are fucking with the wrong dude."

"Call that bitch right now."

"Call who?"

"Your fucking lawyer. Three-way her ass, 'cause I wanna hear her say she ain't get that money. I know who I paid the fucking money to."

I was definitely not in the mood for no bullshit games. "Jewel, I ain't fucking calling nobody, 'cause you full of shit. You been ducking my calls, not calling me—"

Jewel cut me off in mid-sentence. "What the hell are you talking about? I was out of town in New York on business, so I didn't have time to call you back."

"What fucking business?"

"Ghostwriting business."

"You full of shit!"

"Oh, so now I wasn't outta town? Calico, I can fax you the contract that I went out there to sign."

I didn't respond to Jewel.

"So now you don't want to call her. Look, I'm telling you to call the lawyer, so I can hear what this bitch is saying. Now, if you don't want to call her, then that shit is on you. But you better stop blowing up my phone about this bullshit."

"Test me if you want to, Jewel. Keep tryin' my patience. That's all I'm telling you. And you can tell Touch the exact same thing. You think this shit is funny? Some fuckin' playtime because you wanna pretend to act all hood and shit? Okay, let's see who's having fun after I'm done with yo' ass."

With that said, I hung up the phone. I knew there was no need for me to three-way Jewel into my lawyer's office. I had already paid my lawyer the money that I owed her. I paid her that shit out of my pocket, not out of the money that Jewel and Touch were trying to play me for. And I knew that there was no way in hell that my lawyer would ever try to get over on me about no money issues.

But, like I had said, Jewel and Touch could test me if they wanted to. They were definitely fucking with the wrong cat, 'cause I wasn't the one to be fucked with. My temper was rising, and my revenge list was getting longer by the day. Niggas and bitches alike were beginning to take me for a pussy, and it was time I started to make an example out of someone.

Chapter 23

"Label Me Ike Turner"

Touch

I couldn't find Ciara anywhere. Just like her bum-ass friends, her lazy ass wasn't ever about getting off her ass and doing shit. I knew there was only one place that she could be, and that was at her homegirl Monica's house. Sure enough, when I pulled up to Monica's house, Ciara's car was parked in the driveway.

After parking my car in the middle of the street, I jumped out and went to Monica's front door and started ringing the bell like a madman. I wasn't a short-tempered kind of dude. In fact, I had a real long fuse, and I definitely wasn't one to be hitting on no chicks. That wasn't me at all. But with certain bad memories continuing to flashback in my mind, something had snapped. I knew that I was about to cross that line to "woman-beater" status.

I was trying to keep the thoughts out of my head, but I was having no such luck.

Even as I rang Monica's doorbell, I continued to have flashbacks of Ciara fucking one of my workers when I was locked up. My flashbacks continued, as I was reminded of the night I came home and my girl had burned my money and bleached my furs.

Then I was reminded of that phone call I got when Jewel was fucking Calico. My otherwise easygoing nature was gone, leaving me with an anger that I'd never experienced before. I was literally looking to fuck a bitch up, and there was one just behind this door that needed that serious-ass beating.

A voice from the inside asked, "Who is it?"

"It's Touch."

After I said my name, everything went silent for a few moments. Then I heard some rumbling around inside before the door flung open to reveal Ciara standing there in her bare feet, jeans, and a top. She was drinking a Heineken, and in the background, I could hear Judge Mathis on the television.

Ciara looked me up and down. She didn't say anything, but her body language was screaming, "What the fuck do you want?" She then took a swig of her beer.

Looking at her ghettoness just disgusted the shit out of me. I couldn't help but slap that beer right out of her hands.

With no other words being said, Ciara just went crazy and started swinging on me like she was the female heavyweight champ Laila Ali. "You don't be coming in here like you own the place, tryin' to put your fucking hands on me!" she barked, landing punches and scratches to my face, chest, and arms.

I hauled back with one right hook to her jaw, sending her straight to the floor like a rag doll.

I immediately put my foot on her neck and applied as much pressure as I absolutely could, hoping to snap that shit in half.

"Ciara, I'm asking you one time—Did you fuck that nigga?"

Just as I said that, Monica came charging at me with a steak knife. Luckily, I saw her just in time and side-stepped her and grabbed hold of her wrist and bent it all the way back. She screamed out in pain and dropped the knife.

"Ahhh shit!" I screamed as I looked down and realized that my baby mother had just stabbed me in my calf with the broken Heineken bottle. "You fucking bitch!" I yelled. I kicked her in her mouth and proceeded to stomp both her and Monica right there in Monica's doorway. There were no words for the pain I was feeling, but there were many in between all the blows I was inflicting.

Apparently we had been making so much noise that one of Monica's neighbors came running over to see what was going.

I hollered, "This ain't none of your fucking business, miss! We all right. Everything is all right!" and slammed the front door shut.

I picked Ciara up off the ground and flung her across the room, and when I caught up with her, I grabbed her by her hair and punched on her like she was a human punching bag.

Meanwhile, Monica was still on the floor, clutching her wrist and writhing in pain.

"Did you fuck Calico?"

Ciara looked at me with the little bit of energy she had left. She looked as if she was trying to spit on me, but the only thing that came out of her mouth was blood. Through her tears and ragged look, she said, "You're such an insecure pussy. Maybe if you weren't fucking Diana, I wouldn't have fucked Calico."

I looked at Ciara in disbelief, wondering how the fuck she knew I'd fuck Diana.

"Look at you, looking all stupid in the face. Yeah, that's right. Your boy told me. Calico told me all about your little sexcapade with that trick. And after a smack in the face like that, all I could do was fuck the nigga. He laid it on me so damn good. I knew it was worth it."

At that point, I sort of snapped out of the rage that I'd slipped into. My leg was stinging like a bitch. I looked down and saw a patch of blood staining my pants, and there was blood all over my sneakers.

"Yeah, I fucked him! And he wasn't no weakdick nigga like your ass! What you need to be doing is watching your back, muthafucka!" She tried to laugh, but coughed up blood. "From what I'm hearin' in the streets, you a snitch, and Calico is gonna git you." Ciara had enough energy for that last sentence then she passed out.

A neighbor burst open the front door and came inside the house. "Monica, you okay? I already called the cops. They should be here soon."

I looked over at Ciara and started to get angry at her ghetto-ass again, but thankfully my rage had subsided enough to limp out of the house, jump in my car, and pull off.

Before I could make it home, both Sasha and Jewel began taking turns blowing up my cell phone. I really didn't want to speak to either one of them, or to anybody for that matter, so I let all of my calls go to voice mail as I continued on home.

I went straight to my bathroom and applied rubbing alcohol to the gash on my calf that Ciara had caused. "Uggghhhh!"

Sasha had stopped calling me, but Jewel was continuing to blow up my phone.

Through my pain, I finally decided to answer.

"Jewel, what's up?" I asked through clenched teeth.

"Damn, Touch, you sound like you taking a shit or something," Jewel said.

"Nah, that fucking bitch Ciara cut my ass."

"What? When did this happen?"

I went on to explain everything to Jewel, and she made me describe the cut to her.

"Can you see the white meat?"

"Hell, yeah. I see white meat, red meat, and some blue stringy shit."

"Oh Lord! Touch, you ain't gonna patch that shit up with no Band-Aid. I can tell you that right now. You need to take your ass to the emergency room and get stitched up."

I looked at the three blood-drenched towels that I had used to try and stop the flow of blood coming from my cut and realized that Jewel was probably right. "I think you right."

"Okay, so you going now?"

"Yeah."

"Which hospital you going to? I'll meet you over there."

"Sentara Leigh."

"Okay, I'm on my way. Wrap your leg as tight as you can with a T-shirt or some shit before you leave the house, a'ight? I'll be there as soon as I can," Jewel said to me and then hung up the phone.

When I made it to the emergency room, I saw that it was crowded. I figured that I might have to wait for a while, but after I gave the nurse all of my personal information, she came from around her desk and took a quick look at my cut. After examining it for about thirty seconds, she ushered me right into the back where all of the other nurses and doctors were tending to patients.

"That was quick." I smiled. "You letting me skip all those people out there?"

"Well, I'm not sure, it looks like you may have severed muscle tissue. I don't want to have you wait out there for too long and take a chance on you properly using the leg ever again."

I thought about my baby mother. *I'ma kill that bitch!* I followed the nurse, until she situated me in one of the rooms. She told me, "Sit on the bed. A doctor will be right with you."

Thankfully, after fifteen minutes or so, a doctor examined me and determined that although the wound was deep, it didn't affect muscle tissue. "It it was awfully close. We'll get you stitched up and out of here within a half an hour or so."

I nodded my head in agreement. I then lay back on the bed, propped my head up on the pillow, and stared into space. My quiet was then interrupted by my annoying-ass ringtone.

"Leave me alone. Shit!" I looked down at my cell phone and saw Sasha's number pop up. "Hello?"

"Touch, it's Sasha."

"Yeah, Sasha. What's up?"

Sasha sucked her teeth. "See, I knew it. So it was just about some pussy, right? "

I didn't say anything.

"Uh, sir, I'm afraid you can't use the cell phone in the hospital," a nurse said to me.

Thank God. Saved by the nurse, I thought.

"Sasha, listen, I'm in the hospital right now and I can't talk, but I'll call you back."

"Yeah, whateva." Sasha abruptly hung up.

"I'm sorry about that," I said to the nurse as I put my phone away.

No sooner than I had put my phone away, Jewel came walking into my room.

"Hey, pookie face," she said as she walked up to me and gave me a kiss on the cheek.

Jewel was looking good as hell. My dick got hard instantly, just looking at her divalicious self. At that moment, I realized I was actually playing myself by giving a fuck what my baby mother did, and for giving two shits about Sasha and how she felt. I realized that Jewel had everything I wanted and needed in a woman. I knew that I had to make her my girl and that we had to move forward in some type of commitment shit.

"You okay?" Jewel asked.

I looked down at her peep-toe stiletto heels. "Damn, them some sexy-ass shoes."

"I got these when I went to New York." Jewel smiled. "You like 'em, huh?"

Before I could even reply to Jewel, two police officers walked into my room.

"Trayvon Davis?" they asked.

I attempted to sit up as straight as I could. "Yeah, that's me. What's up?"

"Just relax, sir," one of the cops said to me.

One cop went on one side of my bed, and the other cop went to the other side. Each cop grabbed one of my arms and placed a handcuff on each wrist and then proceeded to also cuff the railing of the bed that I was sitting on.

"What the fuck is this?" I yelled.

"Trayvon Davis, we're placing you under arrest. You have the right to remain silent. Anything you say can and will be used . . ."

This is some bullshit! I said to myself as the cop continued to read me my rights. I don't know why, but just then a nervous smirk came across my face.

Chapter 24

"My Time to Shine"

Sasha

When I got back to Atlanta with the hundred thousand dollars, I knew one thing and one thing only. Sasha was going to do whatever the fuck Sasha felt like doing. If I didn't feel like doing shit for the day, then I wasn't doing shit. If I felt like buying new clothes every day, then that's what the hell I was going to do.

As I sat in my bedroom and counted the most money that I'd ever had at one time, I knew that I wasn't going back to Bottoms Up. Fuck that dancer life! I was tired of that shit, tired of the hustle. Tired of lame-ass, crusty-ass niggas feeling up on me and me dancing for them just so I could get money to pay one pissy-ass bill here and there. I was quitting ASAP, and I had one hundred thousand reasons to do so.

Jewel had been calling me from the moment that I had hit the Georgia State line. The bitch didn't give me a minute to breathe before she started hounding me about the money. She even had the nerve to tell me that Calico was pressing her hard and that she was having second thoughts about the plan. She was changing her mind and wanted the money back.

As far as I was concerned, that sounded like a personal problem. Hers, not mine. But I didn't tell her that. Instead, I just kept her at bay and told her that it was too late and that I had gone through with the original plan that she'd agreed to. I told her that she needed to relax until the money was flipped.

The truth of the matter was, Jewel wasn't ever getting shit from me, and I could have cared less if I'd ever spoken to her ass again. She was always the one on top, always the one shining, and finally it was my turn.

Two days after coming back to Atlanta, I had reached out to Touch. The nigga never called me back. I was always the one calling him and blowing up his phone, so I decided to keep calling until I got through to him, just so I could see where his head was at.

"Hello?"

"Don't hang up on me Touch. It's Sasha. We good?"

"You didn't even call me back and you claimed to be in the hospital. What the fuck is wrong wit'chu anyway? Matter of fact, fuck you! What about me?"

Touch didn't say anything. Just like the punk-ass he was, he started bitching up. As far as I was concerned, if it was just about pussy and he had gamed me, then it was all good. All I needed for him to do was to be a man about it and admit the shit. Hell, it wasn't the first time a nigga had gamed me for pussy.

"Sasha, listen, like I told you I'm in the hospital right now and I can't talk, I'll call you back."

"Whateva," I said and then I hung up the phone.

I sat in silence for a while. I was pissed off. The longer I sat, the angrier I got. I was so angry, I began crying tears of fury. All I wanted was to have shit going well in my life and to be in a committed relationship with someone that wanted to be with me for me, and not for any other false motives.

For the first time in weeks, I thought about Rick. Jewel and all my other fair-weather friends always had something negative to say about the father of my youngest child. But one thing that none of them ever understood was that Rick was the only person who ever accepted me for me and not for any other motives, and that was why I was so loyal and always felt indebted to him.

I'd met Rick years ago after I'd finished dancing one night. I was stopping at a local 7-Eleven to grab a soda when he and his boys were there buying up the place. We locked eyes across the aisle, while the other niggas were grabbing shit like it was The Last Supper.

I broke from my trance long enough to walk to the register. Before I could get the money for my soda, Rick told the dude to just add it to the rest of the shit he was buying. I thanked him and headed to my car. I didn't know he was behind me, until I saw a hand reach for the car handle. I jumped back, and it was him.

"I just thought I'd open the door . . . and get your number," he said slyly.

I had to admit, it was a good move, but not that good to give him my number right away. So we talked outside of the 7-Eleven for a couple of minutes longer until his boys started harassing him to leave. I didn't give him my number, but he gave me his and made me promise to call. And we started talking on the phone every day after that.

It took me a whole year of knowing him before I told him I was a dancer. When I finally told him, he never condemned or judged me. Thinking back on it, I don't know why I would think he would be like these other cats out here. He was the only guy that I'd ever been with who didn't try to fuck me the same day, or within the first two weeks of knowing me. Nah, Rick was different. He waited six months before we fucked, and he was cool with that.

I don't know what I was thinking when I listened to Jewel and all of my dumb-ass friends. They didn't know what the hell they were talking about. Rick loved me, and I know that he did. Sure, he had hit some hard times and was going through a rough patch financially, but that was all good. I knew that he loved me and his son, and he'd supported me for years when he was getting money. Now it was my turn to return the favor.

So as my tears of anger subsided, they were quickly replaced by tears of joy that was mixed with regret.

I immediately dialed Rick's number. "Baby, I love you so much," I said to him when he picked up the phone.

"Sasha?"

"Yeah, baby, it's me," I said through my tears. I apologized to Rick for all the put-downs. "I'm just so stupid, always listening to my friends and shit. Now I realize they don't have my best interest at heart, but you do."

"You been drinking, Sasha?"

"Nooo, baby, I wasn't drinking. I'm serious. I was just sitting here thinking about how much I love you. I miss you and I want you to be with your son. I want the three of us to be together."

Rick started to say something, but I cut him off.

"Listen, baby, I did it. I did it, baby."

"You did what?"

"I did what I said I was gonna do. I came down here and I changed things around."

"Sasha, you're not making sense. What the hell are you talking about?"

"I got enough money to get us a nice two-bedroom apartment, and I can pay the rent for one year up front, furnish the place, and get us a car. I can even give you the money to start your business. All I need you to do is just tell me that you'll come down to Atlanta and be with me and RJ."

I was desperately hoping that Rick would say yes. I mean, after all, I had done him dirty by walking out on him and turning my back on him.

"Whoa, I wasn't expecting a call from you like that," he said.

All this information I was giving to him at one time seemed to have him exhausted.

"Baby, just say yes."

Rick was silent for a moment, and then he spoke up. "You know I love you, right?"

"Yes, baby, and I know that you love RJ too."

"So if I come down there, it's just gonna be about me, you, and little man, right?"

"Of course. That's why I called you. Let's start over. Baby, I'm sitting on a pile of money right now, and we can start over and do it right."

Rick finally agreed to come down to Atlanta.

I was more excited than I had been in months.

Whoever said money can't buy you happiness definitely didn't know what the hell they were talking about. I chuckled. All I knew was that I had my hands on some money, and I was happier than a pig in shit.

Chapter 25

"Forced into the Game"

Jewel

I felt like my world had turned upside down after speaking to Touch. He called me from jail. He had been charged with assault and battery on Ciara and her girl Monica. He didn't have a bond at the time, but his spirits were up. He'd already spoken to his attorney, and they were going up for a bond hearing the next day. He was sure he would get a bond. But shit wasn't looking so bright, as far as the charges. The judges in Virginia Beach had no mercy for convicted felons and definitely none for violent crimes.

It's funny how so much could happen in such a small amount of time. In three months alone, I'd met this new cat and was thinking about putting him on my team, only to start liking him. Before that shit could go any further, I get arrested and then attacked in my own home. Next, Touch comes to the rescue, tells me that he loves me, and we fuck. He goes and beats down his baby momma, and gets stabbed. Now he's in lock up.

To make matters worse, my gut feeling was telling me that bitch had bucked on me with the money. At first she was giving me excuse after excuse, and finally it got to the point where she completely stopped answering her phone. Now, I'm out here in the streets alone with no Touch and without one hundred thousand dollars of Calico's money.

In a panic, I picked up my cell to give her one last try.

The automated recording said, "At the subscriber's request, the number that you are trying to reach has been disconnected . . ."

There was no need for me to listen any further. The message just confirmed my fear. The new found gang-stress in me wanted to take the first flight to Atlanta and search high and low for her ass and fuck her up on the spot, but my rational side forced me to sit down and think.

How the fuck am I gonna get out of this one? Come on, Jewel, this shit can't hold you down. I sat on a bar stool at my breakfast bar and sipped on a glass of White Zinfandel as I tried to put together the perfect plan. Unable to come up with anything, I gave up.

With a sudden loss of hope, I walked to my bedroom to try to get a little sleep. As I lay on my bed, I flipped through the channels on the television. I stopped on BET as I caught a glimpse of the letters TMF. *What are these niggas doing now*? I smiled as I thought back to the time I'd spent with them in New York. BET was covering a party TMF had thrown in Miami. The shit was crazy. They had white tigers in cages, searchlights in front of the club, and they arrived at the club by helicopter. *Damn, these niggas do it big!* I thought to myself as I sat and continued to watch.

All of a sudden it hit me. *Wait . . . TMF . . . that's the answer to my prayers.* I rushed to my desk and pulled out the copy of the contract I'd signed when I was in New York. There was a fifty thousand-dollar advance I would receive. It's not all of Calico's money, but it would be enough to help me get shit moving. *This is it, Jewel. Calico never believed that I was that bitch that can make things happen. If everything goes my way, I will show him why I'm not one to sleep on.*

After making a few phone calls and preparing myself to pull a few tricks if necessary, I was sure I could get that all in one lump sum, instead of the usual five disbursements. Then, after I had the cash in hand, I was sure I could convince Red, one of the head niggas of the TMF crew that showed a little added interest in me, to work with me on a good-ass price for some product. So there it was, shit was set. I had a plan. Now all I had to do was put that shit in motion.

I spent the next hour on the phone negotiating and trying to get everyone to agree to my terms. It wasn't easy, but in the end it was well worth it. I was able to convince the publishing company to agree to releasing the entire advance and wiring it directly to my checking account. I was even able talk Red into giving me a killer price, ten thousand dollars for each of those white girls. And on top of that, he was gonna throw double whatever I purchased. So I would have thirty keys.

So then came my next dilemma—getting rid of that shit. I knew Touch had my back, but shit wasn't looking too good for him. I hadn't heard from that nigga since he was arrested at the hospital and called me the next day from jail. So while I waited to hear from him, I decided to give my boy Diablo a call. From what I'd heard, he was doing it big in the A, and holding shit down in Virginia before the spot got hot. So he was known for doing his thing. After all, he was my ex-boyfriend, and I only fucked with dudes that got bread.

"Hello?" Diablo answered right away.

"Diablo?"

"What's up, baby girl?" he said, full of excitement.

"I need you to deal with some things for me."

"I thought your girl was coming down so you could grab some shit from me," Diablo said, oblivious to all the shit that had gone down between me and Sasha.

I updated him on the circus of events that had gone down between me and Sasha, and explained to him the new plan I had. He was ecstatic that he could get the white girl from me for eighteen grand a key. Diablo agreed to purchase fifteen keys right away, and the rest as soon as he moved those. I was sure Touch could handle the rest, but I agreed to Diablo's terms, until I knew what was up with Touch.

Now it was time for me to pull out the next thorn in my side, Calico. But as I was dialing his number, I thought about possibly killing two pesky birds with one large stone.

Calico picked up on the first ring, spewing disgust. That nigga didn't even greet me with a hello. "I hope you calling to say you got my muthafuckin' money, Jewel."

"Actually, I am . . . kinda."

"Kinda?"

I explained to Calico what went down with his money. "Look, I'm just gonna be straight-up and honest with you. Calico, I never tried to game you. I'm not the type to steal from anyone."

By then end of our conversation, I'd managed to turn shit around completely. I was the victim, and Sasha was the thieving bitch. Calico totally agreed with me. I was able to persuade him to forgive me and allow me the opportunity to pay him half in thirty days, and the other half thirty days after that, with interest added, of course.

Sure, in a matter of hours, I would have the money, and the right thing to do would have been to call Calico up and give him his money right away, but I needed some insurance. Shit, the world ain't fair. I ain't fuck him on that money; Sasha fucked me, and in turn, he got fucked. But I didn't know how Calico actually saw it or if he even cared. I knew that the easiest way to keep myself out of a toe tag was to keep him on a deadline date. Before I got off the phone, I commented again that I didn't fuck him over, Sasha did. I made that shit crystal clear to his ass, and he said that he would take care of it and then hung up.

I was instantly afraid for Sasha, but the emotion left just as quickly as it came. She tried to game me with my own rules. Now she had to pay.

Chapter 26

"Money over Bitches"

Calico

Jewel kept her word and finally hit my man Poppo off with all of my dough in thirty days, right before Thanksgiving. Originally she said that she would pay me half in thirty days and that she would give me the other half thirty days after that. So with her suddenly coming up with my money so quickly, I had instructed Poppo to make sure that he kept his eyes on both Jewel and Touch.

News came back to me that Touch, who had completely fallen off the radar for like a month and a half, had suddenly reappeared back on the scene. I knew something was up. I didn't know exactly what, but I knew that what Poppo was telling me was true.

"Calico, on the real, Christmas ain't until next week, but I'm telling you Christmas done came early for this nigga Touch. The muthafucka got one of his homies driving him and Jewel around in a brand new Maybach, and I heard they just purchased this big-ass crib out in the Heritage Park section in Virginia Beach. Jewel and Touch be pulling up to spots like they muthafuckin' Jay-Z and Beyoncé and shit. Yo, one of Touch's man is getting out and opening up the door for them like a gotdamn chauffeur."

I didn't say anything in response. All I did was chuckle into the phone.

"Last night Jewel was rocking a brand new chinchilla coat. It's crazy. They got money from somewhere."

"Yeah, and that sounds like new money," I said.

"They the ones cutting our nuts and giving mutha-fuckas better prices than we can give 'em," Poppo said, confirming what I had already told him earlier.

I couldn't exactly prove the shit because when niggas like Touch get a new connect and that connect is giving them better prices, they hoard that shit and guard that information with their life. And the fucked-up shit is that a muthafucka like Touch, who I was supplying with product, will turn around and start asking my ass if I need his product because the cost was so low.

When I reached out to Touch to see what was up and why he hadn't re-upped in a while with me, he gave me some bullshit excuse about shit being slow and him going to jail for a moment over some baby momma drama bullshit. Yet I had Poppo telling me him and Jewel was driving around, pushing brand new half a million dollar whips and shit.

"I'm gonna be out there for New Year's Eve. I had to lay low and stay off the radar for a minute, but I'ma be back. We gotta get up with each other and break bread when I touch down," I said to Touch over the phone. I made sure not to make any mention of the new money I knew he was getting.

"Yeah, yeah, no doubt. We gonna get up," he said.

"Yo, so what's up with Jewel?"

"Jewel?"

"Yeah, what's up with her?"

"What do you mean?"

"Is she good?"

"Oh, yeah, she good. Jewel is on some whole new get money shit, and she getting it too. She ain't the same Jewel from a few months back."

"Oh yeah?" I replied on the other end of the phone with a half smile. "So she doing it like that?"

"Yeah, she gettin that ghostwriting money. But you know Jewel is always gonna stay fly."

I took a sip of the gin and orange juice that I had been drinking. "Wow! Okay, so I guess I gotta break that bitch off some more dick." I started laughing into the phone. "For real, nigga, I don't how you ain't never hit that shit. She got the tightest and wettest pussy that I ever fucked. And I done had my share of pussy, you know what I mean?"

Touch didn't respond. I had to look at my phone to make sure we were still connected. I thought I had dropped the call or something.

"Touch, you there?"

"Yeah, yeah, I'm still here. So just hit me up when you get back in town."

"A'ight, fool." Just before I hung up I said, "Touch, keep it real with me—You fucking Jewel?"

"Me and Jewel go way back, you know that."

"But, I'm just saying, you sound like you caught feelings when I was talking about hitting that. And, I mean, a nigga will definitely back off and let you have my leftovers, you feel me?"

"Calico, this is the thing. Fuck this money that we getting, fuck breaking bread together and all that shit. If you gonna speak about Jewel, you make mutha-fuckin' sure that you don't speak disrespectful about her, a'ight."

I couldn't help but laugh at Touch and his clown-ass. He was taking shit personal, like the little bitch he was.

"Oh, so that's your boo now?" I said. "It's all good. So, Encore, that's the spot for New Year's Eve?"

Touch didn't answer me.

"Keep your head up, fool," I said, still chumping his ass.

I could tell that Touch had a problem with me. I could sense the shit for some time, and I knew it had been brewing inside of him for a while and was about to come to a head. But it was all good, because now the nigga had cut into my money. I could give a fuck about Jewel 'cause, like a real nigga, I was always on some ol' money-over-bitches shit. But apparently Touch wasn't, and that was a prime example of why he wasn't built for this street shit like I was.

As far as I was concerned it was always about my money, and it will always be about my money. And that was why on New Year's Eve I was gonna see Touch. Yeah, I was definitely gonna see that nigga. He posed a threat to my money, and I had to do what I had to do in order to eliminate that threat.

Chapter 27

"I'm the King"

Touch

Thankfully for me my lawyer and the Commonwealth attorney had worked out a deal where I would plead guilty to the lowest degree assault charge possible and avoid doing any jail time. The judge would grant me time served for the month and a half that I had already spent in jail awaiting my trial, and I would also receive a sentence of five years probation.

I took that deal in a heartbeat. Yeah, I didn't want to deal with no probation and all that came with it, but at least I had my everyday freedom and wasn't locked behind no prison walls. Besides, without the barrier of prison walls, me and Jewel could focus on getting that money.

And leading up to New Year's Eve, getting money was exactly what me and Jewel did. With Jewel's TMF connect, all of my hustler dreams and ambition were being fulfilled. Me and Jewel were like the hood version of Kimora Lee and Russell Simmons. In a matter of a few short weeks, we were doing it up big and, that was only the tip of the iceberg.

I said to Jewel as I opened up the row of black garbage bags that contained one hundred and fifty thousand dollars in one-dollar bills. "You ain't never seen no shit like this before in your life, have you?"

"Niggas in them strip clubs be talking about making it rain, but I'm gonna make it rain up in Club Encore on New Year's Eve. As soon as that ball drops, I'm gonna have all this money drop from the ceiling and rain down on the crowd. Everybody's gonna know that ain't nobody doing it bigger than me and my girl." I scooped Jewel up and hoisted her into the air and kissed her.

"Yeah, but, baby, I don't know if that's a good thing, though."

"Why not?" I asked.

"'Cause we don't need everybody knowing that we doing it up like that. This is all brand new money, and we just started getting it like this. So I think we should keep a low profile, stack our money, and muthafuckas won't know shit, but we'll be rich as hell."

"Keep a low profile?" I laughed. "That shit went out the window when you leased that Maybach and purchased a $750,000 house."

Jewel and I both started laughing.

"Yeah, you right about that. But, I'm just saying, from a jealousy standpoint, it's like when people see that kind of money just being wasted, then they'll know we getting money. And as soon as niggas get locked up and the detectives start pressing they ass for information, guess whose name is gonna come up even if we ain't have shit to do with anything? Yep, ours."

I knew that Jewel was right. Shit, everything I was doing was going against everything I believed in. I'd made promises after my first bid that I was gonna stay humble, well, as humble as possible, and play the game right this go'round. I knew a certain level of flossing always came at a price, and we definitely didn't need to give the feds a reason to start investigating us. And dropping one hundred and fifty thousand dollars in cash into a crowd was definitely a reason to get an investigation going. The authorities would want to know where in the hell were we getting all this money to just blow.

"Jewel, fuck it though. I'ma keep it real with you. I'm gonna do that shit just to send a message to Calico. I want that nigga to know that, yeah, we getting money, and I that I got you on top of it, as icing on the cake."

"Touch, please. You got me, we got each other. Just fucking ignore Calico and his weak ass."

Jewel again was speaking logically and making sense, but I was determined to be hard-headed on this one. See, as far as I was concerned, yeah, it was always money over bitches, but I wanted to let Calico and the whole world know that not only did I have the money, but now I also had the top bitch. I wanted it all.

With my hands in the air like a king before his dynasty, I yelled to Jewel, "Like those TMF cats you so fond of say, 'The world is ours.'"

Chapter 28

"Never Satisfied"

Sasha

Things had been going as well for me as I had ever envisioned. I had money in the bank, I wasn't waking up to no bullshit nine-to-five, nor was I shaking my ass in nobody's strip club. I had my apartment, I had my new furniture, I had my new Honda Accord, and most importantly, I had my man Rick with me.

So with things going well heading close to Christmas, I had decided to go to Bottoms Up just to chill and hang out and say what's up to some of the girls that I hadn't seen since I'd quit. When I walked into the club, I was greeted warmly by a bunch of the dancers. Everyone thought that I was coming back to work. It felt so good to just let them know that, nah, I was just there to have some drinks and be a spectator.

"What's up, baby girl?" some dude said to me as he came up behind me and put his hands over my eyes.

My first reaction was to think that it was one of the patrons who had recognized me from when I used to dance in there.

"Diablo! Hey, baby!" I said after he removed his hands from my eyes and I was able to turn around and see his face.

"What's up? Where the hell you been? You just vanished on everybody."

"I just been doing me," I explained.

Diablo ordered a drink, and the two of us drank at the bar and talked about a bunch of shit. And, of course, he was hitting on me the whole time, but I never gave in to any of his advances.

"So what's up with you and Jewel?"

"Fuck that bitch!"

"Damn! What's up? What happened between y'all two? I mean, she told me some shit, but I don't get it."

"Diablo, you don't need to get it. Like I said, fuck that bitch!"

"Damn! Okay, so I guess you ain't going to her and Touch's New Year's Eve party at Encore."

"Hell no!" I said with an attitude and a look of disgust on my face.

"They doing it real big up there in VA right now. I don't know, Sasha, you might wanna change your mind about not going." Diablo handed me his phone and told me to look at it.

I took hold of the phone and looked at a picture that Diablo had of him, Touch, and Jewel standing in front of a Maybach.

"Yeah, so?"

"Like I said, they doing it big up there. Jewel got the Maybach. She's killing 'em. That party is gonna be crazy."

"Can we please talk about something else? Anything but Jewel and Touch . . . please," I said to Diablo as I finished my drink.

"Okay, so I got another story for you." Diablo looked around from side to side as if he was being watched. "Word around town says that you off-loaded some of the kingpin's money."

"What are you talking about now?" I said, trying to mask my sudden nervousness. *Where did he get this information from?*

"Well, about a couple of days after you came back into town, Jewel gave me a call. She told me how she couldn't get in touch with you, and asked me had I seen you. I told her, 'Nah,' but wondered what happened to that deal I was supposed to work wit' y'all. She told me that she had to find you to find out what happened. Fast forward to the present, and one of my mans an' dem is telling me that Calico is looking for you, and he wants you dead or alive. I just thought that you might wanna reach back out to your homegirl and see if she can try to extinguish the smoking gun that's about to come your way."

Diablo's words chilled me to the bone. With all my thoughts about getting over on Jewel, I forgot that she had that nigga Calico in her back pocket, and I didn't. Fear and anxiety was now showing on my face.

"You know what? I gotta go. I'll speak to you soon." I gave Diablo a kiss on the cheek and darted out the club.

Why, God? Why? Why me? I screamed in my head as I started up my car and peeled off, tears streaming down my face as I pressed my gas pedal to the floor. *I know that bitch worked out a deal with Calico,* I thought to myself.

I knew in my heart and in my mind that couldn't be true. There was no way that Jewel could overcome the six-figure blow that I had dealt to her and recover so quickly and get a fucking Maybach without help from Calico or Touch. No way in hell. That bitch wasn't Superwoman, and her pussy wasn't all that. I know because I had the shit. *Fuck!* I thought to myself as I really began to hyperventilate.

As I pulled up to my apartment still in tears, I realized that Jewel really must have thought that she was hot shit. As far as I knew, the bitch had never even tried to seriously track me down for the hundred thousand dollars. *Who the fuck does she think she is?*

I tried my best to gather my composure before exiting my car and going inside. I couldn't believe how much pain I was once again suddenly feeling because of Jewel. I was so tired of her always being one up on me, I just couldn't take it.

Yeah, I was gonna be at her and *her man's* little fucking party, but I wasn't gonna be there to party. I was gonna personally make sure that she felt some of the pain I was feeling at that moment. Yeah, my pain was more emotional than anything, but Jewel's pain was definitely gonna be physical.

Fuck that bitch!

Chapter 29

"Happy New Year"

Jewel

"Tonight is gonna be crazy," I said to Touch as I reviewed the checklist for the party setup.

Every celebrity from VA was on the guest list, and the VIP area would have a seafood buffet stacked with lobster tails and king crab and endless Armand de Brignac to wash that shit down. Each guest would receive a complimentary bottle of Rosé and a gift bag with party favors. There were dollar sign ice sculptures, and dancers covered in nothing but body paint. They would be dancing in cages that hung from the ceiling throughout the club. And, of course, the ultimate one hundred fifty grand money drop at midnight. I have to say Touch had really outdone himself this time.

Touch looked down at my brand new five-thousand-dollar heels that had arrived just in time for the party. "Nah, these fucking custom-made Christian Louboutin heels are crazy."

I'd had a mold taken of my foot and had chosen the fabric myself, and had the shoes with a matching clutch custom-made for the night of the party. And my dress was tailor-made as well. This was one night I was confident that I wouldn't be duplicated.

"Look at us." I walked up to Touch and fell in his arms as I looked into his big brown eyes that I adored so much. "Who would have ever thought we would be here?"

"You're right." Touch laughed. "I should have fucked you a long time ago."

"Baby, I'm being serious. I mean, look at this." I grabbed a handful of money from the garbage bags and dumped them all over the bed.

"You did this, baby girl. You brought the shit to the table. I just rationed it out."

It wasn't until then that I realized what Touch was saying was true. I did make shit happen. When everything was fucked and I was alone, I made shit happen, using my money and my connection with TMF. For the first time I had some real gangtress credibility.

"Damn, I guess you're right. I never looked at it like that."

"I'm just glad that it's you that I have to build this with." Touch wrapped his arms around me and kissed me softly. "But I still say I should have fucked you a long time ago. Damn, a nigga was missing out. Time to play catch up." Touch pushed me on the bed playfully and rushed to take my clothes off, as if he had no time to waste.

"Stop playing, boy." I hopped on him and straddled my naked body over him. I whispered in his ear, "Your pussy ain't going nowhere."

"You sure?" Touch squirmed beneath me as he got undressed.

"I'm positive."

I could feel the head of his erect penis brush against my clit. That sensation alone made my juices flow. I moved my hips in a circular motion, forcing the head in and heightening the sensation even more.

Touch grabbed my hips, freezing them in position. "How do I know you won't give my pussy away?"

"Baby, I'm not," I said, eager to be released.

I wanted nothing more than to sit on his lap and have all of him inside of me. Each second he prolonged, the more I yearned for him. Unable to last a moment longer, I removed his hand and sat down on him, forcing his entire dick inside of me, and the next thirty minutes was spent in total bliss.

I opened my eyes as I panted, exhausted from a multiple orgasm triggered by the force of Touch's cum rushing inside of me at the peak of my orgasm. In front of me lay the love of my life, and all around him was money. Hell, the thought alone of fucking on a bed full of money was enough to get me wet all over again and go for round two, but time was ticking and we needed to prepare for our big night.

The next few hours were spent on hair and nails for me, and making sure everything was in order at the club for Touch. By ten o'clock were we getting dressed. Normally, we wouldn't be preparing so soon, but this night I wanted to be sure we were at the club by eleven. After all, the countdown was at eleven fifty-nine, and we had to be there for that.

Just as I'd planned, at eleven o'clock we were pulling up to the club. I was surprised to see such a huge crowd so early. The line was already wrapped around the building, and the valet parking was full of high end cars.

When we pulled up, it was like the president and first lady had arrived. Security cleared the doorway, and they pulled out the red carpet. The driver ran around and opened the back door for Touch and me, and we paraded into the club as the onlookers stared.

The club was beautiful as we walked in. It was set up far better than I'd imagined.

Every known hustler and groupie was in the club, yelling out to Touch as we headed to the VIP section toward the back of the club.

"Touch, what up, nigga."

"Yo, Trayvon."

Everything was about Touch. He was the big man in town. As we walked through, I received dirty looks from bitches cutting their eyes and pointing and whispering, while dudes looked like they wanted to kidnap me. Touch was the town savior, while I was the city's most hated.

I held in my irritation as I held my man's hand tight as we walked through the club. Never would I let anyone see me weak.

Once we got to the back, I noticed a big chair that resembled a throne.

As soon as Touch walked up, the club owner said, "Take your seat, homeboy."

Touch dapped him up. "Nigga, you crazy as hell."

"I had to show love. Ain't nobody ever did it big like this in the club yet, so I had them bring this chair in for you. This is your seat for the night."

"A'ight, a'ight." Touch got comfortable as he sat at his throne.

Just then two naked-ass bodypainted bitches came over. They kneeled before Touch and asked, "What can we get for you?"

Touch looked at the club owner, who still stood beside him. "The bitches too?"

"You the king tonight, homie."

"Oh, this is just too much." I walked away to get a glass of champagne from the fountain.

Touch met me at the champagne fountain moments later. "You a'ight, baby?" he asked.

"I'm good. Don't worry about me. It's all about you tonight. Just do you, king," I said sarcastically before attempting to walk away.

Touch grabbed my arm. "Jewel, don't do this tonight, please."

He was right. I didn't want to let the people see us weak. Regardless of what, we needed to put our best foot forward and show them that our empire was strong.

"Okay, no problem." I put on a plastic smile, kissed him on the cheek, and followed his royal highness to his throne.

As the night went on and I downed glasses of champagne, any insecurities I had earlier in the night were gone. Touch and I laughed and danced. With two minutes left until midnight, I caught a glimpse of Sasha. She was talking to the security at the entrance of VIP. My first instinct was to rush over there and beat that bitch's ass. But again that night I had to put my best foot forward. Besides, security was tight, and I was sure there was no way her ass would get past them.

As Touch rushed to grab two bottles of Armand de Brignac, the deejay said, "One minute."

The crowd grew anxious as we all awaited the countdown. With thirty seconds left until midnight, I glanced at the VIP entrance and noticed Sasha was no longer there. *I knew that dirty bitch wouldn't get through.*

Touch handed me my bottle. He tapped me and nodded his head in the direction of the crowd, signaling me to look at someone.

As I pulled the wrapper off, preparing to pop the top, I noticed Calico in the VIP area.

We all counted down in unison, "Ten, nine, eight . . .
zero."

Everyone shouted, "Happy New Year!" and bottles
began to pop. Everything around me was chaotic. The
crowd was going crazy as the money dropped from the
ceiling. It sounded like a combination of fireworks and
gunshots as the bottles and balloons popped uncontrollably.

"Happy New Year, baby." Touch kissed me passionately.

"Look at this shit. Ain't nobody ever did it this big."
Touch then stood up on the seat of the throne. He
yelled, "The world is mine!" and began to pour champagne on all those around him.

I shook my head as I watched. His boys encouraged
him, handing him bottle after bottle, and the soaking
wet groupies surrounded him. The bodypainted bitches
were now virtually naked because the champagne had
begun to rinse the paint away. The more I watched, the
angrier I got. I'd finally had enough.

I called out to Touch. *This world is fucking mine. I
made this shit happen. I'm the queen of this dynasty. I
built the fucking empire.*

Just then I heard a gunshot. In a state of panic, I
looked up at Touch, and we locked eyes. Then, in what
seemed like a split second later, I felt a striking pain in
my head. I collapsed to the floor, and within moments,
I could hear no noise. Everything was still and eventually went black.

CALIFORNIA CONNECTION 2

Dedication

This book is dedicated to my second mother,
Ives Wynter November 8, 1954–January 24, 2009
May your loving memory live on forever.

Chapter 1

"Mad New Year"

Sasha

Click-click. I put a single bullet in the head of my chrome .22-caliber handgun, put on the safety, and then placed it in my purse. I clutched my purse and folded my arms to fight off the frigid winter air as I rushed toward Club Encore in an attempt to beat the crowd.

To my surprise, once I reached the front I was met by a swarm of people. It was pure pandemonium as I made my way toward the entrance. Noticing the attention of the crowd focused on a car entering the parking lot, I paused just long enough to get a glimpse of what was so interesting.

"Look at this bitch," I said, rolling my eyes when I realized it was Jewel and Touch pulling into the club parking lot. I screwed up my face, showing full disgust. My blood was boiling as I watched them step out of their Maybach and onto the red carpet like they were the fucking king and queen of England. From the tell-tale red bottom of her shoes, I knew Jewel had on none other than Christian Louboutin.

Touch wore a suit, and I'm sure it was top of the line as well. I had to admit, he looked sexy as hell in it.

Suddenly, a flashback of the night we fucked consumed me. It was like I could feel his hands gripping
my ass as he forced himself deep inside me. *Damn.*
For a moment I felt my panties becoming a little moist
from the combination of seeing him and reminiscing.

"Excuse me."

My moment of admiration was broken by a ghetto
chick who bumped into me, pushing along with the
crowd in a desperate attempt to get into the packed
club. Under normal circumstances, I would have let
this bitch have it, but this night I had more pressing
issues, so that bitch got a pass.

I burned with envy as Touch and his bitch headed
toward the entrance. I should have been his trophy
wife, the queen beside him on the throne. All around
them stood crowds of people calling and reaching out
to them like the fucking paparazzi, while others just
stood in awe like peasants, wishing they could have one
moment in their shoes. No matter which crowd they
were classified in, the people still went unnoticed by
"the royal couple," as security guards forced people out
of their way to open a clear path for Jewel and Touch to
enter the club. The shit was so sickening.

Realizing I was amongst this crowd of peasants and
paparazzi, I inched my way toward the front of the line,
which wrapped around the building.

"Excuse me, sweetie." I poked out my small but
perky 34B breasts and called out to one of the bounc-
ers who guarded the front door of the club, giving him
my most seductive look. This fat-ass, baldhead, clean-
looking dude just glanced at me and then turned his
head. *Muthafucka!* I couldn't believe this guy.

Still determined to get in, I dug into my purse, by-
passing my gun, and pulled out a hundred-dollar bill.
One thing I knew for sure is that money talks. This time

I didn't even bother calling out to him. I just walked toward the entrance as though I were part of the royal court.

The same bouncer said to me, "This is VIP, ma'am. Are you on the list?"

"Yes, I am," I said, sliding the money into his hand. Moments later, I was walking through the door with no search and no hassle.

I stood in awe as I entered the club. I couldn't believe the sight before me. Although I hated to admit it, Jewel and Touch were really on some celebrity shit. They had definitely taken things to the next level in VA. *Well, at least Jewel will have a hell of a farewell party*, I thought as I walked through the tight crowd, knowing I planned to make this night her last.

I watched the time as I made my way toward the VIP area. It was eleven-fifteen. I had forty-five minutes to make it to the back, where Touch and Jewel were partying. I wanted to be sure I was there to bring Jewel's new year in with a bang—literally. The crowd was going crazy to Busta Rhymes' "Arab Money" when I reached the bar. I purchased a glass of Nuvo and took it to the head to ease my nerves. Then, as an added prop, I bought a bottle of Ace of Spades, to look as though I belonged in the VIP area.

I knew it would be even harder getting past the security guard at the VIP section. There, niggas passed a hundred dollars all night to get in, so I wasn't sure that was going to fly this go-'round. After fighting a crowd of groupies, I finally made it to the entrance of the VIP. The time was now thirty minutes to midnight, so I needed to get in fast.

"Excuse me, hon," I said to the security guard to get his attention.

"Malibu?" He called me by my dance name, causing me to take a closer look at him.

This must be my lucky day. This gotta be a sign that the new year is gonna be my year. I let out a sigh of relief, realizing this guy was a bouncer at a club I used to dance at. I always felt dancing got me nowhere, and nothing but a few fast dollars, but this was one time it was an actual benefit.

"Hey, boo. How you been?" I gently caressed his arm as I spoke. "I'm trying to get back there and celebrate with my girl, Jewel. I just flew in from Atlanta, and I want to surprise her. I just bought this bottle, so we can pop it and bring in the new year together." I put on my best game, all the while flaunting my breasts and putting on a few flirtatious gestures.

The security guard stepped back and unhooked the velvet rope, allowing me to go through.

I headed toward the back of the VIP area and found a quiet spot in the cut, where I could go unnoticed. There I spotted a sexy chocolate dude who screamed the signs of money. Everything, from his designer labels to his blinding diamonds, said, "I am that nigga."

I couldn't take my eyes off his blinding, iced-out watch. If for nothing else but the diamonds, I had to have that nigga. I could picture him naked with nothing but jewelry—chocolate and diamonds, two of my favorites. I also noticed he stood alone. Since I had a few minutes to spare, I used this as an opportunity to possibly get to know him better.

"Hey, sexy," I said. "You look like you need some company."

"Oh yeah?" He looked my body up and down like he had X-ray vision and could see right through my Betsey Johnson dress.

"Yeah," I said with my sassiest attitude, rolling my neck.

"I'm kind of busy right now, but we can exchange numbers and get up a little later." He pulled out his cell phone, and I did the same.

"What's your name?"

"Calico," he said, and then began to read off his number.

"Calico?" I took a deep swallow, hoping I'd heard him incorrectly.

He spelled his name out to me, "*C-a-l-i-c-o*," confirming I'd heard him correctly.

His response floored me. My heart raced, and my breathing picked up. I tried all I could to keep my composure and to keep my shaking hand steady as I entered my number in his phone. I used the name Malibu to protect my true identity.

"Okay, baby, I'll be hitting you up. Enjoy your night, and Happy New Year." I tried to play it cool. I excused myself and rushed out of the VIP and headed to the bathroom. There I gathered myself. *Oh my God.* My brain was racing and I could see my chest moving up and down as I inhaled and exhaled. I didn't have asthma, but I surely felt like I was about to have a damn asthma attack.

As soon as Calico said his name, although I'd never seen him face to face, I knew exactly who he was. He was the same Calico that Jewel used to fuck with, the same Calico that I stole one hundred thousand dollars from months earlier. The most frightening part was, I didn't know if he knew who I was, and if he knew I had stolen his money. I didn't know if Jewel had put the blame on me, or exactly what she'd told him about his missing money.

I looked at my watch, and it was now five minutes to twelve. Regardless of what happened, I was at the club on a mission, and I planned to complete it. So, I pulled myself together. I took a moment to look into the mirror, applied some much-needed lip-gloss, fixed my hair then headed back to the VIP area.

Just as I got through the rope, the countdown to midnight began. I spotted Jewel and prepared to give her that long-awaited gift as I rushed in her direction.

The countdown ended, and the crowd yelled, "Happy New Year!" Everyone went wild, as money dropped from the ceiling.

I watched as Touch stood on his throne, throwing champagne over a crowd of groupies. They looked like scavengers as they dove for the dollars that fell around them. Others just looked on in envy.

No one even noticed me as I took my time inching closer and closer toward Jewel. When I came within a couple feet of her, I tiptoed my way directly behind her. With fire in my eyes, I took a deep breath then delivered. *Bam!* One to the back of her head and she was down.

Simultaneously, I heard a deafening boom. Frightened, I turned around to see a fearless Calico standing with a smoking gun in his hand and the same fire I had in my eyes moments earlier. People scattered in every direction, screaming.

"He's got a gun!"

"Get down!"

"Where's Kita Boo and Tynika?"

Within moments, the crowded VIP area was clear, and all I could see was two lifeless bodies on the floor. One belonged to Touch, and not far from him lay Jewel. I knew who was responsible for Jewel's downfall, and the sight of her actually brought a proud smile across my face. Now, Touch was a different story. I didn't see him get shot, but I damn sure saw the smoking gun.

Luckily for Jewel, I'd decided to deliver a bottle to her head, instead of a bullet. Her man wasn't as lucky, though. Although I'd shared the same fire in my eyes as Calico, I didn't have the same balls. Gunshots in a packed club on New Year's Eve could only lead to jail. Too many eyewitnesses. Hell, I wasn't no career murderer, but I at least knew that shit.

Frantic, I rushed out of VIP, nearly knocking over the security guard on my way. I ran out the side door of the club to get to my car and get the fuck out of dodge. Moments later, I was in my car, peeling out of the parking lot, running over the curb and nearly tearing out the whole bottom of my car.

I sped down Virginia Beach Boulevard toward the interstate, passing six cop cars headed in the opposite direction. I knew exactly where they were going, and I was relieved to know I'd broken out in just enough time.

It wasn't until I reached my hotel room that I felt safe. I kicked off my heels and flopped across the bed. Thanks to Calico drawing so much attention to himself, I was confident that I'd gotten away with murder. He'd set things up perfectly. Any onlookers would be convinced that he was responsible for Jewel and Touch's deaths.

"Damn! What a fucking night," I said to myself as I got comfortable under the blanket and reflected on the multitude of events that had taken place in such a short period.

I couldn't believe I'd actually witnessed Touch getting shot, or even worse, that I'd run into Calico. I pulled out my phone and flipped to his number. Initially I'd planned to erase it. I wasn't sure to what use I could put the number of a crazed murderer, but something in me said not quite yet. One thing was for sure: I had no plans on getting up with him. I had no intention of calling him and no intention of answering any of his calls. This was a dude that possibly killed a man by gunfire in front of an entire club and didn't give a fuck. I could only imagine what he would do to me if he knew I stole his money. I knew I had to get out of Virginia and back to Atlanta ASAP, but not before I got some much-needed rest.

At first I had a little trouble falling asleep, not because I'd hit Jewel in the head with the bottle, but because I wasn't quite sure if Calico would figure out who I was and come after me next. After an hour of tossing and turning, I finally dozed off to sleep.

The next morning, I was awakened by the sound of a ringing phone.

"Hello," I answered in a cracked morning voice.

"Sasha Williams?"

"Yes."

"This is the front desk. It's now twelve o'clock and past checkout. Will you be staying another day?"

"No. I'm leaving now." I hung up before the lady on the other end could respond.

I grabbed the remote from the nightstand and turned on the television. My heart dropped to my feet, and I gasped for air at the sight before me. I shook my head and rubbed my eyes then turned up the volume to make sure what I was witnessing was real. And real it was. I panicked when I saw my face on the television screen.

"Police are investigating the shooting and felonious assault of a popular Virginia Beach couple. They are

asking for your help in locating the whereabouts of
Sasha Williams, the primary suspect in the crime."

I rushed to gather my things so I could get out of the hotel and on the road to Atlanta.

Before I could finish packing, I heard a forceful knock on the door, followed by a gruff bellow. "Virginia Beach police!"

I knew exactly what they wanted. Knowing how they moved and fearing for my life, I didn't even try anything crazy. One false move and they would swear I was reaching for a weapon, and my ass would be dead, twenty to thirty shots to the torso.

"I'm opening the door," I yelled as I unlocked the door. "I'm not resisting."

Several police officers rushed in, busting through the door with guns drawn. They threw me on the floor and slapped the cuffs on me in a single motion that seemed to take only one second.

"Sasha Williams, you have the right to remain silent. Anything you say can and will be used against you in a court of law. You have the right to an attorney . . ." The officer read me my Miranda rights.

"Yeah, yeah, yeah. Fuck you and Miranda! And that can go on record," I snapped as they lifted me from the floor and directed me out the door.

The ride to the Virginia Beach jail was long and uncomfortable. I sat slumped sideways, with my hands still cuffed, in the crammed backseat of the police car. I actually was relieved when we reached the station. I was ready to just get this whole ordeal over with.

From the car, I was escorted straight to the interrogation room and left freezing like a piece of meat in a freezer. I sat alone for forty-five minutes, shivering in this small room with nothing but a table and three chairs. I never quite understood the purpose of having the room below zero or the purpose of leaving you in the room alone for so long.

Finally, a man walked in who introduced himself as Detective Tarver. Almost to the point of going stir crazy, I welcomed the tall, husky, bald-headed white man, who seemed like he should have been playing some sort of contact sport instead of being a detective.

"Sasha Williams, you're being charged with two counts of attempted murder," the detective said as my mind wandered elsewhere.

What the fuck? Attempted murder? You mean to tell me that bitch ain't dead? My first reaction was one of disappointment, but then I really thought about what was being said to me. *Two counts of attempted murder, Sasha. You going to jail, bitch, and you ain't never getting out.* My heart palpitated, and I felt dizzy as I registered exactly what this man was telling me. Okay, with respect to Jewel, of course, I knew I was guilty, and there was no way around it. But, Touch, oh, hell no. That wasn't my charge, and I wasn't wearing that shit for nobody.

"Do you understand your rights and the counts you are being charged with?" the detective asked.

I'd missed all the information he'd said in between, and although I was still in shock, I just answered, "Yes, sir."

"Now, I know you're not a bad person, Sasha. You're a mother of two, and I know you would hate to lose your kids behind this. So I'm here to help you."

I knew the detective was lying. He didn't give a fuck about me or my kids. I'd seen this same scenario one too many times on the A&E series, *The First 48*. I knew what was coming next. He wanted me to help him, and he would help me.

I played along. "Please don't take me away from my kids," I pleaded.

"Well, here's the thing. We know we have enough information to charge you. That's no question. We have a security guard that identified you. He said you all had a conversation minutes before the incident, and you nearly knocked him over when you were fleeing the scene."

"Oh yeah?" I said, knowing exactly who he was speaking about. I couldn't believe that bitch-ass nigga from the strip club had turned me in. I guess he needed a good look in hopes of going from a nothing as a bouncer to a bitch-ass police officer.

"Yep, and right now, both of the victims are in critical condition. If they die, you could be looking at murder, and you will never see your kids again. I don't want that to happen to you, so I'm willing to help you, if you're willing to help me."

The detective gave almost the same spiel I'd hear on *The First 48* time and time again. It was almost comical. I had to wonder if that was a speech all cops learned in the academy.

"So what do I have to do?" I asked, continuing to play along.

Detective Tarver laid out the deal. "There's a major drug ring in Virginia Beach that revolves around Jewel, Touch, and Calico, and we know you were longtime friends with Jewel. So, what information can you give us to bring down their operation? Your cooperation in helping us bring them down can determine the outcome of your charges."

Seeing this as the perfect opportunity to kill two birds with one stone—getting rid of Jewel and Calico—I readily agreed. I hated Jewel and wanted her out of the picture, and I didn't know just how safe I was with Calico, seeing that I'd stolen his one hundred grand.

"Okay. I'll tell you what I know," I told him. "Calico was the main supplier. He brought cocaine from California and flooded the entire seven cities. Touch was his right-hand man, and together they were killing the drug game. But when Jewel got hooked up with the True Mafia Family, better known as TMF, Touch ended up using them as a new link, cutting Calico out.

"Jewel met the head guys in TMF through ghostwriting. They were coming out with a first-time album, and they hired her to ghostwrite a few songs on it. She used the power of brains and beauty to get in good with them. Then when she got her advance money, she purchased some weight from them and gave it to Touch to get rid of. She had it all planned out from the beginning.

"From that point on, money been constantly flowing. But Touch's big come-up brought beef between him and Calico. He ultimately stabbed Calico in the back and stole all his customers."

The detective continued to fish for information. "Do you have any phone numbers, addresses, or can you give us any other people that may be involved in this ring?"

Careful to tell the detective just enough to ease his hunger, but not enough to incriminate myself, we had a deal. By the end of our interrogation session, I had told Detective Tarver that Calico was Touch's shooter and submitted a written statement describing the events from that night.

When it was all said and done, I'd given Detective Tarver what he wanted, and we had a deal. I ended up being charged with only felony assault, but in turn, I would have to testify against Calico as an eyewitness to the shooting. I can't lie, that shit made me nervous as hell, but a bitch had to do what she had to do to save her ass.

Initially, my thoughts had been that Jewel was lucky I hadn't shot her ass, but in the end, it was lucky for me. Although everything in me wanted to see her in a casket, I knew shooting her in the club would have been too risky. Calico, on the other hand, wasn't as smart.

Chapter 2

"Home Sweet Home"

Calico

It never felt so good to be back in Cali. A nigga was dead broke, and every dime I owned was on the streets, waiting to be collected. I was really starting to feel the effects of Touch's little business taking the rise. I had plenty of product I'd bought from across the border, but no one to push that shit. The Mexicans were loading up cats on the West Coast with cocaine, so they could get my same shit for equal or better, making it impossible to move any weight on my side. It was those niggas on the East Coast that would pay top dollar, but that snake-ass Touch had swiped each and every one of my customers. It was hard to even get rid of my shit on the East Coast at this point.

I thought back to when everything was gravy. I would get the shit from the Mexicans and then hook up with my niggas on the East Coast. In only a matter of days I could get rid of everything. Back then, Touch would take half of the work off my hands off the buck. But then that nigga fucked up the business, had to go and get all pussy-whipped and shit. That put me in a hell of a predicament with the Mexican Mafia. I knew those niggas didn't play when it came to their money, so I used every dime to pay them back. A true soldier always knows it's money before bitches.

I was slowly building my money back up though. I can't lie, shit was real, and I ain't even have a hundred dollars to my name, but a nigga felt good to know he was about to be back on top. Putting Touch to rest was one definite way to assure my rise. After I put those hot balls in his ass, I broke out of Virginia the next morning. I hit up one of my little soldiers back in VA to give me the word on the streets.

"Yo!" Poppo answered.

I got right to business. "What's the word on that side?"

"You gotta work on your aim, duke."

"Fuck you mean, bitch nigga?" I asked, slightly insulted by Poppo's statement.

"Bitch?"

I could tell, by his tone, Poppa didn't take much liking to the name-calling, but I wasn't letting up. "You heard me, nigga. And watch your fucking tone." I was the fucking boss, so I needed to make sure he recognized that when speaking to me.

"Whatever you say, duke. But, anyway, that nigga still breathing," Poppo said still with a slight attitude, but he didn't have the balls to act on his aggravation.

"Hell nah!" I couldn't believe the shit I was hearing. I never missed a target.

"Yeah, dawg, that shit was on the news. They say that nigga in critical condition. And I hear they got that bitch Sasha locked up."

"Sasha? Who the fuck is Sasha?" I asked Poppo, the name sounding familiar to me.

"She that bitch that used to roll tight with Jewel. But the crazy shit is, she popped Jewel in the head with a champagne bottle that same night at the club. I hear Jewel in a fucking coma. That bitch, Sasha, picture was on the news and everything, dawg."

"I can't believe the shit I am hearing right now. You mean to tell me that bitch stood right beside me and I ain't even know that was her? Man, I'm fucking slipping. The bitch came over and tried to holla at a nigga; we exchanged numbers and everything. I got the number in my phone right now. No wonder the bitch started to look all sick and pale in the face, like she'd seen a fucking ghost when I told her my fucking name. She real lucky. That bitch has no idea how close she was to catching one of those hot balls along with Touch. One thing fo' sho', next time, that bitch won't slip away from me." Burning up inside with anger, I ended the call with Poppo and rolled a blunt.

After smoking on some high-grade, I dozed off to sleep.

I was wakened by the constant ringing of my cell phone. I looked at the caller ID. It was my attorney, Natalia Bergetti. Worry hovered over me as I answered the phone. She and I had a hate-love relationship. I hated being brought on charges and loved it when she got my ass off.

She called me by my government name. "Michael?"

"What's up? I know it gotta be bad news for you to be calling me."

"Hate to say it, but yes, it's pretty bad. I just got word from one of my contacts that you're being charged with attempted murder on Trayvon Davis, AKA Touch. And to make matters worse, they have an eyewitness. She was the original suspect, but I'm sure she worked out a deal with the detectives to lessen her charges, if she agrees to testify against you. You know they have been out for you for some time now, so if they can't get you on drug charges, they will certainly go for murder. They just want to see you put away a very, very long time."

"A'ight." I let out a deep sigh and then added, "Well, I'll be there to check you in a few days. Let me sort some things out first." I ended the call.

After I hung up the phone, I wondered if my reign as the Teflon man had run out. One thing I did know for sure though. A nigga wasn't turning hisself in. Those bitch-ass Virginia Beach cops was gonna have to find me.

I had a fucking instant headache as I processed everything that was going on. I was already awaiting trial on a fucking Racketeer Influenced and Corrupt Organizations Act charge, better known as a RICO charge, and now attempted murder. I was pretty confident my attorney could work out the RICO charge with a plea or something, but a witness to that attempted murder was no joke.

That shit was real! I'm sorry, but a nigga just wasn't built for a long bid in the penitentiary. Having a guard with horrible breath telling me what to do, being given slop for meals that even an animal wouldn't eat, beating my dick to a *XXL* magazine and having my momma and kids coming up for visits with tears in their eyes wasn't an option for me. I would pay any price for freedom, and believe me, my attorney wasn't cheap.

Besides, I already knew who their little eyewitness was. It had to be that bitch Sasha. Without an eyewitness, they had no case. So, with that said, I knew what I had to do. It was official. That bitch Sasha had to be dealt with. I knew I would be making a trip to Virginia real soon, but first, I needed to go relieve some tension and get these two monkeys off my back.

I decided to go pay my baby mother a little visit. I hopped in my car and headed to her crib unannounced.

"'S up?" I greeted Corrin, my baby mother, as I walked in on her just in time for dinner. She was cooking fried chicken.

"Use that house key I gave you for emergencies only," she barked at me putting emphasis on the word *emergencies*.

"Whatever." I smacked her on the ass. "Where my kids at?"

"At swimming lessons with my mother, like every Tuesday. If you were an active father, you would know that. And I repeat, that key is for *emergencies* only."

I wasn't trying to hear shit Corrin was saying. I had to give it to her though, she was a true ride-or-die chick. She would rob, stab, or shoot a nigga for me. What she truly wanted was to tie me down, but never that. I wasn't that kind of nigga.

"Don't I pay for your rent in this bitch every fucking month?" I snapped back at her.

"Yeah," she replied, facing me, rolling her eyes.

"If something is broke around here, don't I fix it 'cause your sorry-ass landlord don't give a fuck?"

"Yeah."

"A'ight. Then give me the respect that I deserve, woman," I said, coming closer in the kitchen.

"Nigga, spend more time with your son and daughter. After you tote them around the mall, get them something to eat and some toys, you ready to bring them home. It's more to being a daddy than material shit. You care more about popping fucking bottles in the club than being a father. So be a real daddy and start paying my lights, cable, phone and car payment, then I will start showing you more respect around here. And come in here again unannounced like that and I will change the locks."

That shit she was saying was going in one ear and out the other. Every day was the same shit, but this day I wasn't in the mood. All I wanted was some weed, pussy, and food, and that's what I planned on getting.

"Corrin, I don't need this shit from you today. I already got a headache. Your mouth is going to make it turn into a fucking migraine!" I yelled, confronting her.

I turned her around, pulled down her shorts, popped off her G-string, and bent her over. She smelled like sweet vanilla. I quickly loosened my belt and pulled down my jeans and boxers.

"Hmm, I knew you wanted you some pussy. Hurry up before my mom comes with the kids."

I smacked her ass, spread her cheeks, and pushed my dick into her wet pussy. That was one of the greatest benefits of having a baby moms—guaranteed pussy anytime I wanted. Yeah, Corrin bitched and complained about every little thing, but she was always willing to open those legs for me, day or night.

Chapter 3

"Soldier Status"

Poppo

After talking to Calico I was fucking vexed. I had stood by that nigga's side for years, never deceiving him, stealing from him, or trying to shave off his profit. There was no other nigga that had his back like me, and this was the thanks I get? Not wanting to sit and dwell on him and his bullshit, I decided to go to the barbershop and kick it with some of my niggas and fuck with some of the freak bitches that hang up there.

"Damn, nigga! Fuck wrong with you? Coming in the shop like you wanna kill niggas and shit," Mike, one of the barbers, said as soon as I walked in the place.

My feelings must have been written all over my face. "Ain't shit, man. Who in the chair next?" I asked, still a little aggravated.

"You." Mike brushed the hair from the chair, using a cape, then threw it around me.

Once in the chair, and out of earshot of the public, I began to fill Mike in.

"Nah, duke, it ain't no beef shit. I just got off the phone with that nigga Calico, and that nigga be talking to me like I'm some little bitch. He needs to start respecting men. You feel me?"

"Right, right." Mike didn't say much. Him, like most niggas, was too afraid to curse Calico.

The more I thought about things it really started to get under my skin. I had to wonder what the fuck this nigga took me for. After everything I'd done for homie, all the fucking wars we'd been through and I had this nigga back, this nigga was still talking to me like I was some little nothing-ass nigga. I'd been past the toy soldier status. A nigga had his wings now, but Calico couldn't see it. But whether he chose to see it or not, I knew I wasn't gonna be his "gofer" for too much longer. It was definitely time for change.

Although I'd never crossed Calico before, I was really considering it. I was making just enough money to get by working with him. It was time for me to make a come-up. I figured the next time that nigga gave me some shit to deliver, or some money to collect, I was gonna take that shit and flip and make a little money off of it, then pay him. As long as I did that shit quickly, he would never know the difference. After a few flips, I would have enough money on my own to start buying some weight.

Chapter 4

"Living Nightmare"

Jewel

My eyes opened suddenly as I was jolted out of my sleep from the nightmare that kept playing over and over in my head. I waited for my eyes to focus. Slightly disoriented, I could hear a constant beeping and faint voices in the background as well. I looked around, slowly focusing my eyes, and realized I was in a hospital.

That's when the realization hit me that I hadn't been dreaming at all. There really was an accident. I felt like I was beginning to live out my nightmare. I started to panic. *Had I been shot? Where is Touch?* I touched my head and screamed out in pain. *Oh my God! I was shot in the head! Am I retarded? Can I walk? I need a mirror! Oh my God! Please, where's the mirror?* I felt like I was going crazy. I looked around the room frantically for a mirror. I couldn't move due to all the different tubes that were attached to me, so I called for help.

"Help me! Please help me!" I began to yell out for a nurse.

Seconds later a nurse rushed in. "Hi, Miss Diaz. Glad to see you up and alert. I'm Misty, and I'll be your nurse today. Is everything okay?" she asked calmly.

"No. What happen to my head? Was I shot? I need to see a mirror," I said, still in a panic. Months earlier I'd taken a nasty blow to the head, and it was not nice. I was all swollen and black and blue for days. I refused to go through that again.

"Just calm down, Miss Diaz. You were not shot. You were hit in the head with a bottle. You have been in a coma for two days," Nurse Misty explained.

I asked the next most important question. "What about my boyfriend, Trayvon Davis? Where is he?"

"Your boyfriend isn't doing as well as you are. He's in our intensive care unit."

"Oh God! This can't be happening," I said, realizing again my nightmare was reality. "He was shot, wasn't he?"

"Yes, he was. He was shot in the stomach, and the bullet exited through his back, damaging quite a few vital organs in the process. He's currently in critical condition."

As I listened to the nurse and registered what she was saying, my chest began to tighten, and I felt like I couldn't breathe. "I think I'm gonna pass out," I said to her between pants, and the slow, constant, beeping sounds in the background picked up in pace.

Misty tried to coach me back to a normal breathing pattern. "You're panicking. Just relax and take some deep breaths."

"I have to see him, please," I begged the nurse.

"I'll see what we can do. Just give me a few minutes to talk with the doctor." Misty then exited the room.

I watched as she walked out. Misty was a young nurse, a nice-looking black girl, dressed in Baby Phat scrubs, with a big phat ass to match. I'm usually good at judging character, and she looked liked one of those get-money chicks. With that in mind, I needed to keep her far from my man.

"Ouch!" A streaking pain ran through my head, diverting my attention back to my injury.

I couldn't believe what was going on. I couldn't understand how we went from a night of celebrating the New Year, to Touch being shot and me in a coma. The more I played that night over and over in my head, the more the pieces of the puzzle began to come together. Before long I'd recapped the entire night in my head, and I knew exactly what had gone down. I was sure Calico had shot Touch, and Sasha had hit me in the head. Now that I knew the deal, I knew exactly what I had to do. Calico and Sasha had to pay.

Misty returned to the room with a wheelchair. "Miss Diaz?"

"Yes?"

"I'm gonna take you to see Mr. Davis. The doctor wanted you to wait until he was able to come in and do a quick examination, but I convinced him to let me go ahead and take you to see your boo."

We both laughed at her usage of the word *boo*.

"Thanks, girl," I said to Misty as though we were longtime friends. "I really appreciate it."

"Oh, trust me, I understand. I was in your place once. Me and my man were in a car accident, and when I came to, all I wanted to do was see him. So I feel your pain." Misty parked the chair next to my bed and began to prepare me for my trip.

My opinion suddenly changed about her. Instead of looking at her as another greedy street-bitch, I actually saw her as a pretty cool female. She helped me out of bed, and minutes later, I was comfortable in the wheelchair.

Misty swept me off to Touch's room. As we entered the room, I instantly felt the same tightness I'd felt in my chest earlier, and again, I began to struggle to breathe. The sight of a lifeless Touch with tubes coming from every direction and constant beeps of the monitor and inflation of the breathing machine was just too overwhelming for me.

"Why are there so many tubes? What's going on?" I asked Misty between my tears and pants.

Misty rolled me right next to Touch's bed, and I grabbed his hand as she explained his current state and what the different tubes were for. My heart literally ached as I watched the love of my life lay before me unconscious.

"Just leave me here," I said to Misty. "I want to spend some time with him alone."

"No problem, but I must tell you. Detectives have been up here several times to speak with you and Mr. Davis.

They asked that we give them a call when you all regain consciousness."

"I'm really not interested in speaking to no DT right now, or ever for that matter." I kissed my teeth and rolled my eyes simultaneously.

"Well, I'm not going to call them, but I just wanted to make you aware." Misty smiled.

"Thank you so much. You are so understanding. I owe you." I smiled back and then diverted my attention to Touch.

"I love you so much, baby." I caressed his hand as I spoke to him. "I know you can make it out of this. Come on, Touch. I need you here. Your twin girls need you here. Too many people are depending on you, baby." I knew Touch loved his daughters with all his heart, and if anyone could inspire him to fight, it would definitely be them.

I laid my head beside him on the bed. I could still smell the fresh scent of his Vera Wang cologne. "I love you, Touch," I constantly whispered to him until I dozed off to sleep.

***

The next day I was discharged from the hospital with enough pain pills to sedate a horse. I had fifteen staples straight down the center of the back of my head. When I got home, all I could think about was Touch. After calling his mother, situating things at home, and taking a much-needed shower, I got in my car and headed back to the hospital, no more than two hours after I'd left. That's where I spent each day—by Touch's side—until he regained consciousness.

Chapter 5

"Sad Reality"

Touch

"Aaaahhh fuck!" My body ached with so much pain, and it throbbed as though I'd been hit by a fucking bus. I slowly opened my eyes and struggled to figure out where I was.

I heard a familiar voice say, "Touch, baby," and felt a gentle touch on the side of my face.

I turned to my left side to see Jewel sitting next to me. "What?" I struggled to talk but noticed something was preventing me.

"No, no, baby, don't try to talk," Jewel said to me. "There's a tube in your mouth." She then called for the nurse.

I noticed I felt extremely thirsty, as I took the time to examine my body and things started to register. It seemed like I had tubes coming from every hole in my body. I had tubes coming from my mouth, arm, and even my dick.

Shit was really starting to sink in. I remembered getting shot at the club. Although I was shot in a matter of seconds, the events seemed to have occurred in slow motion. I remembered seeing Calico dip in his waist and me thinking, *This nigga got a fucking gun*, knowing he was going to shoot me. My first instinct was to push Jewel to the floor to get her out of danger. The last thing I remembered was locking eyes with her, and then feeling extreme pain to my stomach. And from the way things were looking from that hospital bed, Calico had really fucked me up. But the one mistake that bitch nigga made was to leave me breathing.

Minutes later, the nurse walked in. After checking my vitals and a quick exam, she removed my breathing tube from my mouth. My first request was water. After quenching the severest case of cotton mouth a nigga could ever experience, I began to ask the thousand questions that had been plaguing my mind.

"How many times was I shot?" I forced out the first question.

"Once," Jewel answered right away.

"Where?"

"In the stomach and exiting out your back," Jewel said, confirming exactly what I'd suspected.

"So, how bad is it?"

I watched Jewel's expression change after I asked that question. That was a sure sign a nigga was fucked up.

Jewel came with some bullshit answer. "Baby, don't worry about all that. You're alive, that's all that matters."

"Yo, this me you talking to, Jewel. Don't give a nigga the runaround. What's the deal? Am I paralyzed or something?"

"No, you're not, but you're gonna have to go through extensive rehab to learn to walk again." Jewel dropped her head and began to cry.

There was nothing I could say. So many emotions were hitting me at one time. I was so fucking vex that I let this nigga Calico take so much from me. I was hurt that Jewel had to see me go through this. I felt like shit because, at the time, a nigga was like a fucking baby. Somebody had to feed me, bathe me, change me, and I even had to learn to walk again. What good was I? I didn't know if you could even consider somebody in that state as a man.

"I'm gonna kill Calico," I said, pure hate in my heart and eyes.

Jewel tried her best to divert my anger to positive energy. "Baby, please don't talk like that. Don't even focus on him. Put your energy into your health. We just need to get you better."

"Matter of fact, why are you even here? I can't do shit for you. If I can't walk or even feed myself, I definitely can't fuck you. Plus, we both know how you love money. If I can't grind, the money will be gone soon, which means you'll be out looking for the next cat. Ain't no point in waiting. Just leave now. You ain't gotta stick around because you feel sorry for me, or because you feel like it's the right thing to do. Haul ass!"

"Touch, why are you acting like that? I've been here by your side every day and night for an entire week while you lay here unconscious. I love you and I'm not giving up on you, no matter what!" Jewel cried.

"Did you not hear me? Get the fuck out, Jewel!" I then began to yell for the nurse. "Nurse!"

The nurse rushed in. "Yes, Mr. Davis?"

"Could you have her leave?"

"Mr. Davis, she's been here by your side every day and night."

"So what? Are you gonna make her leave, or do I need to call security?"

Misty hesitated before speaking. "I'm sorry, Jewel. I have to respect his wishes," she said reluctantly. "I'm afraid I'm gonna have to ask you to leave."

"Misty, I'm not going anywhere. He's just upset right now. This is a lot for him to handle."

"Jewel, if he calls security, you won't ever be able to re-enter the facility."

With tears in her eyes and hurt written all over her face, Jewel gathered her things and headed toward the door. "I love you, Touch, and I refuse to give up on you, even if you give up on yourself. I'm standing by your side, no matter what." Her words were followed by the sound of the door closing behind her.

The next few weeks were filled with intense rehabilitation and constant questioning by detectives. At times, I didn't know if the DTs were trying to find my shooter or get up in my business. On the real, this one detective was making me feel like I was the fucking criminal instead of the victim. They kept asking if I knew my shooter.

Of course, I lied and said no. Shit like this had to be handled on the streets. There was no getting the cops involved. But they just weren't happy when I told them I didn't know my shooter. From there they tried to insinuate it was drug activity that provoked my shooter to come after me, like a drug deal gone bad or some shit. These niggas had to be crazy if they thought I would admit to something like that. Needless to say, after two or three of these bullshit interrogations, all contact was off when it came to the police.

Jewel and I had made up. She didn't give up on me. I swear, if she hadn't done just like she promised and stayed by my side the entire way, I would have fucking lost it. In fact, she showed me more love than I'd ever expected. She'd shown me so much that I knew I had to give her all of me. I had to give her a part of me that no other woman ever had. There were times when I felt like shit, less than a fucking man, and I took that frustration out on her, but no matter what, she still was there encouraging me. She was at my bedside each day, feeding me at mealtime. Although she had no proper training, she would beat the nurses to giving me a bath and assisting me to the bathroom. I always knew Jewel was that down-ass bitch, but now I felt like I owed her big time.

Chapter 6

"Here Comes the Bride"

Jewel

"Come on, baby." I helped Touch out of bed and into a standing position so that he could use his walker.

He had made a lot of progress over the past few weeks. He'd gone from being totally dependent to walking, bathing, eating, dressing, and basically doing everything on his own. Although Touch was recovering, I still had a deep hatred for Calico, and I wasn't going to be happy until he paid for his deed.

Touch's mother walked through the front door.

"Hey, Ma!" I said.

Touch's mother would come over periodically to give me a break. That gave me an opportunity to do any errands I may have. I refused to leave Touch alone until I was sure he could bust a nigga ass if he had to. Until then he would never be alone. I'd purchased extra guns and placed them throughout the house for added protection. I'd even gone as far as to teach his mom how to shoot. This nigga Calico had just tried to take Touch's life, and there was no way I was gonna take a chance of him coming back to finish the job.

"Okay, baby, I'll be right back." I kissed Touch and then headed toward the front door prepared to set the alarm on my way out. Although we lived in a prominent high-end neighborhood, crime had no address, so I needed to protect my man at all costs.

"Wait!" Touch called out as though he was in pain.

"What's wrong, baby?" I said in a panic.

"Come sit next to me." Touch patted on a stool at the breakfast bar next to him. "I wanted to wait 'til my mom was here before I did this."

Confused, I slowly walked toward him and sat on the stool as he requested. I watched as he struggled to dig an item from out of his pocket. I immediately reached out to assist him.

"No, baby," he said, resisting. "I got it." He then finally pulled out a small box. "This isn't the way I dreamed of doing things, but this can't wait any longer. You've shown me love that no other woman, other than my mother, has ever shown me. We've shared good and bad times, and between it all, you stood your ground as my ride-or-die chick. Jewel, I love you, baby, and I can never repay you for your loyalty, but I can give you all of me for the rest of my life. If you would accept, I would love for you to be my wife. Will you marry me?"

My eyes filled with water, and it felt like someone was literally tugging at my heart. "Yes, baby. Of course, I will be your wife."

We kissed each other passionately.

My ring was beautiful. Touch had outdone himself. As soon as I'd seen the name Harry Winston, I knew there was no way I could be disappointed. He was a celebrity jeweler, so I knew Touch couldn't go wrong with him. I opened the box to see a 14-karat white gold princess and baguette matching ring and band set with a total weight of eight carats. I immediately placed the ring on my finger and admired it, leaving the band in the box for our actual wedding day.

"Well, it looks like I'm finally getting my wish," Touch's mom said. She'd always wanted me as a daughter-in-law.

Way back when Touch and I were truly platonic friends, I could remember his mother constantly saying, "Boy, I sure wish you were my daughter-in-law."

"Now get out of here and go do your wifely duties. Get me some groceries, woman!" Touch said in a playful tone.

I grabbed my Gucci bag and headed out the door and made my way to Wal-Mart. Like always, the Wal-Mart parking lot was full, and the store was busy like a damn nightclub. I breezed my way through the aisles of the store, picking up items and checking them off my grocery list.

"Yo, Jewel," someone called out to me.

I turned around to see one of Calico's boys that went by the name Poppo standing before me. I unzipped my purse that sat in the child seat of the shopping cart. I wanted easy access to my gun in case I needed to shoot this nigga.

"Yeah?" I responded with an attitude. I didn't know what type of shit he was on, and I didn't want to make the mistake of showing fear.

"What's good with you, baby girl? Still looking good, I see."

I could tell by his body language and his words that he wasn't on no beef shit. In the past, he had tried to get with me, but since Touch had gotten shot, I didn't know what to expect or who could be trusted.

"Whatever, nigga." I blew him off then continued to look for Touch's favorite cereal, Fruity Pebbles.

"Why you keep blowing me off? I been trying to holla at you for a minute now."

I was just about to diss the hell out of this nigga, but then it hit me. Poppo was obviously one of those niggas that was weak for pussy. He had been trying to get with me since I was dating Calico. Every time Calico would send him to pick up some shit from me or to deliver me some money or anything, he would always make a pass at me. One time he even grabbed my ass. I figured, if he would stab his boy in the back during that time, why not do it now? Literally, that is. Plus, I knew firsthand how Calico treated his boys. He treated them like shit. I knew I could easily get in Poppo's head, so I executed.

"Yeah, you have, Poppo, but I'm a boss bitch, and I need a boss by my side. I can't have no nigga that's being bitched out every day by some other nigga that thinks he's the boss."

"Man, fuck that nigga! I'm trying to do a little something on my own, so I can break off from that nigga now. He be trying to play niggas for a little bitch, and I'm getting tired of that shit."

Poppo's simple ass played right into my little game when he said exactly what I wanted to hear.

"So you think all you need is a little drug connect to get away from Calico? Hell, if that's all it takes, I can put you on to a connect, but Calico will kill your ass if he knew you was trying to do your own thing. That shit makes you his competition."

"Man, I'll deal with Calico."

Poppo's words were music to my ears.

"Okay, look . . . this is the deal. You know Touch is fucked up, so he ain't even fucking with the drug game right now. So I'm gonna need a new boss by my side. If you can get rid of Calico to assure we won't have problems, I will put you on to my connect, and me and you can build a new empire of our own."

"Done deal. Say no more. How can I reach you?"

Poppo's weak ass had fallen right into my trap. Just like the average nigga, he was weak for pussy. I knew I could tell him anything and have him eating out of the palm of my hand. Sure, I made him feel like he was the man and I was gonna be by his side, but it was only to get what I wanted, which was Calico out of the way and my man safe. What better way to have Calico killed than to have his own boy do it?

Poppo and I exchanged phone numbers, and I finished up my grocery shopping excited as a kid on Christmas.

Chapter 7

"Indecent Proposal"

Poppo

"Damn right!" I said to no one in particular as I walked back to my car in the parking lot of the Wal-Mart shopping center.

Running into Jewel was a coincidence, but the offer she made had to be a sign that it was time to break away from Calico. But, still, I had to wonder if this bitch was for real. I must admit, her offer did seem too good to be true. Was this bitch trying to set me up? After all, my man did just try to kill her nigga. *Maybe, once I get Calico out the way, I would be her next man.* All kinds of shit was running through my head, but fuck it! I needed the come-up. It was whatever.

Once I got to the crib, I couldn't get that shit off my mind. This would be the perfect fucking come-up. I could be on top, and I knew that's all I needed to get Jewel. I'd wanted that ass for a long time and it looked like my time was finally coming. I stayed up late watching episodes of *The First 48* and eating pizza and drinking Heineken, which eventually got a nigga tired as hell. I slowly began to doze off to sleep.

***

"Poppo, I'm going to ask you this, one time," Jewel stated as she handed me a glass of Nuvo.

She was dressed in a red wife-beater and torn, tight-ass jeans that looked to have been painted on her. And, gotdamn, that ass was phat! We definitely weren't at my place or hers. Instead, it looked as if we were in one of those uppity expensive hotels like the Westin or Loews or something. The room was huge.

I lifted my head from the king-size bed to see pink roses scattered all over the carpet. A Jacuzzi was to the right of me. A tray of all kinds of cheeses, meats and fruits were to the left of me on a table. Yeah, I could get used to this kind of lifestyle. Jewel was definitely high-class and high-maintenance, but a nigga wasn't complaining. I was confident I could keep up with her and supply all of her wants and needs.

"Thank you," I responded as I took the glass from her and took a gulp of the sparkling pink wine.

"Did you have anything to do with Calico's death?" she inquired. "That nigga was found with a rat in his mouth, and his eyes were cut out. Everyone is in disbelief."

"Don't worry about it. Now that he's out of the way, I will take the throne and have you right by my side as my queen." I rubbed her cheek with my hand.

I thought back to the funeral that I'd gone to just to be nosy, and so that I didn't look suspect. Dressed in all black and my Dolce & Gabbana shades, I was playing the part to the hilt. Calico had plenty of people from near and far there to see him off. His mother, baby mamas, and thousands of "side-bitches" were all trying to hang on to the casket as the funeral groundskeepers lowered it into the ground. He had so many bitches there, for a minute I thought a fight was gonna break out.

"Like I said, Calico is gone. It's time for us to get on with our lives," I told her.

"Let's make a toast," Jewel suggested.

"To making money, happiness, and prosperity," I said, touching glasses with her.

"Well, I'll drink to that!" Jewel grinned then took a sip from her glass.

After she took several sips of her drink, she slowly took off her clothes, revealing a black lace teddy. She turned on the DVD player, and the song "12 Play" by R. Kelly came on. I had no idea how she knew this was one of my favorite songs. When she started dancing around and popping her ass in my face, my dick instantly got hard. One by one, she took off each piece of lingerie.

"You hungry?" she asked.

"A little."

Jewel began feeding me a little meat, cheese, and strawberries dipped in white chocolate.

"Now, I'm very hungry," she said before placing watermelon, cantaloupe, and honeydew melon all over my body.

Afterwards, she started eating it off me. I'd never had any girl do this shit to me. Before I knew it, she began licking my balls and deep-throating my dick. I closed my eyes. I couldn't help it and came right in her mouth. And she gladly swallowed.

"Damn!" I woke up with my dick covered in cum.

That was one of the best dreams I ever had. I took that as a sure sign that Jewel was going to be mine for good.

Chapter 8

"Snitch Bitch"

Sasha

"Free at last, free at last! Thank God Almighty, I'm free at last!" I loudly recited the famous words of Martin Luther King, Jr. as I exited the confines of Virginia Beach jail.

After spending three days there, a bitch was happy to finally get out. When I was originally booked on the lesser assault charge after speaking with the detectives, I went to speak to the magistrate about a bond. That bitch nigga denied me bond, claiming that I was a flight risk, since I lived out of state, so I had to wait to get a bond hearing. When I went before the judge, he granted me a $10,000 bond. I got in touch with a bondsman, and he let me out for a thousand dollars.

I waited patiently for my cab to arrive and literally jumped for joy when I saw him pull up.

"Yippee!" I skipped to the cab like a little kid and hopped in the backseat. "The Doubletree Hotel at Military Circle Mall in Norfolk." I directed him to the hotel I'd stayed at during my arrest. I needed to return there to pick up my car.

As soon as the cabby pulled up to the hotel, I paid him, hopped into my car, and made my way to the interstate, headed back to Columbus, Georgia to my parents' crib to pick up my kids. I'd gotten my own little crib in Atlanta, but I rarely spent any time there.

As I was driving, the scene from New Year's Eve kept playing over and over in my head. The two things most disturbing to me were, one, I'd witnessed Touch getting shot by Calico, and two, I was so damn close to death myself. I knew in my heart that Calico would not have hesitated to put a bullet in me just as fast if he knew I was that chick that robbed him of his money. With that in mind, I began to reflect back on the agreement I'd made with Detective Tarver. *What the fuck have I done?* I wondered to myself, realizing I had made a big mistake. *I've just given myself a death sentence. Calico is gonna fucking kill me. I'm never gonna make it to court.*

My brain started racing, and my nerves were starting to get the better of me. If Calico found out I was an eyewitness, and planning to testify against him, he would make sure I didn't have a breath left in my body, come the trial date. As paranoia set in, I began constantly looking in my side-view and rearview mirrors to see if someone was following me. I was beginning to feel like a fucking lunatic fleeing from the crazy house.

For a moment I could have sworn that a tinted-out black Tahoe was following me. I was so shook, my tank was on empty, but I refused to get gas. When I finally was forced, I circled the gas station two times to be sure no one was following me into the station. I pumped my gas and jumped back on the interstate in record-breaking time.

As I continued to drive, my brain was constantly plagued by this whole Calico situation, so I decided to give Detective Tarver a call.

"Tarver," he answered on the first ring.

"Hi, this is Sasha Williams. I just worked out a deal with you on that case involving the shooting at Club Encore in Virginia Beach."

"Hey, Sasha. What can I do for you?"

"Well, I was wondering if Calico would be informed that I will be testifying, because I'm a little worried about my safety."

"Well, we will inform him there is an eyewitness, but we won't reveal who until the court proceedings. But you don't have to worry. Once we get our hands on him, he will not be coming out, and until then, we will do all we can to make sure you're protected. Don't you worry."

"Okay," I said, still not feeling any more confident than I'd felt before the call. Actually, I felt worse.

I knew, after talking to the detective, there was no way I could go through with the deal we had negotiated. These days it was easier to beat the system than the streets. I could buck on court and be on the run and live to tell about it, as opposed to testifying against Calico and not even making it to court.

Now that I'd made my mind up that I wasn't going to court to testify against Calico, nor my charge for that matter, I had to put an escape plan into play. I knew it was nothing to change my look, get a new driver's license and relocate. I could easily go someplace like Jamaica and live with no problem. I knew a few people there. Plus, I would be in heaven, with so much Jamaican dick to choose from.

The only downfall would be leaving my family, baby daddy, and worst of all, my three- and seven-year-old sons, Malik and Jahad, whom I adored. I'm sure I could probably live without my sorry-ass drug-dealer-gone-bad baby daddy, Rick. Hell, he was part of the reason I had to resort to the streets.

I had actually stopped stripping at one point and was a working chick. I had a comfortable life, house, car, and even a rental property. Then this nigga's drug game got fucked up, and he drained me of every penny, leaving me with two foreclosed homes. And soon I was back to stripping and living with my parents. It wasn't until I bucked on Jewel for Calico's one hundred grand that I was able to get back on my feet. So that nigga, I could definitely do without, but it was the thought of being away from my kids that was killing me. Deep inside, I knew it would be too risky to have them with me while on the run.

My plan was set. I just needed to execute. I still had about fifty grand left from Calico's money that I'd tricked Jewel into giving me, but I needed about fifty more. I wanted to have at least a hundred grand cash when I dipped out of the country. It was time for me to get my hustle on, and by all means I intended to. My life depended on it.

I called up my boy Diablo. Originally from Virginia, Diablo used to run drugs hard in VA but had recently moved to Atlanta when shit got hot, after a few young boys that he used as runners got locked up and started snitching. Although I didn't formally meet him until I started working at Bottoms Up, a strip club in Atlanta, I knew of him in VA because his name rang bells. And, of course, like every other baller, little miss Jewel used to date him too.

When Diablo hit the *A*, he started going even harder, making even more money, and eventually becoming one of the top suppliers in Atlanta. He used his drug money to open a club and started getting money from both angles.

"What up, sexy?" Diablo said.

"Hey, boo. I was calling to see if you were hiring," I said, knowing Diablo would know exactly what I meant. I'd done some work for him before, so he knew I was game for whatever.

"Not right now, baby girl. I'm waiting on some family to come up from out of the country. They should be here in a couple of weeks. Check with me then." Diablo spoke in code, saying that he was waiting for his product to come in.

"Cool," I said then ended the call.

The plan was set and soon to be in motion. I just needed to stay alive until then. I planned to use those couple of free weeks to spend time with my boys and let them know how much their mommy loved them, especially since, at this point, tomorrow definitely wasn't promised.

Chapter 9

"Nurse Save-a-chick"

Jewel

Touch had become more and more independent within the past weeks, so I was able to leave the house a little more often than when he first was discharged from the hospital. I was actually to the point of leaving him home alone. He enjoyed the independence of being left alone; it gave him a much-needed ego boost.

This particular day I'd chosen to take some time out for myself so I went to Starbucks. I was sitting in a booth there, sipping on a latte, using Starbucks Wi-Fi Connection on my laptop to look up some different wedding sites, and getting ideas about our wedding. It wasn't that we didn't have the Internet service or a computer at home. In fact, we had several, including the new HP TouchSmart PC. But I wanted to surprise Touch with how I set off our big date, so I didn't need him looking over my shoulders every minute while I was surfing the Web on our home computer.

I was planning on a major scale. I wanted a tailor-made Vera Wang dress, and a wedding setup to mimic a wedding of the royal court in England, with an aged mansion and horse and carriage to match. I'd even considered contacting David Tutera from the television show *My Fair Wedding* to guarantee that it would be a success. Our city wouldn't expect anything less than a celebrity wedding. Hell, we'd already set the tone with our New Year's party, so we had no choice but to continue the trend.

Although we hadn't set a date yet, I wanted our wedding to be the biggest event niggas in VA had ever seen, the wedding that would be talked about forever. I could already see the looks on the faces of all the haters when they see us stroll down the aisle. Our wedding was going to be the hottest shit VA had ever seen. We were definitely going down in history.

Although I'd plan to have an invitation-only event with police as security because there was no way Touch or I could take a chance of a replay from New Year's night, my guest list was already at five hundred. I was sure to invite all of the who's who and keep out all of the "who's you." I was on some presidential shit. I was even checking out some of the pictures of Obama's inauguration on the Internet, trying to get some additional ideas for entertainment, when I heard a familiar voice interrupt my concentration.

"Jewel, is that you? Hey, girl!"

I turned around in my booth and looked up from my laptop to see the nurse from the hospital, Misty. "Oh! Hey, Misty."

"How's your boo, Trayvon?" Misty used the same slang she'd used in the hospital the day we'd first met.

We both laughed, acknowledging that moment.

"He's great! He's walking without his walker now."

"Wonderful!"

"Misty, I just want to thank you for your kindness to us both while we were in the hospital." I reached out to shake her hand.

"That's my job." Misty flagged her hand in dismissal. "Damn, girl! Let me see that ring!" Seeing my unavoidable rock, she lifted my left hand. "Are you and Tray-von getting married?"

"Yes," I said, a Kool-Aid smile across my face. "We're engaged."

"Congratulations! Dang, that rock is heavy. And that diamond's almost blinding me. Whew! When's the big date?"

Before I could answer, my mouth flew wide open, and I put my hand over my heart. I gasped. I had seen Calico walk by the coffee shop in the shopping mall. I had heard he'd skipped town, and probably went back to Cali, but I knew this thing wasn't over between him and Touch. I was sure that was Calico, and I couldn't take any chances of him seeing me, so I ducked my head down in the booth where I sat.

"What's the matter?" Misty looked concerned.

"I think I just saw this dude, Calico."

"Who's Calico?"

"The guy who shot Touch."

"Oh my God. He hasn't been arrested yet?" Misty jumped in front of me in a protective manner as she scanned the area looking for Calico, and for a second, it looked like she was reaching for a gun on her hip.

"No," I said, kind of thrown by her demeanor.

"We better get out of here." Misty grabbed me by the arm. "Let's slip out the back door, and we can take my truck. I'm parked in the back. I'll bring you back to get your car later."

I lowered my head and tiptoed, with Misty blocking my body, as she walked behind me. She led me to a black Tahoe with dark tint. She opened the passenger door for me, and I scooted down into the front seat.

Misty climbed in on the driver's side and hit the gas pedal. "How about if we go to my place and kick it for a while?"

I was surprised at just how cool Misty was. Sure, at the hospital she seemed like a down-to-earth chick, but I never would have expected us to click so easily.

I examined her from head to toe. She was dressed in D&G jeans, sneakers, and light jacket to match. She had her hair pulled up in a curly ponytail. Based on her attire alone, I would have to say, she was my type of female. Even so, I was still skeptical.

Generally speaking, I didn't trust women, and especially after how Sasha stabbed me in the back. But since I was already in the truck with her and she'd practically saved me from Calico, I figured what the hell.

"That's cool. You stay near here?"

"Yeah, not too far."

And not too far was right because, after a few turns and ten minutes flat, we were pulling up to some new three-story town homes off Independence Boulevard.

"These are nice. I didn't even know they were back here," I said as we pulled into Misty's two-car garage.

"Yeah, they're new. It's not much, but it's a cozy little spot, for me alone." Misty walked in the basement of the house from the garage.

It was a huge room with a sitting area, bathroom, minibar, and another area set up with workout equipment. I followed her up the first set of steps where the living room, kitchen, and the master bedroom sat. Giving me a quick tour, she then led me up another set of steps, where another two bedrooms were.

"We can relax in the basement," Misty said as she took off her coat and got comfortable.

We walked back to the basement, and Misty flipped on the flat-screen television that resembled the exact one I had at home, and handed me the remote.

"Watch whatever you like," she said to me, and then headed to the bathroom.

I used that moment as an opportunity to call Poppo. I needed to know what was up with our little arrangement. That run-in earlier was a little too close for comfort.

I called Poppo's phone over and over again, but he didn't answer. Finally I decided to leave a voice message. "Man, what's the deal with Calico? I just saw that nigga at the mall," I said, trying my best to whisper. "Are you gon' do this shit or what? 'Cause, on the real, it's gonna get done with or without you. So you gonna be a player in the game or a fucking water boy?" I knew the exact words to say to get in his head.

After completing my message, I rushed off the phone as Misty walked in.

"Can I make you a drink? I don't know about you, but I need a little something to relax my nerves."

"Ummmm, do you have any wine?" I asked, to see what kind of level she was on.

"Sure. What would you like? White Zinfandel, Merlot, Pinot?"

"How about Moscato?" I said, knowing she probably never heard of it.

"Coming right up," Misty said, surprising the hell out of me.

Damn! I guess me and this bitch really can roll, I thought to myself, peeping her style.

After a few drinks we both were quite tipsy. We spent the next hour chatting like we were two old biddies.

"So, tell me, when is the big date? Are you aiming for this summer? If so, you only have a couple months to plan."

"Well, I'm working on that. I had a late summer date set, but the owners of the historic mansion I'm trying to book aren't working with me."

"For real? Girl, I got all kinds of hookups. Tell me what you trying to do. What wedding scene do you have in mind?"

I spent the next ten minutes telling Misty all about my fantasy wedding, detail by detail.

"Wow! That's sounds beautiful! Do you have a wedding planner?"

"Nope. I thought about contacting David Tutera though."

We both laughed.

"Girl, save your money. I got your back. Wedding planning is my thing. Any event planning for that matter. I used to work for a huge event planning company before I moved to VA. When I got here I had my own company for a while. Then I got so involved in nursing, I let it go."

"Oh my God! What a blessing. I would love to have you be my wedding planner. It must have been meant for us to meet."

"That's destiny."

Misty and I tapped wineglasses as if we were giving a toast and took another gulp of wine.

Chapter 10

"Bitch Nigga"

Poppo

After I dropped Calico off at Norfolk International Airport, I checked my voice mail. Jewel had called me earlier, but I didn't want to answer, with Calico in my presence. I was sure she'd left a message.

"Are you gon' do this shit or what? 'Cause, on the real, it's gonna get done with or without you. So you gonna be a player in the game or a fucking water boy?"

I took the phone from my ear and looked at it. Listening to her message really pissed me off. It was like even this chick was taking me for a bitch. I wondered if I had the word *bitch* written on my fucking forehead, or if that shit Calico had was contagious.

I called Jewel back. My first instinct was to let that little bitch have it, but instead I decided to hear her out.

"Poppo, what the fuck is going on?" she said as soon as she picked up the phone. "You bitching up on me or what?"

Fuck this! This bitch got me fucked up. Without saying a word, I straight hung up on her ass, not thinking twice about it. I thought I had the patience to tolerate the little attitude she was giving, but I guess I didn't.

Ring! Ring!

When Jewel called right back, I put her in her place this time. "Yo," I answered the phone, "you gon' have to bring that shit down a few notches, ma."

"I'm saying . . . I thought we had a deal?"

"Jewel, I'm a man of my word. I got you, baby girl. This shit takes planning. Calm the fuck down. Have a drink or something. Let me do my shit. I gotta do it where there is no repercussions. But if this nigga makes you nervous, then you will be happy to know Calico is on his way back to California. He was only in VA to look for this bitch Sasha."

"Sasha? What he want with her? Don't tell me he dealing with that sheisty bitch!" Jewel snapped.

"Nah, ma, not at all. That nigga want to deal with her on some whole other shit." Then I suggested, "Why don't we meet up? I don't really do the phone thing."

"Okay. I feel you. What about that little Mexican spot off of Newtown and Virginia Beach Boulevard."

Jewel picked a real inconspicuous spot. For sure no one would have ever seen us up there.

"Cool. Meet you there in about an hour," I told her. "When I see you, I'll get you up to speed on everything."

"A'ight." Jewel hung up the phone.

I had decided to meet up with Jewel not only because I wasn't into the phone thing, but I needed to see her face to face so I could read her. Deep inside, I still didn't quite trust that bitch, so I was proceeding with caution.

I knew exactly what my plans were. I was gonna use Sasha to lure Calico to Atlanta, and once I got him there, I was gonna let him have it. I needed to get that nigga in an unfamiliar area. A place where I knew he had no alliance. That would make my job all the easier. I had shit all mapped out, but I was planning to tell Jewel as little as possible, at least until I felt I could trust her a little more.

After leaving the airport, I made a quick stop by Mo Dean's to pick up a few dollars from Murdock, a nigga that owed me money from a little business we'd arranged a few days earlier. I spotted his car as soon as I pulled into the parking lot. Luckily he was sitting in his car when I pulled up. I parked right next to him. I wanted to get shit done quick so I could shoot up the boulevard and meet up with Jewel.

"What up, man?" I said through the car window.

"Ain't shit."

Murdock got out of his car, and I unlocked the doors so he could hop in mine.

"Here you go." He handed me a wad of money with rubber bands separating them.

"What's this?" I always asked niggas how much they were giving me off the jump, to prevent any confusion.

"Five grand for now?"

"Five grand for now? When am I gonna see the other ten?" I asked, a little aggravated that Murdock didn't have all of my loot.

"I got you, Poppo. I just need a little while longer."

"Yeah, okay, nigga." I placed the money in the glove box then locked it. "Do I need to count after you?" I asked, even though I was gonna count the money, regardless of what Murdock said.

"It's all there, man. Have I ever shorted you before, muthafucka?"

"Nah, nigga. You know better than that. Now get out my car. I got shit to do. Gotta make this paper!"

"Gone!"

Murdock hopped out of my car, and I began to back out of the parking spot. I watched as he walked up to the barbershop next to Mo Dean's and started talking to a couple of guys that stood out front. By the time

I reached the end of the parking lot, the police was flooding the place. I busted a right turn onto Virginia Beach Boulevard and never looked back.

"Whew!" I let out a deep breath. I'd just made it. I ain't have shit on me but I wasn't trying to be in that fucking mix up. I turned up the radio and relaxed as I passed Booker T. Washington High School.

Werp! Werp!

No sooner than I thought I was safe from danger, I heard sirens behind me. "Gotdamn!" I said to no one in particular. I pulled over and waited for the officer to come to the car. I watched from my side- and rearview mirrors as he walked up. Then I rolled down my window.

"License and registration please."

"Can I ask why you pulled me over?" I asked as I gave the officer the information he'd asked for.

"I've been following you for some time. I got behind you after you pulled out of the shopping center on Church Street. You were swerving. Have you been drinking today, sir?"

"Yeah, right." I laughed. I knew everything this cop was saying was bullshit. He just needed a reason to pull me over.

"Well, you don't seem drunk, and I don't smell any alcohol, but let me run your license. If everything comes back okay, I'll send you off with a warning."

"Yes, sir," I said, just trying to cooperate. It's when cats act all nervous or aggressive that cops harass their ass even more. I waited and waited for the officer to come back.

After about five minutes he walked back to the car. He had his right hand on his cuffs. After seeing that, I already knew what time it was.

"Could you step out of the car please?"

That was my confirmation. This nigga was about to take me to jail. "What am I being arrested for?" I asked as I stepped out of the car.

"Driving on a suspended license?"

"What?" I asked, knowing what this nigga was saying couldn't be true.

"You had a ticket a few months back that you never paid. It resulted in your license being suspended."

"Nah, man. I paid that," I explained. "I got the receipt in my wallet."

"Save the excuses for the magistrate, man. Watch your head." The officer put me in the backseat of his car.

I was pissed off as I took a quick ride down the street and around the corner to Norfolk City jail. This was truly some bullshit. I had paid that damn ticket and even had the receipt to prove it, and I still was going to jail on a damn suspended license.

When we drove through the gates, the officer escorted me inside the jail and sat me in the holding tank. I sat there patiently as I waited to speak to the magistrate. I shook my head in disgust as I looked at the drunk that sat beside me covered in vomit and piss. Then I glanced over at the prostitute that sat on the bench across from me, smacking on her gum like it was the last piece of Bubblicious on earth. She stared me in the face, constantly giving me the eye. I watched as the people who were getting released walked past me and out the back door. I could only wish I was in their shoes.

"Terrell Johnson," an officer called out to me.

"Yes."

"Right this way, man."

I followed the officer to fingerprinting. Five minutes later my picture had been taken, and I was done with fingerprinting.

I had to see the magistrate next. As I sat waiting on him, I could see his office from the window. Through the crack of the door, I could see some fine-ass chick standing, her hair pulled up in a curly ponytail. She had that good hair, the kind that curled up when it got wet. She was dressed in D&G jeans that was tight to death and gripped her plump ass just right.

Minutes later, she was no longer in sight, and the magistrate was walking into the room. As soon as he was settled in front of me, I explained my situation. I told him that I'd paid my ticket and had the receipt to prove it. Come to find out, the reason my shit was suspended was because, after I paid the ticket to the court clerk, I was supposed to take the receipt to DMV and get my license reinstated. Lucky for me, the magistrate had mercy, and he let me out on a personal release bond, where no bondsman was needed, just my signature saying I will appear in court.

Thirty minutes later, I was one of those people getting released that I'd admired earlier.

I sat outside the precinct waiting on a cab so I could go pick my car up from the pound. Just my luck, the same chick I'd seen earlier came strolling out the precinct door.

"Hey, beautiful." I couldn't let her pass by without saying a word.

"What's up?"

"What's a woman like you doing in a place like this?"

"Handling business. But I'm sure I could guess what a thug like you is doing in a place like this. Your second home, I bet."

That bitch had just gone from beautiful to beast. At that time I realized what they said about a person being pretty until they open their mouth was true.

"You know what, ma . . . I'm not gonna even entertain that bullshit. You have a nice day." I walked away when I noticed my cab had arrived.

Chapter 11

"Always on the Grind"

Sasha

I'd managed to lay low and lived to see another two weeks. Eager to get on my grind, I called Diablo up to see if he was ready for me to work.

Like clockwork, his package had arrived, and he had work for me. I wasted no time dropping my kids off at my parents' house, kissing them good-bye, and hopping on the interstate and heading back to Atlanta.

After an hour of driving, I arrived at Crossroads Bar and Grill, Diablo's newly opened sports bar. Although he wasn't open for business when I arrived, I walked in to see a pretty busy atmosphere. Knowing I was wanted on the streets, I was a little paranoid when walking in.

I immediately located Diablo, and we took a seat in a booth in the corner, from where I had a clear view of everything in the club. Even though there were groups of guys gathered about in different areas, I took a few moments to check out each of them.

First, I scanned a group of guys gambling in one section of the club. None of them looked familiar. Next, I checked out a group that played a game on the PlayStation 3 and none of them looked suspect.

Finally, feeling comfortable, I directed my attention toward Diablo. I asked him, "So what's the deal?"

He told me, "Well, I got a few deliveries you can take care of for me—one in Florida, the other in Alabama, and the last just around the corner in Fort Valley."

"Oh, I got you. All those are around the corner for me. You know I got you."

"Cool. So we'll set you up for Alabama first."

"A'ight," I said, anxious to get my hands on my first little piece of dough, "I'm ready now."

"A'ight den. Let's do this. Drive around to the back of the club."

I did just as Diablo had instructed and drove to the back.

Diablo brought out the packages of cocaine and told me to stand back. I almost fainted as I watched him take off the door panel of my new car. I knew he had to hide the shit in a secure area, but just seeing the door panel off my car like that fucked me up.

Oh, well, it's all part of the game. It'll be well worth it in the end, I thought as I looked on.

I knew in the end everything would end in my favor. That's one thing I always made sure of. My motto was, why settle for milk when you can have the cow? Just like that shit with Jewel—sure, she was a good friend and she looked out for a bitch—but why would I keep waiting for a handout, when I could easily take hers and do my own thing?

Chapter 12

"Back on the Scene"

Touch

"Hey, Touch. What's good witcha?" "Man, you looking a'ight. Can't even tell a nigga got shot." "Long time no see, big homie."

Everybody dapped me up as I stepped on the scene.

Just as I'd done when standing on my throne at Club Encore New Year's night, I held both of my hands in the air in a kingly fashion. "Yeah, y'all niggas know what time it is. The king is back."

I had just walked in "A New Look," a barbershop where all the ballers and street niggas went to get their hair cut. Behind the barbershop was another room with a pool table and a crap table, where men came to smoke weed, brag and talk shit, and lie about all the money they had and bitches they fucked. The truth be known, more business transactions took place there than corporate America handled on the golf course.

The spot was packed, which made my entrance all the more dramatic. The whole barbershop atmosphere made a nigga feel real dapper, just from the smell of aftershave and powder, the sound of clippers, and rap music that played in the background. This was a man's thing. Nothing like a fresh cut and shave to make a man feel like a man. I was already jiggy with my gear and an added fresh cut was exactly what I needed to make me feel like my old self. I hopped in Mike's chair and requested my usual "edge-up." I wanted and needed to feel like "that nigga" again.

This was the first time I'd been out since my recovery. I was determined to go back in public holding my head high, to let niggas know I wasn't scared of the streets. Sure, I'd gotten shot, but I wasn't letting that shit hold me down. I was strapped with my Glock and dressed in the best. Although I only wore a pair of Robin's jeans, a plain beige D&G thermal shirt, and a fresh pair of wheat Timberlands, it was the Louis Vuitton scarf and skullcap that really set it off. I was finally walking with no assistance, free from walker and cane, so I was feeling on top of the world.

As Mike prepared to line me up, everyone gathered around me to shout me out and sincerely seemed happy to see me. They acted like I was Lazarus being resurrected from the dead, which, in a sense, I was, or better yet, like I was some return war hero from Iraq.

These streets were at war, and that ain't no joke. I could have died, fucking with that damn Calico, and I'd planned to dead that nigga as soon as I located his snake ass.

When I finished getting my cut, a few niggas gave me pounds, tapped shoulders, did the infamous hand-shake that all street cats do.

Raz, another heavy drug nigga on the streets, called out, "Hey, I heard you and Jewel gon' tie that knot."

"Yeah, we decided to do that thang," I said, acting nonchalant.

"Word on the streets is, Jewel got a diamond on her finger so big, it's making bitches sick!" Mike said.

"Yeah, sort of like mine." I gave them a glimpse of the ice I was holding.

"Y'all niggas doing it . . . living large," Raz chimed back in.

"What you mean, nigga? I'm trying to be like you," I said jokingly to Raz.

Suddenly the shop was filled with boisterous sounds of admiration and compliments. Everyone stood around and examined my platinum wedding band with my engraved initials boldly lifted across the band. Jewel had picked this ring out to match hers, which was just as large.

"Man, that ring is sick!"

"Damn, nigga! I ain't never seen no ring like that."

The dick riders started to add their praises.

"Hey, my lady says y'all niggas gon' put on the wedding of the century. They say Barack Obama and Michelle's inauguration ain't gon' have nothing on y'all thang. We got our invitation the other day."

This started a round of everyone saying they did or didn't get their invitation.

I held up my hands good-naturedly. "Hold up. I'll make sure Jewel get y'all niggas your invitation. If you don't get one, on the real, everyone here today is officially invited," I said, knowing Jewel would have a fucking fit if she knew I invited everyone from the barbershop. Knowing her, she didn't send them an invite on purpose.

I finally felt like I was in my element again. I was back, back on center stage where I belonged. All of a sudden, the room fell quiet. I was still popping shit with one of my niggas when I heard somebody whisper, "Poppo's here."

I looked up to see that bitch-ass nigga standing in the door, staring at me. In one quick motion, I went for my Glock, which was in the holster hooked on my belt. My first instinct was to kill his bitch-ass, but I knew I was in a public place, filled with snitches. I knew wherever Poppo was, Calico wasn't too far away. I threw my left hand in the air as to say, "What's up?" I didn't want to have to light the barbershop up, but I would, if I had to.

To my surprise, Poppo threw both hands up in the air on some white-flag, I-surrender shit, letting me know he wasn't trying to beef, at least not at that point. I didn't trust that nigga as far as I could see his scandalous ass, though.

"Hey, nigga, you need to relax. Just consider me your savior," Poppo said in a low tone as he passed me.

Everyone's eyes beamed on that nigga Poppo, their ears almost peeled back. Poppo looked just like one of those 2Pac-ass West Side muthafuckas too, dressed in Converse, jeans, and a flannel shirt. This cat was a fucking joke.

"Nigga, what is you talking about?" I screwed my faced up and wondered how his bitch ass could ever be my savior.

"Ask your bitch."

I could feel my temper rising. "What the fuck you say?" I started to rush his ass, but everyone grabbed me and held me back.

Poppo looked at me and said, "I ain't got no beef with you, little homie. Just ask your old lady what it is." With that, he left.

Although I stayed and let the African broad in the shop braid my hair, my mind was churning, and I was burning up inside. *Ain't life a bitch? I almost got killed, my wifey stands by me, then the next thing I know, that bitch is trying to do me.*

Chapter 13

"The Run-in"

Poppo

I walked out the barbershop wondering if I'd just fucked things up. It was bad enough I had missed my meeting with Jewel when I'd gotten arrested, and I hadn't heard from her since. Then I get into a fucking argument with Touch. I probably shouldn't have said shit about nothing, but that shit just came out of nowhere. I never expected to run into that nigga, Touch. Then it was how this nigga came at me. What the fuck was I suppose to do? Bitch up? Nah, I wasn't about to let that shit happen. But I should have been a little smarter about how I handled shit 'cause, if Touch didn't know about the plan, for sure it was gonna bring problems between him and his bitch. I was expecting a call from Jewel soon enough.

Ring! Ring!

My phone rang sooner than I'd expected. I thought it was Jewel. I looked down at my phone. To my surprise it was Murdock.

"What up, nigga? You ready for me?" I said, hoping this nigga had my ten grand.

I'd been waiting some time for my dough, and a nigga was getting restless. For a minute I thought he had bucked on me for my money. I had actually called that nigga a few times and left a couple of threatening messages. Sometimes that's what it took to get a reaction out of a nigga.

"I got a little something for you, man. You can come check me at the Caribbean spot."

"I'm on my way."

It took no time for me to arrive at our usual spot, Mo Dean's. I walked in the restaurant to find Murdock sitting at the bar.

"What up, duke?" I dapped him up.

"Can I get you a drink?" Murdock offered.

"Nah, man. I ain't here for that. Let me get that off of ya, so I can get out of here. You know I don't like hanging around out here. This spot getting hot. I got locked up on some bullshit the last time I was out here fucking with you."

"Yeah, man. The fucking police flooded the joint as soon as you left that day. They had niggas lined up on the wall, searching cats and running IDs. I was lucky though, everything with me was straight. A couple of niggas got locked up for possession, and a few niggas had warrants."

"Damn! That's fucked up. So what you got for me?" I asked, getting back to business.

"Fifteen."

"Fifteen? You only owe me ten. Did you forget you already paid me five? As much as I would love to take your money, I won't do that to you."

"Nah, fifteen hundred." Murdock handed me the small stack of money.

"Fifteen hundred? What the fuck is really going on, Murdock? You trying to play a nigga or what? I feel like you trying to play me." My patience was running thin with Murdock. He'd been holding on to my money way too long now.

"Come on, Poppo. Man, you know I would never try to play you. We ain't never had no problem with money. Trust me, Poppo, I got you, man."

"You said that same shit the last time we met up. I can't keep hearing the same bullshit. You got one week, nigga. Rob somebody. Fuck it! Rob a bank! But do what the fuck you gotta do to get me my fucking dough." I put the little change Murdock gave me in my pocket then walked away.

Days passed and I ain't hear from Jewel about my little run-in with Touch, so I figured shit was as usual. And I wasn't about to call her so she could tell me something different, 'cause once I went through with the shit, she couldn't renege on the deal. Or, in turn, I would have to deal with her and her bitch nigga too.

So Calico was on his way to Atlanta, and like always, I was on my way to the airport to pick him up. But this time I didn't mind, because I knew this would be the last time. I'd spent years flying here and driving there to deliver packages and pick up money while he sat in California and collected the money off of all my hard work, sweat, and blood. Hell, I had a crib, family, and baby mother in Cali that I wanted to spend time with too. Instead, I was always on the road for that nigga, hopping from telly (hotel) to telly, living out of a fucking suitcase.

I spotted Calico as soon as I bent the corner. Like a proud chauffeur, I pulled up with a smile on my face, trying not to show one sign of deceit on my face.

Chapter 14

"Fucked-up Luck"

Calico

I'd never been so happy to get the fuck off a plane in my life. Hours on a plane from Los Angeles to Atlanta with crying babies, stinking-ass niggas, and no weed was straight fucking torture. As soon as I exited the airport and hopped in the car with Poppo, I sparked up the "kush." I took in one deep pull and let it marinate then let it out slowly. Almost instantly a nigga was re-laxed.

"What up, duke?" Poppo greeted me as soon as I got in the car.

"You, nigga. You fucking slipping. You got a nigga on the road and shit when you know a nigga wanted. I'm trying to fucking lay low."

"Speaking of wanted, how the fuck you fly anyway?"

"I flew as Thomas Jones, nigga. I used a fake ID. You know you can buy those a dime a dozen in the hood."

"I knew you had something up your sleeve."

"Nuff of that shit. Where we headed, nigga? And you got yo' heat?" I asked right away, never really trusting Poppo.

He was the reason I was forced to take a trip to Atlanta anyway. This nigga had been slipping lately. I couldn't understand why so many days had passed and this bitch Sasha was still breathing. And when I questioned this nigga about it, he had all kinds of excuses. It wasn't until I threatened to kick his ass that he started acting like he had some damn sense. He'd heard from one of his boys that Sasha was working for his man, Diablo. On top of that, Diablo was about his paper and was looking for a West Coast connection, so he was definitely a nigga I needed to holla at. I figured I could kill two birds with one stone—befriend this nigga, make some money, and set up an easy kill for Sasha's snake-ass.

"I gotta make a stop. Then after that we headed straight to Diablo's spot." Poppo handed me the gun from his waist.

We drove for about fifteen minutes. Then I noticed we were in a rough area. We were obviously in the hood. Niggas were walking around with oversized white tees, jeans to their knees, do-rags and fitted caps. Everybody looked fucking suspect, like they were just looking for trouble. Being that I was on the run, I knew this wasn't the place for me. I was sure the police lived in areas like this hood.

"Where the fuck we at, nigga?" I asked, not feeling too secure with my surroundings.

"Bankhead. Don't worry, this shit will be real quick."

Poppo pulled up to a set of rundown apartments and jumped out the car.

"A'ight, nigga. Just hurry the fuck up." I pulled out the gun that he had given me earlier from my waist and put one bullet in the head.

I constantly monitored my surroundings as I waited for Poppo to come back. I couldn't take the chance of being caught up in some bullshit. I pulled out my cell to check the time and noticed I had a missed call from my baby mother.

One complete minute hadn't passed before the car door opened and I was face to face with a dope fiend carrying a butcher knife.

"Give me your fucking money!" he demanded.

Almost instantaneously, like a reflex, I lifted my gun and pulled the trigger. *Click!*

Nothing. The fucking gun had jammed on me. I knew this was do-or-die, so my mind went straight into survivor mode.

Bam! I busted the fiend in the head with the butt of the gun, knocking him to the ground.

Just then Poppo walked up. "What the fuck is going on, man?"

"Nothing, nigga. Your piece-of-shit gun almost got me killed. That's all."

"What you mean?"

"Just get me the fuck out of here!" I said, pissed the fuck off.

Poppo hit the gas, and we skidded off.

I exhaled and shook my head as I thought about things as we drove toward the interstate. *I knew this neighborhood was bad luck.* Relieved that I'd escaped without injury or jail, I relaxed and unjammed Poppo's little bullshit gun and placed it snug in my waist.

Minutes later, we pulled up to Crossroads Bar and Grill. Although the club was closed, it was still niggas everywhere, cats in one corner playing Madden on the projector screen, another set of cats gambling in the next corner, and the owner, Diablo, in another spot having what looked like a serious conversation with another cat.

Always willing to take a gamble, I immediately started watching the dice game. It looked like Diablo was gonna be busy for a minute, so I decided to get in on the game.

My luck was running good, and I was killing those country-ass A-town niggas when Poppo came over and interrupted the game.

"Diablo, ready to holla at you, man."

With that, I grabbed up my money and walked away. I counted my money as I walked toward Diablo. I'd won fifteen hundred dollars in that little bit of time.

Poppo introduced us, and I carried the conversation from there. There was no need for a bunch of talking. It was understood niggas was there to make money.

"Look, my shit is on point. I can get however much coke you need. I get my shit from across the border, so it's top-notch. I been bringing this shit over from the West Coast to the East Coast for years, and I had VA on lock, so I know can't nobody else make you a better offer." I continued by telling my numbers.

After a short negotiation, we had an agreement. The deal was set, and it was time for me to get the fuck out of dodge. I instructed Poppo to get me to my hotel. A nigga was wanted, and I wasn't trying to spend too much time on the streets.

Minutes later Poppo pulled up to a hotel right off the interstate on La Vista Road. He went in and reserved the room then came back.

"Room one twenty-four," he said and handed me the card key.

I grabbed my bags and went straight to my room. Once in the room, I kicked off my shoes, laid my piece-of-shit gun on the nightstand, and laid across the bed with remote in one hand and dick in the other as I began to flip through the television channels. Moments later, I began to drift off to sleep.

What seemed like no more than thirty minutes into my nap, a hunger pang hit my belly like a right hook. I woke up, grabbed the guest book, and flipped through the pages to see what nearby restaurants delivered. I chose to go with pizza.

I decided to roll a joint while I was waiting for my pizza. I pulled out my deodorant and rolled it until the bar was completely out. Beneath it was a quarter of kush. Then I searched my bag for Backwoods to roll it with.

"Fuck!" I yelled out loud.

I was experiencing a weed smoker's worst nightmare. I had weed and no fucking paper to roll it with. For a second I considered ripping a few pages from the Bible to roll up, but something inside of me just wouldn't let that happen. With the shit I was in, I needed the Lord on my side, so I couldn't take the risk of disrespecting His Holy Word. I could possibly wait until the pizza arrived to smoke, but I knew after I ate I would definitely have to smoke. It was like dessert after dinner.

I called up Poppo. That nigga had to come back and take me to the store or bring me some Backwoods or something.

"Yo!"

I was relieved Poppo answered his phone right away. "Poppo, where you at?"

"Across town. What's up?"

"Man, I need some Backwoods bad."

"A'ight, I got you. Give me about thirty minutes."

Poppo said exactly what I wanted to hear.

Remembering my baby mother had called earlier, I called Cali to talk to my kids as a way to pass time. And that's exactly what happened. I was so wrapped up in my conversation with my four kids and two baby mothers, I didn't even realize forty-five minutes had passed.

As soon as I hung up the phone with them and was about to call Poppo, the pizza arrived. Feeling hungry as a hostage, I decided to eat first and then call Poppo after.

Once my belly was full, I called Poppo, and the phone went straight to voice mail. It didn't even ring. I hung up and called right back. I got the same thing. I tried two more times, and each time I got straight voice mail.

"Fuck it!"

Fed up, I put on my shoes, and grabbed a few dollars. I was trying to lay low and not show my face too much because I was in Atlanta to do Sasha in. Plus, I had that outstanding warrant. But a nigga would straight lose his mind without weed, so I headed out of the hotel and to a little corner store I saw at the end of the street.

I was excited to see exactly what I needed behind the counter as soon as I walked in. I stood in line at the busy store, anxious to get my papers and get back to my hotel room. For three minutes I'd stood in line, and it hadn't moved at all. For a minute, I thought about leaving and going to the gas station across the street, but I figured I may as well stay, since I was already here.

I looked down at my vibrating phone. It was Poppo calling. I wasn't even trying to talk to that fool at this point. I pressed *ignore*, sending him to voice mail. Finally, the line started to move and minutes later I was at the counter paying for my Backwoods to roll up my weed. As I reached for my change and bag, I heard a commotion at the front door.

"Don't move! Everybody, down. Get on the fucking ground!"

Narcotic police agents had flooded the place.

Muthafuckas, I thought to myself as I lay on the ground. Running wasn't even an option. I was surprised when the cops ran right past me and to the back of the store then started bringing out the workers in cuffs, while another officer cuffed each of the customers, searched us, and ran our identification.

How bad can a nigga's luck be? Talk about wrong
place at the wrong time. I had, just by chance, walked
into a store that was a known drug spot. I felt confident
I would be walking out though. Once again the fake ID
had come in handy. One by one the officers had begun
to release the customers that had no drugs on them
and whose names had come back clear.

One of the officers approached me. "Can I get your
ID?"

I searched every pocket for my wallet. *Fuck!* I thought
to myself in a panic. I had left my wallet in the hotel
room.

"No ID?" the officer asked, noticing my frustration.

"Nah, man. I can give you my name, date of birth,
and social, though," I said, knowing I had the information from my fake ID memorized.

I ran off the information to the officer as if it was my
own. He jotted it down and went back to his car to run
a check. I waited patiently with a few others, as another
cop watched over us.

Minutes later, the first officer returned. "Mr. Jones,"
he called out to me, while pulling out his handcuffs.

What the fuck! I wondered what the hell was going
on.

I didn't respond, I just looked at him with face of
confusion.

"We're gonna have to take you in, son. You have an
outstanding warrant out for nonpayment of child support."

*I be damn! I knew I should have stayed my black
ass in Cali. There is no way one man's luck could be
so fucked up!* I already knew what was in store for me.
Once I got to the jail, they would run my fingerprints
and find out who I really was. From there, I would be
extradited to VA. My shit was fucked up. I was going
straight to jail without a get-out-of-jail-free card.

Chapter 15

"The Wedding's Off"

Touch

When I'd gotten home from the barbershop, I'd planned to let Jewel's conniving ass have it. But the rational side of me just couldn't allow that to happen so quickly. It took all I had, but I went on with the days as usual while I decided on the best way to approach things.

I was the type of nigga that liked to have all my ducks in a row, so when I came with it, I came hard. I liked to be confident that it wasn't shit a bitch or nigga could say to lie their way out of things. I knew I was about to make a hell of an allegation, so I wanted to be sure I had my facts straight when I did it.

After running that day at the barbershop through my head over and over, along with all the other shit that had happened during New Year's, I was sure that bitch was on some sheisty shit. My fucking blood was boiling as I waited patiently for her to come in from the beauty salon.

When she got home, she rushed up to me all kissy-poo and shit. She was wearing leggings, a fitted sweater dress that grabbed tight to every curve of her perfect body, and was smelling of my favorite perfume, Viktor & Rolf Flowerbomb. I had to admit, that shit was quite tempting, but that alone wasn't gonna work this day. I had to give it to her though. She was a good actress. She could've won a fucking Academy Award for the act she put on, and she could have really fooled an amateur, but I wasn't buying the bullshit she was selling.

Before I could dig into her ass, I noticed she had some broad with her. I rolled my eyes at this woman, but Jewel didn't seem to pay me any attention. "Who is this?" I grunted, glaring at her new woman friend. I thought Jewel would have learned her lesson with Sasha.

"Oh, baby, this is Misty. Don't you remember? She's the nurse who took care of us when we were in the hospital. And, lo and behold, she does freelance wedding planning on the side. I hired her as our wedding planner."

"We don't need a wedding planner," I mumbled.

Misty must have picked up my bad mood, because she grabbed her oversized Chanel bag and stepped toward the door. "Well, I'll see you, Jewel. We'll talk later."

"Okay, Misty." Jewel walked her to the door and waved to her.

"Bye, Jewel. Talk to you soon."

Jewel turned back to me like nothing was wrong and said, "Baby, come check out my bridesmaids' colors.

They're going to wear lavender. I don't want no loud, ghetto-looking colors. Yeah, baby, this wedding is gonna have class all the way."

I followed Jewel to her computer room, where she had all the latest bridal magazines spread out on the floor, an indication that she had gone too far. Plus, she'd hired a damn wedding planner. I didn't even think she knew all this stuff, but obviously, Miss Bourgeois Virginia Beach Bitch knew her shit, when it came to wedding time.

And worse still, she knew money wasn't coming in like regular. I'd been laid up for a few months now, so I hadn't been doing no work. And the last count I had, this broad had spent about fifty thousand on the wedding, and we ain't even walked down the fucking aisle. Just thinking about it made steam come out my ears.

"And baby, we're gonna have orchids and baby's breath." Suddenly, Jewel looked up, as if for the first time she had tuned into my sour mood.

"Baby, what's the matter?" she asked, her face twisted into a corkscrew of concern.

This made me all the madder, that she could sound so innocent. *Yeah, right, bitch!* "You know what's the matter." I grabbed her by the neck and looked her in the eye.

She looked all surprised and shit. "No, I don't, baby. What is it? I ain't no mind reader."

"I can't believe you'd do me like this, Jewel."

"What are you talking about?"

"I'm out at the barbershop and this nigga Poppo talking shit to me, like you and him running game together."

"What the hell are you talking about, Touch?"

"So you fucking that nigga now?"

"What? I'm with you every day. I sleep with you every single night. So how the hell do I have time to be fucking somebody else?"

"Well, you gon' tell me something. How is this nigga talking about he gon' be my savior?"

"How the hell am I supposed to know what that nigga was talking about? You know he ain't nothing but Calico's little bitch. You can't believe nothing he says."

"Yeah, I should have never fucked with you in the first place. You the one who was Calico's bitch."

"How you gon' throw that in my face, Touch? Did you forget I made us? I'm the reason we have this house, the cars, the lifestyle of the ghetto fabulous. It was my money from ghostwriting and my connect with TMF that got us here! Oh—and who took care of you when you were sick? I even washed your ass for you and wiped it when you had to shit."

"Oh, just a regular Florence Nightingale. I knew you was gone throw that shit up in my face. But, bitch, you didn't have to do nothing for me."

"Nah, I'm much more than a night nurse. Just so that you know, I was hollering at Poppo to save your ass! I promised to put him on if he took care of Calico for you."

"What the fuck I look like to you? You must take me for some little bitch. You really got me fucked up. Do your thing, Jewel. I'm out." I grabbed my keys, walked out the front door, and never looked back.

I was fuming as I drove. I didn't know where I was headed, but I knew I needed to get the fuck away from Jewel. I wondered what type of cat she took me for. *Do I look like some type of weak nigga that need protection?* My weeks of rehab must have fucked her head up. That broad was tripping.

Finally cooling off a little bit I decided to go to one of my old spots, Mo Dean's Caribbean restaurant and lounge. As soon as I walked in, I felt right at home. The atmosphere hadn't changed a bit.

My boy Raz spotted me as soon as I walked in. "Touch, what up, nigga!"

"Ain't shit, nigga." I headed straight to the bar.

I hadn't been sitting a whole minute before I felt someone hug me from behind and caress my manhood. Off the jump, I knew exactly who that was. It was only one chick that came on hard like that, Dirty Diana.

"What up, baby girl?" I spun around on the barstool to face her.

"Looks like you," she said, referencing my standing dick.

"So what you gon' do about it?" I said, knowing exactly how she got down.

"Oh, you know the deal. I ain't trying to hurt you though. I heard you got shot. Everything healed up okay? You know I puts it down, and I don't want to be responsible for no injuries." She giggled.

"I'm strong and long as a horse." I pulled Diana between my legs and squeezed her ass tight, all the while reminiscing about the last time I fucked her.

Diana was a jump-off bitch that I'd fucked one night on a whim. I knew her face from the spot, but I never really paid her much attention. Hell, I ain't even know her name until the night I fucked her. Her body was tight, and the fuck was good, but every nigga with a little dough had ran up in that. I remember when I fucked her. She was on point, but as soon as we were done, that bitch had her fucking hand out for money. Needless to say, I gave it to her, and I would do it again too. Sad to say, but the fuck was definitely worth it.

Damn! Times were good before I hooked up with Jewel and got locked down. What the fuck was I thinking when I asked her to marry me? I was still gripping Diana's firm ass tight.

"Well, you know I'm working, so as soon as I get off—"

"Say no more." I cut her off mid-sentence, noticing my baby mother, Ciara, staring at me from the cut.

Although I missed my kids like crazy and wanted badly to see them, I wasn't trying to see that bitch. That last time I saw her, I had beat the shit out of her and ended up in jail. She, just like Jewel, just had to fuck Calico.

I turned back around to the bar, pretending to not even see her. If it wasn't for my pending case and the temporary restraining order she had on me, I would have gone over there and beat her ass again. There was no amount of beating that could be punishment enough for the line that bitch had crossed.

"Let me get a Grey Goose on the rocks."

"That's on me," one of my boys told the bartender. "Put all his drinks on my tab."

I spent the next hour, kicking it with my niggas and drinking Grey Goose like it was water. Before I knew it, I was fucked up.

"Yo, I'm out, niggas," I said to my boys as I scrambled to get off of my barstool.

"Hold on, nigga. We can't let you drive like that. You just got out the hospital from one injury. We can't send you right back."

"Oh, he straight," I heard a familiar female voice say.

I looked up to see my ex-girlfriend, Lisa. Ghetto spots like Mo Dean's wasn't her thing. "What you doing here?"

"Don't you worry about it. Just be happy I'm here and willing to help your drunk ass," she said, escorting me out the door.

I looked back to see Diana giving me a dirty look. Sure, I wanted to fuck that, but Lisa had taken over. Besides, I knew Diana was guaranteed pussy. I could hit that at any day any time. I was lucky to get an opportunity to get up in Lisa's stuff again because we'd broken up on bad terms. I was even surprised she had approached a nigga.

"Where did you park?"

"That way." I pointed.

Minutes later we were in my car.

"Where to?" Lisa asked.

"To my crib. Don't act like you don't know the way. You used to live there, remember?" I said, thinking back to the times Lisa and I used to kick it.

"Yeah, until you kicked me out for your ignorant-ass baby mother!"

"Yo, I ain't trying to hear that shit." My mind was on one thing and one thing only—pussy.

It was times like this that I was grateful I didn't sell or rent out my old crib out Bayside area, off of Newtown Road. We pulled up to my spot, and I stumbled out the car to the front door. Once inside I fell across the couch, lit up a cigarette, and called out to Lisa, who was heading up the stairs, apparently to my bedroom.

"What you doing, girl? Get naked. You know you giving me some ass tonight."

There was no way she was staying the night at my crib and not fuck, especially since she'd fucked up my plans of getting with Diana.

"I'm going to freshen up. Meanwhile, can you pour me some wine or something to help me relax, please?" she asked while walking upstairs.

"Nah, I ain't got nothing," I replied, shaking my head.

Just then my phone rang. I noticed I had three missed calls from Jewel already. At the time, I wasn't even trying to hear nothing her ass had to say.

Minutes later Lisa had come back downstairs with one of my T-shirts on. I lifted it up, only to see her neatly shaven pussy underneath.

"Excuse you." She pulled the shirt back down then straddled me.

She tried to kiss me, but I quickly turned my head.

"What? I can't get a kiss?"

I threw her on the couch and ripped her T-shirt and underwear off.

"Why you got to be so rough?" She rolled her eyes at me.

"Shut the fuck up!"

My phone rang another four times back to back. I knew it was Jewel blowing me up.

"Touch, you just tore my bra. This is a La Perla bra and panty set. Do you know how much this cost?"

"Of course, I do. Wasn't I the one buying you that shit when we were together? I probably bought this shit you got on now," I replied, cramming my dick into her dry pussy.

I figured she wasn't in the mood yet, but I was sure it wasn't anything the "king cobra" couldn't fix. And, just as I figured, a few minutes later, I was hearing those sweet moans and groans.

"Ride this dick," I ordered after turning her over to switch positions.

I had to admit, this bitch did have some good pussy. After we had finished fucking, she quickly fell asleep.

I tried to, but Jewel kept calling. Knowing her, she was probably trying to hunt my ass down. I was never the nigga to turn my phone off, because I always figured that the one time I turned it off would be the day something happened to my mom or kids and they couldn't reach me.

But Jewel was leaving a nigga with no choice. Once phone call number fifteen had come through, I was forced to turn off my phone to get some rest. *What a day!* I thought, drifting off to sleep.

Chapter 16

"Cheating Death"

Poppo

"Gotdamn!" I yelled as I hung up the phone with my boy.

He'd just given me the news that Calico was locked up. Most niggas would look at that shit as bad luck, but in his case, it was good luck. That nigga ain't even know he was minutes away from death. That fucking arrest saved his life. The reason I couldn't come for that nigga when he was calling me was because I was setting shit up so I could do him in. I was planning to pick him up and take him to the spot and dead his ass later in the day. But this time that nigga got away.

Ring! Ring!

I was surprised to see Jewel calling. I guess she'd heard the news too. "What up, ma?" I answered right away.

"You fucking tell me. That's what the fuck I want to know. What the fuck is up, Poppo?" Jewel yelled in the phone between tears.

I hadn't the slightest idea what the fuck she was snapping about. "Yo, yo, relax, mami. What's going on?"

"What the fuck did you say to Touch, Poppo? He came home talking some shit about me and you in cahoots together, and I can't be trusted. He even tried to say we were fucking! That's crazy, especially since I haven't talked to you in forever. I assumed you were playing games when you stood me up, and now I hear this shit?"

Right then I knew exactly what Jewel was talking about. It looked like Touch had finally broke the news to her. I personally wondered what the fuck took that nigga so long. I expected to get this call days ago. Already prepared for the wrath, I slipped right into character, becoming Mr. Concerned and Apologetic.

"Listen, Jewel. I'm sorry, baby. I didn't mean for shit to go down that way. That was my bad. A nigga wasn't thinking."

"Did you tell him that we were fucking, Poppo?"

"Nah, I would never do that. I'm a man of my word. You got to trust me. Besides, are we fucking?" I laughed.

"Hell, no!" she snapped back.

"All right, then. Bitch-ass niggas tell a whole bunch of people stupid shit like that. I'm a real nigga. Soon, my actions will show you that. I understand if you're sitting on the sideline as a skeptic right now though, especially since the last time we were supposed to meet I never made it. But about that day, I swear, ma . . . that shit was out of my control. I was on my way and I ended up getting locked up over some bullshit."

"Things are real bad for me, Poppo," Jewel cried out. "I'm fucked up in the game right now. I don't know what to think or who to trust. You don't understand the shit I've been through. I mean, look at this shit. Me and Calico use to be together. He was my man, Poppo, and now we're fucking enemies. Sasha was my best friend, and she stabbed me in the back. Touch was all I had, and now that shit is fucked. What the fuck am I supposed to do or think?"

"I feel you, baby girl. I understand you to the fullest. But I'm saying, I'm setting shit up, ma. Please, I just need you to be a little more patient with a nigga. This shit takes time. You feel me?"

"Yeah, but I can only be patient for so long," she whimpered.

"Don't worry. I got chu. Can I bring you lunch, dinner, or anything else that would cheer you up?" I asked in a concerned tone of voice, trying to throw in a little game. I thought it was the perfect opportunity. Bitches always slipped up when they're vulnerable.

"No, thanks. I'll be all right. I'm just ready to get things going."

"I know. I am too, so let me do my thing. You screaming in my ear ain't helping either one of us."

"Okay," Jewel said before hanging up the phone.

I was relieved that I was able to calm things down and smooth shit over.

Chapter 17

"Thin Line between Love and Hate"

Sasha

I was at my parents crib in Columbia when I got the word. I kept repeating the words of Detective Tarver in my head, *"We finally got him!"* That was the greatest news I could have ever heard.

Now that I knew Calico was locked up, I could finally move freely. I still wasn't trying to testify against him, but I'd told the detectives any information I could find out about Jewel and her affiliation with TMF. I figured this was my only opportunity to finally get Jewel out the picture for good. And once she was gone, I would move in on her throne, steal her king, and rule her empire. Finally, I would be the queen that I was destined to be.

I'd planned to only give them information that pointed toward Jewel. Hell, as far as I knew, she was the mastermind behind her and Touch's little fortune anyway. She was the one with the TMF connect. Because TMF was one of the biggest organized drug rings in the United States, I knew that saying those words to the detective would be like music to his ears.

I was still on some get-money shit. I had gained so much trust from Diablo, I'd gone from delivering packages to receiving them at my address for him. I was number one on the team. He trusted me more than he did some of his close boys, which worked in my favor. The more jobs I got, the more money I made.

I had an incoming call from Diablo.

"Hello?"

"Yo, when my daughter gets dropped off at your crib, I need you to take her to VA. Can you do that for me?" Diablo spoke in code. He wanted me to take the package I received at my house to Virginia.

I excitedly agreed. "No problem."

"Cool. Come see me when she arrives."

The timing couldn't have been better. An all-expenses paid trip to VA was exactly what the doctor ordered. This gave me the opportunity to get at Touch.

I packed my bags as I waited for the package to arrive. By the time I was finished packing, I'd received the delivery. I wasted no time packing it up and getting on the road. I ran by the club and hollered at Diablo then hit the interstate.

In eight hours flat I was in VA. I grabbed some food and got checked into my hotel and relaxed a little. I thought about calling Touch, but I wasn't sure how I could go about it. I mean, I did bust his girl in the head with a champagne bottle. I hoped he could look past that and focus more on that one night of perfect lovemaking we had shared.

It took a moment, but I finally got up enough courage to scroll through my phone to give him a call.

"Hello," Touch answered the phone in a fake female voice.

"Touch, stop disguising your voice."

He continued in his fake voice. "Hello. Who is this?"

"It's Sasha, fool."

"What the fuck you want?"

"Damn! It's like that? Why so much aggression?"

"What the fuck you want, Sasha?"

"Well, I'm in the area, and I was wondering if I could come check you. But before you answer, I need you to think about the last time you were in this phat pussy." I paused a minute. "Okay, now that you've had time to think about it, what's up?"

"Bitch, I'm in some phat pussy right now. And I wouldn't fuck your conniving ass with an AIDS-infected dick. Lose my number, bitch!" Touch followed his statement with a click in my ear.

That was the final straw. Touch had dissed me for the last fucking time. I didn't take rejection well. He was definitely going to feel my wrath. If he didn't know, he was about to learn that payback's a bitch. His name had officially been added to the get-back list. I was about to make his life a living hell and benefit from it all at the same time.

I called up Diablo.

"What up?"

"Oh my God, Diablo," I said, forcing out the words between fake cries.

"What's wrong?" Diablo yelled in a panic.

I purposely didn't answer. I just continued to cry uncontrollably, to add more drama to my act.

"Sasha!" Diablo yelled. "What the fuck is going on?"

"Touch robbed me," I lied. "He beat me up and robbed me."

"What the fuck you doing with that nigga?"

"I invited him over to my room to kick it. Once he got here and realized I had the package here, he straight robbed me."

"What? This nigga can't know that's my shit. Ain't no way he would fuck with my shit like that. Let me give that nigga a call."

"I'll call him on three-way. He probably won't answer your call, since he don't know the number."

I dialed Touch's phone.

Touch yelled into the phone as soon as he picked up,
"Bitch, didn't I say lose my number?"

"Yo, nigga, this Diablo."

"Diablo? What the fuck you doing with that broad?
What type of games y'all playing?" Touch asked, confused.

"Nah. The question is, what type of games you playing? What the fuck you doing with my shit?"

"Fuck you talking 'bout, man?"

"Sasha told me you robbed her. That's my shit,
Touch."

"Man, you believe that lying-ass bitch if you want to.
Fuck her! And as a matter of fact, fuck you too for calling me with that bullshit. I'm rich, nigga. I don't need
your little-ass shit." Touch disconnected the call.

"Don't worry about shit," Diablo said to me. "I'll handle this shit with him. You all right though?"

"I'm banged up a little, but I'll be okay."

I was happy as hell that Diablo had played right into
my little plan. I must say, Touch was right about one
thing—I was very conniving and believable.

"Cool. Call me if you need anything."

Chapter 18

"A New Woman"

Jewel

"You have reached the voice mail box of—" I hung up before the recording could finish. Not hearing Touch's voice and wondering what the fuck he was doing and where the hell he was at was driving me crazy. It had been an entire day since our argument, and I hadn't heard from him. I had called his phone nonstop for a whole hour straight, and all I got was straight voice mail. It had gotten to the point that I was starting to worry. I even called his mother, and she hadn't heard from him.

I didn't know what to think. I wondered if he was with another bitch. It was insulting to me, to keep being sent directly to his voice mail. I was starting to feel as if he didn't give a fuck about me or my feelings. *Was he just ignoring me because of the argument, or had he run into one of Calico's boys and was hurt or, even worse, dead?* My brain was racing.

I'd spent the past day sitting in the house, depressed and crying. I hadn't eaten anything or even bothered to wash my ass or brush my teeth. I picked up the phone to call Misty because she'd called several times earlier in the day and I didn't even bother to answer. I just wasn't in the mood for conversation.

"Hey, girl," I said, trying to sound a little upbeat.

"Jewel?" Misty asked, not even recognizing my voice.

"Yeah, it's me. What's up?"

"What's wrong, momma?"

"Girl, I'm down in the dumps. Sad as hell."

"Awwww. What's wrong, boo?" Misty asked, sounding concerned.

I explained to her the drama I had with Touch from beginning to end.

"I'm sorry to hear that. I'm coming over. Get up and get yourself together. We're gonna go out and have some dinner and drinks. Then we're gonna strategize on how to get your boo back."

"Okay. I'm getting up now. Give me about an hour."

"Cool. See you then."

I got off the phone with Misty then drug myself out of bed. I ran myself a hot bath, turned on Keyshia Cole's CD, *A Different Me*, and turned on the jets in the tub and soaked.

Thirty minutes later I was clean as a whistle and actually felt a little revived. I threw on some clothes, pulled my hair into a messy ponytail, and straightened up the house a little bit as I waited for Misty.

Ding-dong!

Misty had arrived right on time. She gave me a hug as soon as I opened the door. "Hey, hon. You ready?"

I wanted to just cry in her arms, but I took a deep breath, sucked it up, and put on a smile. "Yeah, I'm ready."

Misty tried to share words of inspiration as we headed to her truck. "This isn't a pity party," she said. "We're preparing for a victory. You're gonna get your boo back."

We ended up at a bar not far from my house called Pandemonium, which was the perfect atmosphere. We walked in and headed straight to the bar. Misty ordered our drinks as I got comfortable. Still a little shook from the New Year's incident, I skimmed the restaurant, just to get a feel of my surroundings.

"Oh my God!"

"What is it?" Misty asked, startled.

I stood up from my barstool and walked away immediately, totally ignoring her. It was like I was in a zone and no one or anything around existed as I headed toward the table in front of me.

"Well, I'm glad to know you're okay," I said in my most sarcastic tone, my heart racing. This moment, and what I would do and say, had crossed my mind many times, but now that I was faced with it, I didn't know if I was ready for it.

Touch didn't respond. He just looked up at me, disgust on his face.

"Hello? I'm talking to you. I was worried sick calling all over the place for you. I even called your mother."

"I ain't have shit to say to you," Touch said, looking down at his plate.

"You didn't have shit to say? I texted your ass nearly twenty times today. The least you could have done was let me know you were okay. Is that too much to fucking ask for, Touch?"

"I ain't have shit to say to you then, and I still don't have shit to say to you right now."

"What?" I wondered if this nigga had lost his fucking mind. Feeling disrespected, I began to get loud. "What you mean, you ain't got shit to say to me, Touch? After all the shit we've been through, you really don't have shit to say to me?"

The chick that sat beside Touch finally chimed in full of attitude. "Excuse me," she said. "I don't know if you noticed, but we're trying to have dinner here."

"Excuse me? No, excuse *you*," I responded, totally thrown off by this chick's comment. "I noticed, but I just don't give a fuck. Who the fuck are you anyway? I don't know if you noticed, but I'm wearing a ring. I'm trying to have a conversation with my fiancé. Let me repeat that—*fiancé*," I spat back, feeling like I was about to explode.

"Fiancé? Well, he wasn't your fiancé when he was all up in me last night." The chick then directed her attention toward Touch. "I see nothing has changed with you, Touch."

Dazed, I stood motionless as the bitch's words registered in my head. This whole ordeal was hitting me like a fucking freight train, head-on and with no time to run for cover. I had to wonder how we went from getting married one day to my man fucking another chick the next day. The realization sank in that my world was crumbling before my eyes.

It wasn't until I heard the chick say, "Fuck this! I'm out," that I snapped back to the moment.

"Yeah, bitch, that's the best thing for you. Be out."

The chick stopped dead in her tracks, turned around, and staring me in the face. "Or what?"

She was so close, I could feel the heat from her breath. For a moment I thought about getting out the pepper spray I carried in my handbag, but before I could do anything, I felt someone come between the chick and me.

"Or this!" Misty tossed her drink all up in the chick's face.

"We'll cross paths again," the skinny, shapeless chick with weave to her ass said, knowing she was no match for Misty and me.

I wondered how we hadn't crossed paths before. I knew Touch had a steady girlfriend before me, but the

only girl I'd actually seen from his past was his baby
mother. If I had to guess, this bitch probably was his
ex.

"What was that about?" Misty asked.

"Nothing at all. The bitch just got a little heated because I told her to step."

"Oh, okay. I was watching from the bar the entire
time. Everything looked cool, so I didn't intervene, but
when I saw that bitch come in your face, I rushed over.
I would have given her a beatdown if necessary."

We both laughed.

I directed my attention back toward Touch, who was
pulling out money from his wallet to pay for his meal.

"Oh, so you just gonna leave, Touch? We not gonna
talk about this? You don't feel like you owe me an explanation or nothing?"

"I don't owe you shit. I just want to be by myself right
now. I need some space. I'll be coming over to the house
to get my things." Touch dropped a hundred dollars on
the table then walked away, leaving me hanging.

Chapter 19

"Doing Hard Time"

Calico

I opened my eyes and looked around at the bricks and bars surrounding me. "I can't believe this shit." I was hoping this whole shit was a nightmare, but come to find out, I wasn't dreaming at all. My dick ached, my stomach was growling, and I needed a fucking spliff. I hopped off my bunk and headed to the phone. I hit up one of my jump-off bitches from Norfolk.

She accepted the collect call right away. "What's up, baby?"

"Fucked up, shortie. Thanks for taking the call. You know I got you."

"You know I got your back, boo."

"Look, I need you to make a call for me on three-way." "Not a problem."

I then called out Poppo's number to her.

Poppo answered right away, "Yo."

"What up, nigga?"

"Calico. What the fuck is good, man? I heard you got snatched, nigga."

"Man, it's a long story. I'll fill you in on that shit later. Right now I need you to call my people back home and let them know what's up, so they can get shit lined up to get me out this bitch. Then I need you to handle things with your boy in A-town for me. You gonna have to hold down the fort until I get this shit straight. You feel me?"

"Nuff said, nigga. Say no more. You know I got you. I'ma jump on shit right now. Gone." Poppo hung up the phone.

A few minutes later, the recording came on, warning us we had one minute left on the phone, so we wrapped things up and ended the call.

I returned to my bunk and tried to map something out. I knew I needed to get in touch with my moms and baby mother. They were the only ones I could really depend on to handle my money and make sure the lawyer was paid.

I'd learned my lesson about letting jump-off bitches hold money. That situation I had in the past when I was fucking with Jewel had taught me well. I had got locked up and had her collect my money. When it came time for her to pay my lawyer, no money was to be found. I had to straight threaten the bitch to get my shit back.

But, to be honest, this time it was that nigga Poppo I was a little worried about. I swear, lately that nigga had been on some bullshit. I couldn't quite put my finger on it, but it was just something about him that I just wasn't feeling.

After a few days had passed, I went for my first bond hearing, and was denied. I kinda expected that shit though. These muthafuckers wasn't trying to let a nigga out. Hell, I was a major fucking flight risk. My primary residence was "across the fucking U.S." Plus, I had a number of aliases. There was no way these niggas was gonna take a chance with me.

Even with all those odds against me, Natalia, my lawyer, was still talking some good shit. She was confident that I would eventually get a bond, and was telling me it may take more than a couple of tries. One thing about her though, her word was bond. She didn't sell a nigga dreams. She was always on her shit, and never let a nigga down.

It was visiting day, and cats were getting fresh cuts and edge-ups and shit, trying to look fresh for their chicks. I wasn't fucking with none of that shit though. For one, I couldn't see myself sitting between another nigga's legs while he braided my fucking hair. Next thing I know, I ain't getting no fucking visit.

I hopped on my bunk, grabbed my dick and rubbed on it until I fell asleep.

"Burroughs!" the CO called out my last name, waking me.

"Yo!" I yelled back.

"Visit."

Damn! Who the fuck is that? I wondered who the hell had come down to check a nigga. I hadn't even bothered telling no one my visiting day.

I followed the CO to the visiting room. I was surprised to see my mother and baby mother, Corrin, when I walked out. I wondered what the fuck they were doing there and how the hell they knew my visiting day. A nigga was actually glad to see a familiar face. I was grinning from ear to ear as I sat on the steel stool across from them.

"What y'all doing here?"

"What you mean? There is no way I was gonna leave my baby alone in jail all the way across the country."

"Ma, y'all ain't have to come out here."

"Well, we wanted to make sure everything was squared away," Corrin chimed in. "We going to see Natalia and straighten her out tomorrow."

"Yeah, go 'head and pay her. That's the most important thing. Everything else can wait. You talked to Poppo?"

"Nope. That's one reason I wanted to come here. I don't know what's up with your boy. Baby, I know you ain't gonna wanna hear this, but that nigga made a pass at me."

"What the fuck you say? Corrin, don't fuck with me." I felt immediate anger come over me.

"When he came to the house to collect the things to send down South, he kept making little comments about how my ass was so phat and what he'll do to me. And some shit about you ain't gon' be around to satisfy me, so I may as well give it up to him. He was talking so crazy, I had to ask this nigga if he was drunk or on that shit. Then the next thing I know, he grabs my ass. I was sure he'd lost his fucking mind. I had to smack some sense back into his ass.

"After that I gave him the things and rushed him out of the house. I haven't heard from him since. I even called him a couple of times and left messages about the paper, but he ain't called back. He acting like he dodging niggas or something. Then I hear niggas on the streets saying Poppo talking like you ain't never getting out, and he's the new boss. This nigga can't be trusted, baby."

"What?" It was almost like I could literally feel my blood boiling inside as I listened to the words Corrin spoke.

It felt as though my back was up against the wall. I was ready to kill a nigga, but I knew beating another nigga's ass in jail to blow off steam wasn't going to do nothing but add more charges to my rap sheet. One of the worst feelings in the world was knowing a bitch-ass nigga was tripping on the streets and it ain't shit you can do about it.

After my visit with my moms and baby mother, I wondered how the fuck I was going to make it through.

***

Five days had passed, which felt more like months, and the two special ladies in my life had already paid my lawyer in full. As usual, she was on her grind. I knew the time would soon arrive when I would be released from Virginia Beach hell, AKA Virginia Beach jail. And I knew when I was released I'd be on an unstoppable mission to get my fucking money. The first stop on the road would be a visit to check Poppo. I wondered if he was going to like having a gun in his damn mouth, or a knife clinging to his throat.

Chapter 20

"New Man in Town"

Poppo

"What up, Poppo?" Raz gave me a pound as I walked in the barbershop.

"Ain't shit, nigga. 'Look like money, smell like money,' you know the song, nigga," I said, feeling on top of the world.

Now that Calico was locked up, I was the king of the castle. I'd used the product I'd gotten from his baby mother and flipped it a few times. Finally a nigga was making his own money and not taking orders. This was the opportunity I'd been waiting for. From the looks of things Calico was never gonna see daylight, so I was on some real "fuck-you" shit. I had his shit, I was doing what the fuck I wanted to, and I wasn't afraid to let niggas know it. I had a new attitude. It was time for niggas on the street to know Poppo wasn't Calico's little bitch.

I walked through the barbershop straight to the back, where some dudes were playing a dice game. Feeling a little lucky with my new profile, I got in on the game.

Deebo, one of the guys in the dice game, held the dice in front of a chick who was watching the game. "Blow on these dice for me, baby." She blew on the dice. Then he rolled them. "Bam! Seven! Pay up, nigga, pay up!" Deebo hit, and I lost one hundred dollars just like that.

"Damn, baby girl! You must be good luck. Let me rub these dice on that ass this time. Nah, matter of fact, let me rub them on your ass, pussy, and titties."

"Man, shut the fuck up and roll the fucking dice!" I yelled, getting pissed off by the bullshit this nigga was doing.

"Man, fuck you, Poppo!" he snapped back.

Deebo wasn't no big nigga on the streets, but he was known for bullying a nigga and taking their shit. Just like his namesake from the movie *Friday*, Deebo was the neighborhood bully.

"Fuck you say, nigga?" I stood up. If Deebo had the chance to tackle me, it would be "game over."

Deebo stood up now, towering over me. "Nigga, you heard me!"

"Nigga, you better recognize what the fuck is good and step the fuck back. I run these fucking streets, nigga." I had to man up. If I gave the slightest indication of weakness, this bully would have definitely tried to overpower me.

"Whatever, duke. You come in this bitch talking shit like you on top of the fucking world when just the other week you was in here crying like a fucking baby talking about how Calico don't respect your bitch ass. Nigga, shut the fuck up!" Deebo took two fingers and mushed me in my forehead.

When Deebo stood up and mushed me in my head, he had taken shit to the next level. I knew it was either do or die at that point. So, with my reputation on the line, I knew I couldn't back down. I pulled out my gun and gave him one big forceful strike across the face.

Bam!

One hit and the dude fell to the ground.

"Now who's the bitch?" I said to him as blood flowed from his lip.

"Daaaammmmmmnnnn! You just got knocked the fuck out!" Another guy jokingly quoted the words from the movie *Friday* when Deebo got knocked out.

As everyone else busted out in laughter at his antics, I walked away.

The constant joking must have been too much for him to handle because, just as I got to the door of the barbershop, I heard a lot of commotion behind me. Before I could turn around, I heard shots.

Pop! Pop! Pop!

I dove between two cars and pulled my gun out. I looked up to see dude rushing to a car. I shot back at him. *Bam! Bam!*

I watched as he fell to the ground. I wasn't sure where he was hit, but at least he was down. I jumped in my whip and peeled off, never looking back.

Ring! Ring! Not even a whole hour after I'd left the barbershop, I got a call from one of the barbers.

"What up, Mike?"

"It ain't good, nigga. You know old boy ain't make it. The cop was up here and everything, nigga. Ain't nobody but niggas is out to get you, duke. Deebo boys say, as soon as they see you, it's straight gunplay, no talk."

"What you talking about, Mike?" I played stupid, not knowing if the cops were around or if this nigga was trying to set me up.

"I'm just letting you know the deal. Watch your back, homeboy. Watch your back." Mike then hung up.

I really ain't give a fuck if dude lived or not. As long as I was still breathing, that's all that mattered. Fuck him and his weak-ass crew. I'd been bitched out for the last time and wasn't backing down from no nigga, so any cat who wanted could bring it.

And, as a matter of fact, fuck Mike too for calling me with that shit. There was no way he was gonna get me to talk about that shit on the phone. Like I told that nigga, I didn't know what the fuck he was talking about. Right at that point, permanent amnesia had set in. I had no recollection of those events. Who's Deebo? And what barbershop?

Chapter 21

"Get Your Boo"

Jewel

An entire week had passed, and I hadn't seen or heard from Touch. He didn't even come to the house to collect his things. I felt so depressed and hurt. I'd spend days in bed. I didn't even bother to bathe or put on clothes. I barely ate anything, and I'd completely stopped taking my birth control. I figured, What's the use? There was no longer a man in my life anyway.

I would've never guessed in a million years that Touch and I would've ended like this. Part of me wanted to fight for my man, but another part of me hated him. I couldn't understand how he could move on to the next chick so quickly. No matter now much shit we went through, being with another man had never crossed my mind.

I began to think about this new chick sitting on my throne. *If another chick came in, where would that leave me? What about this empire that Touch and I had built?*

The reality of things was really beginning to settle in. The fact of the matter was, without Touch my entire life would change. Sure, I had the connection with TMF and could get my hands on all kinds of coke, but it was Touch who knew how to push that shit and bring the money in, and who invested in real estate and made our money legit.

Truthfully, I knew nothing about the business and wouldn't be able to survive without him. One thing I did know for sure, there was no way I could go from the top to rock bottom—all at the hands of another bitch. The more I thought about things, the more panic began to set in.

Desperately needing someone to talk to, I called up Misty. She was the only person I had in my corner.

Misty answered the phone in her usual perky voice, "What's up, girly?"

"Touch still hasn't come home, Misty. I haven't even spoken to him since that night at the restaurant. I don't know what to think or do. I really think it's over between us," I said, bursting into tears.

"Oh, you poor baby. I'm so sorry. Do you want me to come over?" Misty was so comforting.

"No, Misty. I don't want to keep dragging you into my affairs. I shouldn't have even called you."

"Jewel, I'm here for you. That's what friends are for. Talk to me, honey. For some reason, I feel like there is more to your pain. What's the matter, Jewel? Are you pregnant?"

Between tears, I sobbed. "No, I'm not pregnant."

"Well, then what is it?"

"It's just that . . ." I paused, pulling myself together enough to slow up the tears.

I wasn't sure how to explain my dilemma, but Misty was being so kind, so understanding. Maybe because I hadn't been close to any other woman since Sasha, the next thing I knew, I had blurted out my whole life story. I told her all about me and Touch from beginning to end. I told her how we started off as friends and how we built our empire. I explained to her how Calico and Touch used to be partners in the game and how Calico and I hooked up. I even told her about how Sasha was my friend turned lover and how she turned on me.

"Anyway, I'm afraid without Touch I will have nothing. My life will completely fall apart, and I will lose everything I've worked so hard for." I started wailing with a whole new fresh set of tears.

Meantime, Misty didn't say a word. I didn't know if she was shocked by my story, or what the deal was. Then finally I heard a sniffle that broke the silence.

"Misty, are you crying?"

"I'm sorry. I'm supposed to be supporting you. It's just that you're so much like me. Everything you're going through, I've experienced. I feel your pain, baby. Matter of fact, I'm on my way over." Misty hung up the phone before I could protest.

In thirty minutes flat Misty had arrived. I looked a mess as I opened the door. I hadn't had the energy to do anything to myself. My normally long, thick, curly hair sat in a tangled mess on top of my head.

"Hey, boo." Misty hugged me as soon as I opened the door.

"Hey, girl," I responded in my most depressed tone.

"Wow! You really look stressed," Misty said, noticing my ragged look. "I know what you need right now."

"I need Touch here with me right now telling me we're still going to do the damn thing and get married. He acts like he don't even give a fuck about me. How can he treat me this way? It hurts to the core."

Misty stroked my tangled hair. "Everything will be all right."

I called those five words "the girlfriend's anthem." A true girlfriend sure could tell you that everything would work out, no matter how bleak shit looked. I was grateful that Misty had moved up from acquaintance level to being one of my girls.

"No, it won't," I said, seeing no light at the end of this dark, dark tunnel.

"Yes, it will. We're gonna get your man back," Misty said. "Now, this is what you're going to do."

"What?" I said between sniffles.

"You're going to stop by Victoria's Secret and buy the sexiest negligee you can find. You're going to cook his favorite meal and plan to have a romantic candle light dinner."

"But I haven't heard from him in a week. How can I get him home?"

"You call him and tell him you want to talk. When he shows up, you let him be the man, and think everything is his idea, but then you screw his brains out."

"Oh God. It hurts so bad. I hope this works," I said, feeling hopeless.

"Hon, I know it hurts. I've been there too a few times myself. There aren't too many men who can say they've had my heart. I know you want Touch back in your arms; it's what we both want. But right now, I'm going to get you a cup of herbal tea, so you can relax a little. I brought some over from my place. Give me five minutes, and I'll be right back."

Misty headed toward the kitchen and came back five minutes later with a cup of steaming hot tea.

I took a sip. "Misty, this tea is good." It soothed my scratchy throat.

"I figured you would like it. I drink it when I'm stressed. Next, let's get you cleaned up," she ordered, heading into the bathroom to run bath water for me.

After a few minutes, my bath was ready, and Misty ordered me into the bathroom.

It was like a load had been lifted off my back as I soaked in the tub with the jets blowing. While Misty washed and combed through my hair ever so gently, I closed my eyes, trying to relax. Although it was sort of awkward at first, once I relaxed, it felt good. Misty washed my hair and bathed me as though I was her patient and she was my nurse.

Since I'd been taking care of Touch for a while, it felt good for someone to finally take care of me for a damn change. All washed up and totally relaxed, I climbed out of the tub.

After directing me to lay face down on the bed, Misty didn't hesitate massaging my body with Oil of Olay lotion. Suddenly finding myself in another awkward moment, my body immediately tensed up.

"Relax, Jewel," Misty said. "Everything I'm doing for you, you should do for your man. Consider this a lesson and take notes."

I took a deep breath and slowly exhaled, trying to relax. I closed my eyes and indulged in the moment. I must say, once I was relaxed, I was able to realize Misty was a damn good massage therapist. Her caress was slow, deep, and an enjoyable pain.

"How does this feel?" she whispered in my ear.

I could feel the heat from her breath on my neck. It sent a sexual sensation down my spine. "Mmmm! Better than any massage I've ever had."

"Good. It only gets better." Misty started caressing my neck with kisses and then licking my ears with her tongue. She turned me over to face her.

I knew exactly where this was headed. Part of me couldn't believe what was happening, but then another part of me wanted so badly to continue.

I gave in to my sexual urge, and we began kissing. While our tongues met, Misty took two fingers of her right hand and starting massing my clit. For a split second, my mind couldn't help but to drift to Sasha. She'd once touched me in this same way, and we'd shared similar sexual experiences.

Once our tongues drifted apart, Misty's tongue found its way to my left breast. She went back and forth sucking on my nipple and gently biting it. By now my pussy was dripping wet.

Misty started licking my clit, and before I knew it, I came in her mouth.

"Misty, what the fuck just happened?" I said between breaths. I'd cum so hard, I was nearly out of breath.

"Ssshhh! Don't worry, baby," Misty said gently.

I obeyed and didn't say anything more. I wasn't sure where things were headed next, and honestly, I wasn't too concerned. For the first time in days, I was totally relaxed, and I'd just released a load of tension.

As my worries drifted away, I dozed off to sleep.

Exhausted from all the events of the past days and busting a huge nut the previous night, I didn't wake until the next day.

I woke to the smell of bacon and eggs. I walked in the kitchen to see Misty cooking up a grand breakfast that included blueberry waffles and omelets. With Touch on my mind, a fresh burst of energy, and Misty by my side, I decided to do just as Misty had advised the night before and called Touch.

"Yeah," Touch greeted me on the phone after I dialed his number.

I was nervous as hell. I didn't want to take no for an answer of him seeing me. But Misty was right by my side, coaching me along.

"Hey, baby," I said.

He sighed. "What you want, Jewel?"

"Well, um, I was wondering if you could come over to the house for a bit. I just want to talk," I suggested, keeping my fingers crossed.

"I'll be over in a few hours. I need to get a few things anyway," he responded and hung up the phone in my ear.

I didn't even care that he'd hung up on me. I was just happy he'd agreed to come over.

Three hours gave Misty and me plenty of time to go to the mall to Victoria's Secret and to the grocery store to get two fresh T-bone steaks and a few sweet potatoes to bake. I planned to smother them in apple butter, cinnamon, and nutmeg, just the way Touch liked it. Next, I planned to cut up a tossed salad topped with French dressing and croutons. For dessert, it was going to be apple crumb cobbler.

Walking around in my black lace teddy and five-inch stiletto heels gave me confidence. I felt sexy, like every man on earth wanted a piece of my pussy. I began to rehearse in my mind what I would say to Touch, remembering to watch my tone. The last thing I wanted to do was get him mad and then have him storm off on me like the last time.

Chapter 22

"When a Man's Fed Up"

Touch

Jewel greeted me at the door, "Hey, boo." She tried to kiss me on the lips, but I turned, and she caught my cheek instead.

While walking in the house, I was on my cell phone patching up things with Lisa. I didn't know what Jewel had in mind, but this one night wasn't gonna change how I felt about things between us.

I went into the kitchen to grab a Heineken from the fridge then glanced over at the food that Jewel cooked. *Damn! My favorite*, I thought as my mouth began to water, but I refused to voice it. Instead, I acted like it didn't even faze me.

I noticed Jewel let out a big sigh, I guess, to refrain from getting pissed and going the fuck off on me.

I grinned to myself and continued my phone conversation. "Yeah," I replied, walking over to the living room to sit down on the couch.

"Baby, how was your day?" Jewel inquired.

"A'ight," I responded.

"Well, maybe I can make it end on a wonderful note." Jewel began to massage my shoulders.

She poured vanilla-scented oil in to her hands, rubbed them together to get the oil nice and warm then caressed my shoulders deeply. I couldn't deny, that shit felt damn good too.

"How's that?" Jewel asked, after giving me a five-star full body massage.

"That was on point," I said, finally relaxed enough to notice how enticing her nightie was.

My dick began to rise as I watched Jewel's ass bounce in her thong as she walked over to the bar to make me a Grey Goose on the rocks. I turned on the television and flipped through the channels as I gulped down the drink she'd made me.

"Uuummm . . . is this for me?" she asked, rubbing my now fully erect dick.

I didn't respond. I just gave her a grin and swallowed the rest of the liquor I had in the glass.

Noticing my glass was empty, Jewel immediately grabbed it and headed back to the bar to make me round two. This time before returning she turned on R. Kelly's *and* Jay-Z's *The Best of Both Worlds* CD, lit some candles, and dimmed the lights. Upon returning to the couch, she took the remote from my hand and turned off the television.

As I sipped on my second glass of Grey Goose, Jewel slipped off my pants. She grabbed my dick and started to lick the tip of my head, gently getting it nice and moist. Then she moved down the shaft, licking it up and down a couple of times then continuing to my balls. A tingling sensation filled my body as she engulfed my balls in her mouth one at a time.

By this time my dick was so hard, it felt at though it was gonna explode. Just when I thought I couldn't take anymore, Jewel gripped my dick and began deepthroating it just the way I liked it. I spread my legs, grabbed a handful of her hair, and pushed her face deep in my lap. I closed my eyes and let my head fall back as I absorbed each second of this goodness. One thing for sure, there was no denying that Jewel gave a hell of a blowjob.

"You like that?"

"Suck that shit, bitch!" I grabbed Jewel's hair even tighter, forcing her head down farther onto my rock-hard dick.

"Aaahhh fuck!" Jewel started to gag as my cum rushed out the tip of my dickhead and hit the back of her throat. She sucked off every drip and swallowed like she was eating her favorite ice cream.

That shit was just foreplay for me. I grabbed Jewel and ripped her lingerie off. I pinned her to the carpeted floor and forced three of my fingers into her soaking wet pussy.

"You giving my pussy to another nigga?"

"No, baby. You know this is yours."

"Maybe you giving the ass up." I forced my thumb in her ass.

She screamed out in pain. "Aaaaahhhh! No, baby. No, I'm not!"

Instead of sucking on her nipple, I bit it. There was no fucking lovemaking this night. To make love, a nigga had to be in love, and honestly I felt no love for her at the time. The thought of her betraying me killed all feelings of love I had for her.

"Ah shit!" Jewel cried out. "Touch, you're killing me, baby."

I pushed in even deeper and harder as I began to reach my peak. "Take the dick, Jewel."

"Baby, please pull out. Don't cum in me, Touch."

"Where you want it? You gonna take it on your titties or on your ass?"

"Wherever you want, baby. Just pull it out."

"Aaaaahhhhh!" After I banged the pussy up DMX-style as in the movie *Belly*, I came deep inside her, totally ignoring her request to pull out.

"Touch, you came in me?" she asked, feeling my wetness drip from inside her.

"Yep," I said as I jumped up.

I quickly headed upstairs. I wasn't trying to hear that shit Jewel was talking. If it was my pussy like she had just claimed minutes earlier, then I was free to do whatever I like with it.

I jumped in the shower and freshened up then headed to the bedroom and grabbed some clothes. I made sure I packed enough things to last me for a while. I didn't want to make another trip back over to the house anytime soon.

"Where are you going?" Jewel asked.

I guess me packing and leaving wasn't in keeping with her plans. "Back to my crib," I told her. "I'm out."

"We haven't talked yet."

"Like I said, I'm out," I repeated, and turned to leave.

Jewel ran into the kitchen and grabbed the two plates of food that she had prepared while I was in the shower. "Don't forget your dinner!" She threw the two plates of food up against the wall near where I was standing.

I didn't give a fuck, as long as she didn't throw that shit at me. I heard her on the phone as I continued to gather my last few items.

"Hello, Misty," she said between sobs. "He's leaving."

Not wanting to be a part of the drama, I rushed out the door, slamming it behind me.

I didn't even get out of the neighborhood before my phone started to ring. Assuming it was Jewel, I didn't even bother to answer.

The phone rang another three times. After the third time, I noticed it was a different number, so I answered. "Yeah."

"Hey, Touch. This is Misty, Jewel's friend," the voice said from the other end of the phone.

"Okay. So what the fuck you want, Misty?" I never really got a good vibe from her.

"Touch, we really need to talk. Jewel is talking crazy. I think she's gonna have a nervous breakdown or do something crazy. You both may be in danger. If you have a few minutes, can you meet me at Silverfish? It's a bar down at the oceanfront, on Seventeenth Street."

"I know where it is. Give me about an hour," I said then hung up the phone.

I really wasn't interested in how the fuck Jewel felt, but when Misty said she was talking crazy and we both may be in danger, that shit caught my attention. I was hoping Jewel wasn't crazy enough to try to call the police on a nigga. I didn't play those types of games. I'd had more than one run-in with shit like that from my stupid-ass baby mother.

One hour turned into two hours as I made a quick stop by Mo Dean's before going to the oceanfront, but I eventually made it to the bar. I was surprised to see Misty still there waiting.

"What up, Misty?"

"Hey, Touch. Thanks for meeting me. Have a seat. I'll buy you a drink."

Misty pressed IGNORE on her constantly ringing phone. The wise side of me was pretty sure that was probably Jewel blowing up her cell phone.

"What did you want to talk about?" I asked as I grabbed a seat next to her at the bar and made myself comfortable.

"Well, I wanted to talk you about Jewel. She's been crying constantly since you left. She's hysterical. She's talking like she can't go on another day without you."

Blah, blah, blah, blah. Misty's words began to go in one ear and out the other. I didn't know if it was the two double shots of Grey Goose I'd drank at Mo Dean's prior to meeting Misty or what, but my mind was definitely wandering other places.

Places like all over her body, to be exact. This bitch was sitting with her legs wide open. I had a bird's-eye view of her "camel toe" through her black tights. The sight of her fat pussy instantly made my wood stand up.

"Yo, let me get a Long Island Iced Tea for the lady," I said to the bartender, a drink that was guaranteed to get Misty a little tipsy.

"Thanks. But do you hear what I'm saying about Jewel?"

"What about Jewel?" I asked, knowing I hadn't heard anything she'd said about her.

"Touch, she loves you very much. Look, I don't know the whole story from beginning to end with the two of you, but I do know that right now she's hurting to know that you think she betrayed you, because she didn't," Misty explained.

"Hmm. Is that so?"

"Yes," she declared.

"Let's take a walk," I suggested, noticing that Misty had already finished the drink I'd ordered.

"Okay. I could use the fresh air," she agreed, obviously feeling a little tipsy.

I dropped a few dollars on the bar to cover the tab and pulled out a cigarette to light when I hit the door.

We walked all the way down to Eighth Street, where the tourists and locals were nowhere to be found. By this point the conversation had moved from Jewel to more interesting things. It felt like only the two of us, the beach, moon, and the stars just existed. This was the perfect setting for sex in my mind. For a moment I felt like Jamie Foxx, and I didn't know if I should blame it on the Henny or the Goose, but the more I looked at Misty, the sexier she was.

I kept making subtle passes and small flirtations with her. Although she resisted, I could tell, with a little more work, she would be dropping those tights and lifting her flowered shirt. We made our way back to the bar. We stopped and talked a minute outside while I finished up my cigarette.

"You know them?" Misty said, pointing to a car that drove by slowly.

Unable to see who was in the car, I watched as they drove to the end of the parking lot and turned around. There was no one else in the parking lot other than me and her, so I figured they had to be watching one of us. A part of me wondered if Jewel had hooked up with someone and decided to stalk a nigga. After all, Misty did say she was talking some crazy shit.

I took a long pull from my cigarette as I waited patiently for the car to come back around. The closer it got, the more I focused in on the people inside. It wasn't until they'd gotten up on us again that I'd realized who it was.

"Get—" I tried to warn Misty to get down, but before I could finish my sentence, shots had already rang out.

I jumped to the ground behind a car as I pulled out my gun. From there I shot back. I looked up to see Misty right beside me firing just as many shots.

"Come with me!" Misty, who was like a miniature Rambo, grabbed my arm and pulled me toward her truck.

Moments later, we were in her truck, and the people who were shooting after us had sped off.

"What the fuck was that?" Misty asked, while speeding toward the interstate.

"I'm sorry, ma. I feel real fucked up right now. I never meant to put you in danger like that. I had no idea."

"Danger? I love danger. It's kind of sexy."

Misty had my head fucked up with her response. "Oh yeah?"

"Yep! So who was that? Was that the same dude from the club on New Year's?"

"Nah. It's a little more complicated than that. This is some beef I shouldn't even have. This broad I fucked with one time set me up. She lied to this nigga and said I beat her up, because I won't fuck with her." I told Misty the least I could about my situation with Sasha and Diablo.

"Damn! That sounds like some 'fatal attraction' shit. How long did you fuck with her?"

"For real, I didn't even fuck with her. I just fucked the bitch one night."

"Wow! You must have really put it down for her to be acting like that over a one-night stand. Umph!" Misty cut her eyes at me.

I wasn't a mind reader, but if I had to read her eyes, they were definitely saying, "I wish I could have a taste of that good dick."

"Oh yeah, the dick is good, no doubt, but it's more to it with that bitch. The bitch is just straight grimy. She'll do anything for a dollar."

"So what more is it? Like, how is she so grimy?" Misty seemed really interested in my story.

"To make a long story short, she was Jewel's best friend. I always felt like she was envious of Jewel. She wanted everything Jewel had, the clothes, shoes, jewelry, cars, houses, and even me. Sad to fucking say, but the bitch got all of it. Yeah, she stole from Jewel to get the material shit, but she wasn't suppose to get me. My stupid ass should have never fucked her."

I explained how shit went down.

"So you cheated on Jewel with her best friend?" Misty seemed shocked.

"Nah. We weren't together yet," I explained to Misty, hoping that fucking Jewel's friend wouldn't ruin my chances of fucking her.

"Mm-hmm." Misty grunted as though she didn't believe me, yet it seemed to turn her on. "You're a bad boy." She continued, "Well, I don't think it's safe for you to go back to the bar. I can just take you home if you like."

I readily agreed. "That's cool."

My mind was so fucked up as we drove, I couldn't even think straight. I couldn't believe that bitch Sasha could have gotten me fucking killed. If it wasn't for Misty peeping them out, I could have been bleeding on the concrete. Two times in a matter of a few months I'd escaped death. I couldn't say shit. I just sat in silence.

"Okay, where to?" Misty said, interrupting my moment of silence.

I gave her directions to my crib, and minutes later, we were pulling up in my driveway.

"Would you like to come in?" I offered.

"Sure."

Misty followed me through the door. Once inside, we got comfortable on the couch.

"You okay, Touch?" she asked, noticing the worry on my face.

"Just a little stressed out. This is two encounters with death I've had in a short time. Worse, I could have gotten you killed. Basically, you're the reason I'm here. What the fuck you doing with a gun anyway? And where the hell did you learn to shoot like that?"

"First of all, don't worry about me. I'm used to this, Touch. I've lived this life before. My ex-boyfriend was heavy into the drug game too, so I was ducking and dodging bullets and had to be on point every day."

Something about Misty's statement made me stop and think. *What the fuck she means, "into the drug game too"? Who the fuck said I was in the drug game?* I'd hoped Jewel's ass didn't run her mouth to this bitch. I'd told Jewel time and time again not to trust anyone, especially no bitch. You think she would have learned her lesson from Sasha.

"I know it must be stressful." Misty stroked my face as she spoke to me.

"Stressful ain't the word, ma. When I first got shot, I wondered if I would ever be back to my old self. Now I'm better, and I've got to wonder if I'd live to see the next day. I've got beef coming in every direction, and on top of that, I don't even know if I can trust the chick I was gonna make my wife. Right now I feel like it's me against the world. Real talk." For the first time, I was able to express the shit that had been on my mind.

"Aaawww, you poor baby." Misty wrapped her arms around me and playfully kissed my cheek.

Seeing this as the perfect opportunity, I began to kiss her. And, just like I figured, she didn't resist. I slid my hand underneath her loose blouse and began to massage her breast. One touch of her nipple and my manhood rose to the occasion.

"Uuummm," Misty moaned.

I gently laid her down, and she assisted me in taking her shirt off.

One by one I sucked her breasts, while slowly sliding my hand into her panties. I had to be sure to make each

move right. I didn't want to take the chance of her resisting and deciding not to go through with things.

Once my hands were in her panties, I buried my fingers deep between her fat pussy lips. Feeling the thick-
ness and moisture alone of her pussy made me want
to bust. No longer able to resist, I pulled off my jeans,
slipped on a jimmy hat, and before I knew it, I was all
up that fat pussy I had been admiring earlier.

Chapter 23

"Charge It to the Game"

Sasha

Damn! What a fucking night! I thought as I opened the door to my hotel room. On a whim, Diablo and I had rolled up on Touch. Of course, after I'd led Diablo to believe Touch had robbed me, there was no way he could run into Touch and not defend his shit. I wasn't expecting to be in the middle of a shootout, but even more shocking was seeing Touch come out of the bar with another chick. From what I'd heard, him and Jewel was getting married, and from the looks of things, they were really into each other.

A part of me was actually kind of happy to have the opportunity to fire shots though. Most of mine were aimed at that bitch Touch was with. If I couldn't have him, then no one would. I'd rather destroy the empire than let another bitch sit on the throne.

After our little incident, Diablo had to settle things with the guys I was supposed to deliver the package to. I listened as he talked to them on the phone.

"Yeah, man, I got you," Diablo said. "I know shit got fucked up, but I ain't even trying to hold on to niggas' money. You know what I mean? I'm saying, that's why I'm here now."

Diablo was explaining his ass off. From the looks of things, niggas was really pissed off.

After he got off the phone, I asked him, "Everything okay?"

"Yeah, man," he said with a distressed look on his face.

"You sure?"

"Man, that nigga Touch really fucking my shit up. This is a hell of a loss I'm taking right now, but I gotta straighten niggas to keep business going, ya dig?"

"I feel you."

For a split second, I almost felt bad for stealing from Diablo, but I really couldn't be certain that it was actually guilt that I was feeling, especially since I'd never felt guilt before. The way I saw it, shit happens, so charge it to the game.

After Diablo set his boys straight, he headed back to Atlanta. Me, on the other hand, I had to stay back to find a way to get rid of the drugs I'd taken from him. I hadn't the slightest idea who I could go to.

Determined to get that money, I used my only resource. I headed to the strip club, The Hot Spot. As an ex-stripper, I knew a lot of the local as well as out-of-town drug dealers that hung out there.

Walking into the strip club, I didn't notice too many familiar faces. People would come and go at the strip club all the time. Stripping wasn't a line of work that exactly guaranteed job stability. One day you're there, the next day you're not. One day the money is good, the next day it's not. But even with all those downfalls, bitches still couldn't break away from the strip game. I guess it was the fast money that was so damn addictive. Just like niggas with the drug game, it was hard to let go.

"Malibu, girl, is that you?" a voice called out, addressing me by my dance name.

"It sure is," I replied back to Candy and hugged her.

Candy, her real name Jennifer, was veteran to the strip game. She was actually the person responsible for my pole skills. She taught me how to work that pole in every way imaginable.

"How you been?" she asked, looking me up and down. "You coming back to work?"

Don't you wish, bitch, I thought, knowing exactly what was going through her head.

It wasn't unusual for a current stripper to examine an ex-stripper in such a manner. I knew she was looking for any signs that I was struggling or doing bad. When a chick stops stripping, other chicks seem to think she has this I'm-better-than-you attitude. But in reality the current strippers are jealous of the ex-stripper, because they wish they were in the ex-stripper's shoes and had the same opportunity to stop dancing themselves. So if a chick happens to be one of those females that are fortunate enough to stop dancing and she comes in the strip club, the current dancer is always gonna be looking for something negative to say.

"I'm fine, girl. Just dropping through. I'm not here for work." I put any suspicion Candy had to rest then switched the subject. "How's Lamont doing?"

"Next month he'll be six."

Candy pulled out her cell phone to show me the latest picture of her son. He was a real cutie with his two front teeth missing. Looking at that picture instantly made me miss my boys.

"I'm glad I ran into you. I need a little bit of information and help."

"Whatcha need, boo? You know I got your back."

"What I need to know is, where's the ballers at? Where's the niggas that's moving major weight around here?"

"See that nigga in the corner by the pool table? He goes by the name Murdock. That's one of the heaviest niggas that be coming to the club. That's who you want to get at."

Candy assumed I was looking for a nigga to take care of me or to run some tricks with, but that was better for me. The less that bitch knew, the better.

"Thanks, girl. Do me a favor. Have the bartender send him over whatever he is drinking." I handed her a hundred-dollar bill.

I quickly went to the bathroom to look myself over and make sure my boobs were sitting up pretty and nice. Women would pay to have boobs like mine, but lucky me, I was just blessed with an awesome rack. Besides this fat cat, that was one of my greatest assets, and men couldn't keep their eyes off them.

After his drink arrived, Murdock looked around to see who sent him his bottle of Nuvo. I raised my matching glass of Nuvo to him and nodded my head, giving him a seductive smile.

After twenty minutes or so, I headed over to him.

"Hmm. I'm a little impressed. I ain't never had a female buy me a bottle, or even a drink, as a matter of fact. And you are?" He smiled at me.

I gave him a fake name and grinned back at him. "My name is Cara."

"It's nice to meet you, Cara. So what's up with you, little momma?"

"Well, I got some birds that are ready to move, and word on the streets is, you the nigga I should be hollering at," I explained with much confidence, although inside I felt a little uneasy. Normally I wouldn't take these types of chances, but I needed to get rid of Diablo's product, and fast. My back was against the wall.

"How much you want for them?"

We negotiated pricing. He got over a little, but a bitch was desperate, and anything was a profit for me, considering it wasn't my shit to begin with.

"A'ight den, it's settled. All I need to know is where and when?"

"In an hour, meet me in the parking lot of Military Circle Mall near the movie theater," I said, figuring that was a pretty safe place.

An hour came and went. I swear, muthafuckers didn't know the meaning of being on time. Murdock was running only ten minutes late, but each minute I waited felt like an eternity. I sat there nervous as hell and shaking. This should have been a smooth transaction.

I saw a couple of guys pulling up next to me in an Escalade. I put one in the head and held the gun by my side, just in case some shit popped off. The two unknown guys stood by my driver and passenger door barricading it.

What the hell is going on? Before I could process anything, one of the guys was in my face.

"Roll the window down!" he ordered.

I refused to roll the window down as he instructed.

"Do what the fuck I say and I won't blow your stupid ass up," he explained, holding up a grenade.

A grenade? This nigga can't be serious. I figured this had to be some type of joke so I yelled at him, "I ain't doing shit!"

He giggled. "Your ass will be blown to pieces."

I reached toward the gearshift to put my car in drive to pull off from this stupid-ass nigga.

"Not so fast."

Bling!

Before I could react, my window was broken, and glass was shattered all over my face.

"Hey, Cara, or should I say Sasha," Murdock stepped in and greeted me.

I wondered how the fuck he knew who I really was. "I'm not Sasha. My name is—"

"Yo, I'm not trying to hear shit you got to say. Hand me over that bag,"

Murdock cut me off mid-sentence.

"I am not giving you the drugs."

Bam! Murdock punched me in the side of my face with one hand and pulled me out the window of the car with the other. Then I felt the barrel of a gun pressed against my cheek.

Once my head stopped spinning and the stars before my eyes disappeared, I turned around to see a fucking AK in my face. That's when I started to realize this wasn't a joke at all. These niggas were literally ready for war, and I wasn't gonna put up a fight. I knew this would be a battle I would lose. The thought of my sons were still fresh in my head.

"Put that shit up, nigga. Y'all couldn't wait for an opportunity to pull out the toys, huh?" Murdock barked. "Y'all niggas don't need all that shit for this little bitch."

Bam! I caught another punch to the face.

"Okay, okay, I'll give you the bag."

"See . . . all it takes is a little manhandling." Murdock laughed.

I struggled to my feet and headed toward the car. I opened the front door pretending I was going for the bag but grabbed my gun instead.

Blap! Murdock's boy hit me in the face with the butt of the gun. He'd obviously gotten a glimpse of me heading for my piece. "I told you this shit would come in handy."

By this time blood was running down my face profusely, and my eyes were nearly swollen shut. I grabbed the bag and handed it to Murdock.

"I was hoping you would choose life." Murdock snatched the bag away. He quickly hopped back in his truck and sped off.

Karma's a real bitch. I shook my head in disappointment and exhaled. "Fuck you, karma! You bitch!" I yelled out loud.

I grabbed some napkins out of the glove box and put it on my bleeding wound then put my car in drive and drove away empty-handed.

Chapter 24

"Murder for Hire"

Jewel

Severely depressed, frustrated, and tired of Touch ignoring me, I headed to Applebee's to pick up my favorite takeout order, buffalo wings with extra sauce and extra blue cheese dressing on the side, and French fries. I was hoping it would cheer me up. I'd tried calling Misty several times but couldn't reach her. I figured it would have been nice to have a girls' night out and discuss how things went when she met with Touch. But after calling her four times and texting her six times, I was probably becoming a bugaboo, which wasn't intentional. But I was really anxious to know what Touch had to say.

I have to admit, I was kind of upset when Misty didn't answer my calls, but I had to realize she had a life of her own, not to mention a very demanding job. Basically I had to check myself and appreciate all the time she'd already taken to truly listen about how I felt. Misty had provided comfort throughout my struggles with Touch. What more could a friend ask for?

The hostess greeted me with a smile as I walked through the restaurant door. "Hi. Welcome to Applebee's."

"Hello. I'm here to pick up a takeout order. The first name is Jewel," I explained, taking off my sunglasses.

"It's not ready yet. You're welcome to wait at the bar or right here by the sitting lounge," she offered. "I'll call you when it's ready."

"Thank you. I'll wait at the bar," I replied and walked over to the bar and took a seat.

"Hi. What can I get for you?" the bartender asked in the midst of taking another waiter's handwritten order.

"A pomegranate martini," I replied, hoping a nice drink would calm my nerves. After all, Applebee's pomegranate martini was my favorite.

Since me and Touch's fallout, there were times I couldn't get my hands to stop shaking. It was like my nerves had taken over me and my anxiety level was off the charts. I was still in shock that Touch had actually left me because he thought I was fucking a nothing-ass nigga like Poppo. Plus, on top of everything, he had the audacity to be fucking another bitch, as if that was okay. The thought of this whole situation made my temples tighten. I could feel a tension headache coming on. I was even more pissed that I went through all the trouble to mend things between us, and he comes over and fucks me and leaves, like I was some chick off the streets. I couldn't even get him to talk to me or listen to what I had to say at the least. Deep inside I felt hopeless about my recurring dream of us getting married. I knew there wouldn't be a wedding day.

"I'm here to pick up a to-go order," a female voice beside me said.

I looked up to see Misty standing beside me. "Misty?"

"Jewel! Hey, girl!" She gave me a big hug.

"I've been trying to reach you. Haven't you gotten my calls and texts?"

"Yes, baby. I'm so sorry. I've been so busy. You wouldn't know all the things that have been going on."

"Jewel," another voice called out, interrupting me and Misty's conversation.

"Poppo," I answered, recognizing the voice.

"Hey, what's going on with the beautiful Jewel?" he asked.

"You got that right. I am beautiful," I responded, even though deep down I didn't truly feel that way.

Misty butted in quickly. "Well, I gotta run, girl."

"Oh, okay. I really wanted to sit and talk though."

"I'll call you as soon as I get a free moment. I promise." Misty grabbed her bag and rushed out of the restaurant.

"That's your girl?" Poppo asked after Misty walked away.

"Yeah. Why? You want to holla at her or something?"

"Oh, nah. I already tried. That bitch got a mouth on her that a make a nigga beat her ass."

"Why you say that? What did she say to you?"

"Well, that day I got locked up, I saw her at the jail, so I tried to holla. That bitch started talking some shit about me being a thug, and jail being my second home, straight dissing a nigga. Instead of cussing that bitch out, I just told her to have a nice day and walked off on her ass."

"Damn! Sorry about that. Maybe she was having a bad day. I wonder why she was at the precinct anyway. Hope nothing was wrong. She said a lot has happened to her in the past days. Now I'm worried. Give me a second. Let me call her."

I dialed Misty up.

This time she answered right away. "Hey, girl."

"Hey, Misty. Is everything okay? My friend just told me he saw you at the precinct not too long ago."

"Oh, girl, it was nothing. I had got locked up for a trespassing charge. I had seen my ex-boyfriend's car in front of this girl's house, so I went up there banging on the door, trying to get him to come out, and the bitch called the police on me. You know how that goes."

"Yeah, I do. Okay, hon. I'm not gonna hold you. Call me when you're free. We really need to catch up." I ended the call.

"Why you sitting at the bar by yourself?" Poppo asked as soon as I hung up the phone.

"I'm waiting for an order."

"Let me take care of that for you."

"Thanks." I grinned after the bartender brought my drink.

"Listen, ma, I'm glad that I ran into you. I got some good news for you."

"Well, it's about time. Go ahead, I'm listening." I nodded.

"I thought that nigga Calico was done when he got locked up, but he's going up for a bond hearing in a few days, and his lawyer is confident he's getting a bond. After he gets bonded out, I'm going to personally pick him up and handle things for you."

"Well, as long as you make shit happen, our deal is still good. Once Calico is out the way, I will put you on to one of my TMF connects." I assured Poppo as if my word was golden.

"Bartender, please . . . another drink for the lady. Now, you know I can't let you eat alone. You want to get a table?" Poppo asked.

"Sure." I giggled. It felt nice to have someone paying a little attention to me, especially since Touch wasn't even bothering to look my way.

At the table I noticed Poppo constantly staring into my eyes. "Why are you staring at me?" I blushed.

"It's not every day a man sees something as beautiful as you."

"Wow! You got a little game with you, huh?"

"This isn't game, baby. You can't appreciate those type of compliments because these lames you been fucking with don't know how to cherish a woman like you." Poppo grabbed my hand.

I didn't know how to respond to Poppo's comment. In a way I took it as a diss because he was insinuating I have poor taste in men, but at the same time he was giving me a compliment by saying I was an exceptional woman. Since I didn't know what to say, I didn't say anything at all. I just smiled.

"If you were my woman, I would give you the world. You would never feel pain, hurt, sadness, or disappointment. You would always be on a pedestal."

Okay now, I knew this nigga was putting it on thick. He was talking straight bullshit. "Whatever." I knew exactly how to respond to that bullshit-ass statement.

"I know you feel like I'm just popping shit, but it's cool. I can show you better than I can tell you. That bitch nigga you with fucked your head up."

"Damn! You keep saying shit like I'm some sad case, a woman scorned or some shit. And why Touch gotta be a bitch?" I snapped. I was getting tired of Poppo's little comments, and he had crossed the line talking about Touch. I mean, I wasn't really feeling Touch, but I still loved him, and I wasn't gonna let no nigga diss him, especially no one from Calico's camp.

"Hold on, baby girl. Don't take offense. I'm just saying . . . I don't know what the next dude thought of you, but you're my dream woman, and by all means I would treat you like it. I would never take you for granted."

I thought, *Damn! Who the fuck is this nigga?* He was blowing me away. Just that quick, he'd made my whole attitude change. I didn't know if I'd just never given this nigga the opportunity to see what he was really like or if he was a different Poppo. Back in the day, I would have never even considered him an option, but this nigga really had me going. I didn't know if it was because I was so vulnerable from me and Touch's breakup, or if it was the alcohol, or if Poppo's game was just simply on point. I was actually starting to feel him a little bit. I needed to calm down.

"Miss, can I get another drink?" I was feeling a little tipsy, but I didn't care. After those days of pure hell I'd been through, I deserved to have a little fun. Poppo was saying all the right things, and I was sucking it all up.

"You want some more wings?" Poppo asked.

"Sure." I nodded. Not eating much in days, I guess I had worked up an appetite. When my emotions were out of whack, my body was too. My head, back, muscles, and joints all ached like I had the flu or something, when in reality it was all stress.

The waitress came back. "Here is your drink. Can I get you anything else?"

"Yes, she'll have another order of wings," Poppo said.

"With extra blue cheese dressing," I added before guzzling down yet another drink.

"Coming right up," the waitress said.

"You really want those wings," Poppo commented.

"Yes, I sure do. I probably could eat them all day." I giggled.

"Jewel, shit is about to be right for us," Poppo whispered in my ear, changing the subject.

"Okay." I laughed.

I was in no condition to discuss things further, but I figured he was talking about money. Plus, I had to use the bathroom. All that alcohol I'd drank was going right through me.

"I appreciate your patience with the whole situation."

"No problem. I need to run to the bathroom."

I struggled to get up then stumbled, but Poppo caught me just in time before I fell to the ground.

"Maybe you should cool off with the alcohol. Why don't you go back to my house and chill? Are you all right to drive?"

"Yeah, I'm okay to drive to your house. I need a minute to use the bathroom," I said while he helped me there.

I had to admit, it was sweet that he was so concerned about me. The average nigga would have tried to keep me drinking, so they could get a "drunk fuck" out of me.

Chapter 25

"Making a Move"

Poppo

"Welcome to my home," I said to Jewel as we pulled up to a little spot I'd gotten in Norfolk.

I'd been spending so much time on the East Coast, and in VA in particular, I figured I may as well get a little spot. Hell, with the money I was spending in hotel costs every month, I may as well pay rent instead.

"Oh, this is cute! Looks just like a bachelor's pad." She giggled as we walked into the living room.

My living room was simple. I had a big-framed, black-and-white photo of Tony Montana from *Scarface* on the wall, a black leather sectional, and a fifty-two-inch plasma on the wall. That's all a nigga needed.

"Make yourself comfortable." I handed Jewel the remote then headed to the kitchen to make her a drink. "What you want to drink?" I asked, trying to be a gentleman. If it was up to me alone, I would have given her a shot of Henny straight. That would have made my night go a lot easier.

"Uummm, what do you have?"

"Hennessy."

"That's it?"

"Look, ma, like you said, this is a bachelor's pad. I don't have no little sweet shit or none of that girly shit you be drinking."

"No Hpnotiq, Alizé, or Nuvo? Nothing?"

"Hpnotiq. But if you drink it, you have to drink an 'Incredible Hulk.' " I had to get the Henny in there some kind of way. You know that Henny make you sin, and that's exactly where I was trying to get to that night.

"Okay. Okay. Incredible Hulk it is." Jewel laughed and sat down on the couch, finally submitting.

"Here you go." I handed Jewel the drink then sat on the couch next to her.

"Thank you."

"Like I was saying in the restaurant, shit is about to come up for the both of us."

"Oh yeah? What makes you so sure?"

"Look, baby girl, I got my eyes on the prize, and by all means, I plan on getting it."

"So let me hear a little bit of this plan," Jewel said. "You got me real curious."

"All you need to know is, soon Calico is going to be six feet deep."

"Oh yeah? And what will happen after that?"

I knew exactly what Jewel wanted to hear, so I played along. "I'm going to take the lead and be in charge. I'm already on my way. Since Calico's been locked up, I've been stacking dough and building up my new team. Some of the old team members will have to go because their loyalty will lie with Calico, and I can't have that. My empire will stand strong and make twice as much as his did. All I need is a queen bee like you by my side," I said, already beginning to feel on top of the world.

"Sounds like a good plan." Jewel guzzled down the drink I'd given her.

Ring! Ring!

My phone rang, interrupting our conversation. Normally I would have ignored it, but it was Murdock.

That nigga owed me eighty-five hundred dollars, and I needed that shit, so I answered.

"Excuse me, ma. I need to answer this call," I said to Jewel then walked away. I picked up the call. "Yo?"

"Ready for you," Murdock said.

"I hope it's all there, Murdock. I ain't taking no cuts."

"I got eighty-five hundred for you."

"Cool. Meet me at KFC at Five Points," I instructed Murdock to meet me at a place close to the crib.

"Sorry about that, ma," I said to Jewel as I walked back into the living room. "Want to take a ride with me down the street real quick?" I asked her, knowing this would be the prefect opportunity to show her how I was getting money.

We hopped in the car, and I met up with Murdock at the KFC. He was already there when we pulled up. This time I got out of my car and hopped in with him.

Murdock handed me the money as soon as I got in. "Here you go."

"Eight-five hundred, right?" I tried to confirm, like always.

"It's all there, man," Murdock said. "And to show I'm a man about principle, I added a little interest."

"Thanks, but I don't need interest, nigga. I need you to pay on time." I then got out of his car and got back into mine.

"Count this for me." I handed Jewel the stack of money then pulled off. I watched as her eyes lit up and a broad smile came across her face.

"I don't count money unless it's mine." She smirked.

"Soon enough, baby girl, soon enough," I said, confident that the time when I could throw her stacks was near.

Minutes later we were back at my crib and comfortable on the couch like before.

"Would you like another drink?" I inquired as soon as we got settled. I already had a mixture of the Hennessy and Hpnotiq in a pitcher cooling in the fridge and ready to pour.

"Maybe just one more," Jewel said and turned on the television.

We were just in time to watch reruns of *The Game* on BET.

Ring! Ring!

My cell phone rang as I was making Jewel's drink. Not recognizing the number, I answered the phone in a fake voice. "Hello?"

"You gon' die, bitch nigga!" a male voice said from the other end.

"Oh yeah? You know where to find me," I said in a calm voice. "I ain't hiding." I then hung up the phone. I didn't want to draw any attention to my phone call and take the risk of ruining the mood me and Jewel had set so perfectly.

I'd been receiving those calls off and on since Deebo's death, and ain't shit happen. I had been carrying on with life as usual, and ain't shit jump off. Hell, those niggas knew where to find me if they really wanted some. The way I saw it, niggas was just popping shit, hoping to scare a nigga away.

I returned to the living room and handed Jewel her drink. "Here you go, sweetheart."

After Jewel finished that last drink, I didn't even bother to ask her if she wanted another one. I didn't want to make it seem like I was really trying to get her drunk. Maybe, she was done for the day and night.

I, on the other hand, knew how to hold my liquor and had about five Incredible Hulks with us just sitting on the couch. I was feeling nice and knew Jewel was feeling even better, so I didn't hesitate to make a move on her. I started by gently kissing her neck and feeling on her breasts. I wanted to put one in my mouth, but no sooner than I caressed her soft, supple breast, she shooed my hand away. Not wanting to ruin the mood and totally fuck things up, I eased off.

"How about a massage?" I whispered in her ear and started to rub her shoulders before she could even respond.

She didn't resist, so I took that as my queue to keep going. I took my time, paying special attention to each part of her body as I rubbed her from head to toe. Although I was disappointed and nearly had blue balls, I was glad to have gotten this far. I just hoped the next time things would be different and I would be inside her pussy. I knew it was wet and juicy, and I couldn't wait for a taste. Literally!

Chapter 26

"Sweet Taste of Revenge"

Calico

Weeks had passed, and still no one had heard from Poppo's little bitch-ass. I'd heard he'd gotten into a little beef on the streets and ended up killing the neighborhood bully, Deebo. That shit was a surprise to me. I guess he was really out there feeling himself, trying to act like he was the big man in town. The stories I was hearing about him really had me going. I couldn't believe this nigga really thought he was the boss. I was convinced he had bucked on me for my money and that was how he had his little come-up. I'd spent each day thinking about how the fuck I was gonna deal with him and was just hoping Deebo's boys didn't get to him first.

Bucking on my money was bucking on the Mexicans' money. And I didn't have the army to go to war with those niggas. Hell, I was already skating on thin ice, because Touch had fucked me up. I was just getting back in good with these niggas and wasn't trying to fuck it up all over again.

My first instinct was to just get out of jail, hunt his bitch-ass down, and straight kill him, but then I started to think on a whole different level. After pulling a few strings, I was able to get one of his bitches in VA to give him a call on three-way. I finally had the opportunity to holla at that nigga.

Of course, I had to ask him about that shit with my baby mother first. That was a true violation. There is no way a nigga could feel up one of my chicks and get away with it, especially my baby moms. Then I asked about my money, and about the shit niggas was saying on the streets. And, like the bitch I knew he was, Poppo denied it all. He gave me some lame excuse about getting robbed, when it came to the money. He had managed to collect on half before he got robbed though. I made that nigga think everything was all good and there was no beef. Plus, when that nigga found out I had another bond hearing coming up and I was definitely getting out on that one, he straightened his act up. At first he thought I would never see daylight, so he was trying to flex. But when the reality hit that I was coming home, that nigga switched his whole shit up.

Just like Natalia had promised, I went before the judge and got a bond. I gathered my shit up, preparing to be released. A nigga never felt so happy. Two months in jail was way too much time for a cat like me. It took three different bond hearings for me to get a bond.

The judge set it at one million dollars, with hopes that I would never get out, but it only took one phone call and one hundred grand, and a nigga was on the road the same fucking day.

Now that I was hitting the streets, it was straight to business. I knew Poppo had to be dealt with. Then I had to get to that bitch Sasha before she got to the witness stand. She was the only eyewitness that had stepped up so far, so without her the Commonwealth's Attorney had no case.

When they released me, I walked out the gate and saw my baby mother parked outside.

"Hey, baby!" she ran up to me and gave me a big hug and kiss.

"What's up? I see you really love daddy, huh? You came all the way across the country to get your man. That's why I fuck with you so hard, Corrin." I gripped her ass and pulled her close to me, my dick swelling.

"Damn! Looks like you're not the only one that's happy to see me," she said, feeling my dick stand up against her thigh.

"So what you gonna do about that?"

"You'll see real soon. Get in the car. Let's get to our hotel."

I didn't hesitate to get in the car. Although I was horny as hell and wanted to fuck my baby mother more than anything, I can't lie, my mind was on other shit. Everything in me wanted to meet up with Poppo so I could give that nigga what he had coming to him.

Corrin drove us downtown Norfolk to the Waterside Marriot, where she'd gotten the room. We pulled up in front and let the valet park the car.

The door on the elevator hadn't even closed completely before she was all over me. She grabbed me by my hair, which was now loose because I had taken out my corn rolls while in jail. With a tight grip on my hair, she forced her tongue in my mouth, pushing me against the elevator wall.

I wrapped my arms around her and began to kiss her back just as passionately. My dick was so hard, it felt like it was going to explode. I turned around, pushing Corrin against the wall, then pushed my hands inside her panties. Her pussy was hairless, and I instantly felt her swollen clit between her fat pussy lips.

"Ahhhh, baby," she moaned. "Not in here." She pulled my hand from her pants.

Ding!

The elevator sounded, letting us know we'd reached our floor. Not knowing if someone would be standing in front of us as the elevator door opened, we both gathered ourselves. When the door opened, I followed Corrin to the hotel room.

As soon as we got in, Corrin started to take her clothes off. I followed her into the bedroom. By the time we reached there, she was completely naked. I grabbed her naked body and tossed it on the bed.

"No, baby, it's not time yet. First, you've got to get a shower."

Corrin was tripping.

"Hell nah. You 'bout to give me this pussy. I've been waiting months for some pussy, and you gon' tell me to go take a shower first?"

"Well, I'm getting in the shower. If you want me, you'll have to join me." She hopped up and ran into the bathroom.

I followed her in there. When I walked in, she was already in the shower. I ripped the curtain back and looked at her soaking wet, perfect body. Although she'd had two kids for me, her body was still flawless, not a stretch mark in sight. I pulled off my clothes and got in with her.

As soon as I stepped in, she grabbed a washcloth and soaped it up. Then she began to wash my body. From head to toe, Corrin wiped me down, not missing one spot. Then I stepped under the flow of the water to rinse the soap off.

When I turned around and all the soap was gone, Corrin got on her knees and began to suck my dick. I knew I was backed up, so when I felt the need to cum, I let the first one go and busted all in her mouth. Now that I'd gotten the quick one out of the way, it was time to really give it to her. My dick was still hard after I came.

I turned Corrin around and bent her over under the flow of water beneath the showerhead. I grabbed her by the waist and pushed my dick deep inside her.

"Aaahhh, fuck!" she screamed out.

Her pussy was nice and tight like always. Water splashed off her ass as I banged it. The sound and sight of her ass bouncing up and down turned me on even more. Before I knew it, Corrin had reached her peak, and I followed shortly after. Although exhausted, we both washed off one more time before getting out of the shower.

When we stepped out of the shower, room service was waiting on us. Corrin had ordered steak and lobster tail.

"I knew you would want something nice after eating jail food for so long," she said as she handed me my plate, "so I ordered the best."

"Damn, boo! You almost make me want to wife you up," I said, knowing that was what Corrin always wanted.

"That's what I'm waiting on. What is it gonna take, Mike?"

"Come on, Corrin, don't start. We're having a nice time, baby," I said, not wanting to hear the bullshit.

"Baby, me and the kids need you. This is the second time you've gone to jail. What if you don't get out the next time? What are we supposed to do without you?"

"Man, I ain't going nowhere. I got shit under control. You worrying for nothing." I didn't know why Corrin was so upset.

"See . . . that's what I mean. You think you're invincible. Mike, you're human. You bleed just like everyone else. It's time to leave the streets. You have money. I can work. I'm afraid, if you don't get out now, you're gonna end up dead or permanently in jail."

"Corrin, chill out." I kissed her on the cheek then picked up my phone to call Poppo.

"What up, nigga?" Poppo sounded excited to hear from me.

"I'm on the streets, nigga. Come get me from the Waterside Marriot. Call me when you're outside." I hung up the phone.

"Who was that?" Corrin was in my face again.

"Poppo," I said, my mouth full of food.

"Poppo? How the fuck could you even deal with that nigga, Mike? Especially after what he did to me?" She began to cry.

I hated to see her cry. "Baby, that nigga gonna pay for what he did, trust me. I would never let a nigga disrespect you and get away with it." I hugged her tight.

"Baby, please just don't get into any trouble."

"Don't worry, mama. I'll be back in Cali with you and the kids before you know it."

"You promise?"

"Only death could stop me." I then finished up my food.

Chapter 27

"Unexpected Guest"

Poppo

I'd just gotten a call from Calico to come pick him up. Truth be known, I was kind of disappointed that he had gotten out. I was enjoying being the king and running the castle. But so be it. This just meant I would have to hold true to my word and dead that nigga.

I stopped by the gas station to fill up the car and to grab a six-pack of Heineken for the road. I had a few in the car, but I needed to re-up for the trip. As I walked in, there was a sexy little petite chick that stood at the register. I gave her a smile as I headed toward the freezer to get the Heineken. She smiled back. That's all the confirmation I needed. I already knew I was gonna holla at her when I checked out.

I heard the lyrics of Soulja Boy's song, "Turn My Swag On," blasting from a car stereo outside the store. Shortly after, I heard a commotion at the front of the store. It sounded like a group of rowdy niggas had just walked in.

"What up, sexy?" one of the guys said, obviously speaking to the cashier at the front of the store.

Another one of the boys sang out the lyrics of Soulja Boy's song. He sounded like he was getting closer to me.

Eager to get the fuck out of the store, I grabbed up the Heineken and headed to the front of the store. No sooner than I got to the end of the aisle, I caught eyes with one of the guys. He stood at the other end of the aisle. I recognized him immediately as one of Deebo's boys.

We locked eyes, like a cowboy stand-off, and before I could blink, he fired a shot at me. One hit the case of Heineken, busting the bottles and causing them to drop out of my hand.

I dove to the next aisle and grabbed my gun. I met the guy at the front of the store, and we fired shots at each other, as his boy ran out the front door. Moments later, he followed behind him and jumped in the truck. I ran out the door after them.

On the way out, I noticed the cashier laid out on the floor, blood coming from her chest. She had been shot.

I jumped in my car and followed the SUV Deebo's boys were driving. I got up close enough to them to fire some shots. One shot hit a tire, almost sending the SUV out of control for a second.

I pressed the pedal to the floor, determined to catch up with them. As soon as I got by their side, the driver quickly busted a right turn and ended up losing control of the truck, which flipped over into the ditch.

I pulled over beside them. I saw the driver crawling from the truck and gave him two shots. I was sure that nigga wouldn't be breathing after that.

With no time to waste, I jumped back in my car and sped off, leaving no eyewitnesses behind. I had to make sure I put those niggas to rest, to let niggas on the street know what was really good. It took shit like that to get a name.

Now that I had a couple of murders under my belt, I was sure I would be respected on the streets. Money, power, and respect was all it took to be the boss. I had the money, and with money came power, and now I had finally gained the respect.

Chapter 28

"Handling Business"

Calico

"Gotdamn! What up, big homie?" I dapped up Poppo. "Take me straight to the *A*," I said to him as we hopped in the car.

Once I was in the *A*, Poppo would be easily dealt with. Then I would hunt down Sasha. If I didn't take care of Sasha, I knew I may never have a chance to shower, eat, or fuck on my own will again.

"Damn, nigga! You on a mission. You trying to holla at Diablo, or you trying to get at that bitch, Sasha?"

"My main thang is Sasha, but I'm gonna holla at Diablo too. I gotta do something to make up for that dough you fucked up. How that shit happen though . . . on the real, man?"

"Man, I hooked up with some of these other ATL cats. The first go-'round I gave these niggas half of the shit, and everything went straight. Then next time I met up with them to get rid of the rest, these niggas was on some other shit. They straight robbed me, man."

"What the fuck you doing dealing with them anyway? The plan was for you to deal with Diablo, man."

"I know, but I could sell it to these niggas for a little more."

"Oh, so you was trying to make a little profit of your own. See where greed get you? Nigga, you ain't ready to be no fucking boss, so stop trying to act like one!" I snapped.

"A'ight, duke." Poppo ended the argument.

The more I looked at Poppo, the angrier I got. I'd managed to deal with it nearly the entire drive, but that last thirty minutes was killing me. I was ready to take him out. I was just waiting for the perfect opportunity.

"Yo, can you get a Heineken for me out of the back-seat?" Poppo whined.

"Yeah," I replied, realizing this may be the opportunity I'd been waiting for.

In jail, a nigga can get anything he wants. I was lucky enough to run into this dude that mixed up a number of prescription meds to make this drug that paralyzes a person for at least six hours or so. It was the jail version of the street drug "Special K." Special K was actually a drug used to tranquilize cats.

I popped open a Heineken for Poppo and put in a little bit of the drug and handed it to him. Pretending like I was actually concerned about Poppo drinking and driving, I suggested I take over the driving from that point.

"Man, I've been locking shit down while you were gone," he bragged.

"Oh yeah? How the fuck you lock shit down?" I knew this nigga was a little bitch and didn't have the balls to put a city on lock.

"Nigga, I knocked off Deebo. Niggas thanking me to this day. That nigga was going around taking niggas' money and drugs and shit. Ain't nobody have the balls to stand up to that nigga. But I ain't back down. In-stead, I made that nigga lay down."

"Yeah. I heard about that shit when I was locked up. I wondered what the fuck was going on."

"Nigga tried to bitch me out during a dice game, so I had to let that nigga know. You know what I mean?"

Poppo was going on like he really was the man on the streets.

"Right, right," I said, making him feel a little good.

"Then I got word that his boys were after me. Niggas was calling my phone, threatening me and shit, but I was like, 'Fuck it! Y'all niggas know where to find me. I ain't hiding. So days had passed, and I ain't never see none of these niggas, that is until tonight."

"Tonight? You ran into these niggas before you came to pick me up?" Now I was really interested in what Poppo had to say.

"Yeah, man. I was at the fucking gas station, and these niggas rolled up on me. They started busting shots and shit, even hit the cute little cashier bitch. Anyway, I catch up with these niggas about a mile from the gas station. They had flipped the truck and shit, so when the nigga come crawling out the truck, I hit him with a couple of shots."

"So that nigga dead?"

Totally ignoring my question, Poppo called out in a panic, "Yo, I can't move my legs."

That was my queue. It didn't even take ten minutes before that shit I put in his drink started to work.

"Pretty soon you won't be able to move your arms either." I gave him a devious grin.

"What did you do to me?"

"Shut the fuck up!" I yelled and punched him in the mouth. Afterwards, my hand hurt like hell.

Shortly after, we arrived at an abandoned warehouse. I came across it on our last visit to Atlanta. The only things there were spiders and rats. I pulled

Poppo's still paralyzed body from the car and dumped
it on the dirty warehouse floor. Then I placed duct tape
around his arms and legs. I'd had him purchase all
the equipment prior to picking me up, so we would be
prepared for Sasha. Little did this punk know it was for
him.

In the warehouse, I started cutting him on his arms,
legs, face, fingers, and neck. Finally, I took off his shirt
and cut his chest and stomach open. For a while, I let
him bleed out. That nigga looked petrified. I took my
time torturing him before I began to speak.

"What? You thought you would get away at trying
to duck me and play with my fucking money? Not to
mention, you violated me by putting your hands on
my baby moms. That alone is a death sentence, bitch
nigga! Did you forget where you came from nigga? You
were nobody. I made you, Poppo. When we met, you
were on the corner selling nicks and dimes, nigga. I
opened the doors for you." I kicked him in the head. I
couldn't believe this ungrateful-ass nigga.

"Fuck you, Calico! I ain't your bitch. I just ain't have
the chance to prove it to your ass. You suppose to be
dead right now, nigga. I had plans for you. You never
was suppose to leave Bankhead. If that stupid-ass
crackhead hadn't fucked up, you wouldn't be here right
now!"

"So what the fuck you saying, Poppo? You tried to
fucking set me up?" Furious, I kicked him two more
times.

Poppo began to laugh. Then he coughed up blood.
"Why you think your gun jammed?" he forced out the
words then spat out blood. "I had given the crackhead
a gun to pull on you and force you in the house, then
from there, I was gonna take over. I made sure the gun
would jam because I knew you would pull it out on

him. But like a typical fucking crackhead, this nigga sold the gun and decided to try and rob you at knife-point instead."

"Fuck you, nigga!"

I'd heard enough, so with gloves on and his own gun, I shot him twice in the head and left him as a nice snack for the rats.

Now that I had one task down, it was time to move on to the other. I needed to holla at Diablo. According to Poppo, Sasha was working for Diablo, so I knew as long as I was fucking with him, I was guaranteed to run into that bitch.

"What up, Diablo?" I shouted out the window to him as I pulled up in front of the club.

He spoke to me through the window. "What's up, man?"

"Hop in, so I can holla at you."

Diablo walked over to the passenger side and hopped in. I wanted to waste no time getting right down to business. I knew I would have to come at this nigga right, so I would be able to get the information I needed. But before I could begin to speak, Diablo started talking.

"Yo, nigga, I need you bad right now. I just took a major loss."

"For real? Damn, man! That's how the game go. What you looking for?"

"Well, I was hoping I could give you something, and you match what I buy. You dig?"

"A'ight, I can work with that. But I need to ask you about this chick you work with . . . Sasha."

"Sasha? Man, you don't want to deal with that conniving bitch."

Diablo had just made my job a whole lot easier. I was thinking I was gonna have to act like I wanna use the bitch as a runner or some bullshit, to get info from that nigga, but it looked like Sasha had rubbed this nigga the wrong way.

"What's up with her man?" I asked, wanting Diablo to elaborate.

"She's the reason I'm fucked up right now. I gives this bitch some weight to take to my niggas in VA, and she calls me, saying, this nigga Touch robbed her. So I goes up there ready for war and roughs this nigga up. I shot after him and everything. On top of that, I still had to straighten these niggas that didn't get their shit, because they had already given me the money. So a few days later, I get a call from these same niggas, saying, they just bought some cheap shit from some niggas that robbed a bitch. When they described the bitch, I knew it was none other than Sasha. The puzzle just fit together way too perfectly. The bitch had lied. Touch ain't rob her. That bitch robbed me!"

"Oh yeah? So now you and this nigga Touch got beef?"

"Hell yeah. Now that's some extra shit I gotta deal with, on top of the loss I took."

"I know that nigga Touch. Me and him had a little run-in too," I said, not sharing too much information. "So about this bitch, Sasha . . . have you talked to her?"

"Nah. I don't want her to know I know what's up. I'm trying to get her here so I can deal with her. I've been calling her, telling her I got more work for her, but she dragging her feet getting here. She suppose to blow in tomorrow though."

"How about this? Get her here, and I'll deal with her for you." I offered to take the problem off of Diablo's hands without telling him my personal beef with her.

"Done deal. I'll let you know when she's at the club, and you get at me about that other thang when you ready. Or you gonna send your boy Poppo? Where that nigga at anyway? I been trying to holla at him since that shit went down."

"Poppo? That nigga ain't breathing," I said with no emotion at all.

"Huh? Fuck you talking about Calico?" Diablo laugh nervously.

"I gutted him." Again I had a completely blank face.

Diablo didn't respond. He wasn't sure how to take me. He just stared at me speechless, looking totally confused.

"I'm fucking with you, nigga. He straight," I said, breaking the ice.

"Man, you had me fucked up. I'm gone." Diablo dapped me up and got out of the car.

I pulled out of the parking lot, pleased that things were falling into place.

Chapter 29

"A Day Full of Surprises"

Jewel

It had been weeks since I'd seen or heard from Touch. The last time I saw him was the night he left the house, crushing any hopes I had of us reuniting. Although it wasn't an easy task, I'd managed to stop calling his phone twenty times a day and thinking about him every minute of the hour.

My days were long and lonely, but I was determined to get over him. I did as many things as I could to stay occupied. The house was spotless, because I'd used cleaning as one of my distractions. I'd gone as far as to even clean out our closets, pantry, and cupboards. When I wasn't cleaning, I was working out or at the gym taking a swim.

Weeks earlier, all of my time was wasted planning for my wedding, but since it was pretty obvious no wedding was in my future, I'd stopped all proceedings. I'd even tried to collect refunds on some of my deposits.

Although Touch wasn't around, and there was no money coming in, the bills didn't stop accumulating. Touch and I had accrued quite some debt with our ghetto-fabulous lifestyle, and our bank account was getting smaller and smaller each day. I didn't know what the future had in store. It even crossed my mind to contact my boy from TMF to do a little business transaction of my own.

I checked the mail to see what new bills had come through. As I sat at the breakfast bar and flipped through the bills, my stomach turned. I literally became nauseous. I jumped from the barstool and rushed to the downstairs bathroom.

"Blaugh!" I began to vomit in the toilet.

I'd been experiencing nausea and fatigue for the past couple of days. At first, I thought I was coming down with a stomach virus, but it was too sporadic. I'd even tried calling Misty to get her medical advice, but I had not even talked to her that much since the night Touch left. I'd left numerous messages, but she hadn't returned any of them. She hadn't even returned my text messages. I wondered if I'd done something wrong or if she was mad at me. It was like she and Touch both walked out my life at the same time.

Not knowing what else to do, I decided to try the obvious and take a pregnancy test. I unwrapped the wrapper and placed the tip of the test under a stream of my urine, as the instructions stated. I recapped the tip and washed my hands and waited.

Two minutes seemed like two hours, but when it was over, I rushed over to read the results. I glanced down and read the results. Unsure if what I was seeing was correct, I picked the test up and read it a little closer.

"Oh, God!" I screamed then burst into tears.

I dropped the test on the floor then slid down in a corner of the bathroom. I sat there with my knees bent to my chest and buried my head in my arms and sobbed uncontrollably. I couldn't understand what I had done so bad that God was punishing me like this. In a matter of weeks, I'd lost my future husband, become distant with my new best friend, and now I was going to be forced to raise a child alone. There was no way I was prepared to raise a child. I had neither security nor the slightest idea how to even raise a damn child.

I gathered myself and tried to call Misty again. I really hated to bother her, because I'd called so many times already, but I really needed someone to talk to. I felt like I was literally on the verge of a nervous breakdown.

"Hey, girl," Misty answered right away.

I was relieved to hear her voice. "Hey, Misty. I really need to talk. I've been trying to reach you for some time now."

"I know, I know. I'm so sorry, boo. I've been working overtime at the hospital, so I've been so exhausted. In fact, I'm on my way in right now. I'll call you when I get off."

"Okay," I said, although I was quite disappointed that I hadn't a chance to tell her what was going on with me.

Stressed, exhausted, and just plain old depressed, I drank a cup of Sleepytime tea and laid down for a nap.

Bang! Bang! Bang!

I was wakened by a hard, constant banging on the front door.

Three Virginia Beach police officers were at the door.

"Yes," I answered.

"Are you California Jewel Diaz?" one of the police officers asked.

"Who? No, you have the wrong house." I backed up and slammed and locked the door in their faces.

It was a dead bolt, so they were going to have to break the door down. I ran upstairs to grab my purse and raided the sock drawer to see what cash I had in there. I didn't have much time.

While the cops were desperately trying to get my front door open, I quickly ran downstairs and headed out of the back kitchen door.

A police officer greeted me with a 9 mm gun in my face. "Get down on the ground!" he ordered.

Another one cuffed me. "You're under arrest for conspiracy to distribute narcotics. Where is Trayvon Davis?"

The third police officer started reading me my Miranda rights, as the other officers rushed through the house looking for Touch.

I was speechless. I couldn't believe what was going on. I sat silent as a mouse as those pigs threw me in the police car to take me down to the station.

Chapter 30

"On a Mission"

Touch

Days had passed since I'd fucked Misty, but something about her just didn't sit well with me. I couldn't understand how this bitch was supposed to be Jewel's girl, yet she gave the pussy up so easily. I couldn't help but think about Sasha when I thought about Misty. Those two bitches were one and the same.

I actually started to feel sorry for Jewel. She had the worst luck, when it came to females.

As I pulled into the driveway, I decided to give her a call. Her cell phone went straight to voice mail, so I tried calling the house. When I called the house, the phone rang out until voice mail picked up. It had been a couple days since I'd last received a call from Jewel. I'd originally figured she had finally gotten some pride and decided to stop calling, but when I called her and wasn't able to reach her, something came over me.

Deep inside, I felt something was wrong. I got out of my car and headed to my front door.

"Yo, Touch," my neighbor called out to me.

I stopped in the driveway to speak to him. "What's up, man?"

"The police was at your crib today, man. They was out here asking niggas when the last time you been here and shit."

I didn't know what the fuck was up, but I wasn't taking no chances in finding out. I'd already planned to take a trip to the A to deal with this nigga Diablo, but the information my neighbor shared with me had instantly put those plans into motion.

I didn't even bother going into my crib. After talking to my neighbor, I walked right back to my car and got right back in.

I called up Lisa.

"Hey, boo." She sounded excited to hear from me.

"What's up, baby?"

"Nothing. Chilling. What's up with you?"

"I need a favor, ma."

"Okay. What's up? You know you can always depend on me, even though you be putting me through hell with all your bitches."

"Ah shit! There you go. How many times I gotta apologize?"

"Mmmm . . . maybe about ten to fifteen more times." Lisa giggled.

"Look, on the real, though, I need you to switch cars with me for a few days."

"Oh, no problem. I don't mind pushing the seven forty-five. But the question is, what is your bitches gonna say? I don't want no beef, Touch."

"Everything good, man. I'm on my way over." I hung up the phone.

When I got to Lisa's house, it took about ten minutes for me to bend her over and get a quickie. Then I switched cars with her, and I hopped on the interstate and headed to Atlanta.

My brain was racing the entire ride there. I tried calling Jewel several times, but I still couldn't get her. Then I began to think even harder. I started to wonder if this bitch had set me up. I knew bitches had a habit of letting their emotions take over and doing some crazy shit. That would explain why she stopped calling me and wasn't answering any of my calls.

My mind ran on Misty. *What if that bitch set me up? She knew a little too much about me, and the bitch just came on the scene out of nowhere.* At that point everybody was a suspect. I broke my phone in two and threw it out the window onto Interstate 95.

The longer I drove, the more I was consumed with my thoughts. I tried to listen to the radio and CDs, but nothing could get my mind off this shit. *This is what I get for thinking with my dick. I should have never fucked that girl, Misty. I didn't even know that broad like that. What if Jewel found out we had sex and now she's out to get me? These bitches had me slipping.*

I was disappointed with myself. I was usually on point with shit, but I had to admit, I'd fucked up a whole lot in those past few weeks. I knew when I got to the *A*, I would need to get one of those pre-paid cell phones to conduct my business, but first I needed to pay a visit to Diablo.

It worked out in my favor that I got to Atlanta late that night. I went to a strip club called Bottoms Up that I frequented. I figured I would catch Diablo there. The last time I ran into him, it was at that same spot.

Sure enough, just like I figured, he was there. I discreetly sat in the corner of the club and waited patiently for an hour for him to head out.

I watched him stagger to his car. I pulled out of the parking lot behind him. He was too drunk to realize I was even following him. Plus, I was thankful he didn't take no bitches home with him. The less witnesses, the better for me. Besides, the only one whose head I wanted to put a bullet in was Diablo's.

Diablo pulled up in his garage. Just as he was closing the garage door, I literally rolled my body in underneath it before it shut. When I pressed up on him, his back was turned.

"Nigga, what the fuck you doing here?" he asked before I put my gun into his back.

"You don't get to ask any questions." Without warning, I shot him in the leg.

"Man, you shot me!" he whimpered in surprise.

"Do we understand each other? Next time, I have no problem with shooting you in the throat."

"Yeah, I got you." He nodded, sweat coming from his forehead.

"Take me to your basement." I shoved him in the back with my gun.

I followed a limping Diablo through his house and into his basement. Once there, I tied him up with some rope he had on the counter in his basement and got ready for his execution.

"Touch, man, please don't kill me," he begged. "I got kids."

"There you go again with your mouth." I pistol-whipped him.

"Please," he said, blood pouring down the side of his face.

"Why you think I stole from you, bitch nigga? I run these fucking streets. You really think I need to steal from you?" I asked.

"Sasha told me you robbed her. That shit was worth eighty grand. But I later found out that bitch kept the shit and tried selling it to some niggas in VA. I guess she set us both up, man. The bitch is sheisty. Maybe she was thinking one of us would be in a six-feet-deep grave right now. Please—"

"Nigga, shut the fuck up! Crying like a little bitch!" I untied him enough where he could maneuver his way out of the ropes. Then I quickly dipped out of his crib.

I knew deep inside this nigga was telling the truth. One, I knew how this bitch Sasha moved, and two, just how that shit happened didn't seem right. First, the bitch was trying to get a piece of my dick. Then as soon as I diss her, this nigga was calling up saying I robbed Sasha. That bitch just saw an opportunity for get-back and to make some cash all at the same time.

Chapter 31

"Payback's a Bitch"

Calico

"Yo," I answered Diablo's call, hoping he was gonna deliver the message I'd been waiting for.

"She's ready for you."

"Cool. I'm on my way."

I'd waited nearly two weeks for Sasha to arrive in Atlanta. For a moment I had thought about going to VA to look for her ass. Luckily, I waited a few extra days.

I jumped in my car and headed to the club, where I slid in unnoticed, trying to draw as little attention to myself as possible.

The scene was the same as the very first time I'd gone there. There was a group of guys in one corner playing Madden on the projector screen, another set gambling in another corner, and Diablo was in another spot, having a conversation with another cat.

Just like before, I entered the dice game. After about fifteen minutes, I heard niggas talking about a phat ass that just bounced into the club, so I turned around to check out the ass too.

Bingo, I thought, a smile spreading across my face. That phat ass looked real familiar to me. I was almost certain it belonged to Sasha.

To be sure, I pulled out my cell phone and scrolled down to the name Malibu then hit *send*. Moments later, her phone began to ring, and she started to fumble through her purse to search for it. Already having my confirmation, I hung up.

I sat quiet as a mouse, watching Sasha's every move. She didn't look in the direction of the dice game, so she didn't even notice me.

When I saw her leave the club, I slipped out of the club and cautiously made my way to the car and jumped in. I noticed a staggering Diablo right behind me.

"What the fuck happen to you, man?" I asked as soon as he got in the car.

"I got shot."

"What? Man, get the fuck out of the car! I can't be taking no cripple with me on no shit like this," I said, not willing to take any risks.

"Chill out, man. Everything a'ight."

"Yeah, okay, nigga. Shit get tight, you on your own."

"I can hold my own, man. Don't worry about me."

That ended the conversation as we spotted Sasha loading the duffle bag Diablo had given her in the trunk of her car. I waited until she left the parking lot and followed her for more than twenty minutes, waiting for the right time to let her have it.

"Looks like she's headed to her crib," Diablo said. "We gonna have to be careful because she has two little boys, and sometimes her baby daddy be there."

I watched as she pulled onto a quiet neighborhood street then into an apartment complex. Sasha grabbed her duffle bag and headed into her third-floor apartment.

Minutes later, we grabbed our guns and rushed to her apartment.

I kicked the door in. I was the first to spot her. "Surprise, surprise, bitch!" I said, pointing the gun in her face.

"What the fuck is this?"

Smack!

I hit her hard in the face with the gun, and she dropped to the floor.

"Shut the fuck up, bitch!" Diablo pinned her to the living room wall. "I ought to kill your muthafuckin' ass."

I punched her in the face. "How long did you think you was going to keep playing us and we not figure out your damn scheme?" This bitch deserved to get beat like a dude. She thought she was so fucking slick, taking other people's money.

Diablo still had her pinned to the wall.

"Please . . . my sons are in the other room sleeping. Don't hurt them," she begged, almost breathless.

"Let her go," I ordered Diablo, and she fell helpless to the ground, choking and trying desperately to catch her breath. "I got something better in store for this bitch." I snatched her shirt off, leaving her in her bra. "You want to see what it feels like to have something precious taken from you?" I slid my gun beneath her bra, forcing her breasts to pop out.

Sasha tried desperately to crawl away. "Please don't do this."

Wham! I kicked her one time in the stomach.

As she balled up in the fetal position, I lifted her skirt and began to unbutton my pants. I was gonna teach her a lesson.

I glanced over to see Diablo standing in the corner like a scared little bitch.

I forced her legs open. My dick was rock-hard as I slid her panties off, leaving her completely naked.

"Mommy," a little boy called out, rubbing his eyes.

Without flinching, I shot him in the head one time.

"No, not my baby! Nnnnooooo! He didn't deserve that!" Sasha screamed out, trying to fight with all her might.

Now that shit had turned in a different direction, sex was no longer a priority. I needed to get the money and get the fuck out. Besides, Diablo looked as though he was gonna pass out at any moment.

I kicked Sasha in the stomach again. "Where's the money?"

"My baby!"

"Where's the fuckin' money?" I followed with three more kicks to the stomach.

"Oh my God!"

"Where's my muthafuckin' money, bitch?" I punched her in the head to help her remember where it was.

"All right, all right, I will get it for you. It's in the living room closet," she informed us and began slowly crawling in that direction.

Diablo and I quickly went to the living room and opened the closet door. We began to search through all the shit stacked up in the closet.

"It's near the back," she said between tears.

After ransacking the closet for a few minutes and still not finding shit, I started to feel like this bitch was trying to play me. I turned around, planning to go and shoot this bitch's other son, to let her know this shit wasn't a game, but to my surprise when I turned around, she was gone.

I looked up just in time to see her climbing over the balcony. I started firing shots, and this crazy bitch straight jumped, never looking back or thinking twice.

Diablo and I rushed over and looked from the balcony of the apartment to see a lifeless body covered in blood. I would have shot that bitch again, but from the looks of things, there was no need. That bitch was definitely gone, her body twisted like a pretzel and blood flowing all around her.

Almost instantly, people started to crowd around her and yell out for help. The last thing my ass needed was even more witnesses to get rid of.

Diablo and I got the fuck out of there. This shit was spiraling out of control. We ran down the stairs, but when we reached the bottom, police were already pulling up. There was no way we could make it to the car, so our only option was to make a run for it. Knowing Diablo would only slow me up, I dipped off, leaving him alone. He didn't even resist, and the cops arrested him right away.

The cops were right on my heels.

"Get down! Put down your weapon!"

There was no way I could go down. This time for sure I would never see daylight. Not even Natalia would be able to get me out of this one. So, with no other option left, I decided to shoot my way out. It was do or die.

I stopped in my tracks, turned around, and faced the cops. They all froze and pointed their guns right at me. I said a silent prayer and slowly lifted my gun.

Bam! Bam! Bam! Bam! Bam! Bam!

It seemed like shots rang out forever, my body gyrating and burning all over. I knew I was taking my last breath and this was lights out.

Chapter 32

"Life on the Run"

Touch

Looking down at my watch, the clock read a little after midnight. Going down 95 South was easy and smooth for me, but coming back up 95 North was a muthafucker. At least five damn times, I almost fell asleep at the wheel. The last time I dozed off, I veered to the left and woke up in time to barely miss the deep ridges on the side of the road, which scared the hell out of me. One thing for sure, those things definitely worked. Otherwise, my ass would have come off the highway and ended up in the ditch.

I turned on some country music and rolled down every window in the car as I continued my drive. I knew once I got on Route 58 East, it would be smooth sailing from there.

My plan was to go chill at Lisa's house for a while and lay low. I needed to get my mind right and sort some things out. I called her up to run things by her.

"Hey, boo," she greeted me on the phone.

"You home?"

"Well, I was just about to go out with my girls downtown and barhop. What's up?"

"I want to come through for a while."

"That's cool. I should be back home in a couple of hours."

"Tell you what . . . if you stay home and wait for me in that red piece you wore last time, I'll stop by and grab a to-go order for you at IHOP. Don't worry, I know you like your bacon extra crispy."

"You know that's one of my favorite spots. Let me call my girlfriends and tell them I won't be coming out tonight. Don't keep me waiting too long," she cooed.

"Give or take, I'll be about an hour," I assured her and hung up the phone.

Out of my left rearview mirror, I noticed this black Tahoe had been following me ever since I'd passed Emporia. At the time I was almost to Suffolk. It wasn't unusual for a person to be behind you for a while, because Route 58 was such a long stretch, but I didn't want to take any chances.

I pressed on the gas pedal and moved up to eighty miles per hour. The Tahoe did the same. I moved up to ninety and hauled ass. When I saw they were still keeping up, I was sure I was being followed.

Not knowing if these were some of Diablo's niggas or someone from Calico's crew, I pulled out my gun and cocked it.

I slowed down a little, prepared to bust shots all up in that fucking truck, but to my surprise, as soon as I slowed down, sirens began to go off. I looked in the rearview to see blue and red flashing lights on the dashboard of the truck. It was the fucking police in an unmarked car!

My forehead was sweating, and my heart felt as though it was beating out of my chest, but I couldn't lose focus. I continued to keep my eye on the Tahoe and on the road.

I moved up to ninety-five miles per hour. I wasn't going to let those fucking pigs take me in without a fight, and throw me in a urine-infested cell. I drove like a crazed man, swerving around cars.

In no time I was in Portsmouth. I knew a few spots I could definitely dodge the fucking police in that area, especially since it was only one truck after me.

I didn't know if this nigga thought he was "Supercop" or what, but he never called for backup. Shit like that made me think they wanted to do a nigga in. With no backup, he could kill me and then say it was in self-defense. You never could tell when it came to cops these days.

I noticed an exit ramp a short distance ahead. I hopped on the ramp, doing ninety, not letting up on speed the least little bit.

Just as I was going around the curve on the ramp, I looked up to see a fucking Honda Accord coming the wrong way. It was coming right at me. With no time to stop, I swerved to avoid hitting it.

Unfortunately, the black Tahoe behind me wasn't so lucky. All I heard was a loud crash then I saw the Tahoe go up into the air and flip over at least four times. Then the Tahoe rolled and landed with the tires up.

Damn! That nigga gotta be good as dead. I breathed a sigh of relief.

My next stop was IHOP and then to Lisa's house.

Chapter 33

"Judgment Day"

Jewel

My stomach was in knots as I entered the courtroom and sat at the defendant's table with my lawyer. I didn't know if it was anxiety, or my baby doing flips in my stomach, but I surely felt sick. Minutes later, the prosecutor came and sat across from me at his table. Then came the judge.

I took a deep breath as the prosecution began.

"Your Honor, we would like to request a continuance. There's been a tragic accident. Our key witness has been killed in the line of duty. Melissa Johnson, the lead detective on this case, had gathered an enormous amount of evidence and tapes that led to the indictments for California Jewel Diaz, AKA Jewel, Trayvon Davis, AKA Touch, and several members of the True Mafia Family, AKA TMF. Without her here to testify, the prosecution needs a little more time to develop a stronger case."

My attorney stood up to speak. "Your Honor, the defense would like to request a bond until the next trial date."

"Continuance granted. Bond set at one hundred thousand dollars," the judge said then dismissed court.

Luckily I'd grabbed the money Touch and I had in the stash. Plus, I had gotten refunds on some of the deposits I'd paid for the wedding. That money, added to my little nest egg I had saved up for emergencies, was just enough for me to make bond. Hours later, I was on my way home.

I took a deep breath as I placed my key in the door and walked in my house. A part of me screamed, *Home, sweet home*, while another part of me wanted nothing to do with that house or any of the memories that came along with it. I made my way through the mess the cops left behind while searching the house, and found a comfortable spot on the couch in the living room.

I flipped on the television and heard the reporter say, *"Lead detective in big conspiracy case killed in the line of duty."*

Knowing this was my case they were referring to, I turned up the volume on the television. I watched as they showed the pictures from the scene of the crime. It was a bad accident on the exit ramp of the interstate. They showed pictures of a black Tahoe that was flat as a pancake. It looked like it had flipped over like six times. Evidently the officer was on a high-speed chase when a drunk driver came up the exit ramp and hit her head-on.

When they flashed a picture of the detective on the screen, my mouth dropped to the floor. I rubbed my eyes to make sure I wasn't hallucinating.

"Melissa Johnson was in pursuit of a wanted felon by the name of Trayvon Davis, AKA Touch when . . ."

The rest of the words the reporter spoke were a blur. My brain wandered elsewhere. *Misty, nurse Misty, wed-*

ding planner Misty, my so-called best friend Misty was an undercover police! Everything in me just wanted to burst into tears. *How could I have been so stupid? I knew better. I'd already gone through this with Sasha, and Touch had warned me from day one. But I didn't listen.*

I began to feel like all of this was my fault. I broke the rules of the game. I let that bitch come into our lives, and day by day she tore it up, leaving me facing conspiracy charges, broke, and pregnant, with my baby father on the run.

My heart suddenly ached for Touch, so I called him up.

"Hello?" he answered on the first ring.

I burst into tears. Just the sound of his voice was so comforting. "Touch."

"What's up, Jewel? What's wrong, baby girl?"

"Touch, I miss you. I need you. *We* need you."

"Jewel, I can't even lie to you. I miss you too. I even tried calling you, but you didn't answer my calls."

"Touch, I was in jail. I've been through so much. You have put me through so much. You don't understand how this shit has torn me apart. I went days without eating, and nights without sleeping."

"I'm sorry, Jewel. I swear, I'm sorry. What happened? What the fuck were you doing in jail?"

"The police came here with an indictment on conspiracy charges. They had one for you too."

"Yeah, I heard. My neighbor told me they came to my crib. What the fuck is going on? This shit is crazy."

"Touch, you're all over the news."

"What the fuck?"

"Yes, you are. You were in a high-speed chase last night?"

"Yeah."

"Well, do you know who was following you?"

"No."

"It was Misty."

"Misty?" Touch said in a confused tone.

"Yes, Touch. She was an undercover police officer the entire time. She set us up. I feel so responsible. I should have never let her in. You warned me time and time again. This is all my fault." I began to cry even more.

"Nah, baby. It's not just you. I'm just as much to blame. Now I just gotta make shit right."

"Yes, you do. Please make things right." I then said again, "We need you here with us."

Touch finally caught on. "Why do you keep on saying that? Who is *we*?"

"*We* is me and your unborn child."

"My unborn child?"

"Yes, Touch. I'm pregnant."

Touch didn't say anything, and for a moment, we sat on the phone in silence.

I finally spoke up. "So what do we do now?"

"We be a family. I'm on my way home." Touch hung up the phone.

For the first time in days, I had a smile on my face.

CALIFORNIA CONNECTION 3

Chapter 1

"Snitch Bitch"

Jewel

"Baby, how much longer before you get here?" I asked Touch in my sweetest voice.

"About fifteen minutes," he replied then hung up.

There was a lump in my throat as big as a rock hanging up the phone. I swallowed in an attempt to get it down. With my head hung low, I gently rubbed my stomach and thought about my unborn child.

"Take your positions, guys. He'll be here shortly!" the head detective instructed his guys to man their posts to prepare for Touch's arrival.

"Please forgive Mommy, baby," I whispered toward my protruding stomach. "I just want the best for you."

My palms started to sweat, my heart was racing, and tears rolled down my eyes. Seconds seemed like minutes, and minutes seemed like hours, as I waited for Touch to come home. I knew as soon as he walked through the door they would sweep him away and I would never see him again. My child would be without a father, and I would lose the love of my life. But I also knew with life comes sacrifices, and this was just a sacrifice I had to make. It was either him or me, and there was no way I was gonna give birth to my child in jail.

"You sure you got this?" the police officer asked me as he escorted me from my bedroom to the living room.

"Yes, officer!" I rolled my eyes, sick of the officers constantly checking to make sure I was down for this.

"You just stay hidden in the bedroom—"

"Oh my God!" I yelled, interrupting the officer mid-sentence. "We've been over this too many times." He'd gone over the instructions time and time again. I had it already!

"Just want to make sure you're not having any second thoughts or planning to try anything tricky. If this goes wrong, it's your head, little lady."

Save your threats, asshole; they don't scare me, I thought. I definitely wasn't having second thoughts. At this point it was all about my baby. The only thing I had to worry about was getting the fuck out of dodge when this was all over with because I knew, once Touch realized I was the bitch who got this show in motion, all hell would break loose.

"He's here," I heard another police officer announce from the hallway. I looked out the window to see Touch cautiously walking up to the house. Now I was having second thoughts. The fifteen minutes came sooner than I expected.

The officer quickly whisked me into the bedroom. My nerves were building, and it took all I had to refrain from bursting into tears.

"Honey, I'm home," Touched yelled as he opened the front door, a huge smile across his face.

Within seconds cops came out from every closet, corner, and room in my house, commands coming from every direction as they rushed Touch with weapons pulled.

"Don't move!

"Freeze!"

"Hands in the air!"

Touch was surrounded. Taken by surprise, and with no chance to run and nowhere to escape, he stood frozen. Despite all the warning the cops gave me, I couldn't resist looking out into the living room. All eyes were on him, but his eyes were only fixated on me. There was a cold look in his eyes. A look I'd never seen before. I could imagine it was a look of disgust, hurt, anger, and betrayal. Maybe that's why I'd never seen this look before because I'd never done such a thing to him to warrant such emotions.

Touch yelled out, "How the fuck could you do this to me? After all we've been through, Jewel! You bitch!"

I felt ashamed that I had set him up. I had to keep telling myself it was for my own good, the good of my unborn baby.

With my cover blown, the officers didn't try and stop me when I walked out of the bedroom. They moved him to the kitchen, and I watched as Touch placed his hands on the counter and the officers patted him down.

For a second, I thought I saw a tear in his eyes. Unable to bear the pain, I turned away. "Answer me!" Touch demanded. "Answer me!"

I refused to give him any explanation. Besides, I knew it would only anger him even more.

"It's over, Touch. Say good-bye," one of the officers said. Suddenly, in one cat-like movement, Touch reached in the kitchen drawer, pulled out a small handgun, and *Pow!*

An enormous force slammed into me, and I fell to my feet as a stinging pain ripped through my stomach.

I looked down to see my white shirt soaked with bright red blood.

"Oh my God!" I screamed out in a panic. "He shot me! He shot me!"

My body jolted, and I shot straight up. I was panting and sweating. I was confused as I looked around the quiet room. *Where is the police? Where is Touch?*

I rubbed my eyes and gathered myself. It was then I realized I was still in bed. I'd been dreaming. I breathed a huge sigh of relief as I gathered myself. *Whew!* Why was I having this dream? The vividness of it scared the shit out of me. What did it mean?

Chapter 2

"One-way Ticket to Jail"

Touch

The minute I heard I was wanted for conspiracy I disappeared. I didn't even bother telling Jewel I was getting ghost, I just vanished. Well, not really vanished. I went and holed up at my other girl, Lisa's house. We never went out together, and I never told any of my boys about her. She was my side bitch, and as long as I kept her lifestyle funded, she never complained.

It had been weeks since my disappearance, and I was really starting to miss Jewel. Not a day went by that I didn't think of her and my unborn child. I'd spent days wondering if it was a boy or a girl, and who it would look like, if it would look like my other kids, me, or Jewel.

I was excited about having a kid with Jewel because I knew I would always have access to it. Unlike with my other kids. Their mother was a bitch who never let me see my babies, and it hurt. I wanted the best for all my babies, but this new one was going to get spoiled. I already knew that.

I wondered if Jewel was eating right. I was hoping she was seeing the doctor and taking care of herself. Sometimes I even wondered if the stress of all the bullshit would cause her to have a miscarriage.

Life was truly fucked up, and I had no idea I'd be so miserable without Jewel and my unborn child. Being on the run was for the fucking birds!

When I'd unexpectedly caught conspiracy charges, Lisa was my only hope. I had no place else to hole up. I damn sure wasn't about to go to one of my boys' houses. Those loose-lipped niggas would have told someone where I was laying my head. And a hotel was out of the question because I wasn't about to pay some crazy amount of money to get caught on video surveillance cameras. So I had been laying low at Lisa's crib until I could figure out my next move.

"Have you seen my Ben and Jerry's mint chocolate chip ice cream?" Lisa asked me, a look of disgust on her face.

Lisa had just come home from work. She hadn't been in the house five damn minutes, and she was already tripping. Lisa was cool with being my side chick, but lately she was really starting to annoy a nigga. I don't know what her problem was, but it seemed that since my money had run low, her attitude was all out of whack. I guess my pops was right when he warned me, "Women think you ain't shit when your paper ain't right. But as long as you got money, they respect you."

"Yeah, I ate it a couple of hours ago," I responded, trying my best to keep my focus on ESPN.

"Well, can you go run to the store and pick me up some more? I've had a long day at work, and I was really looking forward to coming home and eating my ice cream," she expressed with some attitude.

This bitch must be on dope. Is she forgetting I am wanted? I looked at Lisa like she was a damn fool. I didn't know if it was that time of the month for her or what, but she was really on some shit lately.

I rarely went out the house, and if I did go out, I was dressed in all black, with dark shades, and a fucking rastaman hat with fake dreads. I wasn't about to go through all that for some ice cream! I wanted to cuss Lisa's ass out for talking stupid, but I stayed calm in an attempt to keep the peace. I needed her crib to stay and only had about two hundred dollars to my name.

I tried to smooth things over. "When my paper gets right, I will pick up anything you want, baby girl."

Lisa snapped at me, "Go do something! Get a job! Because I'm tired of you laying around here."

I already had enough on my plate, so dealing with a nagging woman every day wasn't something I needed. Waiting for the perfect time to make a move wasn't easy. It took patience and planning, because one wrong move could easily get a nigga locked up. I was miserable not being able to move around the way I used to.

With the word on the street that I was wanted, nobody was willing to fuck with me on no business shit. I had no connects. I knew in a time like this I needed to be with Jewel. She was a true rider. She would have found a way to make shit right. Lisa, on the other hand, was selfish as hell and stingy with her money and her pussy.

"You know damn well I can't go get no fuckin' job! So, for once, will you just shut the fuck up with your smart-ass comments? I'm trying to watch the game." I turned the volume up on the TV.

"Nigga, please! I pay the cable bill in this house." Lisa grabbed the remote out of my hand and turned the TV off. "If I have something to say, you damn sure are going to listen." She then threw the remote back at me. That was the last straw. This bitch had been riding my ass for the past week. I couldn't take it anymore. That move sent me into a rage. I grabbed Lisa by the neck and slammed her on the couch. I'd lost it for a minute. It wasn't until I noticed blood all over her face that I snapped back to reality.

When it was all said and done, I'd choked her and punched her in the face, giving her a bloody nose. Realizing I'd truly fucked up, I quickly let her go. I just couldn't control my rage sometimes. I had one domestic abuse case on my hands, and I sure as shit wasn't looking for another.

"You done fucked up, muthafucka," Lisa screamed and ran to the kitchen. She grabbed a knife and started after me.

I picked up Lisa's car keys and ran for the garage. My time with her was up. Time to find a new place to crash.

"Get the hell out of my house! And if you take my car, your ass is going to jail," she shouted as I rushed into the garage and jumped in her car.

I knew what she was saying was probably true, but at the time, I was all out of options. I pressed the garage opener and threw the car in reverse.

Lisa banged on the hood of the car as I was backing out the driveway.

Boom! Boom! Boom!

"Your ass is going to jail!" she shouted. "Stupid-ass nigga!"

I put the car in drive and sped off, leaving her standing in the middle of the street. I looked in my rearview mirror and saw her on her cell phone. I already knew what that meant. That bitch was calling the police. I needed to get rid of her car fast.

I had no idea where to go. I didn't want to involve Jewel in any more of my bullshit, so her crib was off limits. It seemed my only hope was Lexi, my baby mother. She and I had ended on a real fucked-up note—with a domestic abuse rap. In fact, I couldn't stand the bitch, but I had no other choice, so I headed her way.

After twenty minutes of cruising down the highway, constantly looking over my shoulder and making sure to abide by the speed limit, I was at my baby mother's exit. Two more minutes and I would be at her crib. I couldn't believe I had made it all the way here.

I was hoping Lexi would let me in. My plan was to drop the car a few blocks away and walk the rest of the distance to her house. That didn't happen because, as soon as I exited the ramp, blue lights were flashing from every direction.

"Muthafucka!" I yelled to no one in particular.

I wondered how the fuck they had found me. *No use trying to figure that shit out now.* I needed to figure a way out. My first instinct was to jump out the car and run, but my out-of-shape ass wouldn't have made it one block, so I pulled over. My plan was to talk my way out of this predicament.

The cop came to the window and asked for my driver's license and registration. I grabbed the registration from the glove box then began to search for my ID. *Damn!* I realized I had no identification. I had purposely stopped carrying it on me since I was wanted. I had planned on getting me a fake ID but kept putting it off. Now I was really fucked up.

It didn't take long for the cop to slam me against the car and arrest me for driving a stolen vehicle, and assault and battery. *This is some real bullshit*, I thought as I was being hauled off to the city jail.

I'd only been in jail a week, but it seemed like a month. I knew once I got processed and they realized I had those conspiracy charges, there would be no bond

in my future. Because of jail overcrowding I sat in a
holding cell for an entire week. This was my first day
on the block, and I was looking forward to finally having an opportunity to use the phone. I stood in line patiently. It was taking forever, so I kept my mouth shut,
not wanting to start any trouble.

The dude in front of me finally got off the phone. I
had a feeling he wasn't even talking to anyone, that he
was just being a dick and holding up the line on purpose.

The first person I thought to call was Jewel, who'd
been on my mind all week. Hell, just the previous night,
I beat off my dick, thinking about her sexy body and
phat ass. I wasted no time dialing Jewel up. I hadn't really spoken to her since I'd disappeared. There were a
few three-second conversations where I told her I was
alive and safe, but that was it. I was paranoid her phone
was being tapped, so I would always cut it short.

"Touch? Baby?" Jewel yelled into the phone, after
accepting the collect call.

Before I had a chance to respond, I felt a shove in my
back.

"Get off the phone," this dude demanded.

"Fuck you mean, nigga? I been waiting for the phone
for an hour. Get yo' ass in line, duke!" I said, pointing
toward the end of the line.

Bop!

I took a punch to the stomach. Obviously this man
wasn't up for conversation. But I wasn't no punk, so I
gave him a fight like he wanted.

Bam! I hit him in the head with the phone receiver.

Immediately he and I were throwing blows at each
other.

"Yo, yo, yo!" I heard someone yell. "Back up off him,"
the voice calmly said.

The dude I was fighting released his grip and backed up off me. I watched as he skulked away like a dog with its tail between his legs. I looked up to see an old head standing over me. He reached out his hand and helped me off the ground.

"Thanks, man," I said as I brushed my clothes off.

The man walked me over to a nearby cell. "Clear this bunk," he ordered another dude sitting in the cell. The dude immediately got up and left the cell. It didn't take me long for me to figure out this old head ran things in the block and all these niggas was scared of him. "Son, we need to talk," he said to me.

"A'ight." I agreed right away. There was no way I was gonna challenge this cat. "You all right, Touch?" he asked.

"I'll make it. How do you know my name?"

"I know everything about the streets. I heard you were doing some big things, until you caught those drug charges. You kinda remind me of myself when I was your age. My name is Jimmy. Tell me your story, youngblood."

"Nice to meet you, Jimmy. Thanks for stepping in back there, although I coulda handled that dude myself."

"I know, young'un, I know."

"You wanna know my story? A'ight. I been hustling since I was in grade school. My father was a hustler. He left my moms when I was a baby, but he was always around the neighborhood, so I saw him a lot. His daddy was a hustler, and he brought all three of his sons into the game. My pops and his two brothers ran the streets for a while there. Then the cops decided they was enemy number one and shot my dad and arrested my uncles, Mike and Kendall."

"I know those two cats. They doing a bid in the federal pen, right?"

"Yeah, that's them. Damn! That's crazy. How you know those two?"

"We used to run together on the streets. How you think I know about you?"

"I like that. You a smooth nigga."

"Young buck, don't you ever call me that again. I ain't no nigga, you hear? That's the trouble with you young fools today, calling each other nigga this, nigga that."

"Word. I apologize. You right."

"Continue."

"Well, after my pops passed, I figured it was time for me to man up. I started hustling on the streets. It was small at first, but because people respected my old man, I got a lot of help, and my business started to grow. People were paying attention. Including the cops. I was careful, so I operated for years without getting one bust. Then I got a domestic abuse charge on me, and that's when the cops really started gunning for me. They had some big old undercover sting to set my ass up. Now I'm looking at some conspiracy charges."

"Son, you got heart just like your daddy. You and me can do some big things, but you got to keep your nose clean though. You willing to listen and learn?"

"Hell yeah, my nig—yes, sir." Jimmy smirked and nodded slowly. He patted me on my shoulder and walked out of the cell. From that point on, he took me under his wing. He even made plans to put me on to some work when I got out. Things were looking up. Now I needed to take care of all these bullshit charges against me.

Chapter 3

"Free My Man"

Jewel

It had been days since my brief phone call from Touch, so I took it upon myself to call Virginia Beach City Jail and find out their visiting schedule. I wasn't able to make it until the weekend, so Touch was going to have to wait another few days before he could get a look at me.

I made sure I looked my best as I straightened my hair and applied my makeup. I squeezed my plump booty into my tightest pair of jeans, sure to show every crease and curve. I hadn't seen my prince in nearly three months, so I wanted to put a smile on his face.

When I reached the jail, I went through visitor check-in and was in the back visiting with Touch in no time. It was much quicker than the two-hour waits I had endured during my visits to Norfolk City Jail. I barely had time to even start the book I had brought along to read before I was called into the visitors' room.

"Hey, baby!" I yelled and waved as soon as I saw Touch walking up to our designated glass booth.

It was a bitter-sweet moment. While it was great to see him, it was sad to see him under such circumstances. His hair was freshly braided as though he'd just left the shop, and his smile was still gleaming white and perfect. Besides the orange jumpsuit, he was the same Touch I'd always known. He actually might have been a little bit more muscular from the weights he had been lifting.

"What's up, baby girl?" Touch said through the phone receiver. "I miss you so much. You look good." I said, admiring my man and touching the glass that separated us.

"Thanks. You look good too. You got my dick rising." Touch massaged his penis as he spoke. "It don't even look like you have gained a pound. Are you eating okay? You making sure my son, a'ight?"

"Oh, I'm good. Let's not worry about me. The question is, Are you okay in there? Do you need anything? What exactly are your charges, and how did you get caught anyway?" I spat one question after another.

"Damn! Jewel. Hold up. I feel like I'm under interrogation." Touch gave me that million-dollar smile then added, "The important thing is, I'm no longer on the run, and I got a bond. The bond is one hundred thousand dollars. I need you to holla at the bondsman and give him ten grand."

There was an instant lump in my throat and a pit in my stomach. *Ten thousand dollars? Where the hell am I gonna get that?* I thought as I listened to Touch's instructions. Touch must have noticed the worried look on my face. "What's the problem, Jewel? Why you looking all crazy and shit?"

"Well, baby, it's just that I don't have that kind of money." I cringed as I explained, knowing Touch wasn't going to be happy. I was now happy there was a barrier between us.

Touch yelled, "What you mean, Jewel? I left fifty thousand dollars behind when I left the house."

"Touch, it's been three months! We have a mortgage, two car notes, and a shitload of credit card bills." I kept my tone even, but I was pissed. He left me high and dry. What did he expect?

"So you mean to tell me you blew fifty grand in three months? You don't even have ten Gs to get a nigga out?" Touch shook his head then dropped his head down into his hand. Seeing him look so defeated made me feel real fucked up inside. I had to make things right. "Don't you worry, baby. I got this. You will be out by morning. You know I've never let you down before, and I'm not about to start now."

"Now that's the Jewel I know." Touch smiled, his mood instantly brightening.

The brief tension between us subsided. We talked away. About how he was faring in there, about how his meeting this old head named Jimmy. The whole time I just wanted to touch him and kiss him. Before we knew it, our visiting time was up. We tried to prolong our good-byes as long as possible, but the damn COs were being assholes.

"Love you, baby. *Mwah*!" I kissed him through the phone. I was getting emotional but tried to stay strong for my man. It was no use. I couldn't stop the tears.

"Love you too. Take care of my baby boy." Touch then hung up the phone.

I watched his back as he walked away and the heavy steel door slammed behind him.

"Damn it!" I yelled after jumping back into the truck.

I didn't know how I was going to get ten thousand dollars by the next morning. Touch's fifty thousand had dwindled down to a mere four thousand dollars. I knew if I didn't get him out by the time morning hit, they might find out about his conspiracy charges. Then he may never get out. I stayed calm as I thought of my options.

After a few minutes of thinking, I made a phone call. A call I didn't really want to make. *I hope this shit works*, I thought after dialing a phone number on my cell.

"'S up?" Rico said after answering the phone. Rico was a little side item I'd had for the past few months. Before Touch was on the run, we were having problems and had decided to split up. He was seeing other chicks, so after a while, I decided to date too.

And that's where Rico came in. Rico was a nice guy. He worked as an engineer for the United States government. He had dough, and the best thing about it was that it was legit. I usually liked my men a little rough around the edges, but after the shit I'd gone through with Touch, it was time for a change. He was everything opposite of Touch.

"Hey, baby. How are you?" I asked.

"I'm still tired from the ride you gave two nights ago. Other than that, I'm good. What's going on with you?"

"Well, I've some great news." I tried to sound excited.

"Oh, yeah? What's that? You're coming over to ride me again?" Rico asked playfully.

"I got accepted into nursing school, and I start next week." I lied.

"Damn, baby! Congratulations!" Rico said, happy about the news. "You ain't even tell a nigga you had applied for school. I'll tell you what. Let me buy your books for you. It will be my present to you."

That shit was easier than I thought. Little did Rico know, I was prepared to beg, fuck, suck, and do something strange for a little change, but to my surprise, I didn't even have to ask. This nigga offered, so I wasted no time going in for the kill.

"Oh my God! Are you serious?"

"Come on, baby girl. You know I'm big on education. I'm proud to see you trying to do something for yourself. I got you."

"Well, I need about seven thousand to cover everything," I said in a whiny voice.

"No problem. You're worth every penny. Plus, after you finish school, a shitload of money will be rolling in. Come over and get it when you're ready."

"I'm on my way." I breathed a sigh of relief.

I started my truck and headed to Rico's house. As soon as I walked in, he had the money waiting for me. Of course, after giving me the money, he wanted to celebrate my acceptance to nursing school by dicking me down. Normally I loved sex with Rico, but this time I wasn't interested in him touching me at all. My mind was on Touch and getting back with him.

"Baby, I can't," I said between kisses.

"What's wrong? It's that time of the month?"

My initial thought was to agree and tell Rico I was on my cycle, but the one huge lie I'd just told him was enough. My conscience wouldn't allow me to tell another.

"No, honey. I've got some business I need to take care of, and I've gotta do it right away." I gently rubbed Rico's erect dick.

I was about to raincheck his ass and dip out the door, but seeing the look on his face and afraid he would take the money back, I got on my knees and gave him some head. It didn't take him long to nut all over the place. I zipped his pants back up, gave him a small kiss on the cheek, then headed out the door, leaving him drooling at the mouth.

When I got back into my truck, I whipped out my cell phone and called Touch's lawyer. I informed him I had the money for bond and made an appointment for them to discuss his options. Next, I called up a bail bondsman well known to all the guys into the drug game. In fact this bondsman used to be a drug dealer himself, except he was one of those smart enough to turn his drug money into something legit. Sad to say, but even I had to use his services once.

I felt proud as I met the bondsman at the jail. I had exceeded Touch's expectation. I got the money, talked to the lawyer, and got his ass that same night.

I waited patiently for Touch to walk from behind the jail walls. As soon as I saw him, I rushed toward him and jumped into his arms.

"What's up, baby girl?" Touch said as I kissed him all over his face.

"Looks like your dick," I responded, rubbing on his erect penis.

"Yeah, that's all for you tonight." Touch laughed, and we hopped in the car.

The ride seemed like it took forever. All I wanted to do was get home, get naked, and ride Touch all night long. I asked him how he had gotten caught, and he was pretty vague. I felt like he wasn't telling me everything. I wasn't going to push it, because I was just so happy to see him again.

Touch smacked my ass before we entered the house.

"You didn't give my pussy away, did you?" "You know this pussy is yours." I assured him with a kiss.

I was dressed in a trench coat. Touch didn't think anything of it because there was a chilly nip in the air. Underneath my trench coat I wore a skimpy French maid set with a small apron to match. My five-inch stilettos added an extra touch. As soon as we entered through the front door, I dropped my coat.

"Damn, Jewel! You never cease to surprise a nigga. I love that about you." Touch hugged me close.

I could have sworn within seconds his dick grew at least two inches. And it got even harder as I began stroking it.

After Touch stripped right in front of me, I quickly got on my knees and started deep-throating his dick.

He pulled my head in even closer. "Aah, man. Don't stop."

I knew just what it took to send him to the moon. My head was definitely like no other. The key with Touch wasn't my tongue, it was the way I stroked his dick. I could make him come in less than five minutes. But I made sure not to give him too much because I wanted him to last all night.

Touch ripped my lingerie off and carried me up the stairs into the bedroom through the gardenia petals lightly covering the foyer floor and trailing up the stairs leading to the bedroom. My pussy instantly became wet. After he let me down, I pulled him onto the bed. I began massaging him, working my way down to his feet. After his massage I turned on the surround sound CD player. Jeremih's song, "Birthday Sex" started to play. Touch's birthday was a few days away, so this was an early present. I began dancing to the song.

Touch loved to see me feel all over myself. Popping my pussy in front of him was his favorite. Not being able to take the uprising sexual tension, he grabbed me up and lifted me up against the wall.

"Which titty do you want in my mouth while I fuck you?" he asked, sticking his thick penis inside of me.

"The right."

For the next hour we had sex in every position thinkable. He literally put me to sleep that night.

***

For the next few days, Touch didn't leave my side. Besides having sex, all he wanted to do was rub my stomach. After a while, it became quite annoying. He was truly about the birth of his baby. He was convinced it was a boy. I, on the other hand, wasn't so sure.

Meanwhile, Rico was blowing up my phone. He'd been texting and calling me continuously. At first I was playing it off like I was in class and couldn't return his calls or texts. But that didn't work for long. All he did was start calling and texting at night. I was doing everything, from sneaking to the bathroom to text him to making bullshit trips to the store to call him. I was afraid it was becoming too obvious that something was up, and the last thing I wanted was Touch to catch on to what I was doing. I turned my phone on silent and ignored all Rico's calls and texts. Pretty soon I began getting calls from strange numbers and private numbers, but I was on to that trick. I knew it was Rico. He was doing anything he could to get me to answer.

Finally I could no longer ignore it. I figured if I just answered one time Rico would stop calling. I snuck upstairs while Touch was sleeping, so I could answer Rico's call.

"Hello?" I said in a soft tone, trying not to make too much noise.

"Hey, sweetie. Where have you been? I've been calling you for days?" Rico said before giving me a chance to respond. "I'm right in front of your house. I was just about to knock on the door when you answered."

"Oh my God! Rico, no!" I panicked. I felt as though I was gonna shit in my Victoria's Secret G-string. "I'm not home yet. I'm on my way, but I need to stop at the store."

With Touch's temper, if Rico had come knocking, there was gonna be a fight, possibly a death, and it sure wouldn't have been Touch doing the dying.

"Okay, I'll wait for you here."

"No, I'm gonna be a little while. Meet me at the grocery store." I started getting my outfit together.

On my way to the garage I peeped in on Touch to make sure he was still asleep. Luckily I hadn't awaken him, and he was sleeping like a baby. I grabbed my keys off the kitchen counter. From the living room I looked out the window and watched as Rico got in his car and pulled off. I rushed in my car and headed out my neighborhood in the opposite direction.

I met Rico at the store. He'd beat me to the store, since I took the long way from my house.

"Hey, baby. What's going on?" Rico said as soon as I got out my car.

I planned on going the distance with this lie and walking around the grocery store and shopping, hoping to bore Rico into leaving while I shopped for my house. But as soon as I saw his face, I changed my tactic.

I told him, "Listen, baby, you can't come over. This is not a good idea."

"What are you talking about?"

I took a deep breath in. I really liked Rico, so it wasn't easy for me to tell him. "My man is back home." I let out the breath I had taken in and prepared myself for his verbal onslaught.

From the day I'd met Rico, I had told him about Touch. Sure, I should have done things a little different and maybe prepared him for this day, but it all happened so quickly. I was hoping he would just go away on his own, but he didn't. So I decided to just put it out there to keep him from getting killed.

"So that's how it is, Jewel? And to think I really was feeling you. You didn't even respect me enough to let me know what was going on. This is how I had to find out? Cool." Rico simply walked away, got in his car, and pulled off.

Damn! That hurt me more than if he had gone off on me. At that point I didn't know what to think. I expected and would have accepted name-calling or the standard "Fuck you!" but a dude talking calm, no cursing or anything, now that was strange. It unnerved me a little bit.

All sorts of thoughts began to run through my brain. *Could this linger into something else? Do I need to tell Touch so he can protect himself? Hell, do I need to carry a gun to protect myself?* I didn't know if Rico was crazy or what. I'd just taken seven grand from this dude then dissed him. I figured it wouldn't be long before he put two and two together and realized I'd used his money to bond Touch.

As soon as I walked in the house through the garage door, Touch was standing in the kitchen waiting on me. "Where did you go?" he asked after biting into a turkey sandwich.

"To the store," I said, startled.

"So what you buy?"

"Oh, I didn't get anything because they didn't have what I was looking for," I said, unable to come up with anything better.

"It must have been important because you left in a hurry. What were you looking for?" Touch wasn't letting up so easy.

"Huh? What you mean?" I said, trying to buy time to come up with an answer to satisfy Touch and get him off my ass. "What was it that you were looking for at the store that you couldn't find?" Touch repeated, like he was talking to a child.

"Oh, I was just craving for some white Oreos. You know, pregnancy craving." I knew anything about the baby would ease Touch's mind.

"Oh, okay." Touch gulped down a glass of juice and headed out the kitchen. "For a second I thought you had run off to see a little dude around the corner or something." He chuckled. "Don't let me find out," he said as he playfully smacked my ass.

I knew he wasn't joking though. If he found out I had gone to see another dude, there would be hell to pay.

"Yeah, your brother." I played along, relieved he hadn't caught me in my lie.

Throughout the evening the private calls continued back to back. I had to wonder what sane person would spend hours constantly calling a person's phone. Rico was really starting to scare me.

Later that night, Touch and I went to the store to pick up a few things. The whole time while shopping I couldn't help this overwhelming feeling that someone was watching us. Especially as we put our groceries in the truck.

I scanned the parking lot but didn't see anyone. I looked in the large windows of the grocery store, and everyone inside looked suspicious to me. I didn't know if it was paranoia or what, but I was wishing I had a gun at that moment. It freaked me out to the point where I considered telling Touch about Rico.

Just as Touch started the engine and put the truck into gear, someone knocked on the driver's side window. The knock was so startling, I screamed out loud and jumped in my seat.

"Touch, don't open the window," I warned and pleaded at the same time.

Touch looked at me like I was losing it. "The fuck you talking about?" He pressed the button, and the window rolled down. "Damn, dude! You scared the shit outta me and my girl," he said to the man standing there.

"Oh, I'm sorry. It's just that you dropped this before you closed the trunk." The man held up a box of white Oreos."

"Oh, damn! Good lookin', my man. My girl would have been sad not have these at home. She's carrying my son, and she got those cravings." Touch was smiling as he took the Oreo's and handed them to me.

"No worries." The man walked away toward the store.

My heart was racing. I had thought for sure the knock was Rico about to blast away. I didn't know what to do then. I couldn't keep living on edge like this. I had a big decision to make—tell Touch or handle Rico myself.

Chapter 4

"Prank Calling"

Lisa

"Fuck you, Touch!" I screamed as I slammed the picture frame against the corner of the counter, shattering the glass.

I took out the picture of us and ripped it over and over again until it was in tiny little pieces. Tears streamed from my eyes. I couldn't believe this nigga used me for a place to stay, for my money, and for my pussy. I really thought he genuinely cared about me. I'd had his back from day one then he had the nerve to put his fucking hands on me! For a minute I actually felt bad for calling the police on him, but the more I thought about it, the more I realized he deserved to get some time for what he had done to me.

After he flipped out on me I was determined to teach him a lesson. Yes, I called the cops on his sorry ass, but I wasn't finished there. I wasn't going to be satisfied with the cops arresting his ass. He needed to be punished by me personally. His personal life needed some fucking with. Little did he know, I'd been calling his bitch girlfriend, Jewel, whose number I'd gotten from his phone when he was staying with me. I knew the day would come when I could use it.

Ring! Ring! Ring! I called Jewel, expecting the phone to ring out to voice mail like it usually did. I had been calling her over and over again, basically harassing that bitch. I never left a message, I just wanted to annoy her. I hadn't fully thought about what I wanted to do yet. I was just playing some childish games with her at this point. I have to admit it took me back to junior high school when I prank-called people. That was kind of fun.

To my surprise, she answered.

"Hello."

I was taken off guard. I didn't say a word. I quickly pressed the mute button on my television so there was no background noise. Couldn't let her try and get any clues as to who it could be.

"Hell-fuckin'-o!" Jewel yelled into the phone.

Although I wanted to say something to her so bad, I continued to remain silent.

"If I ever fuckin' find out who this is, I'm gonna choke the fuckin' life out of you! Stop calling my gotdamn phone!"

I could feel the fury, yet it was so comical. It was working, I was unnerving this little bitch.

To avoid bursting out in laughter, I hung up the phone. I guess the average chick would call me a scary bitch because I never said anything, but that's the beauty of it all. That bitch had no idea it was me ringing her phone, which was definitely some fun-ass shit. As the day passed, I continued to call Jewel's phone, but she never answered again. For a while all I was getting was her voice mail right away. I guess my constant calling had forced her to turn her phone off.

Bored with the calling, I decided to take things to the next level. I logged on to my computer and did a reverse search using Jewel's cell number, but nothing came up. Then I tried Touch. Still nothing. I needed more information if I was going to take this harassment to the next level.

"Think, Lisa, think," I said aloud to myself as I wracked my brain. "The car registration!" I rushed to the kitchen and grabbed Touch's keys. The dumb ass had taken my car. Guess he wasn't smart enough to realize I would call and report my car stolen.

His car had been in my garage since he was on the run. He'd refused to drive it because he knew that was a sure ticket to jail. I pressed the key and unlocked the doors to his car. I looked in the glove compartment and saw the registration. It was registered to an out-of-state address, but at least I had his full name. I rushed back to the computer. This time I did a search using his full name and date of birth.

"Bingo!" I shouted as his information came up. I'd hit the jackpot.

I paid a $29.95 Internet detective fee. It was well worth it. It listed all of his previous addresses as well as relatives. I was even able to get Jewel's information because it had her listed as a spouse. I leaned back in my chair, pleased with my progress. I felt like one smart bitch. With that said, I decided to call it a night.

On my way upstairs I decided to give Jewel one last call. "Here we go again." I yawned then dialed Jewel's number.

"Hello." Like last time, I said nothing as I sat on the edge of my bed.

"Hello," she said for the second time.

Again, I remained silent and lay back on my bed. Then I heard Jewel say, "Touch, come listen to this shit, so you hear it for yourself."

"Hello?"

Touch was now on the phone. My nerves went straight to my stomach when I heard him. I didn't say a word, but it took all I had.

"I'm muthafuckin' sick of this nonsense," Jewel shouted from the background. "This person has nothing better to do but play silly-ass games on the phone."

"Yo'! Who the fuck is this?" Touch yelled in the phone, damn near bursting my eardrum.

I couldn't handle it anymore. Hearing his voice made me lose my composure. "Your worst nightmare, muthafucka!" I said quickly then hung up the phone.

The plan was for me to keep my identity a mystery, but when I heard Touch's voice, I couldn't remain silent. I turned my lights off and got in the bed. I couldn't sleep as I continuously replayed in my head what had just happened. I was too worked up. My nerves and adrenaline were working overtime.

Wow! Touch is home and didn't even bother to call me. I couldn't believe it. I knew he was probably upset with me about the whole stolen car and domestic violence thing, but I had thought he would at least call and try to apologize. Even if he wasn't sorry, I thought he would try to kiss my ass so that I'd drop the charges.

Guess I was wrong about that. The more I thought about things, the angrier I got.

I quickly dialed Touch's phone after I blocked my phone number from his caller ID. He didn't answer, and I was sent to voice mail. After twenty attempts, I eventually gave up and headed to sleep.

As I drifted off to sleep, I thought, *Touch just can't come in and out of people's life as he pleases. He would be so upset if Jewel loses that sweet little baby of his. Tomorrow, I'll be sure to leave her a little gift on the doorstep. Vengeance is best served shaken up and cold. Touch will pay for what he's done to me.*

Chapter 5

"A Liar's Lie"

Touch

"You ready?" I asked Jewel as she was slipping into a black minidress.

This dress was one of my favorites. It fit every curve of her body perfectly. I watched as she tugged on her dress, making sure everything was in the right spot. My dick rose as I lusted over her perfect body. I noticed Jewel's ass was the same size, but her titties seemed to be two sizes bigger. But the strangest thing was, her stomach was flat as a board.

"Damn, baby! Is my baby boy growing at all?" I questioned. I knew Jewel was only a few months pregnant, but I at least expected her to have a little pudge or something.

"Touch, everybody doesn't get big right away. Some women don't even start showing until five months." Jewel then walked into the bathroom, and I followed behind her.

"Well, have you at least been going to your prenatal visits and stuff?" I was concerned that something might be wrong with my baby. I would never forgive myself if something happened and we didn't do everything we could to prevent it.

"Touch, please! You're driving me nuts!" she shouted, obviously frustrated. "Go watch TV or something. I'll be ready in a few."

Not wanting to have a rocky start to the day, I backed off and did as Jewel asked. As I sat in the living room watching TV, I kept thinking about how happy I was about my child-to-be. I just knew it was a boy. As I came out of my daydream, I noticed the time.

"Jewel, hurry up!" I shouted. "Give me ten minutes," she yelled back. "I'm almost done."

We were on our way to pay my lawyer a visit, and if Jewel didn't hurry, we were gonna be late. Mr. Schultz was all about his business, and time was money. This dude actually charged extra for each minute you were late. I didn't blame him. With the clients he had, he needed to be a ball-buster. I'd been dealing with him since the start of my criminal career, but that made no difference to him. This man didn't deal with credit, good faith, or give a fuck about all the other times I'd paid him up front. Times are now, and he wanted his money right now. I couldn't argue with him. He was good at what he did, and I respected his game.

"Jewel!" I yelled out to her again.

She shouted back, "Trayvon Davis, leave me alone!"

What the hell she could be doing that was taking so damn long? For a minute I wondered if she was stalling on purpose. It wouldn't be the first time she would have done it.

Jewel always hated going to see the lawyer. What she feared the most was the unknown; not knowing how much time I may or may not get was probably driving her crazy. I admit I had put my baby through a lot. Every woman has a limit. I had to wonder if I had pushed Jewel over hers. I constantly thought about blowing the trial and just copping a plea, but my rap sheet was fifteen years strong. There's no telling how long the

D.A. would want to put me away. I couldn't take that chance. I'd rather take my chances with a sympathetic jury and let the chips fall where they may. *Damn! This wasn't how I imagined my life would turn out. I was supposed to be living on some private island by now.*

I got tired of waiting and even more tired of thinking about court and all my problems. I headed to our bedroom to drag Jewel out. As I approached the bathroom door, I could hear her talking.

"I'll call you back." She hung up the phone just as I was walking in the bathroom.

"Oh, that's what's taking you so long. Who was that?"

I was a little heated but tried to stay calm. "One of my girls."

Now I was suspicious. "Girls? You ain't got no girls."

"You don't know what I have," Jewel snapped. "You've been ghost for over three months, remember?"

"A'ight, Jewel. Let's roll," I said, still trying to avoid an argument. She was right. I had disappeared, but now I was ready to make it up. For Jewel and my baby.

"Okay. I'm ready," she replied with a fake smile going through the motions.

Jewel seemed a bit on edge all morning. At first I just figured it was because of our upcoming visit with the lawyer, but the more I observed her, it seemed like it was something more. I started tripping, thinking it had to do with her pregnancy and that the phone call earlier was to her doctor.

I started feeling guilty on our ride over to the lawyer, thinking Jewel deserved way better than this. The funny thing is, I think she had realized it faster than me. But that's life. I learned a long time ago the sun will still rise whether you stand alone or with someone by your side. That's why my loyalty was always to the almighty dollar and the streets. They came before anyone and anything in my life. Now I was starting to re-think that motto. Jewel was breaking down that code.

As we drove, Jewel's phone was constantly buzzing. It was seriously starting to bug my ass. I couldn't even enjoy the tunes on my mixed CD because of it.

"Damn, Jewel! Who the fuck keeps calling?" I asked, annoyed as hell.

"It's that same person that's been calling private. I have answered the phone a thousand times with no-body talking on the other end. You know how it goes, Touch."

"They still calling? Why don't you just change your number, babe?"

"I thought about it, but so many important people have this number, and so many things are going on right now, I just really don't think it's a good idea."

Although I felt what Jewel was saying was a bunch of bullshit and the person calling was whoever she was talking with earlier, I didn't even bother saying any-thing. I didn't have the energy to fight with her at the moment. I was trying to get rid of the drama between the two of us, so instead of slapping the bitch for lying to me, I just turned up the volume and let the music take me into a deep zone.

As I bobbed my head to the words of "6 Foot 7 Foot" by Lil Wayne, my moment of attempted meditation was interrupted by Jewel's constant texting. Now my patience was starting to run thin with her, and I felt like I was gonna explode.

Without hesitation, I snatched Jewel's phone from her hand and started going through her call log and text messages. Jewel had been acting real suspicious lately, and I couldn't ignore it anymore. I knew she had been sneaking to the garage and various places throughout the house to use her phone while she thought I was sleeping. There was no doubt in my mind Jewel was hiding something, and I was about to find out what it was.

I read the text in her phone aloud—"I haven't heard from you. Call me. You did some real fucked-up shit. Jewel, I know you're not in school. You're a fuckin' liar. I would have given you anything."

"Okay, you happy? Now please give me the phone back, Touch," she said, trying her best to stay cool.

"Jewel, who the fuck is Rico?"

"Oh, you want to go there?" Jewel said in a sarcastic tone.

"I'ma ask you one more time—Who the fuck is Rico?"

I had her in a semi-choke hold, causing her to almost hit the person in front of us.

"Get your fuckin' hands off me," she struggled to say, but I wasn't letting up until she answered my question. She pulled the car to the side of the road, and within seconds she somehow pulled out a taser gun.

"What the fuck is this?" I laughed as I released her.

"Now, nigga, *you* listen to me. You fucked up our relationship a long time ago. Then you were on the run while I was alone and pregnant. On top of that, your sorry ass is up for domestic violence charges for another bitch! So, please, I beg you, don't come at me with a whole bunch of questions!"

Damn! I thought as I listened to Jewel. There was nothing I could say in response to that. Everything she said was true. Her words rendered me silent. The only good response would have been to apologize, but there was no way in hell I would have done that at that moment.

"Oh, you quiet now, huh? You don't have shit to say." Jewel put the car in park.

"Nope. No time to talk right now. We'll talk later. We got more important things to take care of," I said, blowing off the conversation then stepping out the car.

"Fuck you, Touch! Go handle your business by your fuckin' self. You've done this plenty of times before. You know the routine." Jewel then drove off.

I didn't have the time or energy to chase after her. I just shook my head in disbelief and began walking to my lawyer's building. Everything seemed to be spiraling out of my control, and I had no idea what to do about it. I wanted to make everything easy for Jewel, but sometimes I got the feeling she didn't want me around. Nothing I did was right.

Fuck it! I thought. *I'll just do me from now on.*

I somehow reached Schultz's building on time. I pressed number eight on the elevator and walked in the office. As I sat waiting to see Mr. Schultz, I thought,

What bullshit is this? He would make me pay extra for being late, but when I was on time, he made me wait and wouldn't give me no damn discount. That's the price I had to pay for having the best attorney in town. I'd rather pay his ass than do time.

The receptionist said, "Mr. Schultz can see you now."

"Thanks," I said while walking toward his office.

"Mr. Davis." Schultz greeted me with a handshake.

"Thanks for taking me at such short notice. Here's your money. It's all hundreds, just the way you prefer." I bit my tongue and didn't say nothing about the double standard.

"You know me well." Mr. Schultz accepted the money and motioned for me to have a seat. "Listen, let's get to it because I don't want to take too much of your time. I've already talked with the district attorney."

"Wow! That was fast. That's why I fuck with you, Mr. Schultz!"

"Yeah, I took her out last night, so I figured I may as well discuss the case while I had her eating out of the palm of my hand. Everything in life is about who you know and how much power they hold. From church to the law, it's all politics, my friend."

"I know all about. I'm just glad to have you in my corner."

"Money talks!" Schultz laughed. "The conspiracy charges will be dropped due to the lack of evidence. As you may already know, the police officer working undercover on your case died in the line of duty. She was involved in a tragic high-speed chase." Schultz cut his eyes at me. He knew it was me she was chasing. He took a sip of his coffee. "The prosecutors hoped to still be able to go on with the case, based on the reports from the officer. But the files from the case have mysteriously disappeared." Schultz cut his eyes at me again. Now I knew nothing about the missing files. I damn sure was glad to hear the news though. "As far as the domestic violence and the auto theft charges, you will have a hefty fine, be required to go to anger management class, and unsupervised probation for a year. So I need you to stay on your best behavior at all times. No fighting, smoking, drinking, or drugs. And if you decide to do it, don't fuckin' get caught. You got it?"

"Damn right!" I said. This was the best news I could have possibly heard. Way better than I'd expected.

"This time, you got real lucky. Your court date is in two weeks. I will have my receptionist send you a reminder in the mail."

"I'll be there. Thanks, man! I'll see you in court," I replied, happy as hell.

I walked out of the office with a big-ass Kool-Aid smile across my face. To my surprise, Jewel was waiting for me in the parking lot with the tazer gun still in her hand. Believe it or not, not even that was able to ruin my joy. With her being pregnant, I knew her hormones were all fucked up.

I gave her a hug. "Thanks for coming back for me."

She looked shocked as hell. She didn't know how to respond to my friendly attitude. She just got in the car and started it up. I had just gotten the best news in my life and didn't want to ruin the moment. I just wanted to go home, smoke a blunt, and lay down. I know Schultz told me to stay away from drugs and alcohol, but I had been up the last two nights awaiting my fate, stressed as a motherfucker. For the first time in months I was stress free! I needed a rest.

The entire ride home, Jewel and I didn't say a word to each other. She didn't even ask about what happened with my lawyer. I didn't know if it was because she was scared to hear or if she didn't care. Either way, that was cool with me. I was finally able to listen to my CD and zone out without interruption. I blasted the radio, leaned my seat back and turned up the tunes of "I'm on One" by DJ Khaled. I sang along.

When we arrived home, Jewel didn't even pull in the driveway. She dropped me off and pulled right back off. I didn't even question it. There was no way she was going to ruin my good mood. I walked right on to the crib and didn't even look back. I figured she was acting out because she wanted a reaction from me. And, more than anything, she wanted an explanation and an apology. True, she deserved it, but I wasn't quite ready to give in yet. She would get what she wanted but on my terms.

When I got in the house, I did exactly as I'd planned. I rolled a blunt, grabbed the remote, and got comfortable in the bed. I hadn't taken two pulls from the blunt before my cell phone rang. I looked at the caller ID, but

I didn't recognize the number. I wondered if it was that bitch Lisa, who had been blowing my phone up on the regular. It was time to put an end to this shit.

"Hello," I answered full of attitude, ready to let Lisa's ass have it.

"Yo, Touch, this is Jimmy. What's been going on?"

"Oh, damn! Jimmy, it's good to hear from you. I just left my lawyer's office, and shit is lovely right now. Those conspiracy charges are dropped. Somehow paperwork got fucked up."

"Like I told you when you were in here, it's all about who you know. You'll be surprised the things people will do for money."

"True, true." I wondered if Jimmy had anything to do with my good fortune. I wanted to ask him but knew that "the man" was probably listening in on the other end. "I need you to check out something for me. My boy Deuce called you on three-way for me. He gon' call you back a little later." Jimmy abruptly hung up the phone. Ten minutes later I got a call from Deuce, just like Jimmy said.

"Talk to me," I said after answering the phone.

"You a cocky muthafucka," the voice responded, laughing.

"Hey, what's going on?" I was hoping I didn't fuck myself by saying that.

"This is Deuce. I don't do too much talking on the phone. Meet me at Tiny's Bar. Can you make it there in thirty minutes?"

"Yes, I can."

No sooner than I hung up the phone with Deuce, I realized I didn't have a ride to meet him. Jewel hadn't returned home yet, and my car was still in Lisa's garage. I needed to get my shit back.

With no other choice, I called a cab. Fifteen minutes later, I heard a horn blow outside. My cab had arrived.

I hopped in the backseat. "Tiny's bar," I told the driver.

"You got it." The fat, greasy-haired, white dude put the car into drive. As I was riding to meet Deuce, my thoughts turned back to my car and Lisa. *I can't believe this bitch has been calling Jewel's phone. How the fuck did she get her number? I've really gotten myself in a fucked-up situation.*

A side of me wanted to go to her house and fuck her up again, but another side of me thought, *Maybe I should bait her in.* After all, that bitch had my car, and if I gave her a little attention, said the right words, I could not only get my car back, I could probably convince her to drop the charges.

I had to clear my mind as we pulled up to the lounge where I was meeting Deuce. I paid the driver and hopped out the funky-smelling taxi. Homeboy needed a shower bad. With two football games set to air that night, the bar was packed. I walked in, grabbed a seat, and ordered a bottle of Guinness. I sat thinking about the risk I was taking, dealing with Jimmy and his friend. I didn't really know these dudes at all. Yeah, Jimmy knew my pops, but what if they were actually enemies and he was setting me up to get revenge? Why was he so eager to help me in the joint? I decided I needed to be on guard while dealing with these dudes.

The fucked-up thing was, no matter how much doubt I had, I had no other choice than to fuck with Jimmy and Deuce. The word on the street was, I was on the run at one point and just got out of jail. When niggas hear shit like that, they scatter away like roaches when the light comes on. No one wants to be seen dealing with a wanted brother. Some real disloyal motherfuckers out here on the streets.

An older dude sat down next to me. "Touch."

"Deuce?" I replied, unsure if this was him.

"That I am. What's up, man?"

"Chilling."

We dapped each other up.

Deuce told the bartender, "Can I get two shots of vodka?"

Dressed in a grey sweatshirt, dingy jeans, sneakers and a Pittsburgh Steelers hat, Deuce smelled of oil, so I assumed his day job had to be working on cars. I could tell by his demeanor that he was old-school just like Jimmy.

"Jimmy must really like you, youngblood," Deuce said. "He doesn't usually take such risks."

"Risk?"

"You heard me right, son. If it was up to me alone, you wouldn't be in on the business. I don't need no youngblood fuckin' up my paper."

"Well, lucky for me, it ain't up to you," I spat, a little offended. "I'm gonna get mine, just like the next man. I don't want to mess with my paper or anyone else's."

Deuce didn't say anything after that. He just stared me straight in my eyes. I wasn't going to be intimidated by him, so I met his eyes with the same intensity. I knew I could probably take him if it came down to fists, so I challenged him with my eyes for him to make the first move.

Deuce ended our little game of chicken by saying, "Well, you have an opportunity to make some money. Are you in or out?" He broke eye contact and took a sip of his drink.

Without even knowing what I was agreeing to, I said, "I'm in."

Our handshake symbolized me signing my name on the dotted line of a contract.

"Well, you start tonight. Don't fuck it up," he informed me. "This is the deal—I'll give you the product, you get rid of it and bring back 50 percent of the profit. That goes to Jimmy."

"Just like that, huh?" It was a hell of a deal, but I was a little leery. It was almost too good to be true, but I couldn't afford to say no. I needed the money, and Jimmy was the only one willing to deal with me.

"That's it. You keep the money coming, and I'll keep the product coming."

Then we made arrangements for me to pick up my first couple kilos of cocaine. I really didn't like working on consignment, but a nigga was broke and needed a start.

I left the bar feeling on top of the world. My case was dropped, and I got put on to a way to make some major cash. This was the best day I'd had in a long time. I hopped in the cab humming the tune of "It Was a Good Day" by Ice Cube.

Chapter 6

"Baby Snatcher"

Jewel

After dropping Touch off at the house, I barely gave him time to close the car door before I sped off. I wouldn't have minded running over his pinky toe in the process. Touch had truly pissed me off! True, I was guilty for not telling him about Rico, but he had the nerve to question me, when he'd been living with another chick! I needed a little relaxation, so I decided to make a last-minute spa appointment. Luckily, I was a loyal customer, and they fit me right in.

"May I help you?" the receptionist asked as soon as I walked in.

"Yes, I'm here for my for eleven o'clock appointment with Miriam," I responded.

POSH was an exclusive day spa with all the trimmings, and Miriam was my favorite. Not only was she a wonderful masseuse, but she was also a great esthetician. I'd planned to get the works. I'd requested a manicure, pedicure, a ninety-minute deep tissue massage, facial, and body wrap.

Although this was supposed to be a time of relaxation, I found myself spending a lot of time thinking about Touch and all his mistakes and fuckups. In the beginning we were a match made in heaven, best friends turned lovers. He was everything I ever wanted and needed in a man. But it seemed like the more money he made, the more problems we had. We ran into a little problem with the law, and things went downhill from there. When Touch and I both got caught in an undercover sting operation, it caused a huge rift between us. He thought I would rat him out, no matter how much I tried to calm him. I got taken by surprise by the investigation as much as he did.

Luckily for me, the charges got dropped because my attorney found a loophole in the law and convinced the judge that the charges against me were illegal. Good thing too. I don't think I would have been able to handle jail. I liked the finer things in life, and prison attire didn't suit my body. At times, I had begun to think I may be falling out of love with Touch. A woman can only take so much. R. Kelly had sent a warning to all men with the song, "When a Woman's Fed Up." Well, this woman was reaching that point, and fast.

"Jewel, now I'm gonna give you a little extra attention and really focus on your head and scalp massage," Miriam said as she let my hair down. "I noticed you're very tense, so I wanted to see if we can release a little tension you have in that area."

"Gladly." I nodded.

This kind of massage was the best part. One simple massage stroke of my scalp started draining my stress, my irritation, and my resentment of Touch. *That nigga should be grateful I been in his corner for so long.*

As Miriam massaged my head with her magic touch, I was beginning to feel totally relaxed, so I closed my eyes. The first person I thought of was Rico. He'd always said that I deserved better out of life, but it was up to me to make it better. The more I thought about it, the more I realized he was right. I needed to make a change in my life. If I wanted the finer things, I needed to go out and get them. I couldn't rely on some street-ass nigga to provide for me.

Despite the fact I fucked Rico over, he still called from time to time and left messages saying he just wanted to hear my voice so he would know I was okay. He was a real gentleman, unlike most of the niggas I dealt with. I started regretting that I'd really fucked Rico over. A couple of times I had thought about calling him, but I was ashamed of the way I had treated him. I knew what I did was wrong.

Lying on the table, fully relaxed, I was considering calling and patching things up with him. Rico showed me nothing but kindness since the day we met. He was beginning to fall for me. I would be able to have the finer things if I went back to him. I began to compare Rico and Touch. *Rico is stable. Touch's sorry-ass damn sure is not. I need stability, no drama, and less chaos. With Touch, I never know if he is really in my corner. The only thing he has been truly been loyal to is the streets. I have always come in second place, which is so unfair to me. Rico seems to be all about me.*

The more I thought about it, the more it became clear that Touch wasn't good for me. *So why do I keep going back to him? I think I might be afraid to let go of him.*

Four hours, later my time of relaxation was over, and it was time to head home.

My anxiety slowly started to rise as I pulled into the neighborhood. I took a deep breath and continuously recited the words, "I will not fight with Touch tonight."

While pulling up to the house, I noticed a box at the front door. Getting excited about the package, I parked in the driveway instead of pulling into the garage, since it would be easier for me to just pick up the package and go through the front door. I'd ordered some Victoria's Secret and was surprised it had arrived so soon. Receiving packages in the mail always improved my mood.

As I got closer to the box, I noticed it was already open. Feeling that someone had opened my package and stolen my lingerie, I began to get angry. *Damn, these grimy-ass niggas out here,* I thought, approaching the box. I quickly grabbed it and glanced inside. "Oh my God!" I screamed and dropped the box in a panic. "It's a baby!"

Inside the box lay a baby with a knife in the heart. Without thinking, I quickly grabbed the baby from the box. I thought that maybe there was still a chance to save it.

The second I touched it, I realized it was a plastic doll. "What the fuck?" I yelled. I was fuming inside, wondering who the fuck would do such a wicked act. The first thing that came to mind was one of Touch's psycho bitches.

I rushed inside the house with tears in my eyes. This was the final straw. I know Touch had fucked a lot of women even while he was with me, but this crossed the line. As soon as I opened the door, Touch was right there.

"Jewel, what's wrong, baby? I heard you yelling." He grabbed me in an attempt to console me.

"Don't touch me!" I yelled, pushing him away.

Touch yelled as he noticed the baby in my arms. "What the fuck is this?"

"What does it look like, Touch? It's a gift that someone left on our doorstep."

"What?

"Yeah. It's probably one of your psycho bitches you be fuckin'."

"Hell, nah. That bitch don't know where we live."

"Ha! Busted, you stupid moron! What specific bitch are you referring to?" I threw the doll at him.

"Damn! Chill, Jewel. I don't know who did this, Jewel."

"Touch, what is really going on with you and that chick you got that domestic charge from? I need to know what's going on. My life could be in danger." I tried explaining to Touch the seriousness of the situation.

"Don't overreact. There's nothing to worry about. I will find the muthafucka that did this and make them pay."

"Oh, really? How would you find this person? Do you have an idea who it is or something?"

Touch shook his head. "I said I don't know."

The thought that someone was bold enough to step foot on my doorstep and leave a bloody doll was crazy. This was way too over the top for me. I felt like I was having a nervous breakdown.

I quickly went into the kitchen and grabbed a bottle of wine with a glass and made my way down to the basement to unwind. "I need some time alone!" I yelled as I walked away without looking back. I didn't even want to look at Touch.

I filled the Jacuzzi up with hot water and bubbles, turned on Kelly Rowland, and filled my wineglass with Riesling. As I sat soaking in the tub, I started thinking about all of my enemies. *But who would be evil enough to do such a heinous thing?*

The first person that came to mind was Sasha, an old friend of mine. She'd done some real fucked-up things in the past, but it had been nearly a year since I'd heard from her. She had just disappeared, and no one knew where she had gone. But something told me it wasn't her.

Then my mind traveled to Rico. After all, I had lied to him and taken ten thousand dollars from him to bail out Touch. He did have a reason to be pissed at me. A small part of me wouldn't blame him for seeking revenge. Any thought I had of getting back with Rico was now out the window. I wondered if he had really flipped his lid. Honestly I had no idea what this man was capable of doing. It's always the quiet ones who are the most dangerous. For a minute I even contemplated telling Touch about Rico; it would only be fair to tell him. Our lives could be in danger.

I took the last sip of my Riesling, turned up my music, lay my head back on my bath pillow, and closed my eyes. I was totally relaxed as the tune of "Motivation" floated through my head. I moved my hand to my midsection as I listened to the words of Lil Wayne.

With each verse I massaged my clit in a circular motion, moving my hips in rhythm with the music. I could feel myself reaching my peak as I imagined sitting on Lil Wayne's face, gripping his dreads tight.

Minutes later, after I'd satisfied myself, a true feeling of total relaxation sent me into a doze.

"How could you do this?" a whisper interrupted my moment of euphoria.

"What did you say?" I looked around the room nervously. I could barely make out the person's voice. "For the first time, in a long time, I actually wanted to treat a woman right, and here you come with the bullshit. Jewel, man, you broke my fuckin' heart." A face finally appeared from a dark corner of the room.

"Rico, I—"

"I didn't fuckin' say you could speak," he said as he pressed the cold metal tip of a gun to my stomach. "I think we both can agree that you have done enough. Right now all your ass is going to do is listen, and when I'm done, I might let you speak."

I nodded my head to let him know I understood very well. My mind was racing, my heart was fluttering, and I was too terrified to move an inch. All I could do was pray Touch would come to my rescue. He was upstairs somewhere probably high and drunk, while this nigga Rico was trying to make this my last living night in the basement.

"This pain is unbearable. I thought you were the one for me. I have a few questions, and you damn sure better answer them," Rico said.

I nodded again, the gun still lodged into my stomach.

"Did you ever love me?" he questioned.

"Yes," I said without hesitation. I didn't love Rico, but I knew at this point it was either do or die. I had to say exactly what he wanted to hear in order to save my life.

"Oh, yeah. So, that dude upstairs, do you love him more than me?"

"Rico, why are you doing this?" I begged.

"Shut the fuck up, Jewel! I didn't say you could speak. Now answer me. Does Touch have more of a special place in your heart than me?"

"No," I said, trying to assure him he was the love of my life.

"Jewel, your ass ain't too convincing. I bet if I had a thousand dollars in my hand ready to give then you would put on a good show for me. You always were about the dollar. I was nothing but kind to you. I wanted to take care of you. All I wanted in return was you to love me and accept me," he stated, becoming angrier and angrier.

"Rico, baby, I do love you," I said as I caressed the side of his face.

"You lyin' bitch!" He smacked my hand away from his face. "Shit ain't gone ever change. You're nothing but a manipulative, gold-digging whore. It is what it is though. Now open wide for me," he demanded as he placed the gun in my mouth.

Pow! The trigger went off, jerking my head back into the wall.

I woke up to the sound of my wineglass shattering on the basement floor. I was in a cold sweat.

"Damn! Rico is haunting me in my dreams," I said to no one in particular.

I gathered myself, grabbed a towel, and got out the Jacuzzi, careful not to step in glass. I headed up the stairs feeling guilty as hell for playing with Rico's emotions.

Chapter 7

"Rude Awakening"

Touch

I answered the phone not knowing who it was. "Yeah."

Its constant buzzing had finally broken my sleep. My neck was stiff from sleeping on the couch, and my head was hurting from all the Hennessy I'd drunk the night before. My hangover was so bad, the entire room was blurry and spinning.

I figured if someone was calling so many times this early in the morning, it had to be important. I hated to be woken up out of my sleep, so I was in no mood for bullshit.

"Hey, boo," a female voice said from the other end of the phone.

I looked at the caller ID. I didn't recognize the number, but the voice sounded familiar. "Who the fuck is this?"

"You know who it is. It's the chick you beat the shit out of then stole her car. Anyway, what did you think of your baby girl? Wasn't she beautiful? She was even dressed in a Juicy Couture onesie with matching socks and hat. Wasn't that little outfit so cute? I would have had her delivered a few days earlier, but FedEx was a little backed up."

Lisa had the sweetest little tone to her voice, like she was shooting the shit with one of her girls. My blood was boiling as I listened to the words this bitch was saying to me.

"Lisa, if you ever muthafuckin' step foot on my property, I promise you, you won't leave this bitch walking."

"Now is that any way to talk to a woman that holds your freedom in her hands? That was a threat, Touch. Did you forget you've already been charged with domestic violence? Now a recorded threat like that was not a smart move, honey." Lisa laughed then hung up the phone.

Her taunting was driving me over the edge. Not only did she have my court date hanging over me, now she had a recording of me threatening her. I felt like I could drive over to that bitch house and choke the breath out of her ass that exact moment.

In no shape to do anything at the moment, I struggled to my feet and headed to the kitchen to grab a bottle of water out of the fridge. I noticed the baby doll on the kitchen counter, and as I walked past, I saw a piece of paper attached to the blanket it was wrapped in. It read: *When life comes, so does death. Time is precious. Take advantage of it while you can.*

I thought to myself, *This bitch is really trying to fuck with my mental. Well, at least now I know who been causing all this chaos. It shouldn't be much of a problem to put an end to this.*

The more I thought about Lisa and the stunts she was pulling, the angrier I got. She was playing me, and it pissed me off. I needed to figure out a way to put an end to her games.

"Stupid bitch! Do she know who the fuck I am? I will kill that bitch." I snatched the doll from the kitchen counter and took it to the trashcan. As I came back from the garage, I met Jewel.

"Why are you yelling at this time of the morning, Touch?" she asked, tying her silk robe together.

"Sorry, babe. I didn't mean to wake you up. Go back to sleep. I just had a little too much to drink. Let's go back to bed." I didn't want to tell Jewel about the call I'd received from Lisa or that Lisa was the culprit behind all the prank calls.

I walked with Jewel to the bedroom and hopped in bed beside her.

"I love you," I whispered in her ear while holding her tight. "And Daddy loves you too, Junior," I said, rubbing her belly.

An hour later I awoke. I wanted to be sure I beat Jewel out of the bed. I wanted to cook her breakfast before she started her day.

I woke Jewel up to breakfast in bed. Although I'd never said the words, "I'm sorry," this was my way of apologizing. I knew the way to Jewel's heart. With her, it was always the little things that mattered the most. Well, money mattered to her most, but the little things came in a close second.

After breakfast Jewel hopped out of bed and rushed to get to the gym. It was Zumba day, and she didn't want to miss it. Before she left, I gave her a much-needed gift.

"Touch, you're giving me a gun?" Jewel asked with the .22-caliber in her hand.

"Yeah. Babe, I think you really need it. Especially after that baby doll incident. I can't be with you all the time, so you need some extra protection. Besides, that little taser gun you got only works close range."

"All right." Jewel nodded. Then she placed the gun in her purse before heading out the door.

I walked back to the bedroom feeling a little reassured. Now my only worry was that one day Jewel would get the idea to use that same gun on me. I was sure there had been plenty of times she imagined killing me.

Now that I was on my way to patching things up with her, it was on to my next task of the day. I needed to get my car from that crazy bitch, Lisa. I knew the chances of me going to her house and her actually handing the keys over without a fight was slim to none. After her phone call I knew for a fact that she would provoke me to do something terrible to her conniving ass. I definitely didn't need a murder charge on top of domestic abuse and auto theft. The more I thought about it the more it seemed that I was going to have to go over there and meet with her face to face.

Chapter 8

"Face to Face"

Touch

The cab driver out front of my house honked his horn to signal he had arrived and was ready to leave. I opened the door and signaled for him to wait one second. It was the same greasy-haired driver I'd had before, and he didn't look too pleased to have to wait.

As I put my shoes on, I had a decision to make. Do I take my gun to Lisa's house, or do I leave it home? I had been weighing my options ever since I'd called for the cab. On one hand there was no telling what that bitch might come at me with, so it would be good to have protection. On the other hand, I didn't want to get caught with a weapons charge if she saw me coming and called the cops. I wasn't supposed to be anywhere near her, pending the outcome of her case against me.

I grabbed the handle of the gun, paused, then decided it was best to leave it home. The gun found its place next to my underwear in the dresser drawer. I was hoping I had made the right decision by going over to Lisa's unarmed.

On the ride over, I went over every scenario I could think of. I would try and talk sense to her, and hopefully she would give up the car easily. If everything went smooth, then I would be sexing this bitch in a matter of minutes. Give her some good dick then talk her into dropping the charges. If that didn't happen, I didn't have any clue what I would do. I needed to play it right. If the bitch pushed it, I wasn't sure if I could control my temper and not give her a beat-down. Force might be necessary to get my car back. The cabbie asked, "You want me to come back and pick you up later?"

"Nah. I'm picking my car up. I won't be needing your services ever again." I handed him a twenty-dollar tip.

His eyes bugged out of their sockets. "Too bad. Not everyone tips as good as you. If you ever need a cab, you know who you can call." I watched him as he drove off down the street. The block was quiet, not a soul around. I looked at Lisa's house and took a deep breath. I tried to keep calm as I walked up to the front door. No use in starting this thing off in a pissed-off mood.

Here we go, I thought as I knocked on the door. I nervously rubbed my hands together as I waited for Lisa to answer. After waiting longer than normal with no answer, I banged on the door a little harder. I looked through the window and didn't see any movement in the house. I went around and looked through the windows of the garage door and saw both Lisa's car and mine. *Why ain't this bitch answering?* I thought.

I circled the house and peeked in all of the windows. Still no sign of Lisa. I had no choice. I was going to have to enter without her permission. What else could I do? She was holding my property, and I needed it back.

Luckily for me I didn't need to break any windows to get in. I knew where Lisa hid her spare key. I was happy not to attract the attention of the neighbors. I reached up and felt around the top of the window frame for the key. *Damn, it's not there!*

I stepped back and looked at the window. I realized I had been feeling around on the wrong one. It was the one closer to the front door. I went to the right window and felt the key immediately.

The key easily slid into the keyhole, and I cautiously and quietly opened the door. Standing just inside the door, I listened carefully but didn't hear anyone moving around the house.

"Yo, Lisa," I yelled.

No answer.

Jackpot! I was going to get my car and all my shit back without having to deal with her crazy ass.

I quickly moved further into the house. My first stop was the kitchen. My car keys were sitting on the counter right where I had left them. I couldn't believe she hadn't even touched them since I had left. In one motion I grabbed the keys and dashed upstairs. I was under a time crunch. I needed to gather all of my belongings and get the hell out before Lisa came home.

The bedroom was a mess, with clothes strewn all over the floor and bed. I opened the door to the equally messy walk-in closet. All of my shoes were under a pile of Lisa's clothes. I threw the clothes into the bedroom and stared at my shoes. I realized I didn't have anything to put my stuff in. The thought of using one of

Lisa's suitcases quickly left my mind. That bitch was likely to say I stole her property and hit me with a burglary and theft charge.

I ran back downstairs and grabbed a few garbage bags from the kitchen. Bounding back up the stairs two at a time, I got a little winded. I paused for a brief moment to catch my breath at the top of the stairs. While standing there, I thought I heard a noise downstairs. I quieted my breathing to pay close attention to the sounds of the house. Satisfied that I was still alone, I continued on, easily filling up two trash bags with my clothes and shoes.

I popped the trunk of my car and threw the bags in and immediately rushed back inside to retrieve the rest of my shit. I still needed to get the flat-screen TV and Blu-ray player I'd bought. Once they were packed in the trunk I slammed it closed. I was just about to get in the car when I remembered the bag of weed I had left behind. *Can't leave the kush behind.* So I went back in one more time.

I came running back down the stairs with the bag of weed in my hand, excited at the thought of getting the hell out of that house and getting high. As soon as I hit the floor at the bottom of the steps, I was attacked from behind.

"What the fuck are you doing in my house?" Lisa jumped on my back like a lioness attacking a gazelle.

I felt my skin break and the blood flow as she sunk her claws into my neck. Caught off guard, the force of her attack knocked me over, and the weed went flying as we both struggled against each other.

Lisa was grabbing, pulling, kicking, clawing whatever she could, to inflict pain. I was trying to regain my bearings and get her off me. She was fighting with the strength of an elephant and the fury of a rabid dog. I was having trouble containing her, and she was getting some solid blows to my head and face. Not only had she scratched my neck, but she drew blood from my ear and ripped my shirt open.

I was finally able to get a good angle on her, and I hauled off on her. The force of my punch sent her flying back.

"You fuckin' crazy?" I screamed.

"What you expect me to do? I go to the store and when I get back there's someone in my house. How you think I'm gonna react?"

"It's me. Not some filthy crackhead breaking into your place."

"You look like a crackhead to me."

"You ain't got to be like that," I said, trying to calm her down.

Her breathing was getting back to a normal rhythm, but she still had a wild look in her eyes.

"Like what? You broke into my house. Fool!" She tried to smooth her wild mane of hair.

"I didn't break in. I used your key to get in. I wanted to surprise you." I took a step toward her.

"You surprised me, all right. I almost killed your ass."

I looked at her seductively and said, "I'd like to kill that ass. Why you think I came over here? I couldn't stand being away from you."

"Oh, yeah?" She smiled.

"I was hoping we could drop all this bullshit between us. Get back to some good lovin' like we used to." I stepped right in on her and stroked her hair.

"We might be able to drop all this. You gonna show me how you want to kill this ass."

I slapped her ass. "You know I do." "Come on then." She started walking upstairs, and I followed. When we got to her bedroom, she started walking toward her closet. I needed to stop her before she got inside and saw my shit gone. "Where you going, babe?" I grabbed her hand.

She pulled away. "I want to put on something sexy for you."

"What for?" I reached for her hand again. "I'll just be taking it off."

"It makes me feel sexy." She avoided my grasp and went to the closet. It took a second, but then I heard it. "Oh no, you didn't. You muthafucka." She came running out of the closet with a shoe in her hand.

I spun on my heels and darted down the stairs, with Lisa in hot pursuit. I went straight to my car and jumped in.

Lisa came running into the garage with a poker from the fireplace. "You gonna pay, you piece of shit!" she screamed.

I put the car in reverse and was halfway out the garage when Lisa swung and smashed the passenger side window. My tires screeched as I swung out of the driveway and slammed the car into drive, but she was able to smash the rear window as well before I could hit the gas. Her neighbors started coming from their houses.

"You're gonna regret this, Touch! You fucked with the wrong woman! Just you wait!" She threw the poker at my car as I sped down the street.

I looked in my rearview and in the distance saw Lisa still throwing a fit in the middle of the street. This bitch was legit crazy. There was no telling what she was going to come back with. But, at least, I had my car.

Chapter 9

"Taking the Law into Your Own Hands"

Lisa

The color bark brown does my body good in this suit, I thought, admiring myself in my full-length mirror. *It's a shame this is the first time I've ever worn it.* I was dressed professionally with a touch of sexiness. I had to have my boobies hanging out just a little. Give them a little glimpse of what they can't have.

Before I left my apartment, I dabbed Versace Blue Jeans perfume behind my ears and my neck. I got a glimpse of my ass as I walked off. *Hell, if I didn't go super-duper psycho on Touch, he'd still be giving it to me from the back.* That nigga was only good for sex, which was what I craved.

When I walked into the courtroom, the most important eyes I cared about was Touch's. I wanted him to see what he had created and pay for what he had done. No one fucking hits me and gets away with it. He didn't even have the decency to apologize to me. That would have eliminated most of this. On top of that, his dumb ass had made it worse by antagonizing me and breaking into my house. I wanted him to get on his knees to beg for mercy and for my forgiveness. I fell asleep easily at night, knowing Touch wouldn't sleep as he constantly thought about what his new life would be like behind bars.

When I arrived in the courtroom the district attorney with his tuna fish breath pulled me to the side. He wanted to go over some last-minute details. I didn't listen to a word he was saying. I was searching the courtroom for Touch, who was nowhere to be found.

"All rise," the bailiff announced. "The Honorable J.B. Gordon."

I was glad this show was finally starting. I was hoping Touch would be the first to go before the judge, so he could be the first to go to jail. I knew the look on his face would be priceless as soon as the judge announced his guilty verdict. And, after it was all said and done, I had plans to visit him in jail just to laugh and gawk in his face. He had to learn he'd fucked with the wrong one. There was no way he could get away with what he did to me. Touch treated me as if I was a piece of shit. No man had treated me like that, and I wasn't about to allow a man to treat me like that. I had been sitting on the court bench for over two hours, and my case still hadn't been called. Getting impatient, I looked at my watch. It was eleven-fifteen, and I still hadn't seen Touch. For a minute, I'd begun to think he'd bucked on court and decided to be on the run and leech off another chick, like he'd done me.

I decided to give him another fifteen minutes to show. No such luck. I gathered my things. I wanted to check the docket to be sure I was in the right courtroom.

Just as I was about to stand, the court doors opened, and Touch and his attorney walked through the doors like they owned the place. Touch was decked out in a suit. He walked toward the front of the courtroom with his hot-shot attorney. Our eyes met, and he looked away immediately. He was trying hard not to look my way. I knew he saw me because I was sitting at the end of the bench, near the aisle. I figured he was still pretty pissed off about the baby doll incident and our last altercation at my house.

We weren't called until after the lunch break. Sitting through all that court bullshit wasn't fun at all. And I was anxious to get it over with.

"The Commonwealth calls Lisa Platow to the stand," the bailiff said.

I stood up and walked to the stand like I was walking the runway in Fashion Week. I positioned myself on the witness stand then looked at Touch with piercing eyes. My eyes were glued on him when the bailiff said his spiel about telling the truth, nothing but the truth, blah, blah, blah. Yeah, I agreed and even nodded my head. But I was agreeing to tell my own version of the truth. Like they say, it's three sides to every story, your side, my side and the truth.

"Ms. Platow, would you explain to the court how you received your wounds?" the Commonwealth's Attorney asked.

"The defendant, Trayvon Davis, beat me, punched me, and kicked me, eventually causing me to have a busted nose," I explained through cries. The night before I'd rehearsed this part over and over in the bathroom mirror, hoping the judge would believe me.

"Is this the first time you have been abused by the defendant?"

"No, it isn't." I pulled a handkerchief from my purse and wiped my tears.

"How often would this occur?" The Commonwealth's Attorney was setting it up to go in for the kill.

"He would assault me in some form at least once a week. The simplest things would trigger it. If the defendant had a bad day or I did something that he didn't like, then he would punish me," I lied.

"No further questions, Your Honor."

Next, it was Touch's lawyer's turn to question me. I knew he was about to attempt to dig into my ass, but I was determined not to lose my cool. The last thing I wanted to do was appear as the mad black woman I knew he was gonna try to make me out to be.

"Ms. Platow, how many times have you filed a police report for these so-called occurrences of domestic violence?"

"I'm not sure," I replied, shrugging my shoulders.

"Well, maybe I can help you out. The only police report I see is the one recently filed along with your stolen vehicle. Never once, prior to this incident, did it mention physical violence. Nor did you go to the hospital. There are no hospital reports at all." Touch's lawyer was really making me out to be a liar.

"I told the cop what happened to me. What more do you expect? I was afraid to call the police prior to this incident, and I was too ashamed to go to the hospital." My palms had suddenly become sweaty.

"Ms. Platow, it's clear to me that you're just a scorned woman trying to get back at a man who you're in love but who's not in love with you."

This lawyer was getting under my skin. Because I was afraid what may come out of my mouth, I remained silent, but I was sure my thoughts were written all over my face as I rolled my eyes.

"Your Honor, based on the huge lack of physical evidence, I move to dismiss this case. This case is frivolous and an obvious fraud." Touch's lawyer walked away. "Ms. Platow, you may step down," the judge ordered.

As I started to walk back to my seat, I realized I had just lost this battle. My hands couldn't stop shaking, not to mention my sweaty palms. Before taking my seat, I cut my eyes at Touch one last time, who sat calmly with a smirk across his face. The mere sight of his smug little ass made my blood boil.

"Please rise for the verdict," the judge announced.

I listened as the judge announced a not guilty verdict for the assault charge and guilty for the stolen vehicle charge. He was sentenced to one year supervised probation. I couldn't believe my ears. Even if Touch was found not guilty on the assault charge, I at least expected him to get time for stealing my damn car.

I grabbed my purse and began to storm out of the courtroom. I met Touch at the courtroom door. "After you," he said then began to laugh.

"Fuck you, Touch!" I yelled, totally losing my mind.

That laugh in my face was the last straw. I took off my five-inch stiletto heels and started beating Touch with it. I got in a few good jabs in his dick and face. Before I knew it, he had begun to bleed, and the bailiff was all over me. Before he was able to pry me off him, I'd managed to bite Touch in the face. The bailiff had saved him this time, but it wasn't over. This was just the beginning. I had it in for Touch, and he was gonna pay. I'd decided to take justice into my own hands. After I made bail and got myself out for contempt of court. Now I was doubly pissed.

Chapter 10

"Woman of Destruction"

Jewel

My hands were starting to cramp as I sorted Touch's money into stacks of ones, fives, tens, twenties, and hundreds. It seemed like the stack of ones was always the smallest. Although I knew it wasn't right, and to some it may even be stealing, I would always take most of Touch's one-dollar bills for myself. By the time I was done, I'd have at least two hundred dollars in ones alone. Believe it or not, he never even missed them. As far as I was concerned, Touch owed me, and I deserved a little gift. Over time those extra ones added up to designer handbags, jeans, and shoes that I loved. And I never once took a fifty or a hundred-dollar bill. I knew my limit, and I wasn't about to push it.

After I separated the money and marked the large bills with a counterfeit pen, I slid it through the money counter. I thought back to those times I used to count each bill by hand. Talk about carpel tunnel and some major hand cramps! It took quite a bit of begging, but Touch finally bought a money counter.

Once I verified the amount and strapped it, I placed the money aside. Then I pulled out all the bills for the month and totaled them up. Things had really gotten behind, with Touch being on the run and then locked up. I was slowly getting out of debt with all the money coming in and was grateful that our bills were finally getting caught up. We would have been out of debt much sooner, but you know I needed to pamper myself. A girl needs her bags, shoes, jewelry, and clothes.

With Touch being in the drug name, it wasn't wise to put anything in his name, so everything fell on me. As soon as we stopped paying the bills, collectors were after me like I'd stolen something. My credit was ruined, and my bank account had a lien.

So I nearly jumped for joy as I grabbed enough money to pay all our past due bills in full. I counted out bills money and put the rest of the money in the vault in the basement. I walked to the vault with a permanent smile on my face.

I know people say money can't buy happiness, but it sure does make things a lot easier in life. Which in turn gives happiness. Not only that, money is the number one reason marriages fall apart, so what does that tell you? I noticed since Touch had been making a little money, things between us were getting a little better.

Our relationship wasn't the best, and we definitely still had our issues, but things were a little brighter. At least we had hope at this point. I still didn't feel we had gained back that love we'd had in the past, and we still weren't quite that dynamic duo of a team as we were in the past either. But I was grateful and hopeful that we were slowly making progress.

Rico had stopped calling and harassing me. Plus, those crazy-ass anonymous calls had ceased as well. I was no longer afraid to go outside to get the mail anymore or packing my gun just to go to the grocery store. I was even starting to feel safe without Touch in the house. I was feeling so good that I'd decided to do something special for him.

I whipped up a T-bone steak and scrambled eggs with cheese, his all-time favorite meal. I purposely had a grill built into the kitchen stovetop. It was nights like these that it came in handy. I popped open a bottle of Moët to enjoy with our meal and lit candles in the dining room, kitchen, bedroom, and even the stairs. Then I turned on some jazz music to create a relaxed mood in the house.

I didn't want to say much to Touch, except how much I truly loved him. Enjoying our food and riding the shit out of him was what both of us needed.

I threw on a flaming red lingerie set I'd ordered from Victoria's Secret and matching five-inch stilettoes. It was something about the color red that sent Touch into a sexual rage.

Just as I was finishing up the meal preparation I heard Touch pull up in the driveway. I turned down the lights and lit the candles on the table. The ones I placed throughout the house were already full flame. I was in need of Touch's dick. I was feeling an attraction for him I hadn't felt in a long time. Maybe it had something to do with all of the sexiness I had created in the house. It even made me think that just maybe the love was coming back.

I hurried to the bathroom to freshen up and give myself a quick look-over. When I was done Touch still hadn't come in the house. I began to get anxious, so I looked out of the window to see what was taking him so damn long. Touch had just gotten out the car, and to my surprise he had roses in his hands. I smiled, knowing this was going to be a good night for us.

I watched as Touch headed toward the front door. After he took only a few steps, I watched him fall down on the ground like he had been shot. Without thinking I grabbed the gun he gave me from the kitchen drawer.

I rushed outside with gun cocked, ready to blast the first thing moving. As soon as I took a few steps out the door, out jumped a chick from the bushes with a huge gun the size of a rifle in her hand laughing hysterically. I didn't know what the hell was so funny, and I didn't have time to try and figure it out. I aimed at her without hesitation and pulled the trigger.

Pow!

I opened my eyes after shooting the gun. To my surprise the chick was still standing there. Evidently my aim wasn't as good as I thought. Guess next time I should keep my eyes open when I fire.

"You crazy bitch!" The girl dropped her gun and hit the ground, covering up in a ball.

I was struggling to cock my gun again and put another bullet in the chamber when I heard Touch scream out, "Jewel, don't! It's not a real gun! She only has a BB gun!" He snatched the gun from me.

That's when I realized what was going on. This bitch had to be none other than Lisa. I picked up a tree branch and started running in her direction. Realizing she was about to get a beat-down of a lifetime, she ran toward her car.

"Your charges may have went away, but don't think I'm going to do the same!" Lisa screamed at the top of her lungs as she got in her car and sped off.

I chased after her. It didn't take me long to recognize I wouldn't catch her, so I gave up. I was furious as I stood in the middle of the street yelling all sorts of profanities at the top of my lungs. I was half-naked and making a fool out of myself in front of my neighbors. I began to walk back to the house, preparing to dig into Touch's ass.

"Jewel!" Touch yelled as I walked back toward the house. "Jewel!" he screamed again and began to rush toward me. "Jewel!" He tackled me to the ground like a football player.

"What the—"

Zoom! A car sped by, interrupting my sentence.

Touch had just saved my life, pushing me out of the path of Lisa's vehicle. That psycho bitch was trying to run me over. That was it. She had finally pushed me to the limit. I wanted to grab my gun and shoot that bitch between her eyes just for fucking with us. I couldn't believe she had the nerve to come to my house. Then I began to wonder how she knew where I lived. My brain became flooded with all sorts of thoughts as I had a flashback to that baby doll incident.

"I can't take this shit no more!" I shoved Touch off of me with all my force. "Because of you thinking with your dick, you put my life in danger. Dumb ass! What if that car had actually hit me? And what if Lisa had a real gun?" I stood to my feet and began to walk away.

"Make her ass go away, Touch," I yelled, looking back at Touch, who was a couple feet behind me.

"It's not that easy, Jewel," Touch mumbled back.

"What do you mean? I've seen you make much bigger problems disappear. Why is Lisa any different? What? You got feelings for her or something?" I demanded to know as we walked in the house.

"Jewel, you're talking crazy. Don't worry. I got this. Go upstairs and lay down. You don't need to be getting all upset. It's not good for the baby."

"Good for the baby? Are you fuckin' serious?" I got up in Touch's face. "How the fuck you gon' part your lips and tell me what's good for a damn baby? Me nearly getting ran over by a fuckin' car isn't good for the fuckin' baby. Nigga, please! Get the fuck outta here!" I shoved Touch in the head.

"Don't put your hands on me, Jewel," Touch said, grabbing my wrist. He had a death grip on it, and I could feel my fingers getting numb from lack of blood flow.

"Or what?" I knew he was serious, but there was no way I was backing down. I was just as mad as he was and ready for war.

"Fuck this!" Touch said then pushed me into the wall while attempting to walk away.

As an immediate reaction, I started punching him in the chest. I had so much pent up aggression, and I was letting it all out on him.

"Jewel, stop!" Touch demanded as he tried holding me down.

"Why don't you stop acting like a fuckin' little bitch and start being a man? The old Touch would have never allowed this to happen. On top of that, I know this ain't the first time that bitch has been here. This is just the first time I've caught you and the bitch in action. Fuck you! You could never be the father of my damn child!"

Those were the last words I spoke before Touch scooped me up and slammed me on the table. I hit my head so hard that I was dizzy. Before that I'd always thought that seeing stars was a figure of speech, but now I know it's real.

I grabbed my head as I rose to my feet and noticed my hand was soaked in blood. Once I realized I was bleeding, it was like I'd immediately become possessed by a demon. I ran to the kitchen and grabbed the first thing I saw. Lucky for Touch it was only a meat pulverizer, but I'd planned to pulverize his ass to death.

"Jewel, put that down, please. I'm sorry," he began to beg. "Ah, damn! Baby, you're bleeding bad. Let me help you." Touch tried coming near me with a towel in hand.

"Don't come near me!"

"Jewel, I know you're mad, and so am I. But right now you're bleeding really bad. Please, baby, let me help you." Touch attempted to grab my arm.

"Get the fuck away from me!" I yelled like a crazed woman then started hitting him all over with the meat tenderizer. The blows landed with thuds. If his arms were a steak, they would be the most tender cut of meat you ever tasted.

When my arms got too tired to swing anymore, I dropped my weapon and ran upstairs. I didn't know where I was going, but my first instinct was to pack my bags, so that's what I did. Touch gave a half-hearted attempt to try and stop me, and that pissed me off even more. Instead he just stood there and watched me pack. I was in a daze as I packed and didn't even realize what I was packing, but once all of my Louis Vuitton bags were full, I grabbed them and headed out the door.

"Jewel," Touch called out to me in his most pitiful tone.

He even sounded like he was crying, but I refused to look in his direction. Keeping my eyes focused on the door only, I walked right past him and into the garage. I hopped in my car and pulled out the driveway, never looking back. "Where the hell am I going to go now?" I shouted at the top of my lungs, tears streaming down my face. For thirty minutes I'd been driving in circles with no place to go. It was times like this I wish I had my mom to run to. My mom had moved back home to Panama years earlier, and not a day went by that I didn't think of her and miss her. She'd taught me all I needed to know about being the materialistic, gold-digging woman I was. I knew she was only a phone call away, but I didn't want to call her with this mess because she would be worried. There was nothing she could've done to help me at that point, and hearing her voice would have only made me sad.

I became lost in my thoughts as I hopped on the interstate, feeling alone and sorry for myself. Everyone I let close to me always let me down.

Sasha, that conniving bitch that pretended to be in love with me, was the first to fuck me over. Then came Misty, who was the perfect friend and played the role so well, I totally forgot Sasha existed. Well, little miss perfect turned out to be a cop. My first true love, Calico, was simply using me to move drugs for him.

Finally, there's Touch, my best friend turned lover, who fucked me over more times than I can count.

The more I thought, the more realized the poor choices I'd made in friends and men. I couldn't understand how one person could get dealt such a bad hand in life. Why was I always letting people take advantage of me? Why did I put myself in these positions? Well, I'd had enough. I was no longer going to be taken advantage of. I turned up my radio and drove along with a renewed confidence.

Before long I'd gotten so wrapped up in the tunes of my iPod that I hadn't even realized 64 West had turned into 95 South, and it was getting close to midnight. Here I was in the middle of nowhere in the middle of the night. I was exhausted and needed a place to crash. Since Touch had been watching me pack, I wasn't able to take all of my cash during my rush to get out of the house. I didn't want to spend a chunk of the money I did have on some fleabag motel.

I wracked my brain trying to think of someone I knew in the area. That's when it hit me—my girl Shakira. She had recently moved to DC. Although I hadn't talked to her in nearly two years, she was my last option. Shakira and I were really close, but our friendship became distant due to the jealous ways of a previous friend of mine, Sasha. Sasha had played me and actually made me think I might be in love with her for a minute. Her conniving, jealous ass got in between Shakira and me and caused us to lose touch with one another. I'd always regretted not patching things up with Shakira, but I was too embarrassed to admit that Shakira had been right about Sasha's sneaky-ass. Shakira had warned me, but I didn't listen. I was too stubborn.

Then when everything started happening with Touch and Calico, I got so caught up that patching things up with Shakira was the last thing on my mind. Sometimes I felt so dumb when I thought about the decisions I made. Actually I attributed a lot of my heartache to Sasha. There weren't many things I could say I regretted, but being friends with her was definitely a big, big mistake.

I grabbed my phone to give Shakira a call, but I noticed I had ten missed calls and six text messages from Touch. My radio was turned up so loud and I was so lost in thought, I hadn't heard any of his attempts. Deep inside I wanted to call him back, but I just couldn't allow myself to do it. I truly felt he was probably still fucking with Lisa. Too bad for him he found out the hard way she had a touch of fatal attraction.

I scrolled to Shakira's number in my cell phone. For a moment I contemplated whether I should make the call or not. I felt guilty for letting time get away from our friendship, but I trusted she was the kind of friend who, if we hadn't talked in a while, would just pick up where we left off. With that final thought, I pressed send.

"Hello," she answered.

"Hi, Shakira. It's me, Jewel," I said softly, unsure how she would respond.

"It's who?" she asked in a groggy tone.

"Jewel."

"Oh, Jewel! Girl, I didn't recognize your voice. Is everything okay?" she asked right away. It was amazing how she still could sense something was wrong, even though we hadn't talked in ages. "Honestly, I'm not okay." I began to cry all over again.

"Aaaawwww, Jewel. What's wrong, honey?"

"It's a long story. My life is in shambles. I just packed up and left Virginia Beach. I've been riding for hours. I'm in your area. Do you mind if I come over just for the night?" I said, just putting it out there. I was so exhausted, I didn't bother beating around the bush.

"Sure. When we hang up, I will text you my address, and you can just put it in your navigation system. I'll be waiting for you. Drive carefully."

"Thank you so much," I responded, grateful she was my savior in a time of need. My attention was directed toward my dashboard after hanging up the phone with Shakira. I had fifty miles before empty. I was feeling tired and drained, so I figured this was probably the best time to pull off, get gas, a 5-hour Energy, and wait for Shakira's text.

I stopped at the BP gas station directly off the exit. My stomach had started feeling queasy, so I used the bathroom and grabbed a snack.

Emotionally, physically, and mentally drained from the day, I was totally exhausted and in a daze as I set the pump and got back in the car.

"Get the hell out of the car!" a man demanded, gun in hand.

"What!" I replied.

My head was spinning. I must have dozed off while waiting for the gas to finish pumping.

"Now!" he demanded.

I gathered myself and jumped out the car as the masked man demanded. I contemplated running away but was afraid he would shoot me if I tried.

He immediately started rummaging through my car. He used one hand to snatch my iPod while using the other to keep the gun pointed directly at me.

My hands began trembling, and my bladder was about to burst. I closed my eyes and silently prayed this dude would take whatever he wanted and leave me alone. I didn't want my life to end this way.

I heard another male voice directly behind me say,

"Yo, come on, man. People are coming." I was relieved that I hadn't tried to run. I probably would have been gunned down by whoever was behind me.

"Shit!" The masked man rushed out my car. He pressed the gun firmly against my temple and down to my neck. "Turn your face," he said. "Don't look at me!"

I closed my eyes and did exactly what he said. The next thing I could hear was him getting into another vehicle and driving away. I let out a sigh of relief as I opened my eyes to see nothing but his mask lying on the ground. My life had been spared, and he hadn't gotten away with anything but an iPod. I was certain God had left me here for a reason.

Just then I felt my phone vibrate in my pocket. Shakira's text had come through. I plugged the address into the navigation system and headed down the road to my new life.

Chapter 11

"On a Mission"

Unknown Person

My counselor asked me, "Are you ready to say the sobriety prayer?"

"Yes." I nodded. This would be the last time I would say that damn prayer and the last time I would see that group. Sad to say, as much I hated that place, I sure was going to miss them, especially my counselor, Frank. He had really helped me get through some hard times. My final night in the center they threw a small party for me. The best part was the confetti cake from Cold Stone Ice Cream Bakery. Even though to this day I felt like I never should have been there, I must say, while there, I learned to enjoy the simple pleasures of life. Before arriving at the center, the police force was my life. Working undercover and taking down the bad guys was what kept me going each day. But when I pissed off one of my superiors and they tried to force me onto desk duty, I fought back. So when I got into an accident, they really fucked with me and told the public I had been killed. Then when they saw I wasn't going away, they went on to say I had drugs and alcohol in my system and hid me in a rehab center. Of course I had drugs and alcohol in my system, I was undercover. I had to do what the people around me were doing. That wasn't uncommon in my line of work at all. What it all boiled down to was, they wanted me off the force, and they were going to get me off by all means. I knew the justice system was crooked, but I never expected to be a victim. After all, I was on their side.

As I walked out of the treatment center, I could only imagine my family or anyone at all coming to greet me outside. With my career as my primary focus, I had no time for children, a mate, or even a pet companion. No one would be coming to greet my sorry ass. The one relationship I did have ended when my life on the force began. Every other relationship I had was all related to my work, so none of it seemed real. During my time at the treatment center I realized there was one person who I might have had some real feelings for.

My reality hit me as I got outside of the building. Nothing but the dust from the cab stopping and greeting me. I said hello and hopped in. As I got comfortable, I was hit with a stench of sweat and smoke in the car. That's when I realized I was entering back into the real world after a year and a half in rehab. The ride home was surreal. I felt like the world had already changed so much. In fact, it wasn't the world that had changed, it was me. I was clean and sober. When I arrived home, I was in total shock. As I walked into my apartment, chills went down my spine. It had been so long since I'd been there, for a moment I felt like I was in an unfamiliar place. That feeling quickly went away as soon as I entered the living room. I stared at the countless plaques and honors on my wall. They reminded me of what I used to be. As I went down the row of plaques, it was a virtual walk down memory lane. I thought back to the many cases I had solved and the awards ceremonies.

There were definitely more highs than lows throughout my career, but the most recent and lasting memory
was the lowest of the low. I was forced off my case and
out of the department.

Thinking of all that went wrong made me feel like a
failure. A rush of anger came over me, and I grabbed
the largest garbage bag I could find and began to throw
all the plaques and awards in there. None of them
meant shit at that point.

I'd worked so hard and was so committed to the
force, just to have everything blow up in my face in the
end really hurt. At first, I wanted to die, but deep inside
I knew I couldn't give up so easily. I needed to survive
this ordeal, so I could redeem myself. So I could repair
my reputation.

The first thing I learned in rehab was that love truly
conquers all. From that day I knew I had to go to my
special person to confess my everlasting love. The
thought of this person was what helped me make it
through. Since I no longer had the force to look forward to, I made this person my daily motivation. There
was one problem—I had met this person on the job,
and we had left on very bad terms.

After clearing my wall of every honor and plaque I'd
received, I went into the bathroom. All I wanted to do
was take a hot shower and wash away the past. The
grime and dirt of my past were weighing me down, and
I needed it lifted. I stopped and looked at myself in the
mirror. I hated the person I saw. I saw a failure.

Looking in the medicine cabinet, I found a pair of
sharp scissors and started cutting my hair then I dyed
it platinum blonde. This was going to be a new beginning. I never again wanted to be reminded of who I
used to be. Finally after cleaning up all the stray hairs
that had fallen in the sink, I took a shower in the hot-

test temperature I could stand. I stood there watching the past fall away right down the drain. It was a new day. After my shower I headed into my kitchen and opened the refrigerator. The stench of moldy milk, cheese, strawberries, and Chinese food almost made me vomit. Again I found myself grabbing a garbage bag. Just like my awards, I tossed everything from the fridge in there.

It didn't take long for me to realize my whole place needed a thorough cleaning, so I turned on the radio and got to it. I cleaned my apartment from top to bottom. When I was done, the place smelled of bleach. I grabbed my bags of garbage and headed to the dumpster. On the way there, I was stopped in the hallway by a voice calling to me from behind. My old self would have been on high alert if someone had called me from behind, but the new me was calm.

"Excuse me," a familiar voice said. I turned around to see the previous love of my life. I was no longer calm. My heart began to beat hard, and a lump formed in my throat.

"Hey," I was so caught off guard, it was the only word I managed to get out.

"Oh, that's the best greeting you can give an old friend?" Jamie said to me while we embraced.

I could have stayed in Jamie's arms forever. It had been so long since I'd felt the loving embrace of a mate. I had no idea what to say to him. We stood there for a second until Jamie broke the tension by grabbing one of the garbage bags I was carrying.

Jamie and I had been lovers for three years. It was a typical passionate affair that just lost its passion. Well, *I* lost my passion for it. I fell in love with something new, my job. I just didn't have time for Jamie anymore. My new lover was more exciting and dangerous. Seeing Jamie brought up so many memories, good and bad. All the bad memories had to do with the way I'd treated him toward the end of the relationship. I didn't know any other way to handle the situation than to be a bitch and make him hate me. I was hoping that Jamie wasn't here to bring up old fights and make me beg for forgiveness. "So what brings you here, old friend?" I asked Jamie as we headed to the dumpster together. "You. I've been keeping up with you. I heard you had been in rehab for a while and you were getting out today, so I wanted to be there to welcome you home. I actually went up to the facility to pick you up, but you had already gone."

"Oh, that was nice of you. I would have never expected to see you." I smiled at Jamie. The thought that he still cared enough to want to meet me made me happy inside. I guess he had forgiven me for my attitude all those years ago.

"So how are you? It's been so long. Did rehab help?"

"I think so. I've turned over a new leaf in my life. I'm feeling clear and conscious for the first time in a long time."

"That's great. Rehab did all that?"

"Yep. I learned to slow down and take it one day at a time. If I don't get it done instantly, I won't die."

"I agree. I haven't learned to accept that concept yet. Maybe you could help me with it."

Jamie never was the type to wait to see how things would work out when faced with a problem. With the smallest obstacle, he would run like a puppy with its tail between its legs. That's one reason why we never worked out. I loved a challenge and faced them head on, even if sometimes too fast and without thinking it all the way through. It was the only way I knew how to operate. Frankly I thought it was kind of bitch-like to run from your problems.

"Listen, umm, I'm starving. Did you have dinner yet?" Jamie asked with a rub to the tummy.

"What are you in the mood for?"

"Pizza loaded with cheese and sausage," Jamie said right away.

"I see nothing has changed." I smiled. "Still the same Jamie."

"You remembered?" Jamie smiled back.

"How could I forget? Now come on up to my place. Lucky for you, I just finished cleaning my house, so I won't need to put your ass to work." I laughed.

Jamie said, "I'm guessing your apartment reeks of bleach."

"Yes, it does." I giggled. "Guess I'm not the only one that remembers old habits."

"Some things in our relationship I will never forget," Jamie said.

We ordered a pizza covered in hot Italian sausage and roasted red peppers. Seeing Jamie again was quite comforting. It was easy to fall right back into a rhythm with him. It was familiar and safe, which was what I really craved at that moment.

After coming out of the rehab center, I thought no one would grace me with their presence. For my whole stay in rehab I thought I was alone, but I had come to accept that. Then out of nowhere came Jamie. I knew one thing for sure, things happen for a reason. I sat there thinking that maybe Jamie and I were supposed to rekindle our relationship, get married, and have a puppy.

We sat there for a good hour just talking and laughing. It was a nice way to reenter society.

"So, what brings you back here, Jamie?" I asked before picking up our plates and placing them in the sink. After Jamie and I had broken up he had moved out of town. He said he had another job in Baltimore, but I figured he was leaving to get away from me. Thinking about it made me feel a bit guilty, but I can't control how other people react.

"I landed a corporate position with a cigarette company in sales and marketing. I couldn't refuse the offer that was on the table. I just moved back. Haven't even been here two days. I'm not even unpacked yet. Boxes are all over my apartment."

"Knowing how you are, they will be there for a while." I laughed.

It felt so good to laugh and be at ease, it was easy for me to fall into Jamie arms. It felt so comforting. It turned me on to be wrapped up in another person's arms again.

Even though, I wasn't ready for sex, we did mess around. Jamie couldn't get enough of my clit. Having an orgasm relieved a lot of tension for me. It had been a while since anyone had been down there, besides my own fingers. After we both had our orgasms, I invited Jamie to stay over for the night.

The next morning I woke up to see Jamie's head on the pillow next to mine. It wasn't until that moment I realized that I'd possibly made a big mistake. I hadn't even been home twenty-four hours and I already had a regret.

This was not the love I'd planned to come home to. It wasn't the thought of reuniting with Jamie that kept me going while in rehab. I wanted to reunite with Jewel. The thought of her was what kept me going.

My stomach started to turn as I thought about how I'd just fucked up. I had to get Jamie out of my house and fast. I needed more time alone to think about what

I was doing with my life. What was going to make me happiest? I thought Jewel was going to make me happiest, but now this little encounter had me all messed up.

"Good morning, baby," I whispered, to wake Jamie.

"Good morning," Jamie said between yawns.

"Not to rush you out the door, but I've got an appointment I have to rush to this morning," I lied.

"Oh, no problem," Jamie said while getting up.

As Jamie got dressed, I went to the bathroom to brush my teeth and wash my face. I had to make it look authentic. I waited in the bathroom for a few minutes extra to give Jamie some time to get dressed and me some time to get my head straight. By the time I returned to the bedroom Jamie was fully dressed.

"Can I leave you my number?" Jamie asked with cell phone in hand.

"Sure." I grabbed my phone and entered the numbers as Jamie called them out to me.

"Will you call me later?" Jamie asked before heading toward the door.

I nodded. "Yes."

"I'm going to be totally honest with you—I want this relationship back," Jamie said, looking me in the eyes and cradling my face.

That was the last thing I expected or wanted him to say. "Let me think about it. I don't want us to move too fast," was the best response I could come up with.

I did enjoy Jamie's company, but I wasn't sure I was ready to rekindle what we had in the past. Too much had transpired, and so much time had passed. We were both different people from back then. I was dealing with personal issues, which I wasn't sure I could do if I had to worry about someone else's issues as well. I looked at life through a different window than when Jamie and I were dating.

"Understandable," Jamie said.

After exchanging a small kiss, we gave each other a big hug, and I watched as Jamie walked through the front door of my apartment. I sat on my couch and tried to figure out why my life seemed to be so complicated. Less than a day from rehab and already I was dealing with drama. I sighed as my thoughts went to Jewel.

Chapter 12

"You've Got Balls"

Touch

"Here you go, Officer Phelps," I said, handing him a fresh box of Krispy Kreme doughnuts. The box also included ten crisp hundred-dollar bills. I laughed to myself as I wondered what it was with piggies and their beloved doughnuts.

Jimmy had at least ten cops on his payroll. When they saw us doing our thing in the streets, they kindly looked the other way. These dudes were even willing to get rid of a body for Jimmy. This kid, Officer Phelps, was a street kid turned cop. He said Jimmy was like a father to him. The longer I worked for Jimmy, the more I realized that this man was and will always be loved in the streets.

Officer Phelps took the box without a word. He opened it up, took out a doughnut, and started eating it. I believe he was just making sure the money was in there. He kept eating the doughnut as he walked away.

I got in my truck and headed back to the spot.

"It's a wrap for tonight," Deuce said, nodding his head as we gathered up Jimmy's cut.

I wrapped the money tight and handed it over to him, so he could make the drop to Jimmy's girl. Happy to be done for the day, I got ghost quick. No way I was going to hang around and have Deuce think of one last errand for me to run.

That night when I got home, I puffed on a couple of blunts while listening to some music. Listening to those songs really had me reminiscing. It seemed every song that came up reminded me of Jewel. Damn, I was missing that girl. Since I hadn't heard from her, I figured she had finally reached her breaking point.

Usually she would have either come home by now or at least contacted me, considering I had blown up her phone with texts and voice mails. I knew I'd done it this time, so I can't say that I blame her. How much can one person take? Truth is, I knew I could be a motherfucking handful at times.

I got so high, I passed out on the couch before I could call Jewel and tell her once more how much I missed her.

The next morning, I got up and went to Waffle House to eat pancakes, and scrambled eggs with cheese and bacon. I was really starting to miss Jewel bad. This used to be one of our favorite breakfast spots. To cheer my spirits up, I went to visit Jimmy. He was turning into a father figure for me. I wish our visits didn't have to be in a prison separated by plexiglass. To maintain a low profile, we would make our conversations brief. Talking in codes made both of us feel a little at ease. No matter how low you talk, you never know who may be listening. Especially the bullshit warden.

"What's up, Jimbo!" I said as soon as Jimmy walked to the glass window.

"You know what it is, youngblood," Jimmy said as he sat down.

"You looking good."

"Yeah, I'd be looking better on the other side of this glass though." Jimmy grinned. "So how's business?"

"Business is good. We're getting the goods in regularly, and the customers are happy. No complaints, boss." I tried my best to answer Jimmy without saying too much.

"And what about the employees, are they staying in line? They coming to work on time and paying off their debts?"

I assured Jimmy everything was in line. "Everything's in order, boss. Don't you worry."

"That's what I like to hear."

Jimmy and I talked about the latest on the streets, and the latest jail talk, then wrapped up our visit. It was always good talking with Jimmy. He gave me good advice and made sure I understood everything that was going on. He had a knack for making me feel better. He was a smart old dude, and I loved learning from him. He was quick with dropping his knowledge on me, and I soaked it all up. He had lived through it all and seen it all, so the dude knew what he was talking about.

After visiting Jimmy, I went back to the crib. I didn't have any work for the day, so I was gonna just relax. Getting some rest was long overdue for me. I had been grinding nonstop for a while and was exhausted.

I was looking forward to a little rest and relaxation, but to my surprise, I couldn't relax at all. My mind was churning with thoughts about Jewel. It had come to the point that everything in the house reminded me of her. Everywhere I looked, there was another memory of her.

I couldn't take it anymore. I dialed Jewel's cell number. The tough guy role was out the door. No more pride for this lion. I repeatedly kept calling her, leaving voice mails and sending loving texts. But no matter how many phone calls or texts I sent, I still got no response. After a while I was actually starting to worry.

This was not like Jewel. I looked at the clock, and it was only seven in the evening. I couldn't sit in the crib any longer. I had been pacing around the house all day and needed some different scenery. My weed was done, and I didn't have shit to drink. Thinking about Jewel and being dry was gonna drive a nigga crazy.

With that, I grabbed my jacket and keys and headed out the door. I was gonna hit a local bar for a few drinks. Hopefully being around people would get my mind off Jewel. Jewel had some crazy-ass hold on a nigga, and I needed to break her grip.

As soon as I walked out the door, I saw a midnight blue Jag pull up in my driveway. I didn't recognize the car and wasn't expecting anyone. I was immediately on guard. My thoughts raced as to who it could be. Was it Lisa? Was it one of Jimmy's associates? Whoever it was, I wasn't getting a good feeling and wasn't in the mood for no bullshit.

"Get the fuck off my property," I stated, pulling my gun from my waist.

"Yo, man. I didn't come here to start any shit," a male voice said. "I just want to know if Jewel is here."

"Who the fuck are you?" I asked with a mean-mug face.

"Rico," he replied.

So this is the muthafucka Jewel had been spending all her time with when I was locked up, I thought. As soon as I heard the name I already knew who he was. I finally was able to put a face to the name. *This muthafucka has some nerve coming to my crib.*

"You got two options, dude. You can get in your car and leave my property, or leave this earth. Which one will it be?" I asked, putting the gun to his temple.

"It's cool, my nig. I'll leave." Rico got back in his car and put the window down. "Just do me a favor and tell Jewel I came by. By the way, you need to be a little more kind to your savior. If it wasn't for me, your ass would still be in that cell, homie. You never know when you may need me again." Then he sped off.

Once I was sure Rico was gone, I texted Jewel, telling her what had just gone down. Of course when she received that text, she called back right away. It pissed me off how she didn't respond when I was spilling my heart out to her, but she wasted no time calling back about Rico. She called me back to back three times in a row before I finally decided to answer.

"Tell me right now what went down with you and Rico," I demanded as soon as I answered the phone.

"This nigga coming to my house looking for you and shit."

"Lower your voice, Touch, or I'm hanging up!" Jewel yelled back.

I ignored her ass because I knew if we were face to face, she definitely would not be acting this gangsta. In fact if she did step to me this way in person, I would have likely slapped her upside her head. No one was allowed to step to me with that attitude and not get checked back into place.

I began to say, "I'm only going to ask you one more time—"

Jewel interrupted me. "He was there for me when you were not, and it was his money that got your sorry ass out of jail. That's all you need to know." She then hung up the phone.

I called her ass back at least ten times, but I got no response. After the second attempt at calling her, she turned her phone off, but I still continued to blow up her voice mail. After a while I gave up.

I sped to the bar angry that I had spilled my heart to Jewel and all she could do was hang up in my face. I needed a drink and fast. Once I reached the bar I

threw back shot after shot until I could no longer feel
the burn. My anger, pain and hurt had been numbed. I
sat there and let the liquor work its magic on my nerves
and emotions. When I was completely numb and totally fucked up, I looked at the bartender, tried to order
another round, and passed out. That's the last thing I
remembered about that night.

The next morning, I woke up not knowing how the
hell I got home. I assumed the bartender either called
a cab or took me home himself. I was going to have to
get my truck later on. I was thankful for a new day and
ready to get on my grind and make some money.

A half-finished blunt was sitting on my nightstand.
I lit it up and took a few pulls as I gathered my morning thoughts. As I sat on my bed puffing on the blunt, I
heard the toilet flush. I jumped out the bed and raced
to the bathroom. I opened the door, and there was a
woman standing at the sink.

"Hey." She smiled. "I'm sorry, but who the fuck are
you? And how did you get into my house?"

"Ah, I'm the one who got your ass home from the
bar."

*Damn, I was fucked up last night! I don't remember
talking to this bitch at all.* "Okay, that's cool, but I don't
know you and you need to get your ass out my house."

"Nigga, please. You don't have to ask me twice. Your
ass was so lame last night, I can't wait to never see your
ass again."

"Fuck you, bitch! You pushin' it." She sauntered past
me like she didn't have a care in the world and walked
downstairs. I followed and watched as she put her shoes
on and made her way to the front door. She turned before she went out and said, "You're welcome for getting

you home safe. Your truck is in the garage. I took what you owe me and nothing more."

"What the fuck you talking about?"

"I'm a prostitute, you fool. I don't give this pussy up for free. Well, last night I didn't give it up. I have two words for you—*whisky dick*." She smiled and closed the door in my face.

She was so calm about the whole thing, it left me tongue-tied. I had nothing to say to her. She had stunned me and left me standing at the door trying to make sense of what she just told me. It took me a little bit, but I realized I had just been suckered and dissed by a prostitute.

Instead of getting mad at the prostitute, I directed my anger at Jewel. She still hadn't come home. I knew her crazy ass was heated, but so was I. My baby had never stayed away from home so long, but I sure as hell wasn't going to give her what she wanted. I figured she probably had the phone right by her side waiting for me to call and make up.

I almost called her but then thought better of it.

Naw, man, I believe I'm going to wait this one out.

I just knew deep inside my baby would be walking through the house door any day now telling me how much she missed me and loved me. Or at least I was hoping she would.

In an attempt to kill time and get Jewel off my mind, I popped in a DVD featuring comedian Mike Epps. He was so funny that my stomach cramped up as I watched him act a damn fool in the movie *Friday*. It didn't' take long for the munchies to kick in, so I made my famous turkey sandwich to tide me over.

By the time I finished eating, it was going on one o'clock in the afternoon, and I still hadn't heard from Jewel. Unable to resist any longer, my fingers began to dial her cell number. Again, it went straight to voice mail. "What the hell!" I shouted out to no one in particular.

I dialed Jewel's number three more times to make sure my hearing was correct. Each time I got the same message, "You have reached the automated voice mail box of—"

"This chick cut her phone off," I said as I pressed end on my cell phone.

The more I sat and let shit marinate, the angrier I got. I couldn't stand it. I called Jewel again. "Yo, Jewel, stop playing. This ain't funny. Bring your ass home. You taking this shit way too far," I screamed in the phone, leaving her a voice mail, then threw my cell phone across the room.

All this stress about Jewel was fucking me up. My temples were pounding, and it felt like my head was gonna explode in a matter of seconds. A headache was coming toward my temples and fast. I decided to lay down and take a nap before I lost my mind and totally flipped out.

When I woke back up, I turned over to look at the time on the clock. It was getting close to eight o'clock. My whole day was wasted worrying about this bitch. I went across the room and grabbed my cell phone from the floor where it had landed when I threw it earlier. I checked the caller ID, and there still was no call from Jewel, but I refused to give her the satisfaction of me calling again. Jewel loved to see me squirm.

She had never been this stubborn, so I was beginning to get a little worried. I was hoping nothing had happened to her. Quickly erasing those thoughts from my mind I convinced myself Jewel would be strolling in the house at least by midnight. Unfortunately, I was wrong. I paced around the house until one in the morning with no sign of her.

Chapter 13

"I'm Watching You"

Lisa

I knew Touch was bound to fuck up and I would be there to catch his ass. After my embarrassment at the courthouse, I was determined to get this selfish motherfucker. So many nights I'd sat and watch him stagger his drunk ass into the house. This particular night I was hoping I would be just as lucky. My confidence was high, and I was ready to serve up some retribution. If things went as planned, I would follow right behind him and enter his house with ease. I had been playing it low for a while, so I knew his guard would be down.

I was dressed in all black with a hoodie on, and I'd been sitting outside Touch's house for hours waiting for him to come home. I felt like a real gangster as I used binoculars to get a bird's-eye view of his house. Since I didn't know how long I would be waiting, I drank no liquids at all. I was craving some water or a tasty appletini. My mouth was dry as shit. I refused to leave my post, no matter the situation. I even put on Depend underwear, just in case I had to pee, but the lack of fluids in my body prevented me from having to piss myself.

"Finally," I whispered as Touch pulled up in the driveway. I slouched down lower in my seat to shield myself from his eyes.

To my surprise, his guard wasn't down at all. That fool was looking all around under the car, in bushes, and even behind the garbage can, all the while carrying a gun in one hand and talking on his cell phone in another. My window was down, so I was able to listen closely as he secured the premises before walking in the house.

From what I was able to gather, he was leaving Jewel a voice message. He had his beg game on, so I guess Jewel had left him. I laughed to myself and waddled in joy with this newfound discovery. *Karma is a bitch, muthafucka.*

I sat patiently and waited another hour before I attempted to walk into Touch's house. The Touch I knew always hit the blunt and drank a couple shots of Hennessy after a long day. This was the little extra edge I needed before making my move. I quietly climbed out my car and walked to the back door. I turned the knob. This shit was easier than I thought. Touch dumb ass had left the back door unlocked.

"Jewel, is that you?" he called out as I walked through the door.

Shit, I thought to myself knowing for sure I was caught. I froze in my steps, not knowing what to do.

"Jewel? Baby, answer me," Touch shouted out again.

With no other option, I cleared my throat and tried my best to disguise my voice. "Yes, baby," I replied.

"Make me a drink, and bring it in here when you come please, baby," Touch begged.

"Okay."

I grabbed a shot glass and sprinkled a drug called Thorazine in it and mixed it with the Hennessy. I'd learned from a criminal-ass friend of mine that it paralyzes the body. I walked up behind him and put the glass to his lips, and he drank it all down in one big gulp.

"I knew you would come back," he said, slurring his words.

Touch was so drunk, he didn't even notice as I pulled out the rope from my backpack and started wrapping him with it.

"I love you," I whispered in a sweet tone as I knew Jewel probably would. Then I pulled the rope tight.

Touch finally opened his eyes. He began to tussle a bit, but it was too late. The medicine had all ready kicked in.

"What the fuck," were the last words he spoke before I stuck it to him hard, like a virgin with no lubrication.

I pulled out a pair of brass knuckles from my pocket and started beating him with no remorse. I couldn't resist fucking with his manhood, so I stomped on his dick. And to wrap it all up, I knocked out one of his teeth. I was sure to leave my mark, just as he'd done to me. To fuck up his mind even more, I ransacked the place to make it seem like I was looking for something. Satisfied with my handiwork, I took one last look around the place. I figured, since I had the run of the house, I would take something as a memento. I deserved it, considering what Touch had put me through.

I quickly snatched up an iPod from the end table and put it in my pocket. Then I went through Touch's pockets and took all his cash.

My last stop was the kitchen. I opened the refrigerator took out a beer and calmly sat and drank it. Now that my mouth had some saliva back, I went back to Touch and spat in his face before walking out the back door.

Chapter 14

"Girl Talk"

Jewel

Shakira and I spent the morning at Tyson Corner, a mall in Alexandria, Virginia. Our first stop was the M•A•C counter. I could have used some more M•A•C makeup, but I simply couldn't afford it. No Touch meant no money. It was times like these that I hated myself for depending on a man for so long to provide for me. Shakira offered to pay for some items for me in the store, but I refused. She had a little daughter to take care of, and there was no way I would allow her to spend her hard-earned money on me. Besides, this was her first bonus check from her job, and I wanted her to only splurge on herself.

While speaking with Shakira about my situation, I realized it was time I made some changes in my life. I didn't know how, but it was time I figured it out. Back in Virginia, being with Touch was stressful. Not only did I have to put up with his erratic behavior, I had constant irritable bowel syndrome. My stomach was always churning for the worse.

While in DC, I didn't feel the churn at all. I felt relaxed. Everything felt easier. Also, there was no looking over my shoulder and wondering if someone was going to kill me or him first. Some nights, I would catch

Touch looking out the window with his gun in hand, waiting and willing to kill anything that moved. I knew this was the life I chose, but it wasn't the way I wanted to live. Now it was time I broke free. I was truly getting too old for the bullshit. Ten years down the road, I didn't want to look back and regret that I'd never made a change for the better.

From the time I reached DC, I'd had my phone turned off, so Touch had no way to contact me. I wanted to be free from the drama, hurt, and pain. To be honest, I had no idea what my next move was, but I was sure it would be a positive one.

Looking at Shakira made me realize what potential I had. I knew if she could do it, I could too. We'd come from the same past and walked the same paths in life.

After browsing the mall a couple of hours, I ended up purchasing a pair of shoes on clearance. For lunch, we went to the Cheesecake Factory. Thankfully, I had a gift card I'd received from my father for my birthday. The total I'd spent for the entire mall day was only thirty dollars and fifteen cents. Being accustomed to spending whatever I wanted, this was a big accomplishment for me, and I couldn't have felt better.

Later that afternoon, we took Shakira's five-year-old daughter, Kelly, to the zoo. It had been years since I was at a zoo, and I was just as excited as Kelly. I always found the animals so exotic and fascinating.

"What flavor snow cone would you like?" I asked Kelly as we walked up to the concession stand. I had a crazy craving for rainbow cotton candy myself.

"Grape, please," she said with a head nod.

"Sure thing!" I smiled as I ran my fingers through Kelly's long, wavy hair. I wondered if my daughter would have such characteristics. Being around Kelly made me second-guess my life decisions and reassess my priorities. I wondered if I had made different decisions in my life if I would've had a child now. I wanted a baby now, so I could raise it to be a respectful, contributing member of society. I became a little sad thinking that I may never have a child.

Shakira had raised Kelly well and taught her respect at a young age. My eyes filled with tears when I observed the loving bond they shared. The most touching time was bedtime. Shakira would bathe Kelly, and after reading her a bedtime story, they both would get on their knees on the side of the bed and say their prayers together.

I couldn't help but think about what it would be like for Touch and I to raise a family together. My thoughts would start out nice enough. Then I would get a vision of Touch walking around with a gun near my baby, and those happy visions would turn into a nightmare.

When the night hit, it was girl time. Shakira called over a neighbor to babysit Kelly, and we hit the road.

"So what's the going rate for a babysitter these days?" I attempted to start a little small talk after being seated. We were dining at Tuna, a local upscale seafood restaurant.

Girl, I don't know. As long as I continue to reload Suzie's iPod gift card and pay her twenty dollars in cash, she's good for the night."

We both started laughing.

"Shakira, I'm proud of you," I had to admit.

"Me?" Shakira said in a surprised tone. "For what?"

"Well, you have got your own place. Your daughter is healthy and happy. You make your own money, and you don't have to depend on a man. All the things I dreamed of."

"Thank you, Jewel." Shakira said, tears in her eyes. She then rose from the table to give me a hug.

"Shakira," I said, surprised at her reaction.

"I really appreciate that, Jewel. You have no idea what that means to me." Shakira wiped the tears from her eyes. "It wasn't easy. A few years ago, I wanted a change from the drug life. I went back to school to become a dental hygienist, and with the help of God, I landed a job right away. Life is all about balance. I've got my Kelly and my job. We are taking it day by day," Shakira explained, looking over at the bar.

"You deserve to be happy," I replied, thinking back to the rough past Shakira had. She was heavy in the drug game because of some shady guys she'd dated, and in order to survive she had to strip.

"And so do you too."

"Sometimes I'm not so sure if I do. I made my bed, and now I have to lay in it," I said, full of self-pity.

"That is not true, Jewel. You control your destiny. You have got to find yourself. Let go of the self-pity and bring that confident, outgoing Jewel I know!"

"I guess you're right. I have sort of lost myself. I've gotta find me and find my happiness in the process. Touch has put me through so much. The fights, the cheating, the mental and physical abuse, and prison have all taken a toll on me. If I told you everything that has happened, you would lose your appetite." I began to tear up. "You know what? The pity stops here. I'm not looking back. I want to look forward from this point on. You're going to be my inspiration." I was fighting to hold back my tears.

"I believe you will change your life." Shakira then hugged me again.

"Yes, I will," I replied, hugging her tight.

"Wow!" Shakira said as she looked toward the bar. "I had no idea dinner was gonna be so emotional!" She gave a grin but seemed a little distracted.

"Shakira, you have been looking at the bar many times. What's up? Is a cutie over there or something?" I asked, no longer able to ignore her constant glares over at the bar.

"Turn around," she said.

I quickly turned around and scanned the entire bar, but the only thing I noticed was the bartender making a flaming drink.

"There, walking out the door."

"Who?" I inquired.

"A woman dressed in jeans and a black sweater. She had a haircut similar to Halle Berry. She was dark-skinned and kept staring in your face the entire time she was on her cell phone," Shakira explained.

"Hhhmm. I don't know anyone that fits that description. Plus, I don't know anyone in this area. Are you sure she wasn't looking at you?"

"No. She was definitely looking at you. Maybe it was a mistaken identity and once she realized you weren't the person, she left."

We both blew it off and left the conversation at that as we enjoyed the rest of our dinner.

As we walked out of the restaurant, I patted my stomach. "Girl, I'm stuffed. That was some good eating." Normally in Virginia my stomach would be doing backflips after a meal like that. Not now though. I was feeling good.

"Yes, I'm stuffed too. The food was so tasty. We have to come here more often." Shakira nodded.

"Where to now?" I asked, yawning.

"Are you tired? I see you yawning."

"No, the night is just getting started for me. Give me thirty minutes, and I will perk back up. The food has got me sleepy. I have a small case of the *itis*." I giggled.

"Well, I want to take you to a place called Pink Dices, a new club in the area. I've heard nothing but good reviews. Plus, if you get in before eleven, ladies get a free drink."

"I'm in! I need a drink, and I love free!" I laughed, giving Shakira a high-five.

"Jewel," a voice called out behind me.

Shakira and I both turned around wondering who the hell would know me in DC. But when we looked around, there was no one else in the parking lot. I began to develop goose bumps. Both of us wanted nothing else but to get the hell up out of there. Chills went down my spine as I wondered, *Did Touch send someone to spy on me? Has he found me?*

Shakira and I darted out of the parking lot. I was so shaken up, I didn't feel like going out after all. My stomach got that queasy feeling I would get back home. My night was ruined by Touch once again. Would I ever be able to live a stress-free life?

Chapter 15

"Unveiling the Truth"

Unknown Person

I hope Jewel didn't see me last night, I thought as I got out of my car. I knew it was likely that she may have seen me because I couldn't stop staring at her. I just couldn't help myself. She was just so beautiful, much prettier than I'd remembered. I wish I could have approached her that night, but the time wasn't right. I needed some time to gather my thoughts and figure out what I wanted to say to her. I was sure that other chick she was with caught a glimpse of me, and she was making my spot hot. That's why I had to dip out so quickly.

Finding Jewel had been much easier than I had anticipated. The first thing I did was to go to all of her known addresses. She obviously was at none of them.

Next, I checked the prison and court records to see if I could find anything out. I saw that her case had been dismissed, and there was no record of her being in prison. So I knew she was still on the outside.

The last thing I did was put a trace on her cell phone. Being an undercover cop, I had associated with many underground types, and the one I needed at the moment was a master computer hacker. He went by the nickname CyberRat because he said he could root around and find any information you needed. It was not even a day before CyberRat came back to me with a general location for Jewel, and more information than I had asked for. He had hacked into her e-mails and found some information pertaining to her looking for employment. I knew this information was going to come in handy. I packed up a suitcase and was headed for DC an hour after I received the information.

Being a cop on a stakeout was one thing, but being a stalker was on a whole other level. I'd made arrangements for Jewel to come into the bookstore, Barnes and Noble, to meet a person named Joel. Because I had access to her e-mails I had replied to her, acting as a potential employer. She answered, and we agreed to meet for an interview. Little did she know, I'd been pretending to be this Joel guy the entire time.

I knew Jewel was about her dollars, and from the sound of her e-mails, her money was getting scarce, so I played on that. I sent her an e-mail guaranteeing her fast money with little risk. I knew it would sound too good for her to pass up.

As soon as I walked in the store, I spotted Jewel sitting at a table in the café. I had come a little early, so I could pick the perfect spot and relax a bit before approaching her, but that plan was out the door. Jewel must have been real hungry for cash to show up this early. Normally, with her attitude and ego, she would show up late, to prove she was in charge.

Seeing her there already threw me off my game. I almost turned around and walked right back out, but

I convinced myself to stay. The opportunity had finally come for me to confess my love. It was what kept me going when I was at my lowest point. I took a deep breath in and walked over to Jewel. I was nervous, and my stomach was turning upside down as I approached her.

"Jewel," I carefully greeted her. She was taking a peek at the latest *Cosmo* magazine.

"Misty?" she responded, taking off her sunglasses. "What the fuck is this?"

"May I please sit down?" I asked, expecting her to decline and possibly even smack me in my face. If she declined, I was already prepared to beg her to listen.

"What the fuck? I thought you was dead?"

"I'm not. It's really me. The force just made that up to try and get rid of me. I've been thinking of you for so long." My eyes watered. I was so happy to speak with her. She hadn't ran off or slapped me. I was hopeful that she felt the same way about me as I felt about her.

"Are you fuckin' serious? Fuck that! Get the hell away from me! You come into my life to get me set up with the feds, and I'm just supposed to fuckin' welcome you back? When I saw your face flash on the news with the words, 'Officer killed in the line of duty,' I was happy that shit happened to you. All the shit I told you, all the times I spilled my guts to my caring nurse, when the whole time you was a fuckin' cop! I trusted you, bitch! You were my best fuckin' friend!" Jewel shouted then stormed off.

I took a deep breath and prayed that the words coming out of my mouth would make her listen to me. "Give me five minutes. That's it. I won't bother you again. Please, Jewel, I'm begging you." I followed behind her.

Jewel turned around, and I braced myself for a smack to the face, but to my surprise, she said, "You got three fuckin' minutes. Don't waste my time. You've stolen enough of my life already!"

"Well, um—" I began to stutter, but Jewel cut me off.

"Oh, and let me guess—You're Joel. Me trying to make some money was a smokescreen for you. What a fuckin' asshole! Wow, look at the time. I've talked for one of your three minutes. You better hurry up. You may proceed now," she said, looking at her watch.

I took another deep breath. "You need to know that I have loved you since the first time I saw you. You were lying there in the hospital, and you looked so beautiful even in such a fragile state. It may sound cliché as hell, but it's the truth. I got kicked off the case for you. My colleagues had a hunch I was tampering with evidence to protect you, and they were right. I'll do anything for you. I was offered a desk job, but I turned it down after getting hurt. The bottom line, I've been suspended until further notice."

Jewel shook her head. "This isn't making sense to me."

"Jewel, I was tampering with evidence so the heat could come off you." "What?"

"I couldn't have you doing prison time. I was never going to testify against you or bring evidence that would lead to a conviction because I couldn't bear the fact that it would split us apart. I was falling in love with you. I am in love with you. I risked everything for you. The force is all I had. It was my daily motivation, and I lived to work undercover. Since it's been gone, I've had a chance to realize there is a life outside of that. You're the only thing I've ever loved, other than being an agent. And that's why I'm here today. I need you in my life."

"So are the police still watching us?" "Yes," I answered honestly. "That's why they faked my death. Touch and you had to believe I was dead so that they could continue their case. The force felt that you guys would get relaxed and feel like your case was open and shut, and soon let your guards down."

"Wow!" She looked off into space.

"Although I'm not on the force anymore, I still have a few friends that keep me in the loop. I refuse to let you get wrapped up in Touch's shit. The best thing you could have done was move out. You need to stay away from him. They want Touch so bad."

"You've lied before, former best friend," Jewel said. "So how do I know you're not lying to me right now? Why should I trust you?"

"Jewel, I love you," I simply stated.

"This is a lot to take in. You've deceived me once. I don't know if I could ever forgive you. I didn't even know you were gay."

"All the signs were there. You just didn't want to notice. After getting hurt, I was placed in physical therapy, and to get through the pain, all I did was think about you giving me another chance. No more lies and deceit, Jewel, I promise. I'm standing here asking for forgiveness."

"I gotta go," Jewel said.

It was obvious she couldn't take anymore. It was just too much for her.

"Can I at least give you my number, and maybe you can call me some time?" I asked with my best puppy-dog face.

"I guess," she responded, pulling out her cell phone.

This was definitely a good start, better than I'd ever expected. I walked out of the store a happy camper. As soon as I got in my car, my cell phone rang. I pressed talk without even looking at the number, excited that Jewel had decided to call right away. I was hoping she had decided to grab a bite to eat and talk about things.

"Hello," I said right away, expecting to hear Jewel's voice on the other end.

"Hey, baby," a voice said.

I took the phone away from my ear and looked at the caller ID. That definitely wasn't Jewel's voice. The caller ID said Jamie.

"Hello?" Jamie said in response to my moment of silence.

"Hey, Jamie. How are you?" I said, a little disappointed that it was him instead of Jewel.

"I'm good. Missing you."

"Awww! How sweet! I'm in the middle of something right now. Can I call you back in a few?" I said, rushing to get Jamie off the phone.

"Sure. No problem," he said before hanging up.

I really wasn't feeling Jamie, or any man for that matter. Since my time in rehab, I had come to terms with the fact that I was a lesbian. I knew, deep down inside, the other night with Jamie was a big mistake. It was a moment of weakness, a test to see if I was really gay. The only good thing that came out of it was, it confirmed my love for Jewel, and that I definitely liked women. I should have never fooled around with him.

He'd just caught me at a vulnerable moment. Somehow I had to get Jamie out my life and Jewel in it. I wasn't sure how I was going to do it, but it had to happen.

I pondered this dilemma all the way back to Virginia. I'd driven all the way from Virginia Beach just to meet with Jewel. As I drove, I thought long and hard about my feelings for Jamie and my feelings for Jewel. No matter from which angle I looked at things, it always pointed back at Jewel. For some reason, I just couldn't let her slip through my fingers again.

By the time I'd hit Seven Cities, my mind was made up. I had to get rid of Jamie. I saw no upside to keeping him in my life.

Chapter 16

"Does Someone Have Voodoo on Me?"

Touch

In all my years of being in the drug game, I ain't never had no fucking body come where I lay my head at and put their hands on me. This is some bullshit, I thought to myself as I looked over my numerous scars and my missing tooth in the bathroom mirror.

I couldn't believe that shit had really happened to me. The fucked-up thing about it, I couldn't remember a gotdamn thing about the previous night. I was seriously going to have to consider not getting so fucked up on booze and weed. What I did know was, it had to be a nigga to do that shit. Sure, I thought about that psycho Lisa, but there was no way that bitch would have the strength to tie me up.

I wracked my brain trying to figure out who the fuck it could have been. I ain't had no beef on the streets, so it wasn't from a business associate. *Maybe it was Lisa and some nigga that did this to me,* I thought as I prepared to hit the road. If so, that bitch was reaching new levels of crazy, and I would need to end her life for that shit.

I was headed straight to the dentist. There was no way in hell I was walking around town looking like a fucking crackhead with missing teeth. As I got dressed,

I continued to think through all the people it might be that fucked me up. That's when that nigga Rico popped in my head. All of a sudden, he'd moved to the top of my list of suspects. If it wasn't for Jewel's dumb ass inviting him into my house, the other night probably would have never happened. If the bitch was so eager to fuck, why couldn't she fuck him at his house?

Fuming from the thoughts of this nigga fucking me up like he did, I called Jewel up. I wanted her to know that she was going to be responsible for this nigga's death. I got her voice mail. I called back to back three more times and got her voice mail every time. The last time, I decided to leave a message.

"Jewel, you know who the hell this is. Answer the phone when I call you. Your boyfriend paid me a visit.

You should have said your final good-byes the last time you saw him because he's dead for sure now!" I screamed in the phone.

I was hoping that message would get her attention. I went to take a leak, and before I could finish the phone was ringing. I knew it was Jewel. I answered right away ready to light her ass up.

"Yo, bitch, you got it coming to you when I see you," I yelled into the phone as soon as I picked up.

"Yo, nigga, this Deuce. What's up with you? Long night last night?" Deuce laughed.

What the fuck he mean by that? Is he referring to me getting a beat-down? Is he involved?

Many thoughts went streaming through my mind. Now I had another suspect to consider. The last thing I wanted to do was to off this nigga. It could cause some major problems with Jimmy and me. Which would seriously affect my money. I didn't even bother explaining my situation with that nigga. We had a brief business talk, and I got off the phone.

Despite the bullshit I was going through, I had to get on with my day. I hopped in my truck and started out the neighborhood. I didn't even get to the end of the block before it shut off on me.

"Damn!" I banged the steering wheel then got out.

I had to wonder if this day could get any worse.

Thinking maybe it was the battery, I popped the hood.

When I got out of the truck, I noticed my gas tank was open with a little note tied to it. The note read, "Sweeter than sugar, baby."

"Damn it!" I yelled to no one in particular. Just when I thought it was over, Lisa struck again.

This bitch is relentless, I thought. I looked down at my ringing cell phone. It was Jimmy.

"Hey, Jimmy. What's up?" I greeted him, trying to maintain my composure on the phone.

"There is a slight problem with our pictures," he said, letting me know there was a problem with the business.

"From my end, there isn't a problem. The pictures seem clear to me. Everything is accounted for," I said, assuring Jimmy that all the figures added up.

"I will be home soon to straighten it out."

"All right. So everything good otherwise?" I asked.

"See you soon," Jimmy responded, cutting me off, and hung up the phone.

I could tell by that conversation that things weren't good. I wasn't too worried because I knew I made sure everything was accounted for at all times. I wasn't no rookie to the game, so I knew to not even be a dollar short when working on consignment. Having Jimmy back on the street was going to be nice. I couldn't wait for his release.

I called up ma dukes to take me to the dentist. I had to get my grill right, but after that, it was pure relaxation. I looked forward to locking myself in the house and drinking a few Heinekens, smoking a blunt, while watching my DVD collection of *Martin*. I had to do something to keep from catching a murder charge. I didn't know if it would be that bitch Lisa or that punk Rico, but somebody was gonna die soon.

Chapter 17

"Making a Change"

Jewel

I finally mustered up the energy to listen to the numerous voice mails Touch had left. I already had an idea what to look forward to. *Bitch* was my middle name to him if he was angry.

Touch barked on the phone, *"Bitch, I know you were behind this. Don't worry. We'll get another battle together. This time, I will be the only one standing. I thought you learned your lesson last time I beat your ass. Sending that nigga to my fuckin' house. Is you crazy?"*

The next few messages after that started off the same way, *"Bitch this, bitch that." Here we go again,* I thought. Others messages followed, but they were kind and sweet, with Touch damn near begging me to come back to him. Blah, blah, blah, it was all the same shit with Touch — Yell at me, hit me then proclaim how sorry you are and how much you love me. I deleted the messages. I was really starting to tire of his stupid-ass. I thought about calling him and chewing his ass out, but I dialed another number instead. Without giving it a second thought, I pressed send.

"Hello," I heard on the other end of the phone.

Although I wanted to speak, no words came out. I didn't really have a reason to call. I was just feeling lonely and wanted someone to talk to. It didn't hurt that I had been intrigued by Misty's offer ever since we'd met at the bookstore café.

"Hello?" the voice said again.

"Hi." I managed to force out one word.

"Jewel?" Misty sounded excited.

"Yes. I had no one else to call."

"Hey, baby. I'm so happy you called. I never thought I would see this day. I'm here for you. What's on your mind?"

"Just going through the highs and lows of Touch. I just checked my voice messages, and it was the same old thing I have been dealing with. It seemed like every other word was *bitch*. Men don't understand how much that word really hurts. I guess they were going-away presents."

"That's crazy. Jewel, I told you, you deserve better. No man should ever disrespect you like that," Misty said, a bit of anger in her tone.

"Plus, he fucked some girl name Lisa and end up beating her or something. They went to court, and he won the case, and now she's out for revenge. This chick came to my house and everything. It was a mess."

"He cheats on you, and now Lisa won't go away. Jewel, this is crazy. I can't believe you are even keeping contact with him. Why don't you get a new phone? I'll pay for it." She sounded so soothing.

"You know how hard it was to hold my composure when Touch told me he had to go to court behind her?"

"I can tell you're still hurting behind all of this. Sounds like you're getting angry all over again just talking about it."

"You're probably right. I feel like a hole has been ripped through my heart. I don't know what to do. I thought he was my best friend, but friends don't treat each other like this, do they?"

"No, Jewel, they don't. My best advice to you is to separate yourself from him. It's the only way you will get strong, independent, and feel more secure about yourself. What can I do to help you? I am here for you, no matter what."

"You're right. It's time to make a change. Thanks for talking to me, Misty. I really need an ear to listen. You always were a good listener, even if it was to try and get information for the feds."

"I am so sorry about all of that, Jewel. Even though I was trying to put Touch away, I would never have hurt you. It seemed like I was interested in what you had to say, because I was. I still am. You are an amazing and beautiful woman."

Misty's sincerity made me cry. No one had been this kind to me in a long while. All the stress of my life with Touch was coming out through those tears.

"Thanks, Misty. You are too kind. I have to be going now. You've given me a lot to think about," I said, wiping my tears.

I was glad I'd called Misty. It felt like the best decision I had made in a while. I found comfort in talking with her. It felt familiar. Before I knew she was a cop, when we would have our conversations, I'd always appreciated her advice. She was so confident and knew the answer to everything. She always seemed to know what to say, and at the right time. Once again I found myself putting my trust in Misty. I prayed to God I wasn't making a horrible mistake like I'd done in the past.

After talking to Misty, it was clear that I needed to go back to Virginia and face my demons once and for all.

I started by calling my lawyer and telling him I needed an appointment to come in and talk to him about my case. Then I called a moving company and my real estate agent. Once everything was in order, I planned to hit the road the next morning.

I woke up the next morning optimistic. I knew I was making the right decision. I said my good-byes to Shakira before leaving. She was a good friend, and I was grateful for her kindness. She was definitely one of a kind, and I felt I would always be indebted to her for accepting me with open arms. "Good luck today. Hope everything goes as planned,"

Shakira said, giving me a big hug.

I didn't want to let go. One part of me was excited to face my past and move on, and the other was scared to death of the unknown.

"I'm sure it will," I assured her as we walked toward the door.

I loaded my car with my luggage then I hopped in. I waved a final good-bye as I drove off.

"Drive safe," Shakira yelled as I pulled off.

Attempting to beat the traffic, I left DC close to six o'clock in the morning. I put on the tune of Nicki Minaj to keep me energized. It seemed like I got to the Tidewater area in no time at all. As I drove through the Hampton tunnel I began to get nervous. My legs were shaking as reality set in. I didn't know if I was truly ready to face my past, but in order for me to have a brighter future, I knew I had to.

My first stop was Norfolk to meet with my lawyer, Eric Dickerson. I told him everything Misty had shared with me. He was grateful for the information but warned me to stand clear of Misty. He thought she may have ulterior motives and not truly there to protect me. I heard what he was saying, but in my heart I felt Misty's motives were sincere. Call me stupid, but I believed her. I trusted her more than I trusted Touch. Touch always vowed he would never do a long bid ever again. Plus, his motto was money over bitches, so why wouldn't he sell me out to stay on the streets and make money? Based on what I shared with Mr. Dickerson, he made a deal with the DA's office. In exchange for my testimony, I would receive immunity. Besides, Touch was the one the city of Virginia Beach and feds truly wanted, not me. I was just a pawn. Touch would do the same to me. *Fuck him. I'll get him before he gets me. This is the new Jewel. I ain't no ride-or-die no more. It's about taking care of myself.*

"Thanks for signing on the dotted line. My office will be in touch," the district attorney said with a smile on his face after receiving my written statement. I'd written a three-page testimony about what was really going down. Which was enough to put Touch away for a long while. Oh well, serves his ass right.

On my way to my next task I felt conflicted about agreeing to testify against Touch. Yes, I was mad at him, but did that warrant me helping to put him in jail? There were some good things about him. I truly feel that he did love me, and if I had to be truthful with myself, I did love him. I had to ask myself if my love outweighed the anxiety and heartbreak he caused me.

I started having second thoughts about my decision to testify. I thought about different ways I might be able to move on, but I saw none. Touch would never let me be at peace. If I wanted a clean break and a fresh start, I had to testify. It was all about me now.

When I pulled up in front of my house, the moving company already had their men and truck waiting out front. With precision and laser-like speed, they moved everything to a storage unit, except for Touch's belongings. I had them move all of Touch's things to the garage. I wasn't so cold-hearted that I would throw all his stuff away. He would have the opportunity to collect his belongings if he wanted. I still had some guilt about my impending testimony. After changing the locks, the garage would be all he had access to. Lucky for him, I didn't reprogram the garage opener as well.

The real estate agent was right on time with the contract and for sale sign for the house. I was going to sell it as is. I had no time or money to fix the house up, and I wasn't really looking for a huge profit. I just wanted all links to Virginia and Touch severed, and that house was the last thing tying me to either of them.

By the end of the day, I was exhausted, but I felt free as a bird. Little by little, I was lifting the burden and weight I had been carrying on my back.

I checked myself into a local hotel for the night. I had planned to head back to DC in the morning. Shakira had agreed to let me stay with her until I was able to get things sorted out. I lay my head down to sleep and vowed to myself that Touch will never have the opportunity to disrespect me again. No more name-calling, no more cheating, and no more physical and mental abuse. I knew I didn't deserve any of that, and I refused to take his shit anymore.

As I lay my head on the pillow and thought about my future, I had a huge smile on my face. Independence suited me well. I was excited about my new beginning.

Chapter 18

"Looking for a Pick-me-up"

Touch

"We had shit rolling tonight, man," Deuce said as we wrapped things up. It seemed like every day business was increasing. The fiends were getting word that we had the best shit in Virginia.

Business was going so well, I had spent the weekend at the spot. I didn't want to take the chance of a nigga fucking up or attempting to pull some old "I got robbed" bullshit. I stayed around to set an example for the young niggas. Show them how a real businessman conducts himself. The blocks we had on lock in Norfolk were definitely paying off.

"Knowing the right people and having good product shows in our profits," I stated as I counted up the last stack of money, verifying it was accurate.

"You right about that. Get some rest. I'm about to do the same." Deuce grabbed the money stacks and put them in the duffle bag.

"I can't wait to lay my head down either," I said as I gathered my things.

I hadn't had a bath or even brushed my teeth the entire weekend. It was like a conveyor belt of fiends coming through the door. I barely had time to breathe. I couldn't wait to get home, get a hot shower, and lay it down in my bed. Of course, I was going to need to smoke some weed before all that.

I stopped at the door and turned toward Deuce before leaving. "Did you need me to do the drop for Jimmy?" I asked.

"Nah, man. Have a good one," he replied, grabbing the duffle bag and heading toward the door behind me.

I hopped in my truck, eager to get home. One of them cats around the way who used to be in the drug game had taken my truck over the weekend and fixed that shit. Lucky for me, he was a good-ass mechanic and was able to get it running again. I was tired as hell and happy that I didn't have to call a cab. On my way home, I started thinking about ways I could use all of the cash coming my way. I needed to set up some sort of legit business to protect my ass from prosecution.

The longer Jewel was away, the more I got used to not having her around. Don't get me wrong. I still needed her in my life, but it was getting easier to deal with. I decided to call Jewel when I got back to the crib and try one more time to get her back home.

When I entered the garage, I noticed a number of boxes stacked up in the corner. Being extra cautious, I pulled my gun and looked around to see if whoever stacked the boxes was still lingering. This shit looked suspicious. After getting out the car, I walked to the boxes. Each one had my name written on it with a black marker. I cautiously opened one box and looked through it. It had my underwear and some T-shirts in it. I started opening each box, and each one contained my possessions. All my shit had been thrown into boxes and put in the garage. It didn't take me long to figure what was going on.

Right away I assumed Jewel was back home and was trying to make some statement. I stormed toward the house. I tried opening the door from the garage, but my key didn't work. So I stomped out the garage door toward the front yard and noticed a for sale sign on the front lawn. That's when it hit me like a fucking freight train! Not only was Jewel making a point and getting rid of my stuff, she was selling the house right up from under me. That bitch had some nerve, especially since I'd paid for the house! That's the fucked-up part about the drug game. You have the money but can't put shit in your name. I'd never thought Jewel would do some shit like that to me.

This new drama gave me an extra boost of energy. Now I was even more determined to get some sort of legit business going. I dialed Jewel's number, this time to let her know she won. I was laying my flag down. I couldn't handle this bullshit no more. There were plenty of bitches out there happy to be my girl. But when I called, I got a recording stating her number was no longer in service. Jewel had changed her number on me. It was at that point I realized she was serious. There was no turning back for either of us. Now I would have to fight her for custody of my child.

I dug through the boxes and found some clothes to last me a few days. I checked in a hotel, got a quick shower, then took a little nap.

After my rest, I was rejuvenated, so I hit a local lounge I used to frequent named Mo Dean's. My episode earlier had me wanting to take out some aggression on some pussy. A halo of smoke greeted me at the door. There were a couple of guys playing pool, but the majority of the people seemed to be watching the game on the flat-screen televisions placed throughout the bar. It was a big playoff game on, and the place was packed with screaming fans. I really wasn't in the mood for a large crowd, but I wasn't about to sit up in a hotel room thinking about all the fucked-up things that had happened in the past few days.

I found a seat in the corner and began to watch the game as I waited for a waitress to come over and take my drink order. Out of the corner of my right eye, I noticed a cutie named Diana I had dealt with in the past. She was heading over in my direction. My dick got hard almost instantly as I thought back to the good times I had with her. She was a freak in bed, and because of it she was given the nickname Dirty Diana.

"A Grey Goose on the rocks," she said as soon as she walked up.

"So you remember, huh?" I laughed. Back in the day when I used to frequent this bar, that was my drink, and Diana was my favorite waitress.

"That's not all I remember. You know I ain't working tonight." Diana grabbed my hand and placed it between her legs. *Damn! Some things never change*, I thought. Dirty Diana was still the freak I'd fucked over a year ago. I said straight up, "It's been a long time. You gonna give me some of that?" There was no need trying to be a gentleman with this bitch.

"Follow me," she instructed, motioning with her finger.

She led me to the bathroom hardly anyone uses in the back. As soon as we entered the stall, Diana began unbuttoning her blouse. With her shirt and bra completely open, she started massaging my dick back and forth with her hands.

"Damn, girl! I like that."

"Come take this pussy, it's yours," she said while placing my hand in her pants.

"I could get into that, but first, you know what I like," I said caressing her face.

"All you had to do was say the word," Diana replied unbuttoning my jeans and letting down the zipper.

That's what I loved about Diana. She got down to the business, with no questions asked. It took this girl no time to whip my dick out and put it into her mouth. She didn't start slow but worked right into deep-throating it. My eyes were rolling in the back of my head. Then Diana jerked me off while sucking my balls. A minute later she went right back to the deep throat. I had to admit, this girl gave the best head of all time.

She suddenly stopped, knowing I was close to coming. "It's time for some pussy," she whispered in my ear.

"We got plenty of time for that when I take you home. Diana, come on now, finish sucking me off. You the best," I said, motioning for her head to come to my dick.

When I came, that girl swallowed every drop. She drained me to the point where I couldn't move. After that I definitely needed a drink. We headed back to the table, and I ordered a Rémy straight.

Chapter 19

"Sweet, Sweet Revenge"

Lisa

Getting revenge on Touch was becoming more like a job. My drive for revenge had turned into damn near stalking him. I considered installing a surveillance camera in the kitchen and the living room of his house when I beat his ass, but I figured it was too risky. I'd spent days driving past his house and sometimes waiting for hours for him to arrive. But I still couldn't get down a system as to his schedule. He never seemed to stick to a pattern. I did notice that before getting out of the car, he made sure his gun was in his hand and cocked. I wasn't taking no chances with that. I knew I would surely end up dead if I tried to ambush him as he arrived home.

For one night I had decided to take a night off and focus on me. It was time I got my mind off Touch and moved on to the next man. I knew I couldn't stalk him forever, but I was having so much fun doing it, I didn't really want to stop just yet. I'd already dedicated too much of my life to Touch, so what was a few more days. I was there before Jewel, dealing with the baby momma drama and all his bullshit. Then we broke up, and he came back, and I accepted him, and we ended up in court. I guess I should have followed the rule,

"Never go back." Well, it was definitely time to move forward, and I wanted and needed some positive attention from a man.

A quick trip to MacArthur Center led me to a BeBe dress with a one-hundred-and-sixty-five-dollar price tag. The original price was two hundred, but my girl who worked there let me use her employee discount. This dress was definitely going to get me the attention I was so craving. It had been weeks since I rode a dick or hung out with my girls, and I was looking forward to doing both.

When I got home I grabbed a bite to eat and relaxed a little before my big night. My relaxation turned into a nap. When I woke up, I took a quick glimpse at the clock. It was eleven o'clock. I was surely going to be late, since I was supposed to meet my girls in a half hour. Now they would get first dibs on all the fine brothers up in the bar.

"Damn it!" I yelled to no one particular.

I jumped up and rushed to the shower. I was planning to meet my girls at Mo Dean's Restaurant and Lounge, a well-known spot in Norfolk where all the ballers hung out.

By twelve I was pulling up in the parking lot. I rushed inside the bar to meet my girls, who were already there waiting on me. I found them right away parked at a prime table where all could see them. I greeted everyone and grabbed a seat. I hadn't been sitting five minutes before the waitress walked up.

"Excuse me," the waitress said to me. "Yes," I replied a little annoyed that I barely had time to settle in and she was already hounding me for my order.

"Here is an apple martini. The gentleman at the bar ordered it for you," she said as she pointed him out. "This is also for you." She handed me a napkin.

I noticed the gentleman's number was written on the elaborate napkin the waitress had just given me. "Thank you," I said smiling. I felt a little stupid for getting an attitude with the waitress.

I then turned to my girls and said, "I guess the expensive-ass dress was worth it!"

"Heeeyyyy," we all said as we toasted to one another.

My girls, Candi and Sharon, were hyped up. I was the first one to get some action from a man that night, and I'd only been in the spot for a few minutes. This man favored the singer and actor, Tyrese. I wasn't going to waste any time heading in his direction. Judging by the mischief in his eyes, I knew this was gonna be a good night, and I was eager to get it started.

"Oh shit," Candi blurted out after I got up out of my seat.

"What, bitch?" I asked in a panic, wondering if I had come on my period and had a big blood spot on my ass.

"Look." Candi pointed to a corner in the bar.

I turned to look where Candi was pointing. Touch was sitting at a table in the corner, and some new bitch was with him. My stomach turned, and my mood changed almost instantly. I thought he'd left me for his soon-to-be baby mother, Jewel. I about near had a conniption fit. The one night I tried to get away from this nigga, he showed up in the same spot I was at. All I wanted tonight was a good time with some big-dick baller, and now Touch had to go and ruin that shit. I just shook my head as I stared daggers at him.

"Lisa, just ignore him. It's all about us having fun," Sharon reminded me, trying her best to get me focused.

"Yeah, you're right." I nodded. At least in my head I knew she was right, but my heart was elsewhere. I started walking over to the Tyrese look-alike, but I couldn't help myself. I had to make a slight detour and walk over to where Touch was sitting instead. He didn't notice me as I walked up because he was too busy spouting his stupid game, but I was definitely about to make my presence known.

"What up, whore?" I said, startling him.

Touch looked up at me. "Lisa, don't start your bullshit tonight. I'm not in the mood." He shook his head.

I said to the woman that sat beside him, "And you are?"

"Diana." She rolled her neck and stood up in my face. "Who the hell are you?"

"I'm Lisa. I just would like to let you know, Diana, that Touch beat me, stole my car, and ate up my ice cream. You're a pretty girl. Find someone else and get rid of this trash in your life."

Truly, she wasn't that cute, but anybody could've done better than Touch. Touch got between me and Diana. "Get the fuck out of here!" he screamed.

"Still the same bullshit with you, Touch. I feel like this is déjà vu. This is the same shit that happened the last time we hooked up in the bar. I don't need drama in my life. You know how to find me when you're drama free. I'm just looking for a good time, drama free. Peace." Diana threw him deuces as she walked off.

Touch turned over the table and put his fist in the air as though he was gonna hit me. The bar went completely silent, except for the sound of the televisions.

"Hit me, so I can haul your ass back to jail," I proclaimed. I was scared as hell and didn't want another busted nose, but I refused to punk down to him, especially since I knew the entire bar was watching.

We stood face to face with Touch's fist raised for what seemed like forever. Touch finally lowered his fist when he realized there were witnesses. Instead of hitting me, he spat in my face. With my finger, I wiped the spit off my face and smeared it on his. Touch was enraged. I had just humiliated his ass in front of the whole bar. I was sure this would take him over the edge. I thought I was about to get an ass-whipping of a lifetime.

I took a deep breath and closed my eyes as I waited for the impact of his fist coming across my face. As I heard him growl, I braced my body for the impending impact of fist on face. Then I heard a crash that wasn't bone against bone. I opened one eye to see Touch had punched a hole in the wall. I opened my other eye as he pushed his way through the crowd.

"Fuck you, Lisa!" he yelled as he went through the bar room door. I rolled my eyes and acted like it was no big deal, but truthfully I was scared. Relieved to have my face intact and needing to regain composure, I immediately headed to the bathroom. While there, I not only washed my face, but I got prepared for all the strange looks I was about to receive when I walked back out. I fixed my hair and makeup, sprayed on some perfume, looked myself in the eyes, and gave myself a pep talk. Holding my head high and poking out my breasts, I strutted out the bathroom like I was walking in a high-end fashion show.

I was surprised at the reaction of everyone at the bar. I didn't notice any strange looks. Most people either avoided eye contact, while some of the girls gave me a pat on my back and said, "You go, girl." "Stand up for yourself." "You a bad bitch."

As soon as I walked back to the table, Candi said, "Damn, bitch! You crazy!"

"*O-m-g*, Lisa!" Sharon chimed in. "I can't believe you did that."

My girls wouldn't shut up about how I'd handled Touch. In fact, it was the topic of discussion for the rest of the night.

Deep inside I was ashamed of my actions. I was never that "psycho bitch" kind of girl, but something about Touch just took me there. It was like he added fuel to my fire. His nonchalance toward me and his selfish attitude had me doing things way out of character. Things could have been different, if only he had just given me a genuine sorry for what he had done to me. Then it would have been so much easier for me to just walk away. But no, his dumb-ass couldn't see that he used me and didn't have feelings for me at all. He was freeloading off my ass and spending all my hard-earned money. Then he goes and lays hands on me! I mean, really? Who does that?

To make matters worse, he was already involved with another woman and lied about it. He had the nerve to treat me as if I had known there was another chick in the picture from the beginning. We all know if that was the case and I was truly made aware of Jewel, he would have never gotten my pussy. I had never played the number two role.

The rest of the night was spent bitching about men. Each of my girls had their own horror stories to tell. Each of their stories always ended up saying that they wished they had the balls to do what I had done. While they were telling their stories I was in my own world. After my run-in with Touch, I had a feeling that our relationship wasn't going to end pretty. Touch was pissed off, and I wasn't about to give up fucking with him. Something had to give, and I was afraid one of us would end up dead.

Chapter 20

"Sweet Seduction"

Misty

I stopped washing dishes and dried my hands when my cell phone rang. It was Jewel calling. I desperately wanted to answer, but part of me wanted to send her to voice mail. I figured playing some games might make her want me more. I'd been on an emotional roller coaster as of late, and my feelings for her were consuming me. I gave in to my desire for her.

"Hey," I answered.

"I did it," she stated immediately.

"Did what?" I asked.

"I left Touch. I finally got the nerve to do it. I've been with him for so many years, it was hard to break away."

I could tell Jewel was trying to hold back the tears. And I certainly was hoping she was able to do so, because I didn't want her to shed one damn tear over Touch. He wasn't worth it. Although I didn't hear crying, I could still hear the pain in her voice. It broke my heart to hear it, and all I wanted to do was reach through that phone and hold her.

"Jewel, I know it was hard, but I'm proud of you for realizing that you deserve so much better."

"I moved everything out of the house and put it up for sale. It was difficult packing most of the belongings I could travel with in my car and putting the rest in storage, but I knew I had to do it. The realtor agreed to call me first thing if she had an offer on the table for me. The money from the sale of the house will help me finance a new beginning for myself. And you're not gonna believe this. I talked to my attorney and signed a statement telling them all about Touch and the business. They're granting me immunity for my testimony. That was the most difficult decision I'd ever had to make in my life, but it was necessary."

"That was very brave of you, but like you said, it was necessary. In order to move forward, you have to let go of the past," I said.

"You're right. I'm tired of looking in the past. Now, I'm definitely looking forward to the future," Jewel said, sounding upbeat for the first time in our conversation.

"Now that's the confidence I like to hear! So what's the plan?" I inquired.

"Well, my best buddy Shakira and her daughter couldn't be happier knowing I am going to be staying with them for a while. Then as soon as the house is sold, I'm going to look for my own apartment. In the meantime, I'll be looking for a legit way to make some cash."

"Damn! Sounds like you got it all mapped out. So here's another question for you that doesn't require as much planning. What are your plans for tonight?"

"Not much. I'm heading to Shakira's now. Probably get something to eat and then decompress after my stressful day."

"Well, before you head in that direction, would you like to come by for a few drinks and unwind? You can decompress over here. I'll cook you some dinner, and we can hang out a bit."

"Sure," Jewel said right away, surprising me.

"I'm near Crystal City. When we hang up, I'll text you the address. You just let your GPS do the rest."

"Sounds good. I'll see you in a little while," she said.

I quickly ran around my place tidying up. I wanted it to look perfect for Jewel. I was so excited that she had agreed to come over and spend some time with me. I lit scented candles, started preparing the meal, and even had time to take a quick shower. Before I knew it, there was a knock at the door. "Coming," I yelled as I rushed toward the door. Before opening it I smoothed my hair, took a deep breath, and put a big smile on my face.

"Hi," Jewel greeted me as the door opened. She seemed a little apprehensive and gave me this look as if I better not dare ask for a hug or touch her for that matter.

"Hey." I acted like I didn't notice her look and directed her to the living room area. "Have a seat." I motioned to the sofa.

"Wow! This is really nice," Jewel said, looking around.

"Thanks," I replied as I headed to the kitchen. "You hungry? I haven't eaten anything today."

The aroma of stir fry filled the air. I knew one of Jewel's favorite dishes was shrimp in garlic sauce, but all I had was chicken, so I improvised. I threw the chicken in a skillet.

"Yes, I am, actually," she responded.

The energy in the room was tight, and I could tell her mind was elsewhere. I needed to lighten the mood, so I popped open a bottle of Moscato and pressed play on the DVD player to Martin Lawrence standup show called *You So Crazy*. Jewel hadn't laughed in a long time, and I was hoping a glass of wine and comedy could fix that.

"Thank you," she said as I handed her the glass of wine.

Minutes later as I was putting the finishing touches on dinner, I heard her laughing. Then I served her my beloved chicken stir fry. I kept the wine flowing and the mood light.

It wasn't long before I could see Jewel becoming tipsy. She had gone from uneasy to relaxed and extra giddy in under an hour. After dinner I took Jewel to the balcony. The cool breeze of the night air was perfect. We looked in into the sky and admired the full moon and countless stars in the sky. I couldn't have painted a more romantic sky. I was feeling relaxed and happy with her.

"Misty, thank you for being there for me. A big dose of laughter and a little pampering was just what I needed." Jewel then downed the last bit of wine in her glass.

"You're welcome, baby. Anything for you." I nodded as I ran my fingers through her hair. I knew I was taking a chance of blowing it, but it just seemed like the right time. The whole night seemed like it was leading up to this. *Damn!* My nipples became hard instantly. I'd waited so long for this moment.

Jewel didn't resist, so I kept doing it over and over again. Eventually she tilted her head back, and I kissed her passionately. We stayed out on the balcony kissing and caressing each other. The breeze blowing between us added another layer of sensuality.

I needed to feel Jewel's skin next to mine, so I led her back into the room and gently slipped off her maxi dress. I massaged her feet and rubbed her whole body down. Jewel dozed in and out of sleep, with intermittent moans.

I moved from her feet and began massaging her legs. Then I moved up to her thighs. Jewel let out a gentle sigh when she realized my fingers had moved to her clit. I continued to massage it up and down with my fingers.

"I love your beautiful breasts," I whispered in her ear. I started sucking the nipple of her plump right breast.

By this time Jewel was soaking wet. I continued to massage her clit back and forth. This time, it was with my tongue while I reached up and gently caressed her breasts. I couldn't believe this was finally happening. Even in my best dreams, it was never this good. Jewel was sexier in person than she was in my fantasy.

It didn't take long before she had cum in my mouth and I was savoring the taste of her juices. I wasn't finished giving pleasure to Jewel. I kissed her sensually before I whispered in her ear, "Just lay back, baby. I'm not done with you yet."

I reached into the bedside table and pulled out my strap-on dildo. After adjusting it around my waist, I pulled her legs up and pushed it inside.

"Hmm!" Jewel sighed again.

"Jewel, I love you so much. Please, let me make you mine," I cooed in her ear as my deep thrusts kept coming.

We made love over and over for hours. It was beyond all of my expectations. I was now fully in love with Jewel. I stroked her hair as she slept soundly after our lovemaking. As I stared at her, I knew what I had to do next. In order to keep all of my focus on Jewel, I had to end it with Jamie immediately. Jewel was the most important thing in my life.

Jewel spent the night with me, and the next morning we had a nice breakfast on the balcony. Some eggs, bacon, toast and coffee were our food of choice. I was afraid that the next morning would have been awkward, but it was totally comfortable. Jewel showered while I prepared the breakfast, and then we had a nice conversation about her future. Although I was thinking it, I didn't ask how I was going to fit into her plans.

I got sad when it was time for Jewel to be on her way back to DC. There was a moment when I almost asked her to stay with me, but then I talked myself out of it. I didn't want to come on too fast and strong. I would enjoy the fact that we had one night together and make sure that there were many more.

As soon as Jewel was out the door, I picked up the phone and called Jamie. It wasn't a conversation I was looking forward to having, but it needed to be done, and the sooner the better.

"Hello," Jamie answered. "Jamie, it's me, Misty." "Hey, Misty! I'm so happy you called. How are you?" "I'm good. I was hoping we could talk." I didn't waste any time.

"Of course, baby. I'll always be here to talk whenever you want."

I could already tell Jamie wasn't going to make this easy. *When someone is treating you so nice, how can you just drop him?* I was already feeling guilty, and I hadn't even told Jamie it was over before it even started. I knew I was going to have to stay strong and stick to my guns if I was going to make the break.

"I want to talk about us. I think—"

"I think we make a great pair. Our first go-around was just a trial. I'm ready for this. For you and me."

"Well, you may feel that, but—"

"Hey, Misty, hold on one second. I have another call coming in." Jamie switched over to the other line without even waiting for me to give him permission.

As I listened to the silence on the other end, I started to rehearse what I was about to say when Jamie came back. The only problem was, everything I was rehearsing sounded stupid. After a few attempts to figure out exactly what to say, I gave up. I was going to have to just go with whatever came out and deal with Jamie's reaction.

Once I stopped my rehearsal, I realized I had been on hold for a while, and it started to aggravate me. Why was I holding for so long with someone I was about to dump? I hung up and went to the bedroom to dress for the day.

When I got to the bedroom I noticed that Jewel had left her panties behind. I quickly grabbed them up off the floor and shoved them into my nose. I inhaled her sweet scent, and memories of the previous night flooded my mind. I instantly went right back between Jewel's legs. Just as I was starting to play with my pussy, the phone rang and shocked me out of my memory.

"Hello," I answered in an agitated tone.

"Hey, it's me. Sorry I was on the other line for so long. There's an emergency at work, and I was trying to solve it over the phone. Looks like I have to go in and deal with it. Can we meet up later to discuss us?"

I really didn't want to meet face to face with Jamie. It would be easier for me to end it over the phone, but I just wanted to get back to tending my pussy, so I agreed. I knew, whether over the phone or in person, Jamie wasn't going to take this well.

"Text me the time and place, and I'll be there," I said.

"Will do," Jamie replied, sounding chipper.

"See you later." As I was about to hang up, Jamie had one more thing to say to me.

"Hey, Misty, I'm glad you called." I could tell there was a smile on his face.

Ugh! I thought. *This nigga is trippin'.* I wasn't looking forward to meeting him later.

I hung up the phone and picked up right where I had left off. My hand went directly to my clit as I lay back on the bed and closed my eyes. In an instant I was picturing Jewel between my legs, and all thoughts of Jamie had disappeared.

Chapter 21

"Wicked Realization"

Jewel

My pussy was aching, along with me feeling sick. Laying on my side didn't help either. A wave of nausea took over. I ran to the bathroom, barely making it to the stool. I vomited so hard, it even came out of my nose. Afterward, I looked in the mirror and realized that I was naked. I cleaned myself up and slowly walked out of the bathroom, afraid of what or who I may see next. There, lying in the bed was Misty, and she was naked as well. *Oh ,shit! What have I done?* I thought to myself. I wracked my brain trying to figure it out.

Bits and pieces of the night before started to come back to me. One of the empty wine bottles was scattered on the carpet. I started to feel nervous and jittery. My hands were shaking, and my brain was racing. *I just had sex with not only a woman, but a woman who happens to be in love with me. After Sasha I vowed I would never do this again. We can't just be friends now. Misty will want more. This all happened so fast. Did Misty take advantage of me?*

I didn't know what to think. I started getting afraid that Misty was still working with the feds, so I didn't want to do anything to piss her off. Instead of running out of there, I stayed around and acted cool. Luckily for me, Misty didn't move when I jumped out of bed to throw up, so I just slipped right back next to her. This time I nudged her a little bit so she would wake up.

"Hey, Jewel," Misty said as she wiped her eyes and stretched.

I smiled. "Hey, yourself."

"Stay for breakfast?" Misty asked. It sounded like a question, but I wasn't sure if she was telling me to stay. I decided it better to stay and try and make her happy. Hopefully this little fling would just fade away. I didn't need no cop pissed off at me.

"Yeah. Let me shower first."

"You shower, I'll cook." Misty put her robe on while I went to the bathroom.

I tried acting as normal as possible throughout breakfast. Misty kept asking me about my future and what I was planning. Not wanting to give up too much, I made up some bullshit about taking night courses. I was pretty vague about the whole thing though.

After breakfast Misty tried to get me to stay longer, but I put a stop to that. Told her I needed to get back to Shakira and take care of her daughter. I breathed a huge sigh of relief when I reached my car. On my way home, Misty began blowing up my cell phone. She called so many times that I shut off my phone. Driving like a bat out of hell, I rushed home.

"Hey, Auntie Jewel, I made you a picture," Kelly said as soon as I walked in the door.

"Thanks, baby." I smiled and gave her a hug.

Shakira could see how upset I was and told her little one to go in her room and color. "Jewel, what's going on?" she asked as soon as the coast was clear.

"I can't tell you. I'm too embarrassed," I replied, crying and hiding my face.

"Listen, there's nothing you can tell me that I haven't already heard. Girl, I'm all ears."

"Last night I went to see Misty. You know the woman that was in the restaurant staring us down? That's her. She was following me."

"Yeah. So you knew her? What she following you for?"

"She's a friend from the past. I don't want to go into all the details, but she was a close friend of mine, until I found out she worked for the police. Anyway, I was vulnerable because I just left Touch. I just went over there to talk, and this morning I woke up in her bed. I didn't mean for this to happen. She is in love with me. I'm not ready for this, let alone with a woman. You know what I went through with Sasha. She even ruined our friendship. So after her, I vowed I would never go there again."

"I understand. You know I know more than anyone what's it like to be vulnerable. Why don't you take a long hot bath and get some rest? I'll make you my home remedy soup. It can sober anyone up. Then we can figure out what you need to do. My first thought is for you to just tell Misty the truth—You ain't feeling her or any woman, especially right now when you are trying to get your life back."

"How did you know I was drinking?" I said, full of shame.

Shakira giggled. "It's on your breath and comin' out your skin."

I playfully smacked Shakira on her shoulder and went to the bathroom for a good soak. While in the hot bath, I began thinking about what Shakira had said. The thing was, I was kind of feeling Misty. She was seeming really genuine and kind to me. I couldn't believe she was still working for the police, with the way she was acting. All of her advice had been to get away from Touch. If she was still looking to get him, she would've wanted me close, so I could feed her information. I just wasn't sure if I was ready to be with a woman full time. Being a lesbian had never seemed like a lifestyle I would live.

As I thought more and more about Misty, I kept thinking, *I could really like this girl.* Which scared me and confused me. The only decision I could come up with was to take it slow and not jump into anything too fast. I was going to make sure to stick to my new motto—It's all about me and what makes me happy. With that thought, I closed my eyes and enjoyed the warm bath. I would deal with Misty later.

Chapter 22

"It's Over"

Misty

As soon as I finished masturbating, I called Jewel. I needed to speak to her about Jamie. She was so strong the way she dealt with Touch that I wanted her to help me through my ordeal. I wanted her to counsel me on how she got her strength, to give me the confidence she had. When Jewel didn't answer, I figured she either didn't hear the phone or wasn't able to get to it in time. I called right back, and the outcome was the same. I continued to call back to back with the same result. The last time I called, instead of ringing, it went straight to voice mail. I didn't want to believe that she had ignored my calls, so I told myself that she must be in a poor signal area.

I got concerned that perhaps something was wrong with Jewel. I turned on the local news station to see if there were any reports of accidents. After sitting in front of the television for an hour listening to the same stories over and over, I turned it off. I was satisfied that Jewel had not been harmed. So then why didn't she answer? We had such a great night together, and the morning was so special. It couldn't be that she was avoiding me.

I didn't have much time to stress over Jewel's actions as Jamie texted me the address of where we were
meeting. I was so consumed with thoughts of Jewel
that I had completely forgotten about Jamie and our
meeting. I took my time getting ready to go out, stalling
for as long as I could. This was the last thing I wanted
to do, but I wasn't going to back down. I always faced
my problems head on and tackled them, and I wasn't
about to change. I slung my purse over my shoulder
and headed out the door, hoping it would go easy.

Jamie was already waiting at the restaurant when
I arrived, which didn't surprise me, since I was a half
an hour late. That was done on purpose to try and piss
Jamie off. My new plan was to try and get him to want
to break it off with me. I figured the bitchier I was, the
less likely he would want to be with me.

"Hey, sorry I'm late. I took a nap and slept a little
late," I said as I approached.

"No problem. I'm just happy you got here. You must
have really needed the extra sleep." He smiled and
went in for a hug.

I kept my hands at my side and didn't reciprocate his
affection. *Damn, that didn't work!* He was acting like
it was fine to be kept waiting. This wasn't going to be
easy.

The hostess sat us at a small booth with a nice view
out the window. If I had been there with Jewel, I would
have thought it to be a romantic spot, but since I was
with Jamie, it was just another place to sit and eat. I
saw Jamie slip the hostess some cash and give her a
look. He must have requested a romantic table when
he arrived and rewarded the hostess for a job well
done. Jamie was pulling out all the stops to try and woo

me. I was going to have to counter his politeness with some downright dirty-ass bitch.

"This place doesn't look very expensive," I said as I sat down.

"Does it matter?"

"It just kind of shows how you think of me. Taking me to a mediocre place." I frowned as I looked around the room.

"Let's go somewhere else," he said, staying upbeat. "Wherever you want."

"No. I don't feel like driving all over town. Let's just get this over with."

Jamie either didn't hear what I said or chose to ignore it. He just shrugged his shoulders and said, "Okay, whatever you want."

Seriously this was not the way I thought he would be reacting. I mean, I was acting disinterested and bored the second I met him, and he seemed immune to it. Damn, he was going to make me work for this breakup.

"It smells funny in here. Are you wearing cologne?" I scrunched my nose and sniffed the air near Jamie.

"I'm wearing my usual CK One."

"Can cologne go rotten?"

"I don't know." He shrugged his shoulders again.

Not even a direct insult was doing anything to upset him. Inside I was going crazy. I wanted this to be quick and easy and make Jamie feel like he was the one doing the breaking up. Nothing was working, but I was going to hold steady with my plan though.

I looked at the menu and decided on a chicken salad. You know I needed to look fit for Jewel, so my diet had started. After deciding, I just sat there and stared out the window, looking as bored as I possibly could. I even sighed a few times to draw Jamie's attention away from his menu.

Jamie placed the menu on the table in front of him and folded his hands together. "So did you see anything you like?" he asked.

"Yes." I continued looking out the window.

"Good. I'm going to have their burger and fries."

"Keep eating like that, you'll get fat."

He chuckled. "I suppose you're right."

I was now furious inside. He wasn't getting offended by anything I was saying. *What is up with this guy?*

Was he that in love with me that it didn't matter what I said? *I might need to rethink this situation. Maybe I should stay with this guy if he was going to let me act how I wanted. He could fund my life, and I could have Jewel on the side.*

The waitress came over and took our order, and I went directly back to looking out the window. I was now thinking about living my life with Jamie and having Jewel on the side. Could I make that work? As I was fantasizing about that life, Jamie interrupted.

"You said earlier that you wanted to talk about us."

"Yeah. Until you so rudely kept me waiting on hold." I couldn't help being rude now. I had come in with that mindset, and now I couldn't drop it. Damn. I wanted to feel Jamie out and see if he would be up for my arrangement.

"I'm sorry about that."

I took a sip of my Diet Coke and proceeded. "About us. I was thinking that we could date but see other people as well."

Jamie looked perplexed. I couldn't tell what his reaction was by the look on his face. He seemed to be thinking it over. He just kept looking at me and not saying anything, which was starting to freak me out.

"So? What do you think?" I asked.

Now it was Jamie's turn to stare out the window. What was this dude's problem? It was a simple question. This non-answer shit was annoying me.

"So?" I asked again.

Jamie snapped at me. "I'm thinking."

"Chill, muthafucka. Don't snap at me."

"I'm sorry," he said.

The waitress came back over with our food and was about to say something, but she noticed the energy at our table and decided to keep her mouth shut and walk away.

As soon as she was out of range I resumed. "Whatever. Just answer me. Yes or no?"

"Is there someone else? Is that why?"

"No."

"Then why would you ask that?"

"Let's just say, I'm keeping my options open."

"Why can't it just be us and no one else? I want you to move in with me. If we both work, we can save up, buy a big house, and have kids."

Jamie reached for my hand, but I snatched it away. His little pussy-whipped act was starting to wear thin.

"Are you trippin'? I have my own place, and I'm damn sure not about to move in with you or start saving money with you."

"But the other night together was so special."

"Oh, shit. You have got to be kidding me. If I wanted to live with a bitch I would."

Those words made me realize that I was crazy to think I could make anything with Jamie work. My heart and soul were all for Jewel.

"In fact, I want to live with a woman. We have fucked, and I am in love with her, not you. You may be acting like a female right now, but you will never replace the real thing. There is room for one woman in my life. Later, bitch. Don't try contacting me ever again."

Before I even had a chance to stand, Jamie shot up from his chair and screamed, "Fuck you," at the top of his lungs, threw his plate of food through the window, and stormed out of the restaurant.

Everyone turned to stare at me sitting at the table alone and in shock. The whole restaurant was completely silent, stunned at what they just witnessed. I sheepishly looked around the dining room at all the customers. I was embarrassed, to say the least.

I tried to stand up and act like I wasn't fazed, but I'm sure I looked rattled. I was planning on walking out with my head held high and a little dignity, but that was stopped immediately. The restaurant manager came over with two waiters and blocked me from leaving.

"Ma'am, I'm afraid you can't leave. Your guest just vandalized our restaurant."

I was snapped back to reality. Cops were going to get involved in this. It would probably be department gossip in a matter of minutes. I had to make sure I wasn't turned into a department joke.

"Yes, I understand. I'm sorry. I was just so stunned, I don't know what I was thinking. Let me pay for the damage and the meal." I pulled out a credit card.

"It won't be that easy. There will be insurance involved, and I'm not even sure how much it is going to cost to fix. We'll need to call the police. I'm sorry."

"No, don't. Please. Let's work it out on our own and not involve anyone else." The manager thought about it for a minute and decided to not call the police. You know I was relieved. We went back to his office and got down to business. We decided that I wouldn't leave until it was all worked out. He called his contractor and explained the situation.

After several hours and several different quotes to fix the window, we came to an agreement. I gave the manager my credit card number to use after the work was finished. I assured him that I would be monitoring my credit statements, and if there was one odd charge, or I was charged one more dollar than the quoted price, there would be hell to pay.

As I was leaving, I spotted the waitress who had helped me earlier. Luckily she was working a double shift. I walked over to her and handed her a fifty-dollar bill.

"I apologize about earlier," I said and walked out embarrassed but free. It was the most expensive breakup of my life.

Chapter 23

"Target on Your Back"

Lisa

I looked down at my ringing cell phone. This was the third time that my girlfriend Sylvia had called me.

Everyone knew not to disturb me when I was tuning into my reality shows, so I wasn't about to answer. This night I was watching *Basketball Wives*. Those were my girls.

I couldn't take the constant texts and phone calls one after the other, so I answered. Luckily, the show went to a commercial. "Hello?" I answered, annoyed.

"Did you get my texts?" she asked.

"No," I replied.

"I figured that much. Because if you did get my texts, you would have been here by now."

Now Sylvia had my full attention. I pressed pause on the DVR, so I wouldn't miss a second of my show. "Been where?"

"Okay, listen to me very closely. Touch is at the club, Tigerland, with some girl. I thought I should let you know. I would have busted him in the head with a bottle myself, but I'm on a date."

"That's okay. Let me do my own dirty work. So is that chick better-looking than me? Is she light-skinned or dark? Is she ghetto or proper? I need details." I wanted to know what I was up against.

"Don't worry. She's no competition. I've got to go. I've been in the bathroom too long blowing you up. I don't want Jarrod to think I ditched him," Sylvia said before hanging up the phone.

Sylvia was a loyal friend, so it was no surprise to me that she'd made this call. She knew how bad I wanted to fuck with Touch. She even tried to tag along and help, but this was my deal and my deal only.

This was one time I had to put *Basketball Wives* aside. I hurried to put on a cute top, jeans, and stiletto heels. I was going to be the shining star of the night, so I needed to dress the part. I grabbed my co-star, my gun, and put it in my purse. If things went as planned, my gun would end up inside Touch's mouth. I was about to take this game to a whole new level. My mouth started to water, thinking about him pleading for his life.

I was happy that Sylvia had called me. We had just talked about how I was aggravated because the past few days, Touch's house was deserted, and that chick, Jewel, was nowhere to be found. I knew doing something to her would have definitely caught Touch's attention and possibly pushed him over the edge.

Every time I thought about how he spat on me and beat on me, I got angrier and angrier. Repressed rage and aggression was taking a toll on me. My hair was thinning out, and most days, I felt jittery. Getting revenge had become crack to me, and I was an addict. I wasn't sure what my end game was with Touch, but I just knew how much satisfaction I got out of harassing his ass.

After getting dressed, I hopped in my car and rushed to the club. Since I arrived so late, the club parking lot was half-empty. Knowing Touch very well, I knew he would be the last to come out of the building. That nigga loved his drink and would always close bars down.

An hour passed, and cars continued to leave the lot one by one. I watched the club door, patiently waiting for Touch. The waiting was making me tired, and I started to doze off when he finally came out with this mysterious girl. They stumbled across the parking lot to Touch's truck. He had her pressed up against the truck while he felt on her ass and managed to feel up her dress. With the way they were going at it, I thought they would have fucked right in the parking lot if so many people weren't around. It made me disgusted to watch them go at it like they were. I had reached my boiling point.

I quietly but quickly got out of my car, took my gun out of my purse, and fired one shot in the air. Instant chaos erupted in the parking lot. People started scattering and ducking to the ground. Women were screaming, and their boyfriends were trying to hush them up.

My second shot was aimed at Touch, but I missed and hit his car window. My third shot, I had a good aim at him. He was splayed out on the ground in plain view. My eyes got as big as saucers. He was going to die this night, and I would finally be able to move on with my life.

I calmly aimed the gun right at his head and started taking steps closer to make sure I hit his ass. Right as I was about to pull the trigger, something hit me like a ton of rocks, knocking the gun from my hands and forcing me to hit the ground.

I scrambled to turn around to see a two-hundred-pound police offer coming at me like a raging bull. Before I knew it, he was on top of me.

"Officer, that man has been trying to kill me," I screamed, spitting bits of dirt out of my mouth.

"Lady, you're the one with the gun!"

"It's for protection."

"Man, y'all just don't know what this girl has put me through. Justice is finally going to be served. I ain't never been a fan of the police, but I'm sure glad you're here tonight!" Touch said, after running over to me.

The cops flipped me on my stomach and handcuffed me. Touch was taunting my ass the entire time. Like he was the one responsible for me getting arrested. That shit pissed me off too.

When the cops helped me to stand up, I tried to go right at Touch. I was kicking like a donkey, just trying to inflict any sort of pain I could on him. I hit him in the leg, but all he did was laugh.

"See, officers? You see what she is like? This bitch is crazy," Touch said, pointing at me.

Meanwhile, the bitch that Touch was messing with before I interrupted them was crying hysterically on the arm of some other dude. I guess that guy saw an opportunity to swoop in, and he took it. Served Touch right to lose that bitch. I got some satisfaction out of seeing that.

The cops put me in the back of the car and slammed the door after me. I started kicking the cage that separated the front from the back. Then I tried to kick out the windows, and when that didn't work, I went back to the cage. All the while, the cops were talking to Touch, no doubt getting his version of the events between us. Which was fine with me, because when we saw each other in court, it would be my word against his. If I was a betting woman, I would put money on me to convince the jury that I was innocent.

The crowd around the parking lot had dispersed by the time the police were done talking to Touch. His little hussy left with the other dude, which made me so happy. I had tired myself out with all the kicking I had done. My right foot was killing me. I was kicking so

hard, I had actually broken a bone in it. I would make
Touch pay for that when I saw him again. I figured if
he caused me to break a bone in my body, he needed
to have a broken bone in his body as well. *Which bone
would it be?* I thought. *I think I'll break his back. Lay
his ass up in bed for a few months. That'll teach him.* I
smiled as the cops got into the car.

Touch came up to the car window before they pulled
off and said, "You getting what you deserve, bitch. You
going to jail, psycho." Then he started laughing at me.

"You stupid muthafucka. I got my revenge on you,
when I snuck in your house and beat the shit out of
you. I had you scared for days." I laughed as the car
pulled away.

Chapter 24

"Family Ties"

Touch

After that incident with Lisa, I made a vow to be extra careful about where I stick my dick. Lisa had me shook. The whole time I was thinking one of Jewel's stragglers had beat the hell out of me that night. Come to find out, it was Lisa all along. I couldn't believe I let a bitch do that to me. I felt like a damn fool. I was definitely going to make sure no one on the street found out about that shit.

When I sat and thought about things, I realized Lisa had been stalking Jewel and me for the entire time since I was dismissed from the assault charges on her. She was bitter, angry, and wanted nothing more than to see me die. I should have known it was her. I had a hunch, but I couldn't convince myself that a bitch would be that crazy or clever.

After that incident I couldn't sleep, tossing and turning in my hotel room all night. The room was nice enough, but I didn't feel like wasting all my money on some bullshit uptight hotel. I wanted to use it to buy me a nice house. The bed in the hotel was a far cry from my king-sized bed I was used to at home.

After tossing and turning all night, I finally looked at the clock, and it was 8:00 A.M. I was cranky as hell from a long night and a lack of sleep. I wanted to stay in bed all day and try to get some shut-eye, but my boy Jimmy was getting out of jail today. That was motivation enough for me to get out of bed and get dressed.

I was happy Jimmy was getting released because I felt like there was so much he could teach me about the game. There was only so much he could teach me from the inside. I knew my street IQ was about to get a bump up. I had visions of even more money coming my way and one day running my own international drug ring.

After a quick breakfast, I picked up Deuce, and we headed over to Jimmy's girl's place, so we could straighten out this missing money. On the ride over, Deuce was in a talkative mood, which was surprising. Normally he was a man of few words. When he did open his mouth, it was only about one thing and one thing only—the year of 1973 when he ruled the streets, and now he walks those same streets. I was sick and tired of his same old stories. It was like he stopped living after 1973. At first, I liked hearing the stories, but after hearing them over and over, I wanted to punch him in his mouth. I wanted to scream, "Shut the fuck up, you old fool!" but I would just tune out instead, and continue doing whatever it was I was doing at the time.

This day he was talking about how happy he was Jimmy was getting out but that he wasn't sure if Jimmy would be able to survive on the streets anymore. He kept talking about the missing money and asking me if I knew anything about it.

"If you took it, you can tell me," he said. "I won't tell Jimmy. You'll just have to split it with me."

"The fuck kinda snake you think I am? I didn't steal shit. My money was always tight."

After that, we pretty much rode in silence. Occasionally Deuce would say some stupid shit like, "I can't wait to see Jimmy."

Deuce started in with his trip down memory lane, but we had gotten to the house before he could really get deep into his 1973 stories. I couldn't get out of the car fast enough. When we walked in the house, Jimmy was sitting on the couch, sipping a glass of Rémy. This old dude was slick. When he saw us, he put the drink down as he stood to greet us.

"'S up, Jimmy! You home, big man," I said after we walked into the living room of his house.

I started to give him a hug, but he stopped me with a handshake. I guess he didn't like to be touched or some shit. He shook Deuce's hand as well. He was acting real cold toward us. I was expecting a warmer return from him. He was mad cool in the joint, so I just expected even more of it now that he was on the outside. Especially since I had been making so much money for old dude.

Before I knew it, a gun was at the side of Deuce's head. When I moved back to get out of the way, the gun was pointed at me. I had no idea what the reason for this show of aggression was. Had Jimmy been playing me this whole time? He set my ass up. He softened me up in the joint, got me connected on the outside, so I could make him money. Then when he got out and everything was in place, he would off me and take all the profits for himself.

"Yo, man, Jimmy—" I said with my hands in the air, wondering what the hell was going on.

"My money is missing, and one of you have it. I need answers," he demanded, cutting me off.

"Jim, it's me, man. I took it. Please, man, just put the gun down." I looked over to see Deuce on his knees, begging for his life, a big wet spot in front of his pants. I shook my head. This nigga was a fucking disgrace. All the talk about how bad-ass he was back in the day, and he punks out like this? At least he could have tried lying for a while, tried blaming it on me, something to save his ass, but to just cop to it so fast, that shit was embarrassing.

"I was shaving ten grand off the money here and there. I have about fifty thousand dollars in the safe. It's all yours. Take it, man. Just don't kill me, Jim. I know it was wrong, and I felt bad about doing it. That's why I told you. I was going to give it back. I promise. You gotta believe me."

Deuce continued to beg like a little bitch, piss running down his leg. I swear I started to smell shit too. Absolutely disgraceful. I couldn't stand watching his ass beg like a woman.

"Man, have some fuckin' pride!" I yelled, annoyed not only by Deuce robbing Jimmy but by his bitch-ass attitude. "You fucked up. Now be a man about it."

"How could you do it, Deuce? We've been friends over thirty years, man," Jimmy said, shaking his head, still with gun in hand.

I looked at Jimmy, and he had a sadness in his eyes. I could tell it hurt him that his good friend had betrayed him.

"You fucked up our bond when you let Touch in. You have never taken to no dude like Touch before, so it was mind-boggling for me. Jealousy kicked in, and I was planning to pin the missing money on Touch. I know I was wrong. Come on, man. Please. Have sympathy on an old friend."

Only mere seconds passed before Jimmy shot Deuce twice in the head like it was nothing. Good thing he did because if Deuce had walked out that spot alive, I'd have killed him myself for trying to set me up.

We silently stood there watching the blood ooze from Deuce's skull. His eyes were still open, and I felt like he was staring at me. I thought, *Good riddance, you thieving bastard!*

Jimmy's face was tight. He looked pained at the sight of his long-time friend lying dead in front of him.

"Come on, let's take care of this," Jimmy said, signaling in the direction of Deuce's dead body.

I took his shoulders, and Jimmy took his feet, and we moved Deuce's body into the bathtub. Jimmy left the bathroom and returned with two saws and a couple of butcher knives. We began the process of chopping Deuce's body into pieces. We wrapped the parts up in garbage bags and placed them into storage bins. We threw them into the trunk, and Jimmy and I drove to the Chesapeake Bay Bridge in silence. I knew this must have been hard for Jimmy, but we both knew the business, so there was no need to talk about it.

Seeing things like this made me never want to get close to nobody. I would hate to have to kill my best friend over some shit like this. In my opinion, there is no room for friendship in this game. I would learn everything I could from Jimmy, but I wasn't going to get too attached to liking this dude. If the day ever came where I had to take him out, I didn't want it to be hard on me mentally or emotionally.

We stopped at the bridge and emptied the trunk, being careful that no one saw what we were doing. It seemed like each splash echoed for miles, it was so quiet.

"That was hard," Jimmy said when all the bins had been dumped.

I didn't say anything. I just shook my head. I didn't know if he meant killing his best friend and chopping him up or throwing those heavy-ass bins into the water.

***

For the next few weeks, Jimmy and I worked the
streets ourselves, never once mentioning what had
happened. It was an understanding that we had. It
seemed to take Jimmy a few days to get out of the funk
he was in after killing Deuce.

Soon, it came out that Deuce wasn't paying people
their agreed-upon cuts. People on the street were
pissed. Deuce would short them and just keep stalling
when they came to get the rest of their money. Word
of mouth about Jimmy's operation was not good. He
was blacklisted; no one wanted anything to do with his
business. Jimmy's empire was fucked up, but I knew
he had every intention of putting it back together, and
I planned on being by his side the entire way.

"Deuce was right about me taking to you so well,"
Jimmy commented one day while we were on the road
collecting money.

"Feeling's mutual, man," I told him. "From day one
I looked up to you. You always gonna be cool with me.
You picked me up in a big way when I was down."

"It's more to it than that. I'm just gon' be straight-
forward with you, man." Jimmy paused for a minute
and looked out the window at the passing buildings.
He continued to look away from me. "Touch, I'm your
grandfather. I'm your father's father."

"What?" I said, shocked and in disbelief. I almost ran
off the fucking road. "My mother told me my father had
passed. I never knew the man."

"Boy, I know. He is alive and well in Connecticut."

I couldn't believe my ears. I had mixed emotions
inside. How could I have gone so long thinking my dad
was dead and this entire time he was living in another
state? Why did my moms lie to me? I couldn't understand why she would do that. Why didn't Jimmy come
to me sooner and tell me who he was? I wanted to hug

him and punch him all at the same time. My mind was going in a million directions. I wanted to cry, I wanted to scream, I wanted to fight. I was crazy confused.

I slammed on the brakes and made a U-turn.

"Where you going, boy?" Jimmy asked.

"I've gotta talk to my moms about this shit, man. I'm all fucked up in the head right now."

We went back and forth for a second about whether that was a good idea, but in the end Jimmy agreed to come with me to my mom's house. I had to know the truth. Growing up without a father because my mother purposely wanted it that way was fucked up.

I raced over to my mom's house, not caring that I was breaking the speed limit and in danger of getting pulled over by the cops.

Jimmy and I walked into my mother's living room. I called out to her. "Mom!"

"Touch, is that you? I cooked some lunch. Do you want"—The bowl of grits in her hands fell to the carpet when she saw Jimmy's face.

"Why? Why would you lie to me about my father?" I asked with tears in my eyes.

"I knew this day would come but not so soon." My mom turned toward Jimmy. She looked defeated. "What did you tell him, Jim?"

"Not much. I'll leave the explaining up to you."

"Trayvon, sit down, baby." My mom pointed to a bar stool that sat at the breakfast bar to the kitchen. "Your uncles, my brothers, used to work for Jimmy back in the day. That's how I met your father. We both were very young when I got pregnant, and I knew my mother would never approve of the baby or him. Momma forced me to live with my aunt in Alabama 'til I gave birth to you, and then I could move back. She was ashamed and didn't want her beloved church members to know I had gotten pregnant out of wedlock. When I returned I learned that your father and my cousin were in a relationship. That tore me apart, Trayvon. You don't understand. I loved that man. When he cheated on me, it killed me. I couldn't bear the pain. From that day forth, I vowed I would never speak to him again."

I felt her pain and definitely understood where she was coming from, but I still didn't agree with her decision. I felt like she had deprived me of a relationship with my father my entire life. So many nights I would lie in my bed and wish I had a dad to talk to, to ask for advice. I may never have gotten into the drug game if he had been around. I should have been allowed to make my own decisions about my father.

"Mom, you should have told me. You just can't make decisions on my life like that," I screamed at her and walked out. I needed time to process everything that was just said to me. I didn't know how to handle all of the emotions I was feeling, so I just jetted.

I dropped Jimmy off back at his house. On the way back to his place, I didn't say a word to him. I was angry with him and didn't want to hear his bullshit at the moment. I told him that I needed a few days off to clear my head. He agreed that it was a good idea. We said a sorrowful good-bye, and I drove back to the hotel, my head pounding from all the emotions and stress I was feeling.

I stopped at the front desk, and they gave me some Advil for my headache. But what I needed right at the time more than anything was to talk to Jewel. She was the only one that could comfort me. She knew how much I had longed for a father in my life. She would be able to understand my pain and anguish. I called the realtor and pretended I was interested in buying the house but would only speak to Jewel. It took a little convincing, but she finally gave me the number.

"Hey," I said as soon as she answered.

"Hey," she said back in a flat tone.

"You busy?" I asked her.

"Not really. Right now I'm free, but I have a doctor's appointment later on today."

"Is everything okay?" I asked, truly concerned that something was wrong with the baby.

"Everything is fine. I'm just going for a checkup." "Okay, cool. Well, can you meet at Mahi Mah's by the oceanfront? I really need to talk to you."

"Okay, I will meet you. But don't try no stupid shit because I won't hesitate to shoot your ass."

Chapter 25

"'Til Death Do Us Part"

Jewel

"Are you sure you don't need me to go with you?" Misty asked, while giving me a hug. "I don't mind."

I had come back to Virginia to go to the doctors and take care of a few things, and Misty was nice enough to let me sleep at her place. Well, I'm sure the fact that we were having sex every night didn't hurt. Anyway, lucky for Touch, I was in town because if I was in DC, I would never have agreed to meet up with him. "I'll be fine," I said with a fake smile.

The truth was, I felt sick to my stomach and vomited again the previous night. At the time, Misty was asleep and didn't hear me. If she knew I didn't feel well, she would have insisted on coming along with me. It was strange, but it felt nice sleeping next to Misty. Plus, she was pampering me constantly. No man had done that to me for a while.

"Just in case I'm not home, here is your own house key," she said, handing it to me. "Thank you." I nodded.

"Have a great day. Hopefully, you won't run into traffic," Misty yelled, as I headed out the door.

I rushed to the oceanfront to meet Touch. I prayed everything would go well, and I could eat and get out in time to make my doctor's appointment. When I walked in the restaurant, I saw Touch right away. The hostess met me at the door. After she sat me down at the table where Touch was sitting, I looked into his eyes. Surprisingly enough, I felt nothing for him at all. I guess, once my mind was made up, my heart had no choice but to follow the same path as well. It's funny, because the way I used to feel when I looked into Touch's eyes was the way I felt when I looked into Misty's eyes.

While we ate lunch Touch revealed the story about his mother lying about his father being dead. The whole story was just so sad. Maybe if Touch's father had been in his life, he wouldn't have turned out the way he did. Listening to the story though, I kept thinking, *Like father, like son.* Touch's dad was a cheat, and so was his son. Still, I felt sympathy for Touch. All the years we were together, he always wished he could see his father. I felt his mother was very selfish and only thinking about herself.

"Listen, Jewel, I need you to come back home. I love you, and I miss you. I'm sorry for everything I put you through. Hearing this story about my father makes me want to be a great father to our baby and a better man for you," Touch pleaded, touching my hand. "Touch, I can't do that," I stated, shaking my head and removing my hand from his.

"Why? We have been together too long to just end it."

"Yeah, that's what I used to think. Touch, you have hurt me so bad. As bad as your father hurt your mother, maybe even worse. At least he never laid his hands on her like you did to me. I'm tired, and I have reached my limit. Besides, the house is going to be sold next week. In fact, I'm meeting with the realtor at the house today at six to finalize a few things. I've moved on with my life, Touch. I moved out of Virginia over a month ago."

"Why would you do that without talking to me first? I understand if you don't want to be with me, but what about our baby? How can I be a father to my child if you're in an entirely different state? It will be like my father and me."

"Enough of the baby talk," I spat, frustrated. It was time he knew the truth. "There is no damn baby, Touch."

"What?"

"You heard me, Touch. I had an abortion, okay. You were on the run, and we were having major problems in our relationship. I didn't know how or when I would see you, and I barely had enough money to take care of myself, much less a baby. There was no way I could bring a child into a situation like that. There was no way I would want my child to have an unstable father like you."

"Bitch!" He reached for my throat.

I quickly jumped up and threw my water in his face. "Don't make me pull out on you," I said, going into my purse to grab my gun.

Touch called me every name in the book using every profanity you can think of. He pushed the table over, and people all over the restaurant began to stare at us.

I pulled my gun out and pointed it at Touch. Everyone in the restaurant scattered. We had a little stand-off, neither of us saying anything, just staring into each other's eyes.

Finally, Touch left with tears in his eyes, but I refused to shed a tear for that fucker. I calmly put my gun away, paid the bill for the little that we ate, and left the restaurant.

On the way to the doctor's office, I started thinking about everything that just happened, and I actually started to feel a little guilty for what I did. I realized by the tears in Touch's eyes that he really wanted a son. Touch had twin girls that he loved dearly, but because of a domestic dispute between him and his baby mother, he hadn't seen them in months. My baby was probably his only hope of filling that void. Now with the news of his father and everything else, he was fragile. I began to get a little choked up as I pulled up to the doctor's office, but again I refused to drop a tear.

I probably should have told him sooner that I'd had an abortion, but I was afraid that he would've put a beating on me when I told him. I didn't know what I would do when the time came for me to have the baby, but I knew I was going to avoid telling him for as long as I could. *Oh well, Touch brought this all on himself.*

The waiting room was empty when I arrived. "Hello. I'm here for my appointment," I announced as I walked to the receptionist's desk to sign in.

"Hi, Jewel. Fill out these forms. Here is a pen. After that, I will need a urine sample from you for a routine check. The urine cups are in the bathroom with your patient information already labeled on it," the receptionist said to me.

I loved this doctor's office. They had everything all ready for me. All I had to do was show up, and they took care of it all. So much better than the ghetto clinics I used to go through. Those places were third world.

"Thank you," I replied, nodding.

On the form, I decided to put Misty's address as my current address. To be honest, I was feeling Misty and had decided to tell her I wanted to move in when I got home later. It just felt right to me. She treated me the way no man had ever treated me. We'd started out as friends, and it was so easy to talk with her. It just seemed natural to me that we would be lovers. Every time I thought of her, I would smile.

With the form filled out and my mood feeling good, I went to the restroom and tried my best to pee, but I couldn't get even a tinkle. I went back to the waiting room for a while to wait it out. Ten minutes later I went back into the bathroom, but I still couldn't pee. I didn't know what was going on with me. I was getting sick a lot, and now I couldn't pee. I was getting a little concerned that there might be something seriously wrong with me.

"Excuse me," I said to the nurse behind the counter. "Do you have any water?"

"Honey, are you having trouble giving us a urine sample?" she inquired.

"Yes, I am." I laughed, a bit embarrassed.

"There's a water fountain down the hall. Drink 'til your heart is content. Wait fifteen minutes, and I'm sure nature will come calling."

"Thank you," I said and headed to the water fountain.

I guzzled four cups of water, and fifteen minutes later I certainly had to pee. The nurse's plan worked. I peed about three times waiting for the doctor to come in. My legs felt cold as I sat there in the gown they had provided for me.

I thought of Misty and started daydreaming about our future together. I hadn't been this happy in a long time. Touch had put me through so much, I had forgotten what happy really felt like.

I was brought back to reality from a knock on the door. I still had a huge smile on my face from my daydream when my doctor entered. "Come in," I said.

"Jewel, sorry for the delay. I had a false alarm with another patient. How have you been?" Dr. Gills started looking over my chart.

"Okay. And you?"

"My kids are growing and eating everything in sight. My husband just bought another motorbike. Life is crazy." Dr. Gills stopped talking as she read my chart. "Well, well, well, looking at your lab work, it looks like you may not be far behind me because you're pregnant. Welcome to the crazy life of husband and kids," Dr. Gills said with a huge grin.

"What?"

We instinctively hugged each other.

"Jewel, I didn't stutter. You're pregnant, honey. And based on your last period, you're about six weeks."

"Wow! Unbelievable!" I said, letting out a loud sigh. I was in a little bit of shock.

"Jewel, you have options, which we can discuss. Now I need to examine you. So if you can just lie back."

My brain was racing during the entire exam. How did this happen? I can't believe I just told Touch there was no baby and there actually was. Now it made sense why I was getting sick so much lately. I can't wait to tell Misty. What will Misty think? Does she even want kids? Even though I didn't know how Misty felt about children, I wasn't afraid to tell her, like I was with Touch. I wasn't afraid of catching a beating from Misty. That was for sure.

After she finished, I requested the nurse perform a blood test to ensure the test results were accurate. Sure enough, the blood test confirmed what Dr. Gills had already told me. Now the reality really set in. I was going to be a mother.

Dr. Gills and I discussed all of my options. I could abort it, but I wasn't going through that again. I could put it up for adoption, but I didn't want my baby growing up in foster homes or going to a bad family. The only option I considered was having the baby and being the best damn mother I could be.

I was so happy when I left the doctor's office. Driving home, I did some calculating, and if my calculations were right, Touch had gotten me pregnant as soon as he came home from jail. I panicked thinking about him. I didn't know what to do. Should I tell him or keep it a secret?

I desperately needed to talk to Misty. Anytime I found myself in a bind or didn't know what to do, she was always my savior. She had the answer to everything.

I rushed back to the house to talk to her. As I walked in, I heard my name, but it wasn't being said to greet me. It was said like someone was talking about me. I paused at the front door. I heard Misty say on the phone, "Jewel has already agreed to testify, so that's a wrap."

I stood at the door and continued to listen.

"The case is solid this time," Misty said. "Captain, no room for fuckup. In fact, I know where Touch is. We can do the sting tomorrow. I can't wait to officially be back on the force."

It felt like my stomach had dropped out my asshole. My head began to spin. My world collapsed in an instant. One minute my future was so bright and happy, the next, it gets crushed by the woman who I thought I loved. I had been used once again by Misty.

I grasped my heart and quickly walked out the house.

I was struggling for air when I got in the car. I felt like I was having a fucking panic attack. I couldn't believe that bitch was using me to get rank back on her job.

Tears began to run down my face as I started the car and pulled off. I didn't know what to think or who to trust. I couldn't believe I'd let this happen again. *Did she even love me? People are always betraying me*, I thought as I drove to the house to meet the real estate agent.

I tried to call Touch, but he didn't answer. I sent him a text asking him to meet me at the house. I wanted to come clean to him about everything, including Misty. He was the only person I felt I could turn to. My only hope was that he would take me back and keep his word about being a better man to me.

"Oh my God! What is he doing here?" I said to myself in a panic.

When I was pulling up to the house, Rico was in the driveway. I almost shit in my pants. I couldn't deal with him right now, on top of everything else. That was the last thing I needed.

Instead of pulling in, I just kept driving past the house. I looked in my rearview to see if Rico had seen me. He didn't seem to react like he had seen me. Thank God for that.

I went to the store to buy a ginger ale to help with my constant nausea. I loitered around the store, wasting time in hopes that Rico would be gone by the time I drove back. I must have looked like a crack addict the way I was pacing up and down the aisles. I just couldn't stay still, I was so worked up and on edge. Everything was happening too fast.

I tried to read a magazine, but it was impossible for me to concentrate on any of it. I threw the magazine down and went back to my car. If Rico was there, so be it. I had dealt with enough shit today. What's one more little drama?

"Whew!" I gave a sigh of relief as I drove up.

Rico's car was out of the driveway. He had left. I pulled in the driveway and waited for Touch. I sat singing along to the tunes of Keri Hilson, desperately trying to keep my mind off my problems. As I sat there, through my rearview mirror, I got a glimpse of Touch pulling up. He parked on the street in front of the house instead of coming into the driveway. *He must be angry with me,* I thought.

As I was opening my car door, I saw Rico rush toward Touch from next door. That's when I realized he hadn't left. He'd just parked his car someplace else. I jumped out of the car and headed in their direction, but before I could reach them, Rico and Touch had already locked eyes, and both pulled out their guns.

"No!" I yelled, as I ran to get between them.

As soon as I reached them, shots were fired. I looked down to see my white shirt turn dark red. Realizing I'd been shot, I grabbed my stomach.

"My baby!" I yelled, collapsing on the ground. Looking up from the ground, I saw Touch come running over to me.

He threw himself on the ground next to me and cradled my head. "Babe, you okay?" he screamed. "Stay with me!"

I was starting to have trouble breathing. I felt like I was going in and out of consciousness. I tried to speak, but I could only moan as blood trickled from my mouth. Touch was crying and rocking me back and forth like a baby. "Jewel, don't give up. I love you. I'm sorry for everything."

I looked into his eyes, and in the faintest whisper, I was able to say, "Baby."

He looked at me surprised. "Did you say *baby*?"

I nodded my head slowly, every movement for me painful at that point. "Are you pregnant?" he asked.

I nodded again.

"Is it mine?"

I nodded yet again and smiled.

I heard Touch say one last time, "I love you."

And the darkness slowly came to my eyes. I couldn't fight anymore, but I was happy to know that Touch truly loved me.

ORDER FORM
URBAN BOOKS, LLC
78 E. Industry Ct
Deer Park, NY 11729

Name:(please print):_____

Address: _____

City/State: _____

Zip: _____

QTY	TITLES	PRICE
	16 On The Block	$14.95
	A Girl From Flint	$14.95
	A Pimp's Life	$14.95
	Baltimore Chronicles	$14.95
	Baltimore Chronicles 2	$14.95
	Betrayal	$14.95
	Black Diamond	$14.95
	Black Diamond 2	$14.95
	Black Friday	$14.95
	Both Sides Of The Fence	$14.95
	Both Sides Of The Fence 2	$14.95
	California Connection	$14.95

Shipping and handling-add $3.50 for 1st book, then $1.75 for each additional book.

Please send a check payable to:

Urban Books, LLC

Please allow 4-6 weeks for delivery

ORDER FORM
URBAN BOOKS, LLC
78 E. Industry Ct
Deer Park, NY 11729

Name: (please print): _____

Address: _____

City/State: _____

Zip: _____

QTY	TITLES	PRICE
	California Connection 2	$14.95
	Cheesecake And Teardrops	$14.95
	Congratulations	$14.95
	Crazy In Love	$14.95
	Cyber Case	$14.95
	Denim Diaries	$14.95
	Diary Of A Mad First Lady	$14.95
	Diary Of A Stalker	$14.95
	Diary Of A Street Diva	$14.95
	Diary Of A Young Girl	$14.95
	Dirty Money	$14.95
	Dirty To The Grave	$14.95

Shipping and handling-add $3.50 for 1st book, then $1.75 for each additional book.
Please send a check payable to:
Urban Books, LLC
Please allow 4-6 weeks for delivery

ORDER FORM
URBAN BOOKS, LLC
78 E. Industry Ct
Deer Park, NY 11729

Name: (please print):_____

Address: _____

City/State: _____

Zip: _____

QTY	TITLES	PRICE
	Gunz And Roses	$14.95
	Happily Ever Now	$14.95
	Hell Has No Fury	$14.95
	Hush	$14.95
	If It Isn't love	$14.95
	Kiss Kiss Bang Bang	$14.95
	Last Breath	$14.95
	Little Black Girl Lost	$14.95
	Little Black Girl Lost 2	$14.95
	Little Black Girl Lost 3	$14.95
	Little Black Girl Lost 4	$14.95
	Little Black Girl Lost 5	$14.95

Shipping and handling-add $3.50 for 1st book, then $1.75 for each additional book.

Please send a check payable to:

Urban Books, LLC

Please allow 4-6 weeks for delivery

ORDER FORM
URBAN BOOKS, LLC
78 E. Industry Ct
Deer Park, NY 11729

Name: (please print): _____

Address: _____

City/State: _____

Zip: _____

QTY	TITLES	PRICE
	Loving Dasia	$14.95
	Material Girl	$14.95
	Moth To A Flame	$14.95
	Mr. High Maintenance	$14.95
	My Little Secret	$14.95
	Naughty	$14.95
	Naughty 2	$14.95
	Naughty 3	$14.95
	Queen Bee	$14.95
	Say It Ain't So	$14.95
	Snapped	$14.95
	Snow White	$14.95

Shipping and handling-add $3.50 for 1st book, then $1.75 for each additional book.
Please send a check payable to:
Urban Books, LLC
Please allow 4-6 weeks for delivery